MW01201825

A Good Girl's Guide to Dominance

BESTSELLING AUTHOR

WS GREER

Contents

Author's Note

First of all, I want to thank you for taking a chance on me and *A Good Girl's Guide to Dominance*. It took me approximately three months to write the 106K+-word novel in your hands, and it was a blast to write. Quite the change of pace from my previous two books, but it was a change that I needed and very much enjoyed. I put a ton of my heart and emotion in this novel, and I'm grateful that you chose it! Thank you so much for your support!

Secondly, I always like to give a bit of a warning before my readers get started on my novels. This is a BDSM romance, and when I write BDSM, it is as accurate to the real lifestyle as the story will allow, which means it is not perfect and it won't fit every person's idea of a D/s dynamic. The dynamic written here is what the characters in the story need and agree to, so please understand that what is written is intentional <u>for them</u>. It is flawed on purpose.

In any good BDSM romance, there will be tons of kink exploration, which could be triggering for readers who've had bad experiences. Therefore, this is your trigger warning.

While all characters and situations are completely fictional, some scenes may imitate reality and be harmful to those who have experienced violence, assault, or traumatic events.

This novel contains graphic depictions of bondage (spanking bench, and a Saint Andrew's cross), impact play (spanking and flogging), and breath play (choking). It is intended for mature audiences only.

This book has more range than any of my others. It's meant to turn you on, make you laugh, and have you bawling like a baby. It's a slow burn, but it's also a rollercoaster ride like no other. Besides the kinky scenes, character development, and highest-tier dirty talk, my biggest emphasis while writing this novel was EMOTION. This one is going to make you *feel things*.

I'm tempted to say more, but I think it'd be better if you just read and find out. So, buckle up and enjoy the ride. Welcome to *A Good Girl's Guide to Dominance*.

Now turn the page ... and embrace your kinks.

Who The Hell Is Rome Giovanni?

One

"God ... your butt is so cute."

The frown that scrunches my forehead nearly sends pain shooting down my face. I don't want to be in my head in this moment, yet here I am, my thoughts running rampant in my brain and filling it with distractions that don't mix well with the feeling in my gut. When this night began, I was looking for something specific, and it's so fucking annoying to realize that it's not here. Again.

His name is Zane. I met him on FET, which is a kink and BDSM dating app I've been using for a while now. I'm not afraid to admit it. A woman like me has to get what she needs, and there are very few apps that provide the type of things that I am into.

I'm a thirty-year-old woman who is not in the mood to play games. Admittedly, I was more willing to undergo the casual hoop jumping that people endure in their twenties. I was engaged to my highschool sweetheart when I was just twenty-one, and it ended after he cheated on me with some skank from his college. Since then, I've been all about being honest with myself, and the truth is that I'm not a vanilla kind of girl. I have kinks and fetishes, and if there is one thing I've learned in the years I've been swiping through dating apps and falling victim to hopeless experience after hopeless experience, it's that the world is full of men who think they are Dominant ... and they have absolutely no clue what the fuck they're doing.

When Zane first reached out to me on FET, I knew what it was for. While FET isn't advertised as a dating app, it is used as one anyway. The only difference is that people on FET are kinksters, and we all know what we're there for. While a casual encounter has the possibility of turning into something more, when someone reaches out to you on FET, they probably want to fuck you. Again, I'm honest with myself, and even though Zane's message was, "Hey, how are you?" I knew what he was really asking. "Are you willing to have a conversation that I hope will lead to us meeting up and having kinky sex?" When I answered, it too had a double meaning. I replied, "I'm good. How are you?" Which really meant, "Your profile picture was cute enough for me to respond. Let's see if the conversation can actually lead to sex."

And it did.

Zane and I chatted back and forth for two weeks on FET. We picked and chose parts of our lives to share with the other, making sure to keep everything casual and unserious before getting into the kinks we hold dear. We discussed our hard and soft limits during our second week of conversing, which let me know that we were officially traveling down the road toward sex. We met for a coffee date at Dunkin' Donuts that went well after seeing that he hadn't lied with his profile picture, and the second date happened today. We met at his place for dinner, which he did his very best to cook. I applauded his efforts although I prefer far more seasoning on my baked chicken, but it was the thought that counted. He tried for me, which was enough for me to consent to *dessert*.

When we left the table and entered Zane's bedroom, he led the way, holding my hand and guiding me over the threshold. My heart jumped a bit when I saw the photo of an older woman on the nightstand next to his bed, but we're not in a committed relationship or anything, so I blew it off. Honestly, the woman looked like she could be his mother, so I assumed it was. I swallowed hard when I saw clothes in a messy pile in the far corner.

Are those clean? Is he doing laundry?

A firestorm of questions ignited as he physically guided me to the bed and made me sit down in front of him. While I looked up at his cute little face with the five o'clock shadow, his blue eyes weren't enough to distract me from how messy the bathroom was. From my spot on the bed, I could see the sink in the ensuite behind him, crawling with toothpaste both old and new, and hair from the last time he trimmed his beard. His toothbrush was on the counter lying lifelessly on its side next to a bottle of mouthwash with no lid.

This is how a Dom lives?

Maybe I was reading too much into it, but when I think of the word Dom, it comes with an image in my mind. I see someone who is put together. Someone who takes care of themselves—because if you can't take care of yourself, how could you possibly take care of a submissive? I see someone who is neat and orderly, someone calm and composed, someone who doesn't get flustered when the temperature rises. I see strength, discipline, and structure. I see a Dominant.

It's certainly possible that I'm asking for too much. I don't know anything about Zane other than the things he has told me. When you're trying to get to know someone, only going off of what they tell you will lead to despair down the road because no one tells you everything. Learning the depths of a person requires seeing who they are, not hearing who they are. What I see here doesn't fill me with excitement.

But I'd made it to this point. I might as well see how it turns out.

I stayed in my seated position on the bed while Zane gazed down at me, his eyes peering into my soul while lust emanated from his skin. I could see how much he wanted me, so I pushed the dirtiness of the bathroom as far out of my mind as I could and ignored the clothes in the corner. I listened when he told me to open my mouth so that he could stick his fingers in, sliding them back and forth over my tongue while he rubbed the length of his cock through his jeans. A smile tugged at the sides of my mouth while watching him because I could see his dick was big from here, and the untidiness of the house notwithstanding, he seemed controlled in the moment.

"You're so pretty," he'd said, still fingering my mouth. "I can't believe I was lucky enough to talk to you on FET. Now, let's see if you're as submissive as you say."

Again, I was ready to start beaming. Don't get me wrong, I've had a few hookups on dating apps in the past, but every one of them left me with a bitter taste in my mouth, and not in the good way. Zane was on a roll. He was smooth and doing his best to maintain an air of confidence. Then he kept talking.

"Turn around," he'd said.

My first thought was that it was a little fast. We'd just come into the room and sat down, and after our many conversations on FET, Zane was fully aware of the types of things I'm into. I expected a little more foreplay, teasing, and maybe a little bondage for our first time together. But I'm the submissive. It's not my job to determine how this scene goes. Hell, I don't even want to. I want to be guided by someone who knows how to lead, so I didn't say anything. I moved my head back enough for Zane's fingers to fall out of my mouth, then I did as he asked. I turned around on the bed, positioned myself on all fours, and pinched my lips together when he quickly pulled my pants down. I hoped with everything in me that he had some spanking in mind, because his fingers in my mouth started the process of making me wet, but he'd need to do more to finish the job.

Still in my black panties, I kept my ass in the air while Zane backed away for a moment. I heard him rustling around, perhaps opening a drawer and searching for something. I wish I trusted him enough to know that if he walked away to grab a toy, he'd return with something he knew I loved, but this is our first time together, and that trust hasn't been cemented yet. So, I turned around to see what he was doing. I saw Zane grab something silver from the drawer and clutch it tightly in his fist, almost as if he didn't want me to see it, then he turned around and walked back over to me.

"No peeking," he said as he reached up and removed his shirt, revealing tight abs and a deep V outlining his waist and plunging into his pants.

I let out a breath and turned around.

"God ... your butt is so cute."

And here we are. I'm not sure how to respond to that. I'm not sure how to respond in general. This is our first time together, and while Zane explained in our messages that he likes to be called Sir, some Doms also like to be called Daddy, or Master. Either way, this is only our second date and our first time in a scene. Zane may be a Sir, but he's not *my* Sir. Not yet at least. That title has to be earned through trust.

"With a butt like this," Zane says, positioning himself behind me. "I think it would look incredible with a little ... decoration."

My eyes widen as I whip my head around and find Zane balancing a silver butt plug in the palm of his hand. He looks at me with a squint in his eyes as he licks his lips, a sudden aura of douche-baggery wafting off of him.

"Burgundy," I say quickly, shaking my head as I turn around and return to my original position on the bed.

"What?" Zane asks.

"My safe word, remember?" I reply, peering up at him. "Burgundy."

"You're saying your safe word *right now*? We haven't even started yet."

I let out a long exhale as my head drops so low that my chin hits my chest. If there is one thing that will test whether or not a person claiming to be a Dom actually is one, it's invoking the safe word. A real Dom will know that the safe word means everything has ended because he or she has gone too far. They will be apologetic and do their best to console their partner, wrapping them in as much comfort as possible to remain trustworthy to the person they care about. Then again, they'd know their submissive well enough to not put them in a position to have to use their safe word.

A fake Dom, on the other hand, will try to make their sub feel bad about bringing the scene to a close. They will use childish tactics, like guilt tripping, in an attempt to coax the sub back into the scene. A fake Dom will feel insulted by the safe word ... and they'll lose their sub forever.

"We've done enough," I reply, standing to pull my pants back up.

"I haven't even touched you yet," Zane informs me as if his fingers in my mouth don't count.

I sigh. "Zane, it doesn't matter. I used the safe word."

"But why?"

"The fact that you don't know is a red flag, but I'll tell you anyway. During our text exchange, I told you I wasn't into any butt stuff. I don't do plugs. It's a hard limit."

His shoulders visibly slump. "But ... I don't know. I thought maybe you didn't like it because you hadn't tried it, or maybe you tried it with the wrong person—someone who wasn't gentle enough. I could show you the right way."

"No you can't. I'm not into butt stuff. Period. Hard limit."

"So you've never tried it?"

"I don't want to try it."

"But every girl I've been with has loved it."

"Good for them. I'm not interested in changing who I am just because people I've never met enjoyed something I've never tried. I'm not budging on this, Zane."

He pushes out a long, frustrated breath. "This is such bullshit. So what? You're going to call the entire thing off now? What did I spend all that time texting you for then?"

When I look over at him, I see an intense scowl on his face and anger in his gaze. This is another sign of an asshole masquerading as a Dominant. He wants to intimidate me now, hoping his display of anger will put me back into a submissive role, but Zane clearly doesn't understand submissives. Just because I am a sub who wants to be controlled and dominated doesn't mean I'm weak or afraid. It's the opposite, actually. I want a Dom who can earn the right to dominate over me, and I will fucking crush anybody who isn't worthy. My submission is not weakness, it is strength of the highest caliber.

"Apparently, you spent all that time texting me so that you could be embarrassed tonight. I'm not intimidated by your annoying glare or your guilt trip over the fact that you messed up. I told you my hard limits, and if you paid attention to any part of our texts, it should've been *that* part. I don't do butt stuff. Never have, never will, especially not for some asshole who can't even bother to clean up a little before inviting a woman over."

"I knew it," Zane snaps, standing up quickly and slamming his hands on his hips. "*I knew* I'd get this sort of attitude out of you. Of course. I should've seen it coming. Fucking prude."

"I guess you should've if you were planning on pulling a butt plug from your fucking junk drawer. How about you stick that up your own ass. I'm outta here."

"Maybe I will," Zane fires back, shocking the hell out of me. "Because I'm not a fucking prude like you!"

"Boy, fuck you," I snip as I head for the door. "How about you get yourself together before calling yourself a Dom, and clean up this nasty ass apartment before you catch salmonella or a staph infection from how gross it is in here. Dirty bitch."

"Fuck you, ice queen!" Zane barks, but I don't waste my time turning around again.

I make sure to grab everything I came with so that I don't have to ever come back to this landfill, and I slam the door behind me when I leave.

Another meet up. Another fake Dom. Another disappointing attempt at finding something real. I couldn't possibly be more tired of this shit.

Dear Diary,

What the hell is going on? My luck can't possibly be this bad, can it? Zane was a nightmare, and what bothers me most is that I didn't see it coming. Unfortunately, too many women understand the feeling of blaming themselves for not being able to see into the future and dodging an oncoming asshole. I know it's not my fault, but I've been at this long enough to know better. Right? I've seen enough and experienced enough pieces of shit to be able to spot them a mile away. At least, that was what I thought before meeting Zane. So many red flags! How does this keep happening to me?

I knew it the moment I walked into his raggedy ass apartment that smelled like blue cheese and Axe body spray. But my desire to find love clouded my vision and I went through with it anyway, spitting in the face of my better judgment. I have to start doing a better job of pointing out the issues so that I can swerve past these wannabes. Here is the list of what Zane showed me.

Dirty as hell

Rude the moment he didn't get his way

Had expectations without clearing any of it with me, which means he's bad at communication—the number one mark of a fake Dom

Ignored my hard limits

Tried to talk me into doing things I clearly stated I didn't want to do

Disrespected the sanctity of the safe word!

Now that it's written in front of me, I can't believe I allowed myself to step foot into his apartment. I need to be more alert to the red flags, because this can't keep happening.

Surely there is someone out there who actually knows how to be a Dom. No, let me rephrase. He won't know how to be a Dom. There has to be a man out there who actually is a Dom. Right? For the love of God, please tell me there are still real Doms out there somewhere!

Two

"**W**ait a minute. Did you say a butt plug?"

Sitting in my best friend's living room, surrounded by all the people I enjoy most, I hang my head in both disappointment and exaggerated shame. I was embarrassed enough just writing about it in my diary, but saying it out loud triples the feeling. The room erupts with laughter, making my pain and annoyance feel lighter. I'm still agonized by what happened with Zane last night, but this is what real friends are for. I expected them to make fun of me for taking another shot at love via the FET app, and in a weird way, I needed their jokes and laughter to help bring out my own. Admittedly, I deserve ridicule at this point because my love life is a joke, and Jazmine, Michael, and Jeremiah never let me down.

"Girl, why do you keep going on those kink apps?" Jeremiah asks, still laughing to himself, his dark brown skin reflecting the lights shining from the TV.

Jaz, as usual, is first to speak up for me.

"Jeremiah, don't act brand new," she says jokingly. "That's just the way Nia is. Our girl is a freak, and she's looking for her fellow freak to match her energy."

"I think that's what Mr. Zane was trying to do with that booty plugger," Jeremiah quips quickly, sending us all back into a fit of laughter. "Girl look, I know you're into what you're into, and I applaud how open you are with it, but when you tell people you're kinky and freaky, isn't that what you'd expect?"

Jaz frowns, but I shake my head at her this time so she knows I'd rather answer for myself. As she and her husband Micheal watch with amused faces, I clear my throat and sit up straight, the wine in my glass threatening to spill on the black couch.

"Not even close, Jeremiah," I answer. "Let me explain how this BDSM thing works. Everything is all about consent. It doesn't matter how much kinky shit I put in a profile bio, none of it happens without my *approval*. So, when I tell someone that anal is a hard limit for me, it means that I will not agree to do that. Ever. Hard stop. Don't even ask, and definitely don't try to convince or lure me into it. Ignoring limits is like the ultimate red flag in the lifestyle. In fact, it's a deal breaker."

Jeremiah nods his head as he pulls his leg onto the couch for more comfort. "I hear you. You know I'm just messing with you. *However*, you don't know what you're missing out on, girl."

With a chuckle I reply, "I'm not surprised you'd say that."

"Hold on,"Micheal interrupts. "So, you had to tell this guy that you're not into butt play, and he still tried to talk you into it?"

"Basically," I answer. "Honestly, I think I might have to take a break from the lifestyle and see what the vanilla life is all about. I've known Jaz my entire life, and her vanilla ass got married before I did."

"Okay, let's not call me vanilla like it's an insult," Jaz jumps in, smiling. "I like to turn my freak up sometimes, too. Just not as much as you. Luckily, Micheal isn't interested in plugging me up."

"Oh my god, I shouldn't have told you guys anything. I'm never going to live this down," I say with a roll of my eyes.

"Bitch, *never*," Jaz adds.

As the group descends into laughter again, I find myself thankful that I have friends like this. Jazmine Barnes—now Carmicheal—has been my best friend since I was seven and she was eight, when our parents moved next door to each other in South Philly. My father greeted hers as the two of them were mowing their lawns at the same time, which led to my dad inviting their entire family over so that the kids could play with toys while the parents played spades. The moment the door swung open and I saw Jazmine standing next to her parents with wide eyes and a smile bright enough to blind me, I knew we'd be friends for as long as we had access to each other. Our parents played that card game until midnight before spending the next two hours just talking about life, laughing loud enough for it to echo down the street. I knew they'd all be friends forever, too, and I was right. To this day, the Washingtons and Barnes hang out at least once a week, and their daughters still do as well, just from different houses now that we're grown.

Jaz has seen me through all of my craziness. When my boyfriend cheated on me in college, she drove to Temple University and confronted him in front of all of his friends. She didn't even give me a chance to tell her not to do it. I called her crying, and the second I said, "Terrance cheated on me," she hung up without uttering a word. Jaz is what anyone would call a ride or die friend, and I love her to death. She has stood by my side through every relationship, wardrobe phase, and hair change, cheering me on as I switched from all black to earth tones, and from braids to goddess locs. I don't know what I'd do without her, which is why I told Michael I'd murder him in his sleep if he ever broke her heart.

Micheal smiled his way into Jaz's heart seven years ago. She'd just turned twenty-five and we went out to celebrate the occasion at Club Asylum, which can be a bit sketchy, but it's still one of the most popping clubs in Philly. We entered the club as a group of women, and left with Michael talking in Jaz's ear while he punched his number into her phone. It feels like the two of them have been inseparable ever since, and I love that for her. Micheal is a good guy who likes to provide and make his woman smile. What more could a girl ask for?

As for Jeremiah, he's the only person from my job at Sandcastle that I choose to hang with outside of work. I've been in marketing since I graduated college, and used my degree to become a marketing assistant at Sandcastle, one of Philly's biggest ad agencies. As I worked my way up the ladder, Jeremiah Arnold was hired just below me. As the loud and proud gay man in the building, I knew we'd hit it off and have lots in common, as I am the loud and proud member of the BDSM lifestyle. People who don't know shit about shit will look at both of us like we're crazy, which is exactly why we love and support each other. We've been friends for six years, moving up at Sandcastle and making a name for ourselves during the day, and embracing people who love us for who we are at night.

Together Jeremiah, Jazmine, Michael, and I make up the world's best friend group. Even though we give each other shit for literally everything, it's all done out of love, and any of us would gladly help the other hide a dead body if it came down to it.

"I don't think you should switch it up, Nia," Michael says, crossing one leg over the other. "You may have had a handful of rough situations, but we all know that this is who you truly are and what you really want, so don't go changing it up now."

"It wouldn't work anyway," Jazmine adds. "You like what you like, girl. Even if you could bury it for a little while, eventually it would dig its way back up, and if you're with someone who's not into it, too, it could cause problems. So, you're just going to have to endure."

I swallow another gulp of wine. "Enduring sucks."

"Maybe it's the apps," Micheal says.

"It's 2024," I reply. "This is how single people meet. What else am I supposed to do?"

"Maybe go to a bar or something," Jeremiah answers.

Michael says, "Hit a club. That's where I met the love of my life."

Jaz smiles from ear to ear as I roll my eyes. "Oh, my god. Just rub it right in my face, why don't you."

"Just saying," Micheal tacks on with a playful shrug.

"I don't know if any of that will work," Jaz chimes in. "I'm not sure if what you're looking for is on an app or strutting around some club, but he is out there, Nia. I know it."

I smile without showing my teeth. "Thanks, Jaz. I hope you're right, because I'm thirty years old and turning thirty-one soon. I'm getting tired of trying to date around."

"You know I got your back, girl, and it's going to happen for you. One of these days, the man of your dreams is going to show up, and he's going to sweep you right off your kinky little feet."

"Oh yeah? And what will this man look like?" I inquire jokingly.

"I don't know," Jaz answers. "But you'll know it when you see him. He'll be exactly what you need: a man's man—a Dom's Dom who walks in and owns the room. He'll worship every inch of your beautiful brown skin. He'll look you in those deep brown eyes and tell you that he respects all of your limits, right before he disrespects you exactly the way you like it."

"Well damn," I say with wide eyes and a smile. "I think we should drink to that."

"Hell yeah. Everybody raise your glass," Micheal says as he stands and moves to the center of the living room. The rest of us carefully get up and join him, pushing our glasses up in the air next to his. "Here's to Nia, and knowing the man of her dreams is on his way with whips, chains, blindfolds, and an unshakable respect for her boundaries. To freakiness!"

"To freakiness!" we all say in unison as our glasses clink together and we knock back our drinks.

I finish off my wine and embrace the buzz as it swallows me. This is what I need right now—friends and a strong buzz—to distract me from the fact that another date went off the rails and there's no hope in sight. Maybe Micheal's toast will be the wish I need to make it all better, because things certainly can't get much worse.

Three

"**D**amn, I'm about to walk out the door. Why are you calling me already?"

"Girl, you need to hurry up and get here. It is going *down* at the office," Jeremiah says over the speaker of my cell as I grab my coffee and head toward the front door.

I snatch my keys off the hook and struggle to pull the door closed as I scoot out backward. "What do you mean? What's going on?"

Jeremiah suddenly lowers his voice to a whisper. "Mr. Thomas is in his office with boxes. So are Eddie and Jake. Everybody is trying to sneak and watch them while they pack up their stuff. The police are standing next to Mr. Thomas's door, watching as he sulks and grabs his belongings. We think he got fired."

"Mr. Thomas can't be fired, Jeremiah. He's the Chief Marketing Officer. He owns the place." I drop down in my seat and close the door, suddenly in a hurry to get to Sandcastle.

"From what I'm staring at right now, he *was* the Chief Marketing Officer," he says as I start up my car and back out into the street.

"What the hell? Okay, I'll be there in ten minutes if the traffic isn't crazy. But, it's Philly so I'll see you in half an hour."

Jeremiah sucks his teeth. "Do yourself a favor and get here faster than that. You don't want to miss this."

My drive to work is as annoying as it always is. Stopped traffic comes into view the second I steer the car toward the highway exit, and I come to a complete stand still behind a forest of brake lights. While I'm stuck, I think about what could possibly be happening at my office. I've been at Sandcastle for nine years, and Mr. Larry Thomas has been the Chief Marketing Officer, or CMO, the entire time. He owns the company and has staffed it with a couple of his annoying ass sons who strut around the place in high positions with the knowledge that they will own it after Daddy is gone. The nepotism alone should guarantee that the Thomases will remain in control of the ad agency for the next few generations, unless they decide to sell. For the life of me, I can't think of what could have happened that all three of them would be departing. Maybe they did sell. But why would they do that?

Working for Mr. Thomas hasn't been all bad. He is your typical boss who thinks he's better than everyone who works beneath him, but he's not racist, sexist, homophobic, or islamophobic, and he doesn't make passes at the women who work there. He has promoted me three times since I started working for him. Considering how ugly the world is these days, things could be a lot worse than him just being out of touch and inconsiderate. We've never had any run-ins that made me want to quit and go job hunting, but the thing about people in the upper class like the Thomas family is that you never truly know them. It wouldn't surprise me if there was a treasure chest of secrets that Mr. Thomas keeps stashed away from us lowly employees. On the other hand, his sons are little pieces of shit who don't deserve the privilege their father's hard work affords them.

Jake is the oldest, and he's as arrogant as he is ugly. While the younger brother, Eddie, just graduated from Temple last year and already thinks he runs the place. He even started sleeping with one of his father's secretaries, and when the relationship fell apart he got her fired. If Mr. Thomas really is leaving, I pray he takes those little fuckers with him, because I'd hate to be stuck working for either of his offspring.

When traffic finally has a breakthrough, I weave my way up the road and into the Sandcastle parking lot as fast as I'm able. I check my phone one last time for messages on FET—I'm a glutton for punishment, I know—and hurry out of the car, jogging all the way to the door. When I step inside, I'm shocked to find exactly what Jeremiah described, the scene still playing out in perfect detail. Larry Thomas and his two sons are in his office holding large brown boxes. Jake and Eddie's offices are already cleaned out. The three of them take their time taking pictures and diplomas off the wall, filling their respective boxes with everything Mr. Thomas owns. I keep my eyes on them as I walk to my office and find Jeremiah standing in the doorway with a puzzled look on his face.

"What the hell is going on?" I ask, turning to the side so I can slide past him. "They're really leaving? No one knows why? This is crazy."

Jeremiah pulls at the bottom of his burgundy button-up to straighten it out, keeping his brown eyes on the unfolding scene in front of him.

"As of right now, no one has been told a thing," he says.

"What about Sierra? She's VP of Marketing, surely she's heard something. Is she taking over?"

"She has been in and out of Mr. Thomas's office, but she hasn't addressed the rest of us. They had a conversation when he first arrived, but it didn't last long and Sierra didn't look happy afterward."

I sit at my desk and start up my computer, hoping that maybe something came down to the heads of each department, informing us of a pending change of leadership. Brushing my locs over my shoulder, I scan my inbox, skimming through the subjects of each new email and finding nothing from Mr. Thomas.

"There's nothing in my email either," I inform Jeremiah as I lean back in my seat. "So, it's a blackout. No new information in or out. Something big must've happened."

"Clearly," Jeremiah answers. "The police being here certainly adds a thick layer of mystery and awe. Surely there must've been a quieter way of doing this if they're trying to protect a big secret. Now they have the eyes of the entire marketing department on them. Were they really expecting us to just go back to wo—"

The sound of my phone vibrating on my table cuts off Jeremiah's last word. He turns around and catches me grinning as I open up the Tinder app to see that I just matched with someone—a dark-haired personal trainer with a perfect hairline and a strong jaw. His skin is caramel brown, just like mine, and he has hazel eyes. In his profile pic, his smile is mesmerizing as he stares directly into the camera lens like it is a person instead of his phone. His name is Marcus, and I swiped right on him two days ago.

"Really, Nia?"

Jeremiah's voice snaps me out of my lust-struck gaze, and I look up to find him staring at me with a twisted mouth.

"What?" I say with a shrug.

"Tinder? Now?" he asks. When I don't respond he continues. "So the butt plug situation wasn't enough to put you on hold for a little while?"

"Okay, number one—no it wasn't," I answer. "And number two—mind your business. A girl has needs, and Zane wasn't even allowed to try to meet them. I'm not a big fan of masturbation, so yes, I'm going to keep playing the field."

Jeremiah gawks at me for a moment, shaking his head. "You do you then, I guess. Good luck with all of that."

"Thank you, because clearly I need it."

Jeremiah and I laugh just as the silence in the rest of the building is finally broken.

"Umm, excuse me. Can I get everyone to gather around for a second?"

Jeremiah snaps his head over as I jump out of my seat to see what's going on. Mr. Thomas and his sons are standing in the center of the office, their boxes placed at their feet while the uniformed officers stand next to the exit watching. Everyone who owns an office leaves it, while the people from the bullpen stand at their cubicles to see what's about to happen. I step out of my office and lean against the wall by my door. Jeremiah goes to his desk in the bullpen and stands behind his chair, clutching it as he awaits the news.

Mr. Thomas stands in the center in a wrinkled white button-up and blue jeans. His thinning hair is a mess and he has newly formed bags under his eyes that stand out amongst the rest of the wrinkles. His entire aura is disheveled, and his sons don't look much better. He clears his throat, his expression one part sadness, two parts embarrassment. Jake and Eddie both look down at the floor as their father begins to address the room.

"Some of you may have already heard the news. Most of you probably haven't. While it would've been easier and less humiliating for me to do this in the middle of the night while you were all at home, I decided to do it now because I wanted to be the one to inform you of what has happened. If you haven't figured it out from the fact that my sons and I have cleared out our offices, I will be stepping down as CMO of Sandcastle. I am leaving, as are my sons, Jake and Eddie."

Groans and gasps crescendo through the space as people start to look around for answers that aren't there. Mr. Thomas gives it a second before continuing.

"This may come as a shock to most of you," he says, his face flushing from the chagrin of his next words, "but I am being indicted on money laundering charges. At the advice of my lawyer, I will not be speaking on the matter, but this clearly presents a major problem for me and my family."

The gasps and groans rise to a roar.

"Try not to get bogged down by the details," Mr. Thomas says with a raised hand that he hopes will quiet the crowd. "Just know that it has been an absolute pleasure to run this company, and I'm sorry that it has come to this.

"What's most important to you all isn't that I'm leaving, it's who you will be working for going forward. There have been a lot of internal discussions as to who will be my successor, and plenty of names were thrown in the hat by myself and the board, including the current VP of Marketing, Miss Sierra Martinez."

Sierra, who is standing at the very front of the crowd in a navy blue pantsuit, suddenly drops her head.

"It was a very tough decision, to say the least, however, it was decided that we would go another route," Mr. Thomas says. "We thought it best that the company get a new shot of adrenaline to catapult it forward. I only want the best for the company I built, and the current department heads are absolutely brilliant at their jobs. I don't want to derail the progress that has already been made. So, with that being said, I'd like to announce that Sandcastle has been sold and will be under new ownership. The new Chief Marketing Officer will be here tomorrow. His name is Rome Giovanni."

Groans turn to whispers as frustration, confusion, and worry spark to life and spread like wildfire amongst the Sandcastle employees.

"Let me assure you all," Mr. Thomas goes on, "that no one has to be worried about losing their job. The mistakes I've made will not cost any of you the careers you worked so hard for. At least, that is the assurance Mr. Giovanni has given me. He's a businessman, and I expect that he will keep his word. The change taking place is happening at the top, and at the top only.

"Sandcastle has had great days and bad days. I'm sorry for the bad ones, and I'm grateful for the great. I hope I was a good boss to you all. My sons and I have learned so much from you, and I know all of you will go on to do magnificent things. I'm sorry it has to end this way, but you're in good hands going forward, and I hope all of us will land on our feet. Thanks very much."

With that, Mr. Thomas and his sons pick up their boxes and begin making their way out. People tap them on the shoulder and quietly wish them the best as they depart, but in just a few seconds, it all ends. The three of them walk out of the building, flanked by the uniformed officers who escorted them in. The door closes behind them and the entire office is frozen in a state of confusion and shock. Jeremiah looks at me with wide eyes, and all I can do is shake my head.

There are a million questions still left unanswered by the impromptu announcement, and while I desperately want to know how things are going to be different for Sandcastle, there's another question I'm dying to ask. There's an answer we all need before anything else happens.

Who the hell is Rome Giovanni?

Four

"**M**oney laundering?"

"I know, right? It's insane," I reply, lowering my face to the oversized margarita in front of me and taking a big sip from the straw.

Jazmine sits across from me with a margarita of her own, still wearing her work clothes—a beautiful royal blue skirt with a white blouse. Her hair is straight and hanging down just past her shoulders, and her makeup is flawlessly applied, putting her gorgeous, blemish-free face on full display for the entire Al Pastor restaurant to see. I'm so glad she agreed to meet me here for drinks after work, because the craziness of my day at Sandcastle was enough to drive anyone to alcohol. The restaurant hums with the voices of people chatting and chowing down on Mexican food, but Jaz and I are only here for the drinks.

"I'm sure Jeremiah was in there cutting up as he watched that scene unfold," she says, fiddling with the orange slice hanging off the side of her glass.

I laugh. "You know he was. Then again, everybody was really in awe. After they left, I don't think anyone got any work done. All we could do was talk about it."

"Was there any more information about the money laundering? He can't just say that and then dip out."

"But he did. He said he caught money laundering charges and that his lawyer told him not to talk about it, and he never brought it up again. I tried to press Sierra for answers, but you know how much of a bitch she is. As usual, she gave us nothing, so we were left to discuss it amongst ourselves and google his name to see what came up."

"And?" Jaz asks, staring at me with wide eyes, fully invested.

"It was vague," I answer. "There was an indictment on money laundering linked to gambling, but they didn't go into detail about it because the case and investigation are ongoing. There wasn't anything in the article about where he was gambling or how much, and I guess the sale of the company was too recent because it wasn't mentioned at all. We were all pissed because we wanted to know about the guy Mr. Thomas sold the business to. I guess we'll find out when he shows up tomorrow."

Jaz frowns. "Mr. Thomas didn't say anything about him?"

"Only that he will be here tomorrow," I answer. "Searching his name didn't give us anything either, which I think is odd. I really hope Larry didn't sell us to some asshole who is going to run the place into the ground."

"Well if he did, you can always come work with me."

"Girl, you know I don't know a thing about banking."

"Yeah, but that's the good thing about me being the manager of First Philadelphia—I can hire who I want," Jaz informs me proudly, wearing her recent promotion very well. "If Larry Thomas can bring in his sons to work at Sandcastle, I can hire my best friend to work at my bank. We can do a friend's version of nepotism."

"Well, you've got a point there," I say. "Let's just hope the guy isn't a piece of shit and it doesn't come to that."

"Make sure you call me tomorrow. I'm going to want to hear all about this new boss."

"Oh, you know I will," I reply.

As I sip my drink down to its final remnants, I lift my phone from the table and open up FET again. The tequila has started to work its magic, and I'm suddenly wishing I had someone to go home to. That's the thing about being single—you don't realize how lonely you are until it really hits you. Back when I was dating Terrance, I was convinced that being single would be much more fun than being committed to someone. I thought everybody who was unattached was out there living their best life, hooking up with new people every other day and never feeling bored or alone. In my head, it was all fun and games for them, while Terrance and I had grown used to each other and too comfortable with taking our familiarity for granted. We always think the grass is greener on the other side until we reach it and see it was just a mirage, the color fading as soon as we give up what we didn't appreciate enough.

I'm glad Terrance and I broke up, and I've certainly had my fun as a single woman, but I'm thirty now. The fun and games have started to turn into stress and drama, and while I'm gladly a kinky girl, it would be so nice to have someone to be kinky with every day. Someone who knows my kinks and has mastered how to play with them, tantalizing and teasing each one until I'm on the brink of explosion. I want someone—just *one* person—who I belong to.

I crave a Dom who knows how to own me and chooses to do it every single day. Someone who can handle emotions and mood changes that come with the ups and downs of life, and consoles me when I'm frustrated before allowing me the freedom to let go. This is why I don't understand when my friends say they're not into kinks or submission. Why wouldn't they want the privilege of letting it all go after a maddening day at work? They don't understand what it's like submitting to someone you trust with your life, and allowing them to remove every stitch of stress from your flesh. Giving it all to a person who can handle it for you, massaging you with pain and pleasure until the world melts away.

Yeah, I'm definitely tired of being single, but there's another part of it that is even more annoying than the rest. Dating around has shown me that the prospects are abysmal. I wholeheartedly want to be someone's good girl, but all I see is men trying so hard to be bad boys that I can tell from a single glance that they are anything but.

"Uh-oh," Jazmine says. When I look up I see her watching me like a hawk.

"What?"

"I see the way you're scrolling through that phone," she says, shaking her head. "You've got that look in your eye."

"What look? I don't have a look."

"Yes, you do. It's that look you get when you're thinking about your sex life."

I laugh nervously. "I don't have a sex life look."

"Oh? Then how come I can tell just from looking at you that you're either scrolling through that BDSM app or swiping through Tinder?"

I freeze, my eyes wide.

"Told you," Jaz says before laughing.

I laugh with her, but when I look at my phone again, everything is a lot less funny.

"I can't help it," I state sadly. "You're so lucky to be married and happy with Micheal. All I want is my own kinky version of that, but these fucking men out here are pitiful. Look at this." I get up from my side of the booth and sit next to Jaz so she can see my phone as I look through FET. "As I scroll, just tell me what you think of the guys you see."

Jazmine nods, and I begin. "Eww. Hideous," she says on the first guy.

I laugh and keep going.

"Why does this one look like he lives under the stairs in someone's basement?"

I try to stifle another laugh as I continue scrolling.

"Nia, what is this?" Jaz inquires on the next guy. "There's no way these are the men on the dating app you're on so often. This guy says he's into blood play. *Blood* play? Is that what I think it is?"

I nod. "Yes, it is. We don't kink shame, so I'll just say that's not for me and move on."

"Okay. Well, this guy is cute in a sort of 'I was raised in the wild by rabid dogs' kind of way. But what is primal play?"

The waitress brings me a second margarita while I laugh at another of Jaz's insane insults. Once I can breathe again, I try to explain the answer to her question.

"He wants to be the sub in a primal scene," I begin. "Meaning he wants to be hunted like prey, captured and tied up. The chase turns him on. It's definitely a thing and can be pretty hot when done right, but I don't want a guy who is a sub, or who looks like they were raised in the wild by rabid dogs."

I keep scrolling, and every man that comes up is greeted with words of disgust from Jazmine.

Gross.

Terrifying.

Ugly.

Lives with his mom.

Broke.

Married and trying to cheat on the low.

Has never been to the dentist.

Looks like he's into making poisons.

On and on it goes until I finally give up and close the app. I set the phone down and lean against Jaz's shoulder, fake crying.

"If I have a sad face when looking at my phone, this is why," I say. "Being single fucking sucks."

"Clearly," she replies. "You need to download more apps, because that one is filled with nothing but trolls."

"But that's the thing, Jaz. That's the way it is on all of them," I tell her as I pick up the phone again. "However, I did just match with someone on Tinder."

Jaz nearly spits out her drink trying to speak. "Damn, why didn't you start with that? You got me out here looking at all these creatures on FET when you matched on Tinder? Let me see."

Laughing, I open Tinder and show Jaz the personal trainer I matched with just this morning. When she sees him, she smiles.

"Okay," she exclaims. "Marcus Graham. Brown skin, hazel eyes, nice smile with straight teeth, neatly trimmed beard. He's cute, Nia. When are you linking up with him?"

"I don't know," I say with a shrug. "I got the match when I was at work this morning and didn't have time to think about anything but the craziness at the office."

"Well what are you waiting for? You're off work now."

"Yeah, but ... I don't know. I sort of wanted him to reach out to me first."

She scoffs. "Girl, it's 2024. A woman is allowed to make the first move."

"I know that, but I'm a submissive, Jaz. I want a dominant man who can take the lead, and that means showing me that he's interested."

"Matching with you didn't show you that he's interested?"

"You know what I mean," I shoot back. "It'd just be nice if he reached out to me first. A message would let me know that he's *really* interested. Swiping right on me just means he thinks I'm attractive. Now that we've matched and he knows I found him attractive, too, he should be ready to make the first move."

"So, matching put the ball in his court?"

"There's no *ball*," I joke. "I just want to wait a little bit and see what he does. If he doesn't message me by the end of the day tomorrow, I'll write to him. Okay?"

Jaz nods as she sips her drink, finishing it and waving off the waitress so that she doesn't bring her another one.

"Okay," she answers. "Look, all I'm saying is that when you want something, sometimes you have to reach out and grab it. I'm not saying Marcus Graham is *the one*, but you have a little opportunity here. Don't let it slip away by being stubborn."

I nod my head before sipping my drink again. I know Jaz is right, but at the same time, I'm not interested in settling. As much as I may have to reach out and grab what I want, it has to be worth reaching for. It has to be worth grabbing. It has to be what I want, and I want a *real* Dom. Sadly, even after matching with Marcus, I'm starting to think they no longer exist.

Dear Diary,

A Dominant would make the first move.

Here I sit, after a night out with my bestie, and Marcus from Tinder hasn't reached out yet. What is he waiting for? I get so tired of trying to explain this to people, but there are certain things I expect from a man claiming to be a Dominant.

A Dom wouldn't be moved by what year it is. He wouldn't be put off by the idea that women are more vocal about what they want now. He'd respect that fact, but he'd also understand that labeling himself as a Dom would conjure specific expectations. I can't think of a single scenario where a submissive would reach out to a Dom first.

Sure, it's 2024 ... but what the fuck? 😐

Five

My drive to work feels a lot like the first day of school. I'm nervous as I take the same exit I do every day, and anxious as I park my car in its usual spot. Everything is as normal as it always is, but my nerves are piqued as I get out of the car and start walking in. I don't know what awaits me inside, and I'm hot from the stress. This is it. Today is the day we meet the new owner and CMO of Sandcastle.

When I enter, nothing looks different. Everyone is working as usual, but when the door opens everyone's head pops in my direction. All of the eyes in the room land on me and I freeze, wondering what the hell is going on. When they realize it is just me, everyone goes back to what they were doing. Just like me, they are all waiting for Rome Giovanni to arrive.

I walk down the narrow pathway on my way to my office with my eyes on the floor. The click-clack of keyboards fills the air, mixed with low voices having conversations about work and phone calls with clients. I see Jeremiah working at his desk just a few feet from my door, but his eyes are glued to his computer so he doesn't realize I'm here. Before I step inside, I take a glance toward the CMO's office. The lights are out and the door is closed. So nothing has changed since yesterday. I let out a sigh, flick on my lights, and make my way to my desk.

As the start of the day unfolds, I go through my normal routine of firing up my computer and sifting through emails from clients. Usually, there are plenty of messages from Mr. Thomas about Sandcastle's agenda, but now there is nothing. It's actually weird to see my inbox devoid of any of his instructions, demands, and expectations, and I can't help but wonder what it will look like once Mr. Giovanni arrives and takes over. Will he cuss us out via email if things aren't going well? Will he flirt with the women he thinks are prettiest? Maybe he'll flirt with the men. As one of the two Directors of Marketing, I will have to work closely with him. How will he treat me? Will he hate me? Will I hate him? If we don't get along, will we have arguments? Will he call me out in front of my coworkers or pull me aside to speak privately? What if he's an old racist who refuses to accept working with a Black woman? What would that mean for me? Demotion? What would it mean for Jeremiah, a gay Black man? Termination? Lawsuits for discrimination? Exactly what will my life be like now that Mr. Thomas is gone? Will the grass be greener, or will it be the mirage?

With another long exhale, I lean back in my chair and try to calm myself down. The man hasn't even arrived and I'm already driving myself insane with worry and made up scenarios. Maybe he'll be wonderful and nice. Who knows? All I can do is wait and see, and just like every other employee out there, I'll be on the edge of my seat the entire time.

Once I'm done scanning emails, I pick up my phone. I haven't received any messages from my Tinder match, which sucks, but I have gotten a couple on FET. I hold out hope as I navigate to the app and check the messages, only to find that they are from men interested in race play. Like I told Jaz yesterday, I don't knock anybody's kinks, but that is absolutely not something I'm interested in.

"Still sowing your wild oats?" Jeremiah's distinct voice says from the doorway. I find him beaming at me as he leans half his body into the room with a wide smile.

"Trying to," I reply. "I'm clearly in a drought when it comes to FET, and I haven't heard from the guy I matched with on Tinder. My email doesn't have anything new or interesting since Mr. Thomas's departure, so I'm actually bored. What's going on out there in the bullpen?"

Jeremiah steps into the room and plops down into one of the black and gray accent chairs next to the large window in my office that looks out into the bullpen. He's dressed in a shiny black button-up today, looking as dapper as he always does.

"Everybody is anxiously waiting for the new CMO," he tells me. "People are in there stressed out. One girl said she found a Facebook page of a guy named Rome Giovanni, and he's some old Italian guy who looks mean. Another girl said she found a young guy with the same name on Instagram, but his page was completely blank. Then, Martha from brand marketing, said she found a Twitter account with a guy who was at least sixty. His page didn't have any posts, but she could see his likes, and every one of them was for an underage girl."

"What the fuck?" I exclaim with disgust.

"I know, right? There's no proof that any of them are right, but so far it doesn't look good."

"That's just great," I reply sarcastically as I get up from my seat and walk to the door to stare out into the bullpen. Everyone looks busy, but I see plenty of eyes shifting over to the entrance before going back to work. "Do you have any expectations?"

"I don't even know," he answers. "As long as he isn't a homophobe, it really doesn't matter to me. You're the one who has to work with the CMO and VP regularly."

"That's a very unfortunate fact," I say. "Simon and I could have our hands full if the guy's a douche."

As soon as I get the words out, Simon Sampson walks into the room in a white T-shirt and khaki pants. His face is covered in stubble and I can see the anxiety seeping from his pores as he eyes me and Jeremiah.

"Have you seen or heard from Sierra this morning?" he asks, placing his hands on his hips like he always does when he's nervous.

"I haven't," I answer. "I can only assume she's either sick, running late, or out with the new boss."

"She's with him," Simon says as if the fact makes him upset. "She told me last night that they were going to meet early this morning before coming here. I told her that I wanted to join her so that I could be introduced to the new CMO, but she hasn't responded to any of my texts."

"Why were you trying to meet him before everyone else?" Jeremiah asks, frowning hard as he stares up at Simon.

Simon scoffs. "I'm a director of marketing. It's important that I make a good first impression."

"You mean you wanted to make an impression *first*, before anybody else—meaning Nia—could," Jeremiah shoots back without missing a beat.

Simon's eyes dance over to me, but they don't linger.

"That's not ... no, that *isn't* why," Simon lies.

"Sure, Simon," Jeremiah says as he rises from the chair and speaks to me over his shoulder. "I'll see you later, Nia."

"Later," I reply.

Simon's eyes are wide as he looks at me. "What he said is totally not true, Nia. I wouldn't do that."

I have to laugh, because Simon Sampson is well-known in Sandcastle as the office brown nose. We all are aware of the fact that he kisses the boss's ass, and will throw any of us under the bus if he thinks he can benefit from us being run over. It's nothing new, and I've learned to not let it bother me.

"It's fine, Simon," I reply dryly. "Did Sierra tell you anything about the new boss?"

"Unfortunately, she didn't. Honestly, she didn't seem to know much about him herself. It was Mr. Thomas who set it up for her to meet Mr. Giovanni this morning so she could show him around the place. I guess Larry didn't tell her much either."

"Damn. Nobody knows anything about him."

"Nope. I really wish Sierra would have answered my—"

Simon cuts his sentence short as his head nearly breaks to look at the entrance door. Sunlight beams into the office in a long white streak as the door opens, and everyone in the building stops moving. Simon and I step into my doorway, cramming into the small space to get a peek of who might be coming in. Is this it? The moment we've all been waiting for?

The first person to walk in is Sierra Martinez. Her brown skin looks golden in the sunbeam, her lips plump and covered in dark lipstick, her hair wavy as it careens down her back, and her brown eyes focused on someone behind her. She holds the door open while the rest of us hold our breath. Then, he enters.

The air in the room is sucked out along with the oxygen in my lungs. We all see him at the same time, and I swear he is the only thing moving. He's the only thing *alive* in the entire building, and my forehead is blanketed with wrinkles as I gawk at him in confusion.

He's at least six-foot-two—maybe even six-three—with broad shoulders carrying a fit frame, but not overly muscular. His black hair is perfectly styled and almost looks wet, but when he instinctively runs his fingers through it, there is no residue coating his hand. His jawline is the strongest feature on his tanned face, and it is covered in a perfectly trimmed, well-kept beard. His lips are pink and full, drawing my eyes to them when he sucks the lower one into his mouth, biting it before letting it flop back out again. The gray suit he's wearing looks tailored to his body—not too big, not too small, but perfect for him and him only. His light brown eyes scan the room, and even though he's moving at a normal speed, it feels like he's in slow motion. The rest of the world has stopped turning in order for him to make his entrance, and it is more grand than I ever could have imagined. The man is absolutely stunning.

Everyone gawks at him as the door finally closes and he begins following Sierra. She leads him down the path, only stopping to explain what he's seeing.

"This is the bullpen," she says in her strong Spanish accent. "Managers, individual contributors, and everyone who is entry-level works here. Directors of marketing, advertising, brands, social media, and products all have offices—as well as you and I, of course. I'll introduce you to everyone soon, but let me show you to your office first."

He doesn't reply verbally, only with a subtle nod. Sierra spins on her heel and begins down the path again, and my heart starts to hammer. The walkway runs directly in front of my office, which means he is going to see me. We are going to be face to face, if only briefly. I don't know why, but I'm more nervous now than I was when I thought he could be an old racist. Shit. Should I go back to my desk and act like I'm hard at work? That's what Simon would do—look like the hardest working person in the building—but even he is frozen solid. My feet won't move. I'm stuck in cement with my eyes glued to his face. Before I can even shift an inch, his eyes find me as he and Sierra approach.

"G ... good morning, Sir," I hear myself say.

Why? Why the hell did I say that?

Again, he doesn't reply with words. He nods at me, but the look on his face isn't polite or inviting. In fact, I'd say his gaze is menacing. So much so that I involuntarily take a small step backward. I couldn't move myself, but the stone cold stare in his eyes forced me back with nothing more than a look.

The moment passes as he and Sierra keep going. The entire office watches as Sierra walks into the CMO office and turns on the light. Mr. Giovanni walks in behind her, and she steps to the side to allow him access to everything that is now his. Even Sierra, who is usually so bold and headstrong, looks anxious and quiet around him. She moves like a servant, pointing out things to the owner of every item in the building. I've never seen her look so meek, even when standing next to Mr. Thomas. It's clear that the man she's showing around now *is not* Mr. Thomas. They couldn't be more different, and even Sierra knows it.

The door to the office closes, and sound and air finally re-enter the building. Everyone in the bullpen comes back to life. Mouths pop open and jaws hit the floor. Smiles take over the faces of quite a few of the women and even a few men, and when I look at Jeremiah, his eyes are saucers.

We stare at each other, both of us clearly thinking the exact same thing, but Jeremiah is the only one to say it out loud. He speaks my thoughts into existence with the exact level of enthusiasm that I hear inside my head.

"Holy fucking shit."

Six – Rome

When the door opens, I see more than just a room full of people who will be working for me. I see opportunity. I see my vision for my future and the vision my father always had for me ... before. My purchase of Sandcastle is about more than just owning the business. It's about who I am as a person and who I want to become. It's about being great and making my parents proud ... and Natalia.

I spent the early part of my morning with Sierra Martinez, the vice president of Sandcastle. At Larry Thomas's suggestion, she and I met up for coffee and talked about the ins and outs of the company. She did her best to break it all down for me, and also gave me the impression that she really knows her stuff. She will be someone I can rely on going forward. Seeing as how this is the first business I have ever owned, I'll need someone like her to help me along the way. I'm ambitious but also inexperienced, so her expertise will certainly come in handy. However, her eyes have a habit of landing on me and staying there. Her gaze is strong and enticing to say the least. I can tell she has a Type A personality and is a control freak. Perfect. She's the opposite of anything I'll ever want, which means she won't be a distraction.

I see the way they look at me when I walk into the building. They have probably been wondering about the man who swooped in and bought the company, stressing themselves out about the kind of boss I will be. They stare hard, their mouths agape as I walk past them on my way to the office, and I'm not the kind of person who wants to shout out some sort of cheerful greeting or motivational speech. I'm not in the mood to smile or act in a way that is different from who I really am. All of them should get used to seeing this face and the expression on it. It is the real Rome. I am steel—cold and hard at all times. I don't want to be friends or think of my new employees as my family. This is business, and business only.

"This is the bullpen," Sierra says as I look out into the crowd of people in their cubicles.

Some of them stare at me in a way that lets me know exactly what they are thinking. No matter. Once they get to know me, they'll stop.

"Managers, individual contributors, and everyone who is entry-level works here. Directors of marketing, advertising, brands, social media, and products all have offices—as well as you and I, of course. I'll introduce you to everyone soon, but let me show you to your office first."

I nod at Sierra and she continues to guide me down a path of gray hardwood that leads to all of the offices on the perimeter of the bullpen. I follow her lead, doing my best not to make eye contact with anyone just yet. When I'm ready to address them I will, but until then, they can stay on pins and needles.

As we walk, the path takes us past the first office. Two people stand on my right, squishing themselves into the doorway as they gawk at me with unblinking eyes. One is a man who either needs to shave or learn how to care for his beard. He is wearing khaki pants and a glaringly fake smile, and the little nod he gives makes me want to frown in response. I don't know who he is here, but I hope he is not someone I have to work with regularly.

Next to him is a woman with mesmerizing brown skin and strawberry brown locs that hang down to her waist. Her almond-shaped eyes bore into me, and my gaze drops down to her seductively plump lips as she speaks.

"G ... good morning, Sir."

Now I'm the one who is staring, but I shouldn't be. There is something about her, though. Something intriguing that threatens to make me stop walking and start saying things I shouldn't. Her eyes never move from mine, even when she takes a step back as though she's afraid of being too close. I know she's waiting for a response, but the look on her face is like she's waiting for ... a command.

No. I'm not here for that, and I refuse to let myself get sidetracked when this journey has just begun. So, I force myself to move on from her, pulling my eyes away without uttering a single word. When I reach the office, Sierra is already waiting for me. She steps aside so that I can move about the room where I will be spending most of my time as I try to take this business to heights it has never seen before. I want it all to be bigger and better than ever, and as I take inventory of everything in the office, noting the things I will want to change now that it is mine, I know that I'll be successful. I will run this company the same way that I run my life.

I am dominant. I am in control at all times, and anything standing in my way will be pushed aside. This company will be the biggest ad agency in Philadelphia before I'm done with it. All I have to do is remain focused ... and ignore the girl who called me Sir.

Red & Green Flags

Seven

"This looks great, Jeremiah. Let's make the image on the right a little smaller, though. It's taking focus away from the product to its left."

I stand behind my chair and desk as Jeremiah sits in my spot with an ad he designed on my computer. The image is almost complete and ready to move up to Sierra for final approval, but we just need to tweak it a bit before submitting.

With Mr. Thomas gone and the new boss, Rome Giovanni, taking a guided tour to every single department, there isn't anything to do but continue working on the projects we had going before the change happened. We've already lost six clients since news of Mr. Thomas's indictment spread like wildfire, and we can't lose any more. As distracting as it was to watch Mr. Giovanni enter the building looking like a fashion model worthy of a seven-figure contract, Sandcastle still has work to do and commitments to honor if we want to keep the company standing. That won't change, no matter who is seated at the top of the pyramid. But just because I'm trying to continue getting work done doesn't mean I'm not still mesmerized by what I saw.

The image of him stepping through the door still weighs on me, repeating in my mind on a sexy little loop between my instructions to Jeremiah. With all of the expectations I had in my head before he walked in, I never thought he would look *that* way. Mr. Thomas was fifty-two years old and looked every bit of it and then some. He certainly didn't age well, but Mr. Giovanni is either aging like a demigod or he's only in his thirties. Even with his tailored suit covering his physique, it was clear that he is in great shape and takes care of himself. I would bet that he doesn't miss anything—his finger and toe nails clipped at all times, his hair always kept in perfect shape at his scheduled barber appointments, and his apartment spotless every single day. If he pays that much attention to detail, what will it mean for Sandcastle? What will it mean for me?

"How's that?" Jeremiah asks, leaning back in the seat so I can see the entire screen.

I scan the image, nodding my approval. "Perfect. Save it, and then send it to Sierra from my email—not that she is going to see it any time soon."

Jeremiah chuckles as he saves the image. "Yeah, she's too busy escorting the new king around. I don't blame her, though. I want to be close to him for as long as possible, too."

Once the email is sent, Jeremiah spins around and looks me directly in the eyes.

"I've been trying not to say anything," I tell him, "but my professionalism is hanging by a very thin thread."

He scoffs. "Fuck that thread. I can't believe he had the audacity to come up in here looking like the world's most flavorful snack. I was awestruck, taken aback, and flabbergasted."

"Well, that makes two of us then, because I was *befuddled* myself."

"Downright *bewildered* by that man's beauty." Both of us fall into laughter like high-school kids at a pep rally before Jeremiah adds, "I didn't see a ring on his finger either. Maybe you should make a move, because *girl*."

"With the boss? I don't think so. Maybe *you* should," I reply.

"No way. I'm not about to have these bitches in here whispering about me behind my back," he responds. "Plus, that man is *not* gay. He's very well-dressed, but you know I can tell. The only one of us that has a chance is you. So, go out there and make us proud. Unless, of course, you're already committed to Mr. Tinder."

"Ugh, he hasn't even messaged me yet. I'm telling you, I'm cursed to be single for life. Tinder isn't popping, FET is a wasteland, and you know I can't sleep with our boss—not that he'd be interested in a kinky girl like me anyway."

"Oh, you've got a point there," Jeremiah says with a wince followed by a laugh. "Your freaky ass might scare the man away as soon as you ask him to engage in breath play."

I frown and let out a fake wail. "The thought of that man with his hands around my throat could literally make me cry. What I wouldn't give."

Jeremiah laughs. "Girl, you are a mess. So much for professionalism, huh?"

"The thread has snapped."

My friend and I laugh together, but the moment is cut short when Sierra Martinez steps into the bullpen and addresses the group. Her voice booms through the open area and slithers into each office, her accent on full display.

"Ladies and gentlemen," she shouts. "If everyone could get to a good stopping point in your work and gather in conference room A, I'd appreciate it. Mr. Giovanni would like to address us all."

Jeremiah's eyes widen as my heart begins to speed up. I don't know why I would be nervous to have a meeting with the new boss. Is it because of how he looks, or because I'm still worried that he might be an asshole? It's usually the pretty ones that are assholes anyway ... although Mr. Giovanni isn't really *pretty*. He's more ruggedly handsome, with a stern demeanor and intense glare that would bring any woman to her knees, and I am any woman.

Everyone slowly makes their way into the large conference room. The department heads take seats at the front of the table while the less seasoned employees fill up the back end and the chairs lined up along the wall. Once everyone is settled, Sierra enters the room first, walking up the aisle and sitting in her usual spot to the right of the head of the table, followed by Mr. Giovanni.

All elegance mixed with hardness, he struts in, his face devoid of anything that would give away his thoughts. He is emotionless yet carefree as he walks to the front of the room and comes to a stop behind the seat at the head of the table. Everyone watches intently, no words spoken as his presence turns up the dial of intensity in the room. My nerves come roaring back because I'm so close to him that I can smell his cologne every time he moves, the masculine fragrance hypnotizing me from two chairs away. I gawk at him just like everyone else as he comes to a stop, unfastens the buttons on his jacket and removes it. I swallow back a gasp as he neatly places the jacket on the back of the chair, his toned muscles making their presence known beneath his white undershirt and black tie. Then he sits, interlocks his fingers on the table, and lets his eyes slowly connect with everyone around him. He starts on the opposite side of the table, intentionally making eye contact with everyone before finally reaching my side. Our eyes meet, he pauses briefly, I freeze and swallow hard, then he moves to Sierra next to me—and I've never seen a man command a room the way he has this one.

"*Buongiorno*," he finally says.

I pinch my lips together so hard I expect to draw blood. His fucking voice ... and he just spoke Italian. Is this a cruel punishment from God? Am I being tested? Why on Earth would he look that way, sound that way, and speak Italian? How am I—how is *anyone*—supposed to not look at him sexually when this is how he presents himself?

"As you all are well aware by now," he goes on in English while losing no sexiness whatsoever, "I am now the owner of Sandcastle. I'm sure this change has seemed very sudden to you all, and I just wanted to take this opportunity to come and introduce myself as the new Chief Marketing Officer. My name is Rome Giovanni, clearly I'm Italian, and I was born and raised right here in Philadelphia.

"It may not seem like it from the way I came in this morning, but I'm one of you. I've been in marketing and advertising since I graduated college at the age of twenty-one. I'm thirty-five now, and I've enjoyed all fourteen years of my career. Up until about six months ago, I was a Director of Marketing at Bell Liberty Marketing. Some ... *changes* occurred in my life that put me in a position to be able to leave BLM, take a break from work, and then move into business for myself. I'll spare you the details of how it all played out, but I'm very happy to own my first business and looking forward to working with all of you."

He pauses to clear his throat, and the entire room waits on pins and needles for him to begin again, his tone and confidence mesmerizing us all.

"I'm sure you're all wondering what kind of person you'll be working for after being employed by Larry, who was ... well, he was indicted for using this company to launder money, but I'd like to assume he was a good boss to you all despite that."

Finally, there is movement in the room as people fidget after hearing Mr. Thomas being disparaged. Sure, he got caught up in something illegal, and we certainly disliked his sons, but he wasn't a bad guy.

"I have a feeling that Larry and I are quite different," Mr. Giovanni goes on. "I'm very direct and straightforward. It's not a leadership style, it's just who I am as a person. I'm demanding, and when I want something done, I expect it to be. I'll never tell you I'm going to do something and then not follow through, and I expect the same from you all. I want us to be able to communicate with each other without fear, shame, or embarrassment. Open communication is the most important aspect of my life. We will talk constantly and honestly about what we expect from one another, and that absolutely includes what you expect from me. While I am experienced in this business, I am not an experienced business owner, so I'll be relying on your honesty to help me be better. We're counting on each other to make Sandcastle grow and fly higher than it ever has.

"Which leads me to my next point. I'll spend the rest of today learning the ins and outs of the company. I'll comb through the current contracts and finances, and evaluate our business practices with Miss Martinez, and I'll strategize how we can make Sandcastle the best ad agency on the east coast. I'm a very competitive man, and I don't want companies like Bell Liberty outdoing us. We will be the best at what we do because I want to be the best at what *I* do. While I am strict, admittedly, I'm not a hypocrite. I intend to lead by example and be open about my desires and plans for our future, and I won't waste any time doing it.

"First thing tomorrow morning, I'll have a meeting with the department heads. I want to be brought up to speed about every client we presently have, and who we're pitching to in the future. I know the company has taken a hit with the indictment. Some clients have already jumped ship, and more are threatening to do the same, but now that I'm here and leadership has been solidified, we're going to change all of that. Those who have left us will regret it, I can promise you that. Tomorrow, we look to the future. I appreciate you all coming, and I look forward to getting to know each and every one of you. Thank you very much."

With a subtle nod of his head, Mr. Giovanni gets up from his seat, re-dons his jacket, and walks out of the room. There are no corny jokes or words of motivation we all have come to expect from Mr. Thomas. He leaves coldly and doesn't look back once he's at the door. It happens so quickly that people look around at each other, wondering if it's really all over. It's not until Sierra gets up that anybody else begins to do the same.

I'm not sure how to feel now that it has come and gone so quickly. On one hand, he's so goddamn attractive I can barely focus on anything else. On the other hand, he took a shot at Mr. Thomas and admitted that he's strict, competitive, and highly ambitious. In my experience, people who make a point to explain how straightforward they are tend to be the biggest assholes, using their "straightforwardness" as an excuse. *I'm not mean, I'm just direct.* I hate people like that, and now I'm working for one. He's gorgeous, but ... fuck.

As my fellow employees filter out of the room and I try to regain my bearings from our first meeting, I place my hands on the arms of my chair and lift myself up to leave. Jeremiah does the same and shakes his head.

"Well, I don't know what I was expecting, but I'm not sure it was that."

I push my chair in and meet him at the door. "Me either. He's ... intense."

"Something like that. While I can get behind some of the stuff he said, there were parts that made my face scrunch up. There's a chance we could be working for a prick."

"I desperately want that to not be true," I reply. "He wants a meeting with the department heads tomorrow, which means I'll get to see what he's really like first thing in the morning. I'll be anxious the rest of the night thinking about it. I have to admit I'm a bit disappointed."

"Me, too," Jeremiah agrees as we exit the conference room.

As we step out, I feel a tiny vibration in my pocket and hear a familiar chime from my phone. We keep walking as I pull it out and tap the notification, but the words halt my steps. Jeremiah sees me and turns around.

"What's wrong?" he asks.

I keep my eyes on the phone, still reading. "Nothing."

"Then why are you looking like that? Family emergency?"

"No."

"Then *what*?"

"I got a message on Tinder," I answer, finally looking up. "It's Marcus. He wants to take me out for drinks tonight."

Eight

"I can't even explain to you how fine this man is. When he walked in, it was like everything in the room went silent. All breathing stopped. The AC shut off. Lint stopped floating in the air—all to stand still and watch this man enter the building. I was stunned, Jaz. *Stunned.*"

The gasp my best friend lets out is loud enough to echo in my room even though she's on the phone, and I nod as if she can see me. I'm glad I described him well enough for her to understand, because Rome Giovanni's beauty needs to be appreciated. Asshole vibes aside, Jaz wanted to know about the new boss once he finally arrived at Sandcastle, so it was my responsibility to call her the second I got home to give her all of the tea.

"This is *not* what I expected," she says over the speaker. "I held out hope that he was at least a nice guy. I wouldn't have thought he'd be a thirty-five-year-old business owner with a gorgeous smolder. So, what was his personality like?"

I finish slipping into my leggings as I answer. "Commanding. When I say this man knows how to own a room, I mean *this man knows how to own a room*. When he gave his speech at the end of the day, you could hear a pin drop between each sentence. Everybody was locked in while he was speaking. He may have said a few things that made us sit up a little straighter and arch an eyebrow, but he didn't shy away from it."

"Uh-oh," Jaz says. "Made you arch a brow? What did he say?"

"He sort of shitted on Mr. Thomas," I answer truthfully. "Instead of giving him credit for building Sandcastle, he mentioned the indictment and how we've lost a few clients since it happened. People weren't really feeling that. He also said that he's demanding.

That's the sort of thing people should learn from working with you, but I guess I can appreciate the warning."

"A gorgeous, commanding man who owns the room the moment he walks in. Hell, if he's into BDSM you may want to think about marrying him."

I scoff before laughing. "There is no way that man is into BDSM. I could only imagine him ..."

As the words come tumbling out of my mouth, a thought hits me. I realize as I'm saying it that Mr. Giovanni's personality is exactly the type I would expect from someone who is a lifestyle Dominant. Not that all Doms are built the same. They certainly have different characteristics that should mesh with their particular version of being a Dom, but if we're talking stereotypical traits, Mr. Giovanni fits a very specific mold. If I was writing a checklist in my diary, it would include everything I saw him do when he walked into the building. Add on the way he carried himself into the conference room and took control of it with nothing more than self-confidence and body language, and my list would be thorough and complete. But ... there's no way.

"Are you thinking about it?" Jaz inquires, and I can hear every bit of the smugness in her tone. I'm sure she's smiling like the Cheshire cat at this very moment.

"Ugh ... no," I lie, doing my best to shake away the thoughts as I stand in my mirror and contemplate touching up my makeup. "I don't have time to get caught up dreaming about the new boss. I have a *real* date to get to. No need for imagination."

"That's right. I saw your text. Tinder Man finally hit you up. So, where are you guys going?"

"To King's Cage for drinks," I reply, dabbing my cheek with a small brush. "I was so excited when I got his message that I actually agreed to meet up *tonight*."

"No point in wasting time finding out whether he's a psycho or not?"

"Facts. So, I'm leaving here in a minute to meet him. Just finishing freshening up."

"I *can't wait* to hear how this goes," Jaz says. "I hope this is a good one."

"It better be, because my patience with these men is running *very* thin. Wafer thin, paper thin, on thin ice. Every *thin* I can think of."

I finish my touch-ups and pause to do a final assessment before walking to my body mirror to appraise my outfit. Once I'm satisfied, I grab the phone and carry it with me as I head for the door.

"Well, don't let me hold you up," Jaz says. "Good luck with Tinder Man. Call me if he gets weird and you need me to pull up or ring your phone with a fake emergency."

"Thanks, girl. I will," I reply. "And stop calling him Tinder Man. His name is Marcus."

"If he sticks around and earns the right, then I will call him by his name. Totally up to him. Call me later. Love you, girl."

I roll my eyes as I laugh. "Love you too."

Once the call ends, I start up the car, take a deep breath, and head for the highway. Here goes nothing.

"So, what do you do for a living?"

Marcus Graham is every bit as handsome in person as he is on his Tinder profile. He's tall, at least to me—six feet will always look like a giant compared to my five-five—and he's one of those men who looks fantastic with a bald head. His beard is shaped up and groomed, and when he smiles it's blinding, his perfectly straight veneers lighting up the room like high beams. As a personal trainer, it's no surprise that he's in great shape, with boulder shoulders that stand out in his one-size-too-small-T-shirt, and he has great posture as he sits next to me. He certainly isn't overdressed in black sweats and a shirt, but neither am I, so no foul there. He smells good, makes direct eye contact, and isn't afraid to be close to me, leaning in as he speaks. I'd say my first impression of him is a good one. The room didn't stop when he walked in, but he definitely has potential.

"I'm in advertising and marketing," I reply.

"Oh, nice," he replies. "I have a friend who also does that. He's a marketing coordinator at Bell Liberty. Denver Rhoades. You know him?"

I shake my head. "No, but he has a very interesting name. Was he born on the side of the road in Denver?"

Marcus laughs, albeit a little too hard. "That's a good one. No, he's from Philly. I'm not sure why his parents named him Denver considering their last name. Anyway, it's cool that you're into marketing. Do you like it?"

"I like it well enough. I enjoy doing it and it pays a living wage, which is rare these days, so I'm happy with it. What about you? You like being a personal trainer?"

"I do," he replies. "I was big into fitness before I got into it. I figured it'd be a great life getting paid to do something I already love, so I started training some of my friends. Before long it blew up into a whole client list and business."

"That's awesome. What were you doing before you made your passion your business?" I ask, bringing my vodka cranberry to my lips.

"Selling drugs," Marcus replies, peering at me with a blank stare.

I freeze, my glass pressed against my mouth as I stare at him.

Marcus waits a moment before chuckling loud enough to draw a few eyes over to us. "I'm just messing with you. Wow, you really believed me. The look on your face was intense. No, I wasn't a drug dealer. I worked at a car dealership. I was a car salesman. I got you, though."

I take two big gulps of my drink before forcing myself to laugh along with him.

"Yeah, you got me," I say, hoping it doesn't sound as sarcastic as it feels. "Anyway, how long have you been on Tinder?"

"Not long," he says before sipping his beer. "I had a relationship end about six months ago, and I took a little time to myself after that. Now I'm back in the game, but I'm not your average guy. I'm into ... well, maybe I should just say that I noticed something very specific on your profile that caught my attention."

"Oh, yeah? What's that?"

"In your bio, you wrote, 'In the lifestyle,'" he says.

I put my drink down and turn to face him. This is the part of the date that I was looking forward to. It's always cool to go through the generic ice breakers, asking simple questions to not seem too forward or impatient. But it's the meat and potatoes of the convo that *really* matter, and this is it.

"You noticed that, huh? Are *you* into the lifestyle?" I ask. Most people have no idea what we mean when we say "The lifestyle." If Marcus is into it, he'll understand. If not, I'll know there won't be a second date.

"I am," he answers confidently. He takes another pull from his beer, emptying it before setting it down and eyeing the bartender for another. "I take it you're a submissive?"

"I am. I take it you're a Dom?"

"Proudly," he says, full of confidence. "And I'm looking for a submissive woman I can settle down with. I know that it takes time, and I'm at a position in my life where I can finally slow down and have the patience necessary to be in it for the long haul with someone who understands what I need."

"I see." I fight to keep from smiling as I go on. "That's very similar to how I feel about life and love. I'm not getting any younger, but because of what I'm into as a sub and the lifestyle I choose to live, it has become increasingly difficult to find anyone worth my time, energy, and effort."

"So, you want a man to Dom over you?"

"If he's worthy of it," I answer. Now it's my turn to be confident. "I'm not a weak person. The man I choose to be my Dominant will have to be someone who is even stronger than me. They'll have to know how to take the lead and know when to, which means they'll understand when to pull back, too. A D/s relationship is give and take just like a vanilla one. It takes a lot of understanding and wide open communication to pull it off, but if you want it enough and can manage it, it can be the absolute best version of love that there is. That's what I want. The rest of the world can have their vanilla thing, and the judgmental people who turn their nose up when the word kink is mentioned can keep their toxic relationships and sky high divorce rate. I want a singular person who isn't afraid to immerse themselves in the darkest shade of romance."

Marcus smiles from ear to ear. "The darkest shade of romance. I like that. I like that *a lot* actually." As the bartender finishes refilling his beer, Marcus takes it directly from his hand and raises the glass in the air. "To the darkest shade of romance."

I grab my cocktail and tap it against his glass. "To the darkest shade of romance."

We both drink while maintaining eye contact, and I finish mine, loving the fact that this date has gone so well. Maybe this is it. After all this time and plenty of horrible dates to make this seem like a dream come true—is Marcus what I have been looking for?

He sets his drink down and leans in close. "If it's okay with you, Nia, I'd really like the opportunity to get to know you better. I'd like to spend more time with you. Maybe I can prove myself worthy of being the man you call your Dom."

I smile as I nod.

Oh, shit. This might really be it.

"Yeah," I say as my stomach explodes with butterflies. "I think I'd like that, too."

Dear Diary,

I just came back from a date, and ... holy shit! Did that just happen? Marcus was good looking, confident, and putting on a masterclass of Dom vibes. He knew the lingo and seemed to fit right into my idea of what a Dom is supposed to be like. He was perfect.

PERFECT!

It's true that he took a while to reach out to me, but that's probably because he was working, which is a good thing. I want someone who has to get up and go to work in the morning just like me. Someone who has to do things by a schedule because they are driven and motivated by success. Success takes time and hard work, and Marcus seemed to be all about that. He even works for himself as a personal trainer.

I usually open these pages, click my pen, and complain until the ink runs dry. But not tonight. Marcus has made me flip the script. All of the signs were there, and the only flags he displayed were green ones. He even tried to make a joke. It may not have landed with me as hard as it landed with him, but that's okay. He was trying. I loved it, and can't wait to do it again.

Is this it?

Can he be the Dom I've been searching for?

I'll let you know!

Nine

C onference Room B isn't as big as Conference Room A. While the latter is used for big meetings that are usually more like briefings from company leadership, this room is made for brainstorming. When we're in here, it's to strategize and have group discussions with department heads and the key players of Sandcastle. Here, we decide what road the company will travel down, so I know this gathering with Mr. Giovanni will not be like the last one. That was more of an introduction. This is our first *real* meeting, and I am far more nervous now than I was yesterday.

As anxious as I am, I'm still riding high from my date with Marcus last night. He was such a gentleman our entire time together, and we spent the evening laughing and talking about our careers. To my very pleasant surprise, I enjoyed being around him. While his sense of humor is different from mine, he and I are actually on the same page, especially when it comes to the lifestyle. He's a Dom looking for a submissive to spend his life with, and I'm a sub in search of a Dominant. We didn't get into anything too specific, and we're certainly not officially dating yet, but last night was the way I would want any first date to go. I left with a smile on my face and excitement in my heart about seeing him again soon, which quickly turned into heart-racing anxiety about this meeting and being in the same room as Mr. Giovanni. I hate how seeing him and being in his presence once has his image locked inside my mind, even overshadowing Marcus's adorably bright smile, but I digress.

I can feel the tension in the air—it's thick, like trying to breathe train smoke—as we await Mr. Giovanni's arrival again. Every department head is here and so is Sierra, but even she looks nervous. I sit next to her and watch as she twirls her fingers around one another, staring down at her hand with a blank expression on her face. Even when Sandcastle went through a rough period that resulted in a handful of people being laid off a couple of years ago, I never saw the VP look this apprehensive. She timidly glances at the door every now and then before going back to her fingers, and it makes me wonder what kind of conversations the two of them had yesterday as she showed him around.

"You good, Sierra?" I ask with raised brows.

Sierra Martinez and I are strictly coworkers, meaning we don't talk about anything outside of work-related topics. She's a strong woman who cares about her job and reputation, and I've never seen a break in her façade. She went through a divorce about a year ago, and never allowed herself to look stressed or flustered by the drastic change taking place in her life. She came out of it with her head high and her sights set on becoming the world's best advertising and marketing VP, never even mentioning her personal life to any of us or complaining about how difficult it all was. I would have been impressed if I didn't feel so bad for her. Everyone should be allowed to show emotion sometimes and there is no way she went through all of that without feeling something.

"I'm fine," she says coldly, keeping her eyes on her fingers.

"You sure? Because you look nervous," I reply, pushing my locs over my shoulder and sitting up straight. "Everybody in here looks like they're awaiting sentencing."

Sierra sweeps her flowing black hair out of her face so she can look around the table. She sees the same thing I do. They're all on edge. Even Simon looks timid, staring at the same spot on the table in his white button-up covered with a navy blue vest. He is the one who is usually most confident, depending on his ability to brown nose to keep him ahead of the pack.

"Everyone will be fine," Sierra says. "I just ... he ... he's intense and difficult to read. That's all."

"That's one way to put it," I reply. "What is it about him that's so appealing and terrifying at the same time?"

Sierra whips her head over to me. "You find him *appealing*?"

"Don't you?"

We lock eyes briefly, and I see something in hers that knits my brows together. In her glare, there is an intensity that's brand new. She looked anxious before, but what I see now is not anxiety. It looks a lot more like resentment.

The door swings open, cutting off our little staring contest and drawing our eyes over to Mr. Giovanni as he calmly strides in wearing black slacks and a white button-up of his own. Unlike Simon, he isn't covering his with a vest. Mr. Giovanni's highest two buttons are undone, exposing the top of a chiseled chest that has clearly been built by extensive exercise. His sleeves are rolled up to just below his elbow, and I find myself staring at his forearms as he walks in and grabs the chair at the head of the table. Veins pop through his skin and travel from the top of his forearm down to his wrist like a river displayed on a map. It takes real effort to pull my gaze away, only to slowly look up at his face and see his strong jaw and beard pointed right at me. My eyes continue to climb up his face until the moment our eyes meet just as he sits down. It's like he's peering into my soul as he settles into the chair.

"*Buongiorno*," he says.

Fuck.

"Good morning, Mr. Giovanni," Sierra replies after clearing her throat, greeting him for all of us.

He glances at her very briefly before looking around the room. Each person stiffens and sits up straight when his gaze reaches them.

"This morning, I want to talk about the future," he finally says. "As I promised yesterday, I spent the evening combing through our contracts, client list, and finances. I'm happy to say that Sandcastle does operate in the positive. We do make a profit. However, as I sifted through our client list, I was not impressed by what I saw. We have tons of contracts with small-time businesses and entities, but nothing that stood out as a landmark contract. So, I will pose my question to you all, the true operators of Sandcastle. Why are we so small? Why do we do business with small-time companies and never make a big splash?"

All eyes turn to Sierra, who swallows hard as her brow furrows.

"Well ..." she clears her throat, "Mr. Thomas thought it was important that we continue to partner with local companies to boost the South Philly economy and community. He believed that if we brought in enough clients, then it wouldn't matter how small the contracts were. He would rather have a lot of smaller, local businesses on board than a handful of out-of-town-ones."

Mr. Giovanni sighs, his eyes falling to the table. "Larry did business that way because it kept the eyes of law enforcement off of him. Smaller businesses are under less scrutiny. It allowed him to launder money through Sandcastle while he gambled and got into debt with the casinos and loan sharks in Center City. It sounds nice to only want to work locally, but how good is it for the local community if the money they spend ends up in a casino in the middle of Philly anyway?"

"Mr. Giovanni," Sierra begins again, straightening her spine for a fight, but he cuts her off.

"Stop calling me Mr. Giovanni," he snips. "My name is Rome. Please address me as such."

Sierra pauses as if she's worried she is being tested. Mr. Thomas always wanted to be called by his last name. He saw it as a sign of respect for someone his age, but Sierra is forty-one to Mr. Giovanni's thirty-five.

"Okay. Umm, Rome," Sierra corrects herself, her face unsure of whether to smile or frown, "Mr. Thom ... Larry ... *Mr. Thomas* believed in supporting the local community."

"He believed in supporting his gambling addiction," he fires back without hesitation or the slightest bit of emotion. "As a result, Sandcastle barely makes a profit, while Bell Liberty makes more money and attracts top tier clientele. Are you all aware that they landed Nasir Booker?"

"The romance author?" Simon asks, finally pulling some attention away from Sierra, who looks like the pressure of Rome's inquiry has her ready to run out of the room.

"Yes," Mr. Giovanni replies sharply. "The New York Times bestselling author, who travels around the world for the promotion of his novels. All of his advertising in Philly and the entire Delmarva area is controlled by Bell Liberty, our direct rival. That doesn't bother any of you?"

Mr. Giovanni goes around the room, locking eyes with everyone, but no one speaks up. More than likely, no one even thought about the competition. If Mr. Thomas didn't make it a point to bring up who the company was competing with, nobody else was going to.

"I have a proposal," Mr. Giovanni says, not waiting for an answer. "The way Larry wanted to do business has departed with him. He will not return, nor will his way of thinking or his business practices. From now on, Sandcastle will look to rival every company in the industry, especially those on the east coast. We need something new. Something fresh and exciting that shows the clients who haven't already left us by the wayside—thanks to Larry—that we are primed for business and ready to work with major companies who have big pockets. We are no longer in the little leagues, and our next client will have to be big enough to prove that we were not crippled by Larry's departure."

Sierra lets out a long breath before asking, "What did you have in mind?"

"There's a casino coming," he starts, which immediately makes Sierra's eyes widen. "It's called Golden Diamond, and it is scheduled to start construction very soon. This casino is more than just a casino. It's a hotel, a nightclub, and a venue for concerts, comedy specials, and even musicals. Golden Diamond will invigorate the economy for all of Philadelphia, not just South Philly, and whoever picks them up as a client will have work forever, a flagship deal that will be a beacon for companies looking to expand, and a massive payday big enough to provide bonuses to every employee just in time for the holidays."

At the mention of money, everyone's eyes double in size. Silence envelopes the room as people's faces change. It's not that any of us were hurting, but there isn't a person in this world that is going to turn down a raise. Mr. Giovanni may be as cold as ice, but he's clearly smart. He knows how to motivate people, because the tide is already turning in his favor.

"That's an interesting idea," Sierra says. "But if I'm not mistaken, that casino is owned by an even more interesting person."

Mr. Giovanni nods his head, his gaze icing over as he glares at Sierra.

"Wait," I say, finally speaking up with a raised hand. "Who is it owned by?"

Mr. Giovanni hesitates before sighing and answering, "Nix Malone."

My eyebrows raise to the top of my face while gasps and muffled moans fill the room with indistinguishable noise.

"Nix Malone?" I answer, my brows sky high. "The same Nix Malone who is a very known affiliate of Solomon King, the biggest, most violent gangster in the city?"

"Yes," Mr. Giovanni says.

"Sir," I say with a chuckle. Mr. Giovanni stiffens at the word, making me think he doesn't like it, so I correct myself. "Mr. Giovanni, you said you're from Philly, right?"

"Rome," he snips. "Call me Rome. That goes for everyone who works here. Now, yes I am from Philly."

"So you know who Nix Malone and Solomon King are?" I ask.

"Yes."

I wait for a second to see if Mr. Giovanni ... Rome ... understands exactly what he is saying. I watch his face, wondering if he truly gets it, but he never wavers.

"Rome, everyone in the city—police, politicians, judges—they all know that Nix and Solomon are gangsters who have never been caught red-handed. Their money is not good money. They make it illegally. Are you sure you want to work with people like them?"

He eyes me carefully, sucking his bottom lip into his mouth as he scans me. "What's your name?"

"Nia Washington," I answer. "I'm the director of marketing."

"One of two," Simon quickly chimes in. "I'm the other."

Rome glances over at Simon with a fiery glare before returning to me.

"Nia," he says, and I try not to shiver at the sound of my name on his lips. "Nix Malone has never been charged with anything, at least not since he was a teenager. Rumors do not dissuade me."

"But are they really rumors?" I go on, undeterred. "This is a *known* thing. They're just so good at what they do that they haven't been caught yet."

"Say that again," Rome demands, his eyes never leaving mine.

"Say what?" I question with a frown.

"The last sentence you said."

"They're so good at what they do that they haven't been caught."

"They haven't been caught doing anything," he says, driving his point home. "If they haven't been charged with a crime, then what you speak of are just rumors. Club Asylum is owned by Solomon King, and it's one of the biggest nightclubs in the city, is it not? So big, in fact, that I feel safe in assuming that even you've been there."

My jaw tightens as I'm forced to answer. "Yes, I have."

"The companies who do business with Solomon King and his club are not going up in flames, are they? There are no shootouts or police raids at any of his places of business, are there?"

Heat fills my limbs and begins burning toward my heart. "No."

"Right. And have any of you heard of a five-star restaurant in Center City called The VP?" Rome asks, this time addressing the entire room.

"I have," Loretta, the brand director admits.

"Good. Do you know who owns it?" Loretta shakes her head. "Nix Malone. He has been the owner of that restaurant since it opened in 2017. It has never been shut down. It has never been found to be involved in any illegal activity. The VP hasn't so much as failed a health inspection since its doors opened with Nix Malone cutting a giant gold ribbon with photographers snapping shots for the media. Maybe they are what you say they are, but when it comes to business, they clearly know what they're doing."

"So, Club Asylum and The VP are owned by two *well-known criminals*," he continues, eyeing me directly now. "Yet, neither of those establishments have been named in an indictment or found to be a hub for criminal activity. That's interesting, because the only company that *has* been named in an indictment that I'm aware of is the one you work for."

The room goes silent, and my skin feels like its temperature has skyrocketed to a thousand degrees. Pinpricks stab my face and my heart drums with humiliation as everyone looks at me before looking down at the table, clearly embarrassed for me.

Rome stands up and places one hand on the table. "I know this is new for you all. You're not used to going after bigger fish. But now that there is no illegal activity taking place at Sandcastle, we will not shrink ourselves. We will grow, and we'll be unafraid of taking risks."

"This is a really *big* risk," I say before I can stop myself.

"Yes, it is, Nia," Rome replies. "Even if you're not okay with taking it ... I am. This is the move I want to make, and I'll gladly take full responsibility if it goes wrong. If this hurts the company, it will be my fault, not yours. Because I'm in charge. It's important that you remember that."

He takes a moment to stare at me, his eyes sparkling with something unreadable before he looks away to address the room.

"We're going after Golden Diamond. Accept it, brainstorm with your teams, and prepare pitches. Whoever is chosen will pitch directly to Nix Malone ... with me. They'll have a chance to land the biggest account in Sandcastle's history. It's a huge deal, so I suggest you all get started. See you soon."

With a final nod of his head, Rome turns on his heel and walks to the door. He places a hand on the handle, pulls it open, and pauses to peer at me one last time before walking out.

Ten

Leaving the conference room feels like stepping out of a sauna. The air hits me and I realize how hot I was in there. What was that? The way he looked at me was beyond intense, and while I want to be mad about it—I wish I was disgusted by the way his eyes gravitated to me and refused to look away—I honestly can't explain my emotions. I dislike how he embarrassed me in front of my coworkers, but the way he looked at me nearly overshadows it. There's just something so hypnotic about his gaze—the way his jaw flexes as he stares. It's like being locked in place by invisible hands that don't allow me to do anything but stare back ... but fuck him for making me look bad, and fuck him for the idiotic idea of working with a known criminal.

Rome's plan of pursuing a new contract with Golden Diamond casino is beyond insane, and it's about so much more than Sandcastle's history with finding local companies as partners. Going for a bigger clientele isn't a bad thing, and I'd almost expect it from him since he admitted that he's competitive and ambitious during his introductory meeting yesterday. But attempting to team up with people we *know* are sketchy is not a good idea, and no smoldering look will ever make it one.

After taking a quick second to gather myself in front of the conference room door, I bite my lip as frustration grows in my chest. I'm so annoyed by everything that just went down that I need to let it out. I have to talk about it with someone who I know will understand and be supportive of my feelings, and there is only one person working at Sandcastle that fills that role.

"You won't believe what just happened in there," I say to Jeremiah the second I reach his cubicle.

He's facing his monitor, so he never had a chance to see me coming at all, which leads to a wide-eyed, bewildered expression as he spins his chair around. His clean-shaven face looks up at me with a furrowed brow as his cup of coffee steams behind him on the desk.

"Now you know it's too early to come over here confusing me, Nia," he says, slow-blinking like he's too tired to stay awake.

After a sigh, I reach around him and grab his coffee, forcing the cup into his hand. "Then drink this and wake up, because I have to tell you how our first meeting with Mr. ... *Rome* went."

"Rome? Y'all on a first name basis now?" Jeremiah asks before carefully sipping from his Sandcastle mug.

"Apparently, because he demanded to be called by his first name," I explain. "He even had a little attitude with Sierra and me about it."

"Oh, for real?"

"Yes, and that's only the half of it," I continue, my annoyance climbing and raising the volume of my voice without me knowing it. "I think the asshole vibe has been confirmed. This man is off the chain."

Jeremiah frowns like he's disappointed. "Seriously? Goddamn it. The last thing I wanted was for Mr. Thomas's replacement to be a pain to work for."

"Then you better buckle up, because not only is he an ass, he's also so ambitious that he's willing to risk Sandcastle's doors closing so he can work with Nix-fucking-Malone."

Jeremiah nearly spills his coffee from sitting up so fast. "What?"

"Yeah, you heard right. Nix Malone is having a new casino built in Center City—you know, with his blood money—and *Rome* wants us to pursue the ad contract. He even wants us to do pitch wars to see who will be *lucky enough* to go meet Nix Malone in person to pitch our idea. The man is crazy."

"Does he know who Nix Malone is?"

"That's exactly what I said! Apparently he does, he just doesn't care. He says everything we know to be true about Nix and Solomon—everything all of us practically grew up hearing—are just rumors. He thinks because they have never been indicted that they must be good businessmen. When I mentioned their known illegal activity, he chastised me and threw Mr. Thomas's indictment in my face in front of everyone in the room. It was humiliating, so now I have to call Jaz and have her come slash his tires for trying to make me look like an idiot in front of my peers."

When I finish ranting, I look down at Jeremiah and find him frowning at me.

"What?" I ask with raised hands.

"Damn, girl. He has you wound up *tight*," he says playfully.

"What are you talking about?"

"I've never seen you this amped up after a staff meeting before," he expounds. "He wants to pursue bigger fish. That's not the worst thing in the world, although it's crazy to team up with Nix Malone. But why are you so personally bothered? You're damn near sweating just standing here."

I sigh and roll my eyes. "I'm not *personally bothered*. I just don't like the way he talks to people, or how he looks at me."

"Looks at you? Oh, wait. Is he a perv?"

"No, it's not like *that*," I try to explain, but the words won't align right inside my head. "He just ... he has this way of looking at me that ... fuck, I don't even know."

Jeremiah's eyebrows rise so high I think they'll float off his face.

"Oh, you *like* it," he says.

My brows nearly touch from furrowing so hard. "What? No I don't. I hate it."

"But do you, though? You might be able to lie to anybody else in this building, but don't forget that I know you, girl. I know *exactly* what you're into, so don't play. He's so fine that you're feeling some type of way when he stares at you, huh?"

I roll my eyes again, harder this time to really be convincing. "Oh my god, shut up. Okay, yes he is gorgeous—annoyingly, breathtakingly, frustratingly gorgeous—but that doesn't mean anything. He's my boss, and I had a great time with Marcus at King's Cage last night. So, you can just chill with all of that. I don't like being stared at, I don't like being put on blast, I don't like the idea of crafting a pitch to work with a criminal, and I don't like *Rome*. If I'm feeling any type of way, it is all of those things rolled together. Got it?"

"I got it," a voice replies, but it's not Jeremiah's. I look down at him and realize he's staring blankly over my shoulder.

My heart beats like a military drum as I slowly turn around and let out a quiet groan as I come face to face with Rome.

His light brown eyes connect with mine once again, sucking the air from my lungs and putting me right back in the sauna.

"Mr. ... Rome," I stammer like a complete idiot who is definitely about to be fired.

"Mr. Rome? That's a new one, but Rome will do just fine," he says calmly—*too* calmly. He's absolutely about to fire me.

"Rome ... umm ... what's up?" I ask, doing my best to play it all off and hoping he didn't hear any of what I just said.

"Oh, nothing much," he answers. "Just standing here listening to you. You have quite a lot of feelings about me ... and the meeting we just had."

Fuck. That's it. It's over. I just ruined my career over a sharp gaze and Nix Malone.

"Oh my god. Rome, I'm so sorry," I say with as much sincerity as I can muster.

Rome raises a hand. "No, there's no need to apologize. I could tell you were frustrated in the meeting so I came to make sure you were okay. Clearly you're still upset, which is unfortunate. However, it's important that you remember what I said back there. If my idea about Golden Diamond doesn't pan out, it's not on you. If I'm wrong about Nix Malone, that's not on you either. This is *my* plan, and it's your job to buckle up and go along for the ride the CMO puts you on. So, there's no need to be so affected by it. You voiced your opinion and feelings to me in front of everyone—which I admire—now all you can do is go along with it. It's not personal, so let's not make it seem that way. Okay?"

I hesitate a moment, waiting for the other shoe to drop and for Rome to laugh as he loudly terminates my employment right here in front of Jeremiah. But he doesn't. He just stands there, waiting for me to answer him.

"Okay," I reply softly. "Thanks for your understanding."

"You're welcome," he says. "Thanks for your honesty in the meeting. However, it's also important that you know I don't like being talked about behind my back. I know I'm the boss, plus I'm literally the new guy here, so it's bound to happen. But I don't like it. If you have something you want to say to me, come say it, just like you did in the meeting. Just remember what I told you about me being the boss. In fact, let's make sure you don't forget it. Now tell me, Nia, who is in charge?"

I swallow hard, mortification gripping me by the throat. "Y ... you are."

He nods, licking his pink lips. "Say it again."

Our eyes lock together, and I swear to God, everyone in the bullpen fades away. The walls turn black as all sound disintegrates into nothing. All I can see is him as he stares at me, never once focusing on anything else. So many men have trouble maintaining eye contact, but not Rome. He blinks as though he is unbothered, but he doesn't look away. It's like I'm the only person in the room to him, and suddenly my embarrassment turns to something else entirely.

"You're in charge," I repeat with a shaky breath. My body fizzles like a freshly opened soda, and I'm suddenly ready for him to drink me.

One side of Rome's mouth pulls up, and I think I'm about to see him smile for the first time, but he pushes it away.

"Good girl," he says, pulling a gasp from my throat and intensifying the gravity in the room before continuing. "As long as you can remember that, I think we'll be fine. I also have faith in you, Nia. I think you're going to do great with this pitch, and I very much look forward to hearing what you come up with to land this client. Be as passionate as you clearly are, and you can't go wrong. I believe in you, so go get it."

"Yes ... uhh ... thank you," I stutter, totally shocked and disoriented by how all of this just went down.

Rome performs his signature head nod and turns on his heel, walking away without looking back.

I stand there for a moment in complete disbelief. The carbonation of my insides slowly fades away as I stare at the ground, shaking my head before turning around to see Jeremiah's astounded face. His mouth is open, his eyes wide and twinkling like starlight.

"Can you believe that?" I ask before letting out a breath.

Jeremiah's eyes somehow grow wider. "Can I believe how unbelievably intense, unnerving, and *hot* that was? Uhh, no I cannot."

"*Hot*? What are you talking about?" I inquire, but I already know *exactly* what he's talking about.

"Don't play with me, Nia," he says. "We both know what I'm getting at. I know you saw that. Shit, I know you *felt* it, because I wasn't even involved in the convo and *I* felt it."

"Felt *what*?"

"That not only are *you* into *him*, completely and easily excited by the way he talks to you and carries himself," he says. "But, from where I was sitting during that little exchange, he's into you, too."

"Oh lord," I force myself to say with another eye roll. "I don't have time for this. I have work to do, and so do you. We need to research Nix Malone, his restaurant called The VP, and every detail we can find about Golden Diamond, so that we can put together a pitch. I'm going to focus on that and *nothing else*."

Jeremiah nods slowly, his lips pursed before saying, "Whatever you say."

I force a smile as I turn around and walk into my office, but when I sit down at my desk, I don't even touch my computer. I sink into my chair and stare into space as my mind struggles to think about anything other than Rome and the way he just spoke to me. He made me say that he's in charge, he had me repeat it, and he called me a fucking good girl.

Suddenly I'm not thinking about the meeting at all because he has put something entirely different on my mind.

I don't know how or why, but my new boss is giving off some very powerful Dom vibes, but I know I must be looking too far into it. Surely I'm just projecting my ideas of the perfect Dom onto him because he's so attractive and in a position of power. That's clearly the case, because the chances of him being an actual Dominant are slim to none. There's no way he is into the lifestyle.

No way.

Eleven

I've spent the last two days scrounging up every bit of information I can find on Nix Malone and his dealings. To my surprise, he has his hands in a few things I never knew about, including a foundation he set up for needy children in Strawberry Mansion. At first, I thought it was a front—something he used to launder his money to make it even harder to track. I figured a man like him would have no problem lying on kids to further his own agenda. However, after doing a little digging, it turns out that the foundation is real and it helps thousands of kids in Nix's hometown eat lunch at school every day. It doesn't make up for the fact that he is rumored to have robbed multiple banks and made a few of his enemies vanish into thin air, but not everything about him is all bad ... I guess.

I've also gone the last two days without saying a word to Rome. As we prepare our pitches to present to him, everybody is busy with work. There have been no meetings or accidental run-ins in the breakroom between him and I. Nothing significant has happened since he called me a good girl, which truly annoys me. I guess he's not as into me as Jeremiah thought he was.

The only thing of significance that has happened in my life is Marcus. He and I have texted back and forth the past two evenings after work, and I remain pleasantly surprised by how well it's going. He's such a sweet guy and I can tell we're getting a little closer. We're developing a few inside jokes and are becoming more comfortable trading sexual innuendos. It's obvious that he likes me, which is why I smile when I look at his face as he sits next to me at Empire Tavern.

The bar is unusually crowded for a weekday. Country music blares from the speakers while people fill the room with the sound of conversation and good times. A dance floor in an adjacent room is filled to the brim with people doing whatever jig accompanies this song, and the smell of beer and vape smoke fills the air as Jeremiah finishes off his first beer of the night. He sets the glass down with a thud and signals for a refill to the bartender, who is busy with customers on the far side.

"I wish he would hurry," Marcus says.

"He's just busy," I reply. "You looking to catch a decent buzz after a bad day at the office? Or should I say gym?"

Marcus grins. "Nah, I don't really have bad days at the office, Kitten. I think I love my job too much to have a bad day. I just like to play hard after I work hard. How about you? You've barely touched that Long Island iced tea."

My fingers tighten around the cold glass of my drink. "I see. But isn't drinking counterproductive to working out?"

He nods with a playful shrug. "It is, but don't let this fool you. I don't drink often. In fact, the last time I had a drink was when you and I went on our first date. Coming out with you is an occasion worth drinking for. It's like a celebration."

I want to smile, but it evades me.

"Thanks," I say. "As far as my day is concerned, it was just more of the same. I'm filling my time with research into the infamous Nix Malone. I have to prepare a pitch to try to land him as a client."

"Nix Malone. *The* Nix Malone?"

I nod. "Yeah. The one and only."

"Damn. Your boss is hardcore for trying to reel him in."

"My boss is definitely ... something."

Marcus chuckles. "Not a fan?"

"I don't know. It's honestly too early to tell since he just took over a few days ago. We'll see how the pitches go. If we don't bring in the client, that will tell us all we need to know about him and his temperament. So, time will tell."

"True. In the meantime, how about you sip some more of that drink."

"Are you trying to get me drunk, Mr. Graham?"

"Nah, I would never," he says, playfully, gesturing toward himself. "I've never been that guy. I'm the guy who is much more concerned about your well-being. I'm usually asking totally different questions."

"Oh? I'm intrigued. What kind of questions do you ask?"

"Well, Kitten, how much water did you drink today?" he asks.

I try my absolute best not to get hung up on the fact that he has called me Kitten twice, but it is a struggle.

"Umm, not much," I answer. "Maybe a little around lunch time."

"Oh. See? That won't do. You have to take better care of yourself, Kitten. Hey, bartender!" Marcus suddenly shouts. The bartender finishes with another two customers before making his way over to us. "Geez, man. You've been ignoring this side of the bar. Anyway, can I get another beer, and some water for my girl? Thanks."

I twist my lips together as frustration makes me tense.

"Wow," I say, doing my absolute best to stay jovial. "Being a little presumptuous, aren't you?"

"Just looking out for my girl's health," he replies, all confidence. The bartender brings the beer and water and sets them down in front of us. "Here, drink this instead." Marcus slides my Long Island iced tea away, and pushes the water in front of me.

The muscles in my face become rigid like plaster has replaced my skin, and heat rises from my belly like a furnace. I didn't ask for water, I hate the pet name Kitten, and if I order an alcoholic beverage, I'd like to finish it.

Against my better judgment, I take a small sip from the water. "Yeah, that's great and all, but I'm going to finish the Long Island, especially since you paid for it." I pull the glass of alcohol back over.

Marcus navigates my barbed wire scowl with a playful smile. "That's cool, that's cool. Just know that once you and I are officially together, if Daddy says drink the water, you're going to drink the water."

"Daddy?" I exclaim with eyebrows as high as the clouds.

"Yeah, that's what I like to be called."

"Are you a Daddy Dom?"

Marcus's forehead turns into a graphic display of wrinkles. "What do you mean?"

"Are you into DD/lg?"

"I don't know what that is," he replies. "Do I have to know in order to like being called Daddy?"

I shrug, but I'm much more bothered than the gesture suggests. "I guess not. Daddy has become a name that plenty of guys like to be called. All I'm saying is that I'm personally not into the DD/lg vibe. I don't do age regression or anything like that."

"You think I want you to call me Daddy because I'm into age regression? It has nothing to do with that."

"I didn't say it did," I snip. "I'm just letting you know about the Daddy Dom, little girl dynamic since you said you didn't know what it was."

"It's not that deep," he fires back, his face flushing with annoyance. "I just like being called Daddy. Let's not make it an issue, Kitten."

The world tumbles off his tongue once again, and it is the straw that breaks the camel's back.

"Why do you keep calling me that?" I snap, gesturing wildly with both hands.

"Jesus, what's the big deal?" Marcus questions, clearly angered by the quick change of tone. "Kitten is just a pet name I like to use."

"It's not one that *I* like to use," I reply. "Not to mention the fact that I am not yours, Marcus. You don't get to call me a pet name without even asking if I'm into pet names at all—which I am, just not *that* one—and you can't force me to drink water simply because you said so. I know that we're trying to work toward a relationship where you're my Dom, but we're not there yet, and we won't ever be if you can't understand why controlling behavior of any kind at this stage is a giant red flag."

"Wow," he exclaims, leaning back. "I didn't see this coming. All I was trying to do is show you that I could be a good Dominant for you. I wanted you to see me in the act a little bit. You know, give you an example of how I get down in the Dom role."

If there was any wind left in my sails, the breeze has completely stopped now. Disappointment fills my insides and spills out like an overfilled well.

"You wanted me to see you *in the act*? You wanted to give me an example of how you perform the *Dom role*? Damn. You're not the only one who didn't see something coming."

"And *now* what are you talking about? I swear, Nia, it's starting to look like you're searching for reasons to sabotage this thing we're trying to build."

"It's the complete opposite," I answer. "I want it to work, but I also need it to be real. Being a Dom isn't an act or a role for you to play. It's who you are for real on the inside. It's a part of your *real* personality, and it doesn't have to be forced. You don't put it on and take it off whenever the mood suits you. A *real* Dom acts like it even when they don't realize it. They give off Dom vibes every day, all day without thinking about it at all. In fact, other people see it wafting off of them even before they do. That's what I want, Marcus, and unfortunately, tonight has shown me that that's not who you are."

"But it is who I am," he tries to explain, but I raise a hand to cut him off.

"It's not, and that's okay," I tell him as I prepare to get up from my seat. "Someone who doesn't know the lifestyle in and out like I do will be fine with you wearing the skin of a Dom every now and then, but that doesn't work for me. I appreciate your kindness over the last few days, but this isn't going to work between us. I'm sorry. I'm going to go."

"Are you serious?" he asks as I stand.

"I am. Take care of yourself, and good luck in all of your future endeavors."

While Marcus stares at me in disbelief, I grab my wallet off the bartop and walk away. I thought he could be the one, but time will always reveal a true Dom. Unfortunately, it will also expose the fake ones. You just have to be paying enough attention to recognize the red flags.

Dear Diary,

What is it about fake Doms wanting subs to drink water all the time? Is that written in some bullshit book about how to act like a Dom to get what you want out of women? I don't understand it, and I'm so goddamn tired of having to deal with these boys.

I know Marcus was trying, and at first it was appealing. I liked that he was putting forth so much effort, but then the TRYING was all I could see. He was trying so hard that it became obvious how unnatural it all was. I don't want my man TRYING to be a Dom. I need him to just be it. Be himself!

I'm a torturous merry-go-round that will not stop spinning. Every revolution is the same, showing me the same thing over and over again——the same boys with the same flaws playing on repeat. It feels like a never ending loop of shit, and I just want it all to end. I felt so close with Marcus, but continuing to talk to him would've required me to make concessions about what I'm looking for. I would have had to settle, and listen to him command me to drink fucking water when I'm not even thirsty.

Maybe I'm being too picky. I can admit that, but I can also admit that I don't care. I'm a thirty-year-old single woman who has been through a minefield of bad relationships, stepping on them and blowing myself to smithereens too many times for me to count. I will not stop being picky just to allow some moron who watched two of the three Fifty Shades movies and didn't read any of the books to take command of me. My submission is too important, and I cherished the lifestyle too much to operate within a tainted version of it.

So, Marcus is gone and I'm back to square one. Back to wondering if true Doms exist and what it takes to find one.

The saddest part about all of this is that I feel like I've been near someone who feels like a true Dom to me. I've been in the presence of a man who makes me shrink with just a look, while also making me want to be under his control. I've looked into eyes that pin me in place, and watched a man command a room like a general. I've seen someone act like a Dom without claiming that he is one, and I know how it made my insides feel.

But he isn't in the lifestyle and he isn't mine, so there's no point in mentioning him here. I'll see him at work and that's all, so I can't allow myself to dwell on it. I'll just accept the fact that I'm not even in the talking phase with anyone, and hope that it all gets better.

What am I talking about? There's no fucking hope.

Twelve – Rome

When the expansive gray door opens, my best friend and I just look at each other for a moment, both of us glad to see the other but unaware of how to show it. Nikola Collazo stands in the threshold of his gorgeous, three-story home and stares at me, a tiny smirk pulling up the side of his mouth before he snatches me into a hug.

"Why haven't I heard from you in so long, huh?" he asks in my ear. He squeezes me, emotion seeping through his flesh.

"Sorry," I say in a low tone, because I don't have a solid answer that will satisfy him right now. However, that's why I'm here. I needed this—to see him after everything that has happened. If there is such a thing as completing the grieving process, being at Nikola's house would be the final step to the achievement.

After another fifteen seconds, he takes a step back to look at me. I'm not dressed in anything fancy—just black sweats and a white T-shirt that is soaked with sweat.

"You look good," he says. "But you smell like shit."

I grin. "I just came straight over after a run. Sorry I forgot to change into my Gucci shorts, button-up, and sandals so we could be twins. I know that I've failed you. Will you ever be able to forgive me?"

"Maybe one day, but right now all I can do is wallow in disappointment." Nikola stares at me blankly for a moment before both of us laugh. "Shut the fuck up and get in here, Rome. You want a drink?"

"Nah, I'm good," I reply as I step inside, Nikola's hand still on my shoulder, sweat and stink be damned.

"No? Okay. Let's go out back then. Isabella will kill me if I let you stay in here with that stench wafting off you."

"It's not that bad."

"Oh, it is. Come on."

Nikola leads me down an eggshell hallway that eventually curves and goes through his living room. After all his ridicule, I do my best not to touch his lavish off-white couches or even the light-brown tables surrounding them. I turn sideways and slide past the plants that he has watered by his housekeeper every day, and make sure to only look at the tan paintings on the wall. Never touch. Isabella's rules.

Once we make it outside, Nikola pulls out a white chair for me to sit on before adjusting one for himself, and we both sit at the black table with a massive obsidian umbrella opened above us. A gigantic shadow covers us entirely as we lean back in our seats and smile at each other.

"It has been months, Rome," Nikola begins. "I stopped trying to call two months ago because I got tired of being sent to voicemail and never getting a call back. I've sent you dozens of messages since the funeral, which was six months ago, by the way."

"I know full-well how long it's been," I reply curtly. I don't mean for my words to be as sharp as dagger tips, but they poke Nikola anyway. I even see it when he winces.

He sighs and adjusts in his seat like I've already made him uncomfortable. "I know you do. I didn't mean it as a reminder of how long it's been since he passed. I'm just saying I've been trying to reach out, but you've evaded me. I've known you my entire life, *mio amico*. Isabella and I have both been worried, but it's good to see you back up and running. I even hear you've gone into business for yourself." As I nod, Nikola mirrors me and does the same. "That's incredible, man. Well, tell me about it."

It took me this long to return to Nikola's house because I knew we would be having this conversation. It is one I've been wanting to avoid, which is why I've been operating on my own since my father died half a year ago. After the funeral, I became a recluse until enough time had passed for me to be better. When someone you love dies, even the simple task of talking to people feels like the heaviest of burdens.

"Shortly after the funeral," I begin, hating this conversation and needing it at the same time. "Dad's lawyer contacted me about the inheritance and will. There was a lot to go over, which fucking sucked, but as his only child I ended up with everything—the house, the store, the restaurant, and all of the money."

"Well, it's not like he was going to give it to someone else. You were everything to him," Nikola reminds me.

I nod and am shocked that it feels painful. "I know. I'm not sure what I expected, but when it was all said and done, the total for everything was *a lot*. Dad took great care of himself and his businesses, and I finally understood why he was always on me to do the same. Everything he'd worked for was now mine, and I didn't know how to feel about that. That's why I dodged you and everyone else. Losing Mom at nineteen, Natalia at thirty, and now Dad at thirty-five was just too much to bear. You're the only person I love who hasn't fucking died on me, yet I couldn't bring myself to talk to you. I was just in a dark place.

"I practically drank and fucked my way through the first four months after the funeral and handing down of his assets. I was at a new club every night and with a new woman every week, making sure to never commit to anything or anyone. I just wanted to drift without any sense of direction, and that's exactly what I did. But eventually I hit land—woke up one morning and found some random chick next to me, and thought about how disappointed Dad would've been to see me that way. That's really all it took for me to get up and start trying to figure out how to get my shit together and navigate my way through a world in which he no longer exists. It was fucking tough, but I eventually got up, stopped drinking, started exercising, stopped fucking random women, and started making moves. I sold the house and both of his stores."

Nikola's eyebrows jump up. "Really? Wow."

"I know," I say with a raised hand. "I know how much he loved his convenience store and the restaurant, but there was no way I was ever going to heal if I had to spend my life managing the places I practically grew up watching him own and operate. That was his thing, not mine. I got my degree in marketing for myself, not just because Dad wanted me to help grow his businesses. They had to go, just like the house. I took out everything I wanted to keep, but that was all I needed. With the three of them sold, the money skyrocketed even higher and I felt a little better. It was good to say goodbye, as much as it hurt."

"What made you decide to go into business for yourself?" Nikola asks. The look on his face lets me know that he's listening intently and really cares. Time hasn't dissolved our friendship in the slightest. I'm happy about that. Six months shouldn't be able to compete with thirty years.

"A combination of what he wanted for me and what I needed for myself," I answer. "It just so happened that as I was looking for something to purchase for myself, the owner of a marketing and advertising agency was indicted for money laundering. I guess he was a gambler who started working with some sketchy people and got himself caught up. He was forced to separate from his company, and I was more than willing to swoop in and take it off his hands."

"Advertising and marketing," Nikola says with a nod of his head. "Nice, bro."

"Yeah, it's called Sandcastle, and I officially took over a few days ago. Got the lay of the land from the VP and have had a couple of meetings regarding the direction I want the company to go. I may have ruffled a few feathers with my ambition, but that's no surprise."

He laughs. "Definitely not. It's good to see that your time at Bell Liberty wasn't wasted. You went from being a director there to running the show for their competition. Well played."

"Thank you. It really was just perfecting timing. Now all I have to do is not burn the place down. I'm really motivated now that it's all said and done. It took me a long time to get back to a good place, and now that I'm mostly there, I want it to be as successful as possible. I feel like Mom and Dad are watching me, so it has to go well."

Nikola reaches over and slaps me on top of my hand. "That's great, bro. I'm fucking proud of you. You're really doing it."

"Yeah, I guess I am. I mean, I'm not one of the biggest stock brokers in Philly like *somebody* I know, but I'm doing alright."

"Well, we can't all be perfect," he says with a playful laugh.

As the two of us share a happy moment, the back door slides open as Nikola's wife, Isabella, comes out to join us. She looks beautiful as always in a loose red dress. Her long brown hair flows behind her as she comes out, her eyes landing on me and immediately misting over.

"Where have you been, you fucker?" she greets me. I stand up to meet her embrace, and we hug for a moment before she steps back and punches me in the arm. "You had us worried to death, you know that?"

"I'm sorry," I reply, smiling. "I didn't mean to leave you guys hanging. I just needed some time to myself to recover from it all. You two are all I have left in this world, and as much as I love and need you both, it's also really sad and took some time to get used to. I know everybody dies, but it has really felt like death has been hungriest for the people I love most. It was hard, but I'm doing a lot better now."

"That's so good to hear, Rome," she says. "I'm thrilled to see you back on your feet."

"It's good to be back," I say as I sit down. "And it's good to see you both. I love that you two are still going strong after ten years of marriage."

"Uh-oh," Nikola chirps loudly. "It sounds like someone is ready to settle down after their brief departure from the rest of the world."

Isabella doesn't hesitate to jump right on that bandwagon. "Oh, my god. Yes! Please tell me you're finally dating someone seriously, and that I can expect an invitation to your wedding sometime very soon."

I nearly tip my chair backward from leaning back so far, trying to get away from the idea of marriage.

"What the hell just happened?" I joke. "A wedding invitation? I love you, Isabella, but no way. Not *anytime* soon. I'm not even dating anybody right now. After Dad's heart attack, I just messed around and had flings. *A lot* of flings."

"Jesus, Rome, that's all you've ever done since ... Natalia," Isabella says, her voice full of exasperation. "Aren't you tired of that life?"

"She was my wife," I shoot back. "It may have been for only two years, and she may have died from that fucking aneurysm four years ago, but Natalia was my wife, and getting over her has been impossible. I've gotten to the point where I can enjoy someone else's company for a short period of time, but love has been tragic for me, so I've been dancing around that shit."

"I understand," Isabella says. "So, you're going to be single for life?"

I shrug. "I don't know. I see you two and how happy and successful you are as a couple, and it makes me want it for myself. My mom and dad had it, too, before Mom died. Dad never got over her passing either. But, I'm anxious for better things now. All I can say is that I'm open to it. Alright? Is that enough to make you happy?"

Isabella sighs. "For now, I guess. But at some point, I want you to bring someone over here for us to meet. I want to see you in love, and unafraid of it. I don't want you running for the rest of your life."

"The day I introduce you two to someone will be the day I know without question that I've met *the one*. You guys are the closest thing to family that I have left, so I'm not going to just bring any random woman over, but that doesn't mean I'm running," I say, but I'm not sure the last part is true.

"Okay, so if the right woman came along, you'd be open to settling down?" Nikola asks as he reaches over and takes his wife's hand in his.

I eye him carefully. "You know I have very particular tastes. *Very* particular." Nikola smiles, knowing *exactly* what I mean. "So, if I met someone who could meet those particulars, then yes, I'd be open to the idea of settling down." Isabella gasps and goes into a solo applause, clapping enthusiastically. "Oh, stop. She would have to be *perfect*, Isabella, because that's what Natalia was. Whoever this mystery woman is, she would need to be perfect for me in every way."

"That's a pretty big requirement, Rome. Are *you* perfect?" Isabella asks, to which Nikola grins at me. He and I both know that Isabella is the one who always keeps everyone on their toes.

"I'm not saying she has to be perfect," I try to explain. "I mean she has to be perfect *for me*. She would have to check off every box I have, and I would want to check off hers. I've met some new people since I finally started coming outside again, and if one of them happens to be everything I want, then I promise you both that I will go for it. I won't let the past stop me."

Nikola and Isabella look at each other, suspicion and disbelief swirling between them like a dirt devil. I know they don't believe me, but I mean it. I think I've finally spent enough time on my own, living the widower bachelor life, and after all that has happened, I think I'm ready to settle down. It is something else I know Mom and Dad would be proud of, so I tell myself that I won't run from it if it approaches me. At least I think I won't. Who knows—maybe I've already met exactly the right person.

A Dominant Man

Thirteen

"I would like to propose a toast," Jaz says, her shot glass of tequila raised high in the air. Michael, Jeremiah, and I raise our glasses to hers. "To our girl, Nia. When it comes to relationships and finding the man of her dreams who can match her freak, she is clearly cooked, but she holds onto hope and never gives up on her dreams. We could all learn a thing or two from her when he comes to perseverance. May the next man she finds be the BDSM king she has waited her entire life for. To Nia!"

"To Nia!" the rest of the group shouts, while I force a smile that is part annoyed, part fed up, and part thankful for them.

The four of us stand in Jaz and Michael's kitchen listening to a smooth playlist of relaxing R&B and soul music that Micheal has effectively labeled as "Chill Shit." Currently, H.E.R. croons over a beautiful track about how every time she tries to leave, something keeps pulling her back. It's ironic, because that's exactly how I feel after another failed attempt at finding a Dom.

Everything with Marcus started off so great, but he eventually showed his true colors, revealing that being a Dom is something he does in his spare time and whenever he finds a woman who wants it in the bedroom. I'm beyond disappointed with how it ended, and there's a part of me that wants to erase every single profile I have across all dating sites and social media, but every time I try to leave, something keeps pulling me back. Whatever it is that I'm tethered to, I wish it would just let me go.

As the group moves to the small bar stools that surround the beautiful gray granite island in the center of the kitchen, the tequila in my stomach mixes with my dismay and makes my body feel tightly wound. They all sit, placing their glasses in front of them while the tequila bottle is pushed to the middle like a centerpiece. Personally, I wish I could have the liquor all to myself. While work is going fine, I suppose, I still don't like that I'm being forced to research a man who I know is a criminal. Everything feels rigid in my life right now, and maybe a good drunken night would be exactly what I need to loosen it.

As my friends get comfortable, I grab the bottle and slide it over to me, filling my shot glass and knocking it back with no hesitation. No toast required. The glass slams back onto the island as I wince from the taste. When the process is finished, I pause as I realize all of them are watching me with wide eyes.

"Damn, girl. You alright?" Jaz asks, laughing.

"I'm fine," I lie. "Let's see if talking about other people's sex lives makes me feel better about mine. Jeremiah, you go."

Jeremiah's hand flies up to his chest as he points to himself. "Me?"

"Yeah. So, are you dating anybody? In the middle of a little fling?" I ask, already prepared to reach for the bottle again because my buzz is taking far too long to take hold.

Jeremiah looks stunned and stammers like English is his second language. "Umm ... uhh, okay. Well, let's see ... I've actually been dating someone by the name of Gerald for about two months now."

"Oh, you have got to be kidding me," I say, letting my head fall back until I'm staring at the ceiling.

Jeremiah laughs. "Sorry, girl. When it comes to struggling through relationships, you're riding that wave all by yourself. At least, for now anyway. We all know I've had my own issues with finding something long term. I hope it works for me and Gerald, but it's still really new, so time will tell."

Even though my throat is still burning from the last shot, I snatch up the bottle and pour another. Everyone stares as I do it, their faces a mix of shocked and entertained. I don't even care. I'm thirty years old and perpetually single, with an extra helping of constant disappointment to go along with it. I understand their staring, because I'm sure my circus act of a love life is captivating. If I wasn't the one going through it, I would stare at the cinematic event, too. Who doesn't love a great tragedy?

I tilt my head back and pour the liquor in my mouth, my face scrunching from the fire engulfing my throat, then I slam the glass down to turn my attention to Jeremiah.

"Alright, we get it, Jeremiah," I say sarcastically. "You're in love, and my life is a running joke that has everlasting stamina and will never stop running. Great. Just tell me what color we're wearing for the wedding. Okay? Awesome. Moving on! How about you two?

What's going on with the Carmichaels? Going down a particularly bumpy road these past few months? Sleeping in separate bedrooms? Does Michael snore so much that you accuse him of doing it on purpose?"

Jaz frowns so hard I think her face will shatter.

"Damn, Nia," she exclaims. "What are you doing, hoping we split up because your love life is off the rails?"

"Ugh, no," I reply, faking like I'm crying but suddenly feeling the sting of real tears. "Of course I would never wish anything like that. I love you guys so much, and you're such a perfect example of how a loving marriage is supposed to look. But, that's the problem. I see you two and it is a constant driver of my desire, and an immovable reminder of what I don't have. If you guys split up, I wouldn't know what to do with myself. On one hand, I'd lose all hope for love in this life, and on the other, I'd struggle to find peace because I'd be on the run from the police for killing Michael. So basically, my life would be ruined if you got a divorce."

Jaz's stone face softens into a subtle smile. "Nia, I honestly am beginning to think that maybe you're just trying too hard. You want it so badly that you think every time you meet someone that they could be the one. That's very unlikely, especially in today's social-media-driven world. Everybody is so fucking fake, and all these apps have done is empower people to be pricks and hide who they truly are behind a screen. I hate to sound like one of those thirty-plus people who think so little of today's generation, but you're probably better off doing it old school."

I think to reach for the tequila again but decide not to. Instead, I sit back and listen to my best friend. "What do you mean?"

"You need to remove the bullshit filter of apps and meet someone in person," she answers. "You'll have a much easier time getting to see someone for who they really are if you're face to face. Now, it's not a one hundred percent guarantee, because people will always be full of shit. However, there's nothing better than meeting someone in person, instead of your first communication being typed messages."

"So, what are you suggesting? That I go to clubs and bars, hoping men will approach me? I use apps because I'm in the lifestyle, and I know I'm not going to find that randomly in a club."

"You could go to a BDSM club," Michael interjects. "I heard there's a place in Center City called The Black Collar. It's a BDSM exclusive spot that, apparently, is popping.

I've heard some crazy stories. You'll definitely find someone who's into what you're into there."

Jaz cuts her eyes over to her husband. "Now how the hell do you know about that place?"

"Oh, stop," Michael says playfully.

"*Anyway*," Jaz goes on after rolling her eyes. "Michael and I will talk about that later, but he might be right. Maybe go to a club whose patrons are into the lifestyle, too. I promise it'll be better than using those apps."

"Or, maybe she has already met him," Jeremiah jumps in, pulling everyone's eyes over to him.

"What?" Michael asks.

"Who?" Jaz adds.

"Don't," I demand.

Jeremiah smiles. "Rome Giovanni."

"The boss?" Michael asks.

"Oh, the boss," Jaz says.

"No," I say with a scoff.

"Yes," Jeremiah continues. "I saw the way the two of you interacted the other day, and it was fucking hot. You're clearly feeling him, and like I told you then, it was pretty obvious to me that he's into you, too. He called you his good girl."

"Oh, shit," Michael exclaims.

Jaz gasps as her head snaps over to me, her eyes wide with delight.

"He did not call me *his* good girl," I correct Jeremiah with a raised finger. "He just said good girl after I said what he wanted me to. Big difference."

"I don't think there's that much of a difference," Michael says.

"Trust me, there is," I reply.

"To be honest, Nia," Jaz says. "Everything you've told me about your boss has made it sound like he is exactly your type."

"First of all, I don't know what you're talking about," I reply. "Secondly, even if Rome was exactly what I'm looking for, he's not into me, and I highly doubt that he's into the lifestyle, which is an absolute necessity for me. I'm a submissive woman. I want a dominant man."

"And what about Rome tells you that he's not a dominant man?" Jeremiah asks. He glares at me like he already knows I won't be able to come up with an answer.

I try to think of something—anything about Rome that would suggest that he's not the kind of man who could be a Dom. I picture the way he carries himself when he walks into a room, and the thought alone makes me want to sit up straight. I remember the way everyone responds to his presence, everybody focusing more and giving him their undivided attention. I think of the way he maintains eye contact, never feeling the need to avert his gaze out of fear or nervousness. When he speaks, everyone listens, and it feels like more than just his position as CMO and owner of Sandcastle. The way he commanded me to repeat that he was in charge, and called me a good girl when I did what he asked ... that will never be erased from my memory. Try as I might, I can't think of a single thing that Rome does that doesn't carry the aura and essence of a Dominant.

When it's clear that I can't come up with something, Jeremiah just smiles at me, nodding his head proudly.

"Maybe you should go for it," Michael suggests. "I know he's your boss, and the people at your job would probably feel some type of way about that, but fuck them. It happens all the time."

Even Jaz agrees. "I wouldn't usually suggest trying to sleep with your boss, but I know you. This isn't about hooking up with him to get a promotion. We all know you're looking for the real deal, and from what I understand, he sounds like he just might be. Don't let fear block your blessing, girl."

I take a second to soak it all in, shaking my head in disbelief about what I'm considering.

"Fine," I say. "I'll test the waters, but I'm telling you all, he's not a Dom. He may act like one and carry himself like one, but that's just because he's a man who's in charge. He owns the company. There's nothing more to it than that."

"And what if there is more to it than that?" Jaz asks.

"There's not."

"But what if there is?"

We lock eyes, both of us knowing what it could mean if Rome was a Dom and he and I hit it off. Jaz just wants what's best for me. She wants to see me happy just as much as I want to be happy. She has always been in my corner and the foundation I could stand on when I felt like I was losing my footing. I trust her, and the look in her eyes tells me I should go for it.

I let out a long sigh.

"Then I guess we'll see what happens," I say. "But I'm not holding my breath."

Fourteen

I've been on pins and needles the entire day. As I try to occupy my time with research into Nix Malone, I find myself taking unnecessary breaks to step into the doorway of my office just to steal glances at Rome as he works in his. He sits at his desk in black slacks with a matching tailored button-up fastened by silver buttons. His hair is neatly styled as usual, as is his beard that he keeps fairly short.

I wonder if he knows how god-like he is. He moves about his business as if it's the most important and least important thing in the world to him, reviewing documents with Sierra with a face that looks both intrigued and impartial simultaneously. When she asks questions, he doesn't respond with suggestions. He's direct and straight to the point, like his way is the only way—she doesn't have an option unless he tells her she does. Fuck. He's mesmerizing ... and all I can think about since I left Jaz and Michael's house last night. Thanks to them, my heart pounds and rattles my internal organs every time I look at him, wondering when I'll get the chance to make my move.

What even is my move? How will I know when it's time to make it? Damn it. I should've never listened to them. Now I'm stuck until I know for sure that he's not interested in me.

Between the ridiculous and unnecessary trips to my door to look at Rome, I do manage to get work done. I spend some time with Jeremiah, going over ads from previous years that Sandcastle has done for other businesses, but finding that none of them were related to gambling—probably because Mr. Thomas was already involved with it behind closed doors and didn't want to be seen aligning himself with it publicly in any way. So, there's not much to go on as far as related campaigns are concerned, but at least I know I'll get to create something fresh. Four other teams are prepping pitches, and while I don't like anything about Nix Malone, I want to win the pitch wars. I decide that in order for me to pitch this properly, I have to let go of my preconceived notions about Nix. It isn't about him. It's about the customers who will make the casino everything that Nix hopes it will become. Once I clear my head and heart of frustration about Nix, I see a clear vision and begin working toward it.

"Hey, Jeremiah," I shout from my desk loud enough for Jeremiah to hear it at his cubicle. In a few seconds he's standing in the doorway, eyebrows raised. "Make sure we don't put Nix's name on any part of this pitch."

"You don't want to mention the owner?" Jeremiah asks.

"Not once," I answer. "I've got a feeling that other people will aim their pitch toward him because everyone knows who he is and what his reputation is, which would attract a certain kind of person. It's sort of like Club Asylum—everyone knows that it's owned by Solomon King, so going there feels like stepping into a jungle full of wild animals. You're on edge the entire time because you know there are dangerous people lurking. Well, that's the last thing I want for this pitch. It is not our job to attract rich criminals to this casino. We want to attract *everyone*. So that will be the foundation of our pitch. No Nix Malone."

Jeremiah looks up at the ceiling, thinking it over.

"Okay," he says, nodding. "No Nix Malone."

He walks away and I spend the next hour crafting a pitch around Golden Diamond and its prestige. I get into the zone, and the only thing that pulls me out of it is when I see people in the bullpen getting up and walking out.

Lunch time.

Proud of the direction of the pitch and how much work I managed to get done, I get up from my desk and head to the breakroom. I know I have a turkey sandwich waiting for me there, and I plan to bring it back to my office and close the door to enjoy it. I take my time, walking slowly so that most of the people who go into the breakroom have already filtered out by the time I arrive. By the time I leave my office, half the building has cleared out, while the other half are enjoying their lunch hour at their desk.

I make my way into the breakroom and find only two people in it, which is better than the handful I usually have to force my way through. As I enter and open the fridge, both of them leave while my hand is reaching in to grab my sandwich, and I smile when I find myself alone. I know I'm not the only one who likes life better when there are less strangers in my presence. I open my carrying case to make sure that the sandwich is still safely inside along with my chips, drink, and a side of turkey gravy. Once I'm satisfied that I haven't been stolen from, I turn to leave ... only to come face to face with Rome as he enters the room.

My pulse quickens to a blistering pace as we make eye contact, and while I'm worried that my eyes are bulging out of my head, Rome is as calm as ever. His unfazed demeanor doesn't waver for a second as he walks in, his eyes staying on me as he comes to a stop at the fridge and grabs the handle.

"Good morning, Nia," he greets me, his deep voice like a massage to my ears.

"Good morning, Rome," I reply, stepping to the side even though he's not even close to me.

I watch him reach into the refrigerator and grab something to drink. He cracks open the can, spins around, and leans against the counter, his eyes on me like a predator watching its prey.

"So," he says before I manage to force myself out of the room. "How's the Golden Diamond pitch coming along?"

I clear my throat to give myself an extra second to gather my thoughts as memories of last night flood my mind like tsunami waves. Is this it? Is this the moment I test the waters with Rome and see if he's into BDSM?

"Uhh, it's going well," I reply honestly. "I had a little trouble at first, but I think I may have had a breakthrough this morning. Jeremiah and I are making progress and I'll be ready to go for pitch wars."

The side of Rome's mouth lifts, but not fully. Why does he seem to work so hard at denying me his smile?

"That's great," he replies with a nod. "What was the trouble you were having?"

"I'm sure you can guess," I say, angling my head down to cut my eyes up at him.

"Ah, the client himself."

"Bingo."

"But you pushed your way past it and had a productive morning. That's what it's all about. I knew you could do it, and I'm sure your pitch will be phenomenal. Can't wait to hear it."

"Well, I appreciate your faith in me, even when I wasn't sure I had it in myself," I say, to which Rome licks his lips and makes me feel off balance when I'm not even moving.

"Of course," he says. "I see something in you, Nia. I can't quite put my finger on it, but whatever it is, it makes me believe that you're special. Not everyone has the level of passion that you possess. I'm the same way, really. Sometimes it gets in my way and I have to take a step back in order to figure out how to use it to my advantage, but once I put it all together, I feel unstoppable. I think I see the same thing in you."

My eyebrows lift. "Wow. I'm not even sure how to respond to a compliment like that, but I do appreciate it. You're very observant."

"Only with things that earn my attention," he replies, his eyes magnetized to mine.

I drop my gaze to the floor, because keeping eye contact with him can be overwhelming. He's so good-looking it should be a crime. Why is he allowed to walk the streets while looking like this? Plus, he seems to say all of the right things. Who does that?

When I look up at him again, I decide that this is it. This is the moment I've been waiting for, and if I don't do it now, I might not get another chance to find out. He seems to be in a good mood, even a little flirty if I'm being honest—so why not do it now and find out once and for all? Nervousness creeps up my neck with tiny fingers coming to choke me, but I lift my head and force the words past their grip.

"You have to stop," I say.

Rome tilts his head. "Stop what?"

I let out a sigh, stand up straight as if I'm preparing for battle, and keep talking. "You have to stop looking at me like that."

His head stays tilted as his eyebrows knit together. "Like *what*?"

"Like *that*," I answer firmly. "Maybe you don't know that you do it, but I highly doubt that. You have a certain look, and it ... affects me."

"I have a look that affects you?" he asks as if he can't believe what I just said.

"Yes, Rome," I reply. I'm too far gone to pull it all back now, so I take a deep breath and dive into the deep end. "Look, I'm a submissive woman, and that look on your face is a prime example of what I'd expect ... and want ... from a dominant man. It's alluring. It's attractive. It's fucking intoxicating, and you're my boss so you have to stop looking at me like that, because it's driving me a little crazy."

Rome stops moving like my words have just frozen him solid. He gawks at me, his eyes large, round, and unblinking, and I swear I can see the gears grinding in his mind, screeching to a smoky halt as everything falls apart. I don't have to be a psychologist to know that I've clearly dismantled whatever he has been thinking by admitting to him that I'm a submissive. Without him saying another word, I know that I already have my answer. Rome is *not* into BDSM, and he most certainly isn't into me.

"You're a ... submissive?" he manages to ask through a tightly clenched jaw.

"Yes," I admit proudly. Just because he isn't into it doesn't mean that I'm required to be ashamed. "So, I think it's best if you could just stop gazing at me like that, and then I can stop wondering what thoughts you have lurking behind those eyes of yours. I don't mean to be rude, and it's clear that I've rattled you a bit with this admission. I apologize for that, but I just need you to stop for my sake. Okay?"

As if a spell has finally been broken, Rome's eyes fall off of me and drop down to the floor. I have absolutely no idea what he's thinking, but he looks like a man who just watched his life flash before his eyes—like I just ruined a plan he'd been working on his entire life and he's watching it all come crumbling down before he could even begin to carry it out.

Seeing this broken expression on his face doesn't make me feel good. I may be proud of who I am and the lifestyle that I'm into, but I'm also still a woman in search of the type of love and happiness that would make my world complete. Learning that Rome, like everyone else I've been into, will not be the one for me is like a cramp in my stomach—I can walk around fine, but I still feel it, and it fucking hurts.

I watch him slowly nod his head, accepting the shocking revelation.

"Okay," he says.

Both sad and satisfied, I grab my stuff and utter a final word. "Okay." Then I leave Rome and his thoughts in the breakroom to entertain themselves.

Fifteen

Sitting in the same conference room as Rome after telling him to stop staring at me two days ago is difficult for more than one reason. On one hand, it's a challenge to sit so close to a man who looks like Rome, knowing I seemed to have fractured his mind by admitting that I am a submissive. The simple fact that he has that information is enough to cover my skin with goosebumps every time he saunters into a room. I've always been loud and proud of the fact that I'm in the lifestyle, but there's something about *him* knowing that fills my mouth with saliva, and I have to keep swallowing it when I see him. I could quench my own thirst with how much I'm gulping now, because we are only separated by two chairs once again, and I can smell his cologne from here. Not to mention that he's especially stunning today, having the audacity to wear all-white—pants and a V-neck shirt that shows off his chiseled chest like artwork at a gallery. It's fitting, really. Rome truly is a work of art.

On the other side of this arduous situation is the fact that I have to keep my head down with my eyes laser-focused on the wood table in front of me. It's not because I have a pain in my neck that keeps me locked in place, or because there is anything interesting on the table. It is simply because after the break room incident Rome absolutely has not stopped staring at me. Every time I look up, our eyes are somehow drawn together. There is suddenly a powerful magnetic field between us, and his brown eyes keep pulling me in. Even when I manage to stare straight ahead, I can feel his gaze on me like the sun beaming through a magnifying glass and burning a hole right into my skin. His intense glare causes a sizzle that forces me to look his way, and the next thing I know, we're in a goddamn staring contest.

I don't understand it. When I first told Rome that I was a submissive, I watched him deflate. I witnessed the moment wind was taken out of his sails. His beautiful eyes suddenly lost some of their luster, and the intensity in his gaze drastically turned down, becoming nothing more than a whisper. Now, it's on full blast. Why? He clearly wasn't into it, so what is the point of gawking now? I hate it, and the fact that I find it so unbelievably alluring only makes matters worse. This is the morning of pitch wars. How the hell am I supposed to focus with him staring at me like that? Here's an even better question; why doesn't he look at anyone else the way he does me?

I've been working on the Golden Diamond pitch for a week now, combing the internet in search of anything I could find about the amenities of the hotel and casino in a desperate attempt to find a platinum needle in a haystack. I had to push my discomfort aside so that I could work my hardest, because Nix Malone could never make me want to do less than my best. Contrary to how it all began, I want this account. I've always been good at crafting pitches, and I want today to be no different. I'm a competitive person, no doubt, but I'm also intrigued by the idea of pitching my campaign to Nix Malone with Rome sitting next to me. He said that whoever he chose to deliver the pitch would do so with him, and there's a part of me that is dying to see him in action. I imagine his ability to command a room would work wonders in the field, at least that's the answer I give when I question why I want to work more closely with him.

Unfortunately, I'm not the only person at Sandcastle vying for the Golden Diamond account. Simon sits across from me in a baby blue top that is covered with vanilla ice cream cones, and I can see the determination on his pale face today. He keeps his gaze trained on the papers neatly stacked in front of him, still trying to memorize whatever pitch he crafted, but he looks more like a student who thought cramming for the test the night before was better than studying for it.

Three other people are seated at the table as well, each one going over their proposals with notecards or through apps on their phone, but I try not to let them distract me. Rome is distraction enough. Instead of watching them, I go over my own pitch in my head over and over again until Sierra walks into the conference room and takes her seat to Rome's right. Everyone's attention shifts from their pitches to Rome as he stands and centers himself behind his chair.

"*Buongiorno*," he starts. "Thank you all for being here. As we've known for a week, to-day is all about preparing to pitch Golden Diamond Hotel & Casino. This is a potentially major account, and you all have been working diligently over the past few days to come up with the best pitches possible so that Sandcastle wins it. Sierra and I are looking for something new, fresh, and exciting that will let the public know that Sandcastle is not a sinking ship since our former captain went overboard. We're sailing faster than ever, with our sights set on new horizons. While I will be consulting with Sierra on today's decision, the choice is ultimately mine. It is me who you have to impress. So, give me your best. Good luck to you all. Let's start with you, Simon."

Simon pinches his lips together as Rome sits down and focuses on him solely. A tiny ball of sweat pierces the skin on Simon's forehead as he stands up, and perches itself there. It doesn't move as he grabs his papers and bounces between focusing on them and peeking at Rome.

"Umm, good morning," he says, awkwardly trying to look at everyone. "Thank you, Mr. Giovanni, for the opportunity to present this pitch to you. I hope you will find it appealing enough to be chosen to represent Sandcastle in the coming weeks."

Rome raises a hand and furrows his brow. "Simon. I've asked you all repeatedly to call me Rome, and there's no need for the formality or the introduction. I know who you are and that you want your pitch to win, so let's just begin. Shall we?"

Simon clears his throat before wiping away the bead of sweat that has still refused to fall. He brings both hands to his papers and wets them accidentally with his sweat.

"Right, of course. Forgive me," he says, alternating between nodding his head and shaking it. "Umm ... Golden Diamond. As is expected from a businessman like Nix Malone, Golden Diamond will be a premier hotel and casino that will attract the highest rollers that all of Pennsylvania has to offer. It will contain luxury suites fit for a king ... or queen ... umm ... and it will be a beacon for artists and musicians to display their talents before massive paying audiences. Ultimately, it will be unlike anything Philadelphia has ever seen before from an entertainment standpoint.

"Nix Malone is known for his lifestyle of lavishness and mystery, and his casino will embody both mystiques with perfection. The casino floor will be decorated with frills and futuristic games—from brand new slot machines, to online gambling, to in-person tables of poker, black jack, and roulette. Sports betting will also be front and center, allowing customers to not only sit amongst the extravagance, but also take part in it by risking it all for immediate payouts. They can watch the game they have bet on right there in the theater room, with its one hundred massive TVs.

"Uhh ... Golden Diamond will be not only Philadelphia's premier hotel and casino, but all of Pennsylvania's. Golden Diamond—welcome to the life of luxury."

Simon clears his throat again and takes his seat, showing off the world's fakest smile to Rome as he awaits the verdict. Rome stares at him a moment before turning to Sierra. The look he gives her is one that silently asks, "What the hell was that, and is this the best this company has to offer?" There's also a bit of, "What the hell did I buy?" sprinkled in for good measure.

Embarrassment seeps through Sierra's perfectly applied makeup as she quickly turns from Rome's judgmental gaze and looks at Simon.

"Thanks very much for that, Simon," she says as nicely as she can, considering how horribly the pitch was. "If your pitch is chosen, it will need some refining and polishing. But, we'll cross that bridge if and when we get there. Let's move on. Nia, please present your pitch."

Even with all of the preparation I did, nervousness still ignites in my stomach like fireworks. The entire room focuses on me as I stand up with empty hands, but it only takes a second before I feel the sizzle again. Without having to look down at him, Rome's glare prods the side of my face, begging me to look over and acknowledge him. I want to, because he is so pretty to look at and I want to know more about what his gaze means, but this is about more than that. This is the career I had before I ever knew who Rome Giovanni was, and I will not squander it just because he's hot.

Instead of unnecessarily clearing my throat or sweating profusely, I simply take my time. I plant both feet squarely on the floor, take a deep breath and let it out slowly, lick my lips so that they're not distractingly dry, and clear my head of anything that could throw me off. Nothing else exists but the pitch. After a brief moment of silence that forces everyone to the edge of their seat, I begin.

"Golden Diamond Hotel & Casino is not about one person. It is about everyone, but most importantly, it's about *you*." I make sure to look Rome and Sierra in their eyes as if I'm speaking directly to them. They are the customers I want to attract. "The two thousand, top of the line slot machines are jaw-dropping, but they are nothing compared to winning *your* first jackpot. The one hundred TVs to watch games and track the bets you've made are awe-inspiring, but they dwindle in comparison to the feeling of watching *your* bet pay out, making *you* the winner and center of attention as if standing in the middle of your own living room. There are thousands of luxurious rooms in the hotel, but the only one that matters is *yours*. In Golden Diamond, *you* are the monarch to which the rest of the world kneels.

"The world's biggest acts will grace the grandiose stage and entertain the masses, but nothing is more exciting than *your* first experience in the grand hall, feeling up close and personal no matter which seat *you* choose. Fifteen fine dining restaurants await *your* arrival, ready to treat *you* with the utmost respect and care, serving *you* the most mouth-watering meals you've ever tasted. *You* are their number one customer and you will be treated as such every time you visit as if you were the owner, because *you* are the leader. *You* are the VIP. At Golden Diamond, you are royalty."

I make sure to smile and nod so that they know I'm finished, before sitting down and finally allowing myself to lock eyes with Rome. He looks at me with a wrinkled brow, a combination of confusion and awe tattooed in his expression. I don't even know what to think as he stares, and I can also feel Simon watching me. I turn to look at him and he looks furious, as if I just stole something near and dear to his heart. He glares at me momentarily before staring down at his damp papers, squinting at them as if they are the reason his pitch was a disaster instead of himself. Sierra is the only one who doesn't look at me like she wants to torture me, but before she can speak, Rome tilts his head to the side and says something that makes the world stop spinning.

"I don't need to hear anything else."

All attention falls from me and jolts over to him.

Sierra's eyes nearly bulge out of her head. "I'm sorry? What do you mean?"

"Exactly what I said," Rome answers before standing up. "That pitch was perfect, and I don't need to hear another one. At Golden Diamond, you are royalty. Yeah, that's it. Nia, you're pitching to Nix. You and I will discuss parameters and his schedule as soon as he is able to put Sandcastle on his books. We'll talk more soon. Thanks, everybody."

Excitement rages in my gut like a roaring river, but I'm too shocked to even react. All I can do is watch as Rome starts walking toward the door without regard to anyone else. It's Sierra who speaks up and slows his steps.

"Rome, we have three more pitches to review," she says, sounding as shocked as everyone in the room looks and surely feels by this sudden change.

Rome stops at the door, but only briefly. "No, we don't. I've heard everything I need to hear, and I couldn't have come up with a better pitch myself. So, that's it. Nia will pitch. Thank you all for coming. Phenomenal job, Nia. Truly. Congratulations."

Rome shows no sign of hesitation as he turns around and walks out of the conference room.

"Thank you," I say loudly as the door slowly closes behind him.

Sierra turns to face me, and the look of satisfaction she held just moments ago has been replaced by something much more sinister. I don't know what the hell just happened, or whether I should be excited or terrified, but my heart races all the same.

Sixteen

W hen I return to my office, my nerves are still standing on edge and my heart continues to race. Did that just happen? He picked me? Rome picked *me*. But why? As thrilled as I am that he chose me, there's also this other part of my brain that needs to know what led him to make this decision, effectively shunning the other three people who were set to give pitches for the Golden Diamond account after me. Plus, he undercut Sierra, deciding I would deliver the pitch without consulting with her. The meeting ended in a firestorm of confusion and tension as angry glares were hurled across the room back and forth like grenades. Rome was confident and defiant, Simon was distraught, and Sierra ... she looked at me like she wanted me dead after Rome made his choice without her. It had never felt better to lower my head and leave the conference room.

Still reeling from the break-neck-pace of it all, I find my way to my desk and drop into my chair. There is so much going on I can barely wrap my mind around the sum of it. After telling Rome that I'm a submissive and to stop staring, he turns up the dial and intensifies his gaze. Then he picks me for the pitch on the spot. My god, he is impossible to read, and I'm left floating adrift with a strange new sense of desire for him and frustration at the lack of answers. But does it even matter anymore? I'm pitching Sandcastle to Nix Malone and aiming to reel in the biggest account this company has ever had. I acknowledge how important and monumental that is, and I wish I could say that I did it all on my own, but Rome was the one who selected my pitch. As much as I made it happen, so did he.

"How did it go?" Jeremiah's voice slices through my thoughts. I look up at him, and he winces at the sight of my facial expression. "Damn. You didn't get it? That's alright. You didn't want to have to talk to Nix Malone's criminal ass anyway. And fuck Rome for not choosing you. That pitch was great, and if he can't see that, he's dumb as fuck. Beautiful ... but dumb as fuck."

My frown slowly shifts into a thin smile. "I appreciate that you're ready to have my back at the drop of a dime, but that's not it. I actually did get it."

Jeremiah's eyes light up. "What? You got it?"

"I got it."

Jeremiah runs into the room, whirls around my desk and wraps his arms around me from behind, squeezing my shoulders like a bear.

"I knew you would get it!" he exclaims proudly. "I'm so proud of you ... of *us*. We killed that pitch, and I knew you would deliver it like the fucking boss you are. Yes, Nia! Represent, girl!"

I laugh as he takes a step back and forces me to give him a high five, my smile fully developed now. This is why I love my friends.

"Okay, so tell me all about it," he says, finally moving to the front of my desk and sitting down in a chair. "How were the other pitches? Trash, I'm sure."

"Well," I start, already shaking my head from how crazy the story is. "Simon went first, and he was a train wreck—couldn't get his thoughts together, was sweaty, stammering, and just didn't seem well-prepared. Rome looked like he was ready to have him thrown out of the building the second he was done."

Jeremiah laughs. "Good. That's what that little brown nose gets. Okay, who went next, and did they do better than Simon's sweaty ass?"

"I was next," I reply behind a laugh. "I delivered it exactly how we planned, making sure to pitch directly to Rome and Sierra, and when I was finished, Rome said he didn't need to hear anything else. He chose me to pitch to Nix right there on the spot, then he got up to leave. Sierra tried to remind him that there were three more presentations, but he didn't care. He picked me and left. That's it. End of story."

Jeremiah's eyes bulge. "Are you serious? I know it was good, but damn. He chose not to listen to the others? Girl ... now you know."

"Don't even start," I cut in quickly before the rest of his words can make me even more confused and flustered. "He said he couldn't have come up with a better pitch himself, so let's not make it seem like he picked me because he's into me."

"I mean ... if you say so."

"I do say so. You just said that we killed the setup, so don't try to take it back now. Plus, I don't need you thinking that when it already felt like Sierra was thinking it. She was pissed about Rome's quick decision and looked at me like it was my fault."

Jeremiah turns his head to the side, looking at something I can't see from my desk.

"Oh, for real?" he asks. "Could that be the reason she's speed-walking toward your office right now?"

"What?" I respond, but before he can answer, Sierra is standing in my doorway, her face still stiff from the meeting.

"I need to talk to you," she demands before looking down at Jeremiah. "Alone."

My friend doesn't hesitate to jump up and exit the room. The second he's gone, Sierra steps close to my desk, placing both hands on it and leaning forward.

"Exactly what the hell is going on here?" she asks. The VP of Sandcastle stares daggers into my soul, making me feel wounded without any physical pain.

"I don't know what you're talking about," I reply.

"You think I'm blind?" she goes on, even madder now. "I was sitting right next to you, Nia. I saw the way you were staring at Rome. The two of you couldn't have been more obvious, which means the situation couldn't be more clear."

"What situation?"

"You're trying to fuck the new boss."

My mouth drops to the floor. "What the hell? Have you lost your mind? I'm not trying to fuck anybody."

"Bullshit," she snaps. "You're giving him "Come fuck me" eyes, and then he chooses you without listening to the three other pitches that could potentially have been better, and he does so without consulting me. I'm the goddamn VP of marketing, and you two are making moves behind my back. I don't think so. And I bet you think I don't see the bigger picture."

"Bigger picture? Sierra, you're way out of line," I reply, which is far less confrontational than the words I wish I could say.

"Am I? Is it out of line to say that I know you want my job?" she asks, shooting the words at me like an accusatory revolver.

"What?" I fire back, nearly yelling. "I've never said that I wanted your job."

"You don't have to," she blurts, pointing a finger at me. "You've been ambitious through your entire tenure here, climbing the ranks at the speed of light, and your next logical move is to replace me. I'm not dumb, Nia. I see it."

"Clearly you *are* dumb!" I snip, standing up quickly, my ability to remain calm and professional evaporating in the heated moment. "I'm happy where I am, and there isn't a person in this building who could say that I've uttered a single word about wanting to replace you as VP. I can't believe you've drawn these dots in your mind and then connected them all on your own. You're paranoid, but that has nothing to do with me."

"I see the way he looks at you!" she says, nearly screaming it and drawing all attention to my office.

Is she doing this on purpose? There is no reason to be saying this so loudly. It's like she wants everyone to think I'm sleeping with Rome to get ahead. What a bitch.

"How about you keep your goddamn voice down?" I growl, stepping around my desk so that we're face to face. "You made this crazy shit up and now you're trying to get the entire office to think it, too. I'm telling you here and now that I do not want your fucking job, now take your messy ass out of my office right now."

"What's going on?"

Sierra and I both snap our heads over to the door, and find Rome standing there with a bitter scowl on his face. His eyes bounce between the two of us, his brow furrowed, and his gaze as intense as the sun. When neither of us answers, he focuses on Sierra.

"You're the second in command here," he says to her in a calm, controlling, and intimidating voice. "This is how you behave? Screaming unfounded accusations at a subordinate with the door wide open? The entire building can hear you. You have the nerve to disrespect not only Nia, but me as well. I know we all just met each other, but I expected so much better from you, Sierra."

She releases a long, shaky breath before saying in a newly weak tone, "I'm sorry, Rome. I let my temper get the best of me. It won't happen again."

"I hope not," Rome replies. I swear the look in his eyes has us both pinned to the floor, and he's not even speaking to me. "You'll find that I am a very patient man, but I have no tolerance for childishness. I value maturity, and what I witnessed here was anything but. I just started here, Sierra, and it'd be a shame if I fired you after ensuring Larry that no one would lose their job. Are you going to make me go back on my word?"

Sierra's eyes quickly fill with tears that don't fall. "No."

"Good. Now get out."

Sierra lowers her head like a scolded dog and doesn't even look at me again as she walks out, turning her body to the side to scoot past Rome. I stand by my desk in amazement, gawking at Rome as his eyes slowly shift from Sierra to me. He takes a step forward and makes my heart rev like an engine.

"I'm sorry about that," he says after an exasperated exhale. "I'll speak to Sierra more about her professionalism later. She should know better."

I sigh. "Yes, she should."

Rome smirks. "I'm glad we agree. Believe it or not, I didn't come here to throw Sierra out of your office. I actually came to ask you a question."

"Oh?"

"Yes. Are you free for dinner anytime soon?"

The revving of my engine-heart picks so much I think it'll explode. "What? Dinner? After everything that just happened?"

"Relax," Rome commands, gesturing with his hands. "This is a *business* dinner, Nia. You and I need to discuss how we will approach the pitch with Nix Malone. As you already know, he is a very complex character. Now that it's official that you're pitching, I want to make sure we cross every T and dot every I, and I want this account for Sandcastle far more than I care about Sierra's strange paranoia or the potential rumor mill. If we don't win this account, the company could close its doors. We need this. So, this is a professional dinner to discuss the pitch and the client. Make no mistake about that. Okay?"

Fuck. How am I supposed to say no to this opportunity? The owner of the company is asking me to a business dinner, but Sierra just came in here and made sure that anything involving Rome and I will be heavily scrutinized. Thanks to her, they will all think I'm sleeping with him to get ahead. Is there literally anything in the world worse than a jealous, hating-ass bitch like Sierra? She has put me in a lose-lose situation that I have no choice but to partake in. If I turn down the dinner, Rome will be pissed and I will jeopardize the pitch. He is a busy man during our work hours, and he doesn't have time to stop completely and talk about one account, so it makes sense to take time away from the office to strategize. If I accept the dinner, it will look like I'm confirming Sierra's accusations. Either way, I'm screwed.

I let out a long sigh. Fuck it. If I'm going to be screwed, I'd rather be screwed and have job security while bringing in the biggest account in my company's history.

Fuck what they think. Fuck Sierra.

"Okay," I say to Rome. "Let's go to dinner."

Seventeen

I can't believe any of it. Even though we're here, seated in a restaurant that is ironically named Giovanni's, and Rome is across the table lifting a glass of water to his plump lips, I still can't believe that he and I are actually here together. I wonder what Sierra would say if she saw us now. Rome's black button-up would surely have her tense—the way his sleeves are pushed up to his elbows, showing off thick, striated forearms that keep grabbing my attention like cleavage. The way he looks at me over the edge of his glass would definitely make a vein pop out of her neck, and my dark green dress would probably send her to the morgue. The slit alone caused a stir between a few couples as Rome and I were escorted to our seats and men's heads kept turning in my direction. The women they were seated with shot glares across the table that were as cold as the ice in their drinks. There would be no stopping the rumor mill at Sandcastle if anyone from there saw us now, and although we're here to discuss business, it looks like something more.

It feels like something more.

Could it be something more?

"This is a nice place," I say to Rome, looking around the small, cozy establishment with its dim lighting and authentic Italian feel. A large fireplace burns in the center of a display wall across the room, casting a shadow of romance over the dining area as a plethora of delicious aromas fill the air.

Rome nods and smirks. "Thank you. It has been a while since I've been here. It's good to come back and see it still going strong."

"How'd you find this place?" I ask. "It's the little hole-in-the-wall establishments like this one that always have the best food."

He nods again, his eyes dropping to the table briefly before climbing back up to me.

"It was my father's," he replies. "He definitely always made sure the food was incredible and truly Italian."

"Really?" I say with raised brows. "I guess that explains the name. So your father is a business owner, too."

"Was," he retorts quickly. "He passed away fairly recently."

A sudden wave of guilt washes over me. "Oh. I'm so sorry."

Emotion and pain settle into Rome's body, sinking his shoulders and quickly erasing the aura of invincibility he's usually covered in. I watch it all fall away and be replaced by a melancholy gloom that darkens the room.

After a moment, he shakes his head. "Don't be. So, tell me about yourself."

My brows raise, and I may have whiplash from how fast he changed the subject from his father to me. With agony hanging from his face, it's clear that the topic of his father is still with him, but it's a wound he'd rather ignore than discuss.

I clear my throat, trying to move away from the topic instead of asking the morbid, obvious questions everyone thinks of when hearing a loved one has passed. How did he die? Were you two close? How are you coping? Are you okay?

"You want to know about me?" I inquire instead of uttering the questions I *really* want to ask. "Shouldn't we be talking about Nix and the pitch?"

"We will," Rome answers. "But I just took over as CMO and I haven't had the chance to sit down with each employee and get to know them. I'm not some heartless asshole who only wants to get work out of the people at Sandcastle and nothing more. I'd like to know a little about everyone, but with work going on it gets hard to have a private meeting with the entire company. Since I've got you here, I figured I may as well learn who you are. How'd you end up at Sandcastle?"

So he wants to get to know me, but only because he's a boss trying to learn about his employees. As I told Jaz, Michael, and Jeremiah, every sign points to Rome not being interested in me. I'm sitting across from him in the sexiest dress in my closet, but his demeanor is still the same as when our paths cross at the office. Strictly professional.

"Well," I start, "Marketing was the career path I chose in college, so it only made sense when I graduated to find a job in the field in which I'd just obtained a degree. There's no special story linked to a parent or how I fell in love with marketing at a certain time. It's just the thing I chose to do."

"So, you don't love it?"

I shrug. "I enjoy what I do and I love being creative, but I still think of it as work. It's not like I enjoy it so much that I'm doing it in my spare time at home. Trust me, this will be the only time I talk about my job outside of the walls of Sandcastle."

He chuckles with a barely-there smirk. "I can respect that."

"How about you?" I ask.

"Fairly similiar," he replies. "I got my degree for a couple of different reasons, including helping my father advertise this place, but I ultimately wanted to do my own thing. I ended up at Bell Liberty and worked my way up, but disagreements with management slowed my progress. I'm ambitious, and sometimes it rubs people the wrong way when it looks like you're going to bite off more than you can chew."

"Wait a minute. Hold on. You're *ambitious*? You? No way," I quip.

I giggle at my own joke, but then something else happens. As I laugh and ignore my own cringiness, both sides of Rome's mouth lift up, his lips part slightly, his perfectly white teeth show, and he finally unleashes a full smile as he looks directly at me. I'm so taken aback by how gorgeous it is that I stop laughing. My own smile fades away and I just look at him. As if I needed another reason to find him attractive. This is the icing on a cake that was already perfect, and butterflies explode in my stomach as I realize just how drawn to this man I really am. I know he's not in the lifestyle, but I want him anyway. I don't know what that says about me, but I don't even care. Rome Giovanni may be the most gorgeous man I have ever seen in my thirty years on this Earth.

"Funny," he says, still beaming. "I know it's obvious, but I'm not ashamed of it. My father was always on me about being an entrepreneur and having my own businesses. He wanted me to take over the two that he owned, but I wanted more. I saw a chance to fulfill a dream when Larry Thomas got indicted, so I took my shot and hit the mark. I wouldn't be sitting across from you right now if I wasn't ambitious."

I nod along, still stunned by his smile even as it dissipates. "I hear you. Well, you're certainly shaking things up at Sandcastle."

"Is that a good thing?"

"It's too early to tell. Trying to bring in a Nix Malone account is definitely ... something. If it all works out, you're a genius. If not ... well, I guess you will have bitten off more than you could chew, and Sandcastle will suffer because of it. Time will tell."

Rome smirks as he nods, but I can't tell if it's because he's agreeing or another reason.

"You're a straight shooter aren't you?" he asks.

I shrug. "When I don't have to worry about it getting me in trouble."

Rome keeps nodding, active thoughts keeping his body in motion. "You're interesting, Nia, I must admit. You're honest, which is refreshing, and you have smarts to go along with your passion. When you put it all together it's quite formidable. I can see why you've done so well at Sandcastle. I can also see why Sierra would be threatened by you."

I roll my eyes before sipping my wine. "Ugh. I don't even know where all of that came from. Sierra has always been very robotic, but she and I have never had drama like the shit she came into my office with."

"It came from you," Rome says. "She must've had a thought or feeling about you before now, but your pitch, and my reaction to it, was enough to push her over the edge. Your presentation was perfect. I understand her concern for being replaced. Although it's unwarranted, your talents being on display made her question her own. I don't like it, but I get it. You were phenomenal."

My smile is filled with blush that reddens my cheeks. "Thank you. Jeremiah and I are a good team."

"I see that. Did the two of you discuss how you would present the pitch if you actually won?"

"Not really. I figured we'd cross that bridge when we got there, and there was no guarantee that we ever would."

"True, but now you're here, about to cross a very shaky and unpredictable bridge. Are you ready?"

I nod. "As ready as I'll ever be. You'll be there with me, though, right?"

"Of course."

"Good. Because we both know Nix's reputation, and it wouldn't surprise me if he's rude when he doesn't like what he hears. I imagine someone like him has no fear of acting ridiculously when he isn't a fan of something. Who the hell would ever tell him to stop?"

"I would," Rome answers quickly, his gaze trained on me. "While I am aware of Nix's reputation, I would never allow him to disrespect you in any way. You don't have to worry about that."

With wide eyes I ask, "You're going to stand up to Nix Malone?"

"If I had to, to make sure you feel safe? Yes."

A smirk crawls onto my mouth as I look at Rome for signs of joking, but he never shows any. His face doesn't twitch and he definitely doesn't laugh. He gives no indication whatsoever that he's kidding, only a stone face and a fiery gaze.

"You're serious?" I ask.

"Of course. Why wouldn't I be?"

"Because it's Nix Malone. He and Solomon King are the most feared people in this city. Why would you think you could stand up to them?"

"To make sure that you feel safe," he says again, this time with emphasis to make sure I get it. He even lifts his eyebrows and stares at me, really pushing the point.

Rome is as serious as a heart attack. It's so incredible that he would be serious about this that all I can do is giggle. It just keeps coming, doesn't it? The looks. The demeanor. The Dom vibes. He clearly has money since he bought Sandcastle and we're currently sitting in a restaurant that his father owned. He's polite and doesn't shy away from complimenting me, then turns around and tells me how he would defend me against the city's most notorious villains. He is practically piling on the unfairness at this point.

As I laugh at my thoughts and shake my head, Rome's head tilts as the waiter comes to the table to take our orders. We breeze through our selections and have our glasses of water and wine refilled, and the second we're alone again, Rome smirks.

"What was so funny?" he asks.

I shake my head again, still in disbelief of it all. "It's just ... you. It's ... I don't even know how to explain it—or if I should."

He watches me without speaking, waiting patiently for me to continue, and the silence makes me feel obligated to keep going.

"Look," I say, my brows raised. "It's like I told you in the breakroom the other day. I'm a submissive, and you just carry very Dominant vibes. I'm sure you're not into it or whatever, but saying that you would protect me from known gangsters and then gazing at me with that look on your face is just unfair. You're too much, and Sierra has already caught me staring at you, and I have been through the ringer with men in my private life. I ... ugh ... let me stop. I should've never ordered wine before dinner."

Rome lifts his brows to the top of his forehead, a tiny smirk tempting his lips. I'm so embarrassed at how I just let all of that out, all I can do is lift my wine glass and knock back what's left of it, wishing it could make him forget everything I just said. If only being wine buzzed came with magical powers of amnesia. Unfortunately, it doesn't, and Rome looks at me with an amused expression on his face.

He shakes his head slightly, thoughts clearly running rampant in his mind, and I'm convinced that he is about to get up and walk out. Surely this is over, and it wouldn't surprise me if he decided that I shouldn't pitch to Nix after this humiliating display I just put on. I should spare myself the embarrassment and walk out before he has a chance to say anything that will make me feel worse, but I sit and wait, my body on the tracks in front of an oncoming train.

"That's twice that you've said that to me," he says. "You're a submissive. What does that mean to you?"

I eye him cautiously, wondering what road he's about to take us down. I've never been asked that before, and I'm not sure what to make of it.

"What does being a submissive mean to me?" I repeat, baffled by the question. "Do you know what a submissive is?"

"Yes," he replies flatly and with no hesitation. "I know what it has come to mean to the rest of the world, and I know what it means to me, but I want to know what it means to you."

My brow furrows because ... why is he asking me this? Even more importantly, what is my answer?

"I ... why?" I stammer, the muscles in my face tensing and making me scowl. "I don't understand the question."

"Is it really that complicated? I would think that someone who's willing to admit to a virtual stranger that they're a submissive would at least know what it means to them."

"I *do* know what it means to me," I reply, almost defiantly.

"Okay. Then what?"

"It means," I begin quickly before forcing myself to slow down. I don't know where this is going, but it suddenly feels important that I answer correctly. "It means I'm a woman who craves a man she can trust. When I say that, I don't mean in the typical sense. Everyone wants a partner they can trust to not cheat and to treat them with kindness and respect. That's a given. What I want is something more than that. I want a man I can trust with my pain, both metaphorically and literally. I want someone who deserves my submission—someone who has earned it by proving themselves to be reliable, authentic, and authoritative. I want to kneel for someone who I know will always stand for me—someone willing to fight and die for me, remain peaceful and live for me, take all of my pain and frustrations away and make me forget that the world exists. I need someone whose back is strong enough to carry the weight of my emotions and concerns as well as their own. I need someone who doesn't judge me, but grows with me instead. Someone willing to explore ever-changing feelings and passions with me as we grow old together and become closer with the passing of time. I want to give myself to someone in every way possible and allow them to use me, hurt me, love me, break me—because I can always trust that they know exactly how to put me back together again. It requires someone who knows each and every single piece of me and how they all fit together, because I want to be shattered and broken apart so that I can forget the world, and then be restored by the one person capable of building me back up."

When I'm finished talking, Rome doesn't speak. He looks at me, but not the way he usually does. Now he looks as though he is in awe. He licks and bites his bottom lip as his eyes shift downward and back up again, and I suddenly don't feel like he's not into BDSM anymore. At a minimum, he's intrigued by what I just said. At most, there's much more to him than I thought I knew.

"That enough of an explanation for you?" I ask.

He nods. "Yeah, that was ... you're incredible."

My mouth was open to speak again, but his words snap it shut. What did he just say? Not *it* was incredible. *I'm* incredible. Me?

"You're so confusing," I admit aloud, shaking my head.

"Why do you say that?"

"You're so layered, and it fills me with an infinite number of questions about who you truly are. You just asked me about submission and what it means to me. Then that response. I just don't know what to think about you."

Rome releases a sigh and sits up straight. "You want to know more about me?"

"I'd love to," I answer.

"Okay," he says, then his eyes find mine and never leave. "I asked what submission meant to you, and the answer is important to me ... because I'm a Dominant."

Five seconds tick by before I breathe, blink, or think.

"What?" I say.

"Since I was twenty-one, so it has been a while," he says. "That's why I asked about what submission meant to you. I understand it. I've dealt with it and nurtured different variations of it more times than I could count. I understand it more than most, so when you mentioned it the other day in the breakroom, it took me by surprise. I'd been pushing it down while I recovered from the tragedy of my father's death, but you ... hearing you admit it openly and proudly ignited it again."

My heart feels like it pumps it off-beat, the rhythm confused by this admission. I should have known. From the moment he walked through the doors of Sandcastle—the way he dressed, the way the entire building seemed ready to bow and kneel for him, the intimidating way he carries himself and looks at people, his ability to be brutally honest before flipping it over and dishing out compliments without shame. It all points to this. He's a Dom. I should've known it and now I do, and yet I still can't believe it.

I try my best to not let this new information get the best of me. Yes, he's stunningly attractive with all of the characteristics I look for in a Dom, but I can't let him know that I'm lusting for him from across the table. So I push my astonishment down into my belly, swallowing it while it tries to wiggle its way back up my throat like a live worm.

"Interesting," I force myself to say. "In that case, I played your game. Now play mine. What does being a Dominant mean to you?"

Rome smiles wide, stealing the breath from my lungs in an instant. I even let out a tiny gasp from the sight of it, but thankfully he doesn't hear it.

"A submissive making demands to a Dominant. That's interesting."

"You're not *my* Dominant," I reply, grinning like the devil.

"Well played," he says, nodding in agreement. "In that case, it means everything to me."

"Wow," I exclaim with raised brows. "That's about as vague as it gets."

His smile slowly fades away, and I swear the room darkens.

"It's all of who I am," he says. "Every bit and piece of me, from head to toe. The control I crave on a daily basis, the way I conduct my business, the way I speak to people, the way I look at people—I can't help any of it because being a Dom is who I am on the inside. I couldn't turn it off if I tried, and trust me, I've tried.

"I want to be trusted to take the control I so strongly desire. I want it given to me, handed over like a delicate flower that will die if I don't care for it perfectly. I want to know someone so thoroughly that I'm just as knowledgeable on who they are as they themselves, if not more. I want to inflict pain. I want to cause damage and bruise skin, and I want to nurture it all back to perfect health so that it is stronger than it was before.

"Submission is the greatest gift I can ever be given, because it means I've earned the right to be someone's entire world, and entrusted with the honorable task of caring for it in whatever way they need. I'm their protector. I'm their deviant. I'm their god. I'm their devil. I am the air they breathe and blood that flows through their veins. To my submissive, I am everything. Therefore, being a Dominant is everything to me."

My lips slowly part as awe takes over my body. The words in my brain float around and rearrange themselves into unintelligible sentences, so I don't dare try to speak. I can only stare, dumbstruck by Rome's response.

"You shouldn't do that," he says, lowering his head and cutting his eyes up to meet mine.

"Do what?" I manage to ask in a breathy tone.

"Stare at me like that," he answers, throwing my own words from the breakroom back at me. "You're not the only one who is affected by a gaze. If you keep it up, dinner will not be what I want to eat."

Did he just fucking say that?

I don't change my facial expression. I can't. I've lost all control of my body, especially what it desires. I know it's unprofessional. I know what everyone in the office will think and surely talk about. They will drag my name through the mud and stomp on it. I will become a villain to them, while Jaz, Michael, and Jeremiah will sing my praises as my life becomes a rollercoaster ride with the highest of highs and lows that sink to the depths of hell. I know how crazy it will be, but I don't care. I can't. Because I've never wanted a man as much as I want Rome. So I keep staring at him until he knows it just as much as I do.

He sees it in me. I can tell from the way he locks eyes with me, his tongue rolling against the back of his bottom teeth while he thinks things I wish I knew.

"Should I take you home?" he asks, but we both know he's not requesting to end the night. He's asking to start it.

All rationality goes out the window. I don't think about the pain of the past or the pressure of the future. I am only in the now, and right now he is all I want.

"Yes," I reply. "Please."

Eighteen – Rome

This isn't the first time I've driven a woman back to her place after a night out together. I've done it plenty, never feeling the way I do right now. I've had sex, made submissives kneel for me and orgasm all over my apartment before driving them back to theirs and repeating the process. I've had one night stands and spent time at BDSM clubs simply to find someone to keep my bed warm, only to kick them out at the first sign of light. This isn't new to me, but smiling while sitting across from a gorgeous woman is. Feeling like I'm having a good time and that I'd like to have it again *isn't* normal, and I don't know how to feel about that.

I know it has been four years since I lost Natalia, but I was never truly interested in anyone in the quiet and lonely aftermath of her death. Liking Nia makes me feel like I'm upsetting the spirit of the wife I've been hanging onto for all this time. But now that we're in Nia's parking lot, what am I supposed to do? I don't know if I should be here, but I can't think of any other place I'd rather be.

"So," she says from the passenger seat, looking at me with those gorgeous brown eyes. Her locs hang beautifully over her right shoulder, leaving her left exposed. Her brown skin looks as smooth as velvet, and the amount of it she is showing is almost too much to bear. It calls out like a siren beckoning me to the sea, and I am desperate to dive in. With almost no effort at all, Nia is the epitome of perfection.

"So," I say, as the war between my head and reinforced heart becomes more violent. My insides turn to jelly when I look at her, like I'm looking over a ledge hundreds of feet in the air.

She glances down, just as nervous as I am. "Are you coming inside?"

Fuck. What are you doing, Rome?

"Umm," I start, my self-control coming loose and flapping in the wind. "Do you *want* me to come inside?"

After a moment, she smiles. "Yes. Please."

Fuck.

Why does she have to keep saying that? The word *please* flowing out of her mouth is like the most enticing honey dripping from her lips. It sounds so fucking good, and of all the words in the English language, nothing ruins me more than that one.

In this lifestyle, the entire world revolves around consent. It doesn't matter what has been discussed or how sexual previous conversations have been. Without consent, there is nothing. Nia and I could have discussed all of our kinks and most filthy desires in graphic detail at that table, and I never would have attempted to lay a finger on her without her consent to do so. The word *please* is the ultimate consent. It is the mother of all begging, and if there is one thing I fucking love, it is being begged.

My heart has massive walls built around it. Whether I wanted to or not, my love for Natalia became a construction crew in my chest and blocked off my heart with concrete barriers so that it would still be preserved for my deceased wife. My brain, on the other hand, has just lost all control. My will to fight has vanished and my confidence restored just from the look on her face and that word singing from her mouth. I lick my lips as I give into the desire, and when she smiles again I know I'm not turning back.

"Say that again," I demand, before sucking my lower lip into my mouth.

Nia grins, knowing exactly what I'm talking about, and she leans into it.

"Rome," she says, lust pouring from her eyes. "Come inside ... please."

I let out a sigh that releases all of my ability to stop myself into the air. "Okay."

Both of us exit my car and walk up to Nia's front door, my heart racing with each step. I watch her hips sway in her dark green dress, and it makes me want to pick up the pace. I'm teetering on the edge as she inserts the key and opens the door, and the second it closes behind us, our lips finally touch, clashing in a passionate kiss.

I am completely undone as our tongues dance together. We stumble through the house, kicking end tables and the legs of couches before coming to a stop in front of one. Nia's hands roam my body like she's in a hurry, as though she has waited her entire life to press her fingers into my skin and tear at my clothes. My cock responds to her touch, throbbing as it hardens in my pants, but this isn't how I want it to happen. I was listening when she said she has been through the ringer with men in her private life. I won't be just another tale she tells about how bad her love life has been. No matter what happens between us after this moment, I will be the one she remembers most. I will be the memory that makes her stop during her day and get lost in her own mind. Her entire body will memorize the feel of mine before this night is over.

"Stop," I command, taking a step back and sinking into the part of me that I hide from the rest of the world. I let go of the façade and take off the mask I wear every day when I'm in front of people who wouldn't understand or simply don't need to know, and I become who I truly am. I let the Dom in me step forward and harness control.

Nia freezes immediately. Her hands remain perched on my belt, but she doesn't move, looking up at me with raw passion in her gaze. Her body trembles with a need to keep going, but restraint is the mark of both a good Dom and a good sub.

"Put your hands at your sides," I tell her, testing the waters. How far is she really willing to go? Have her issues with men been caused by the fact that she's not a good submissive? I'm about to find out.

Nia licks her lips, her eyes never leaving mine as she slowly lowers her hands.

"Good," I reply with a smirk. "You want this?"

"Yes," she answers.

"You want to submit to me?"

"Yes."

"You want me to be your Dom tonight?"

"Yes."

"Then say it."

She lets out a breath and says, "I want you to be my Dom tonight."

"No," I reply, shaking my head. "If you want it, I need to know it without even a shadow of a doubt. You'll have to beg. So say it."

I watch as realization washes over Nia like suds in a shower. She's not here with whatever men she dated before. She is not in the presence of a fake Dom or a boy who read a book and thought they could play the part. I am real. I am what every Dom strives to be.

"Please be my Dom tonight," she begs.

The sound of her consent fills me from head to toe with desire, nearly sending me plunging into Dom Space. Her words mixed with the sound of her voice is the ultimate aphrodisiac, and I can't get enough of it.

"Do you want me to undress you?" I ask, already aware of the answer but wanting to hear her say it.

"Yes," she replies.

"Say it."

"Rome, please undress me."

"Good," I say as heat envelopes me. "Now don't move."

As I lick my lips, I reach up for the strap on Nia's gorgeous dress, pulling it off and letting it dangle from her shoulder. When I remove the other side, the dress immediately falls to the floor, revealing her perfect body. When I say perfect, I mean gorgeous in every sense of the word. Not unblemished or completely unmarred, or skinny without the slightest hint of fat. I mean impeccably flawed with curves fit for a grown woman. I mean cellulite that I want to run my tongue over, and dark spots that call to me like a beautiful voice in the wind. With each and every so-called flaw that a broken society would have the gall to turn its nose up at, Nia is absolutely perfect.

"Fuck," I whisper to myself before speaking louder. "You're so unbelievable I can barely stand to be close to you. I feel honored, like your presence is my gift from the stars. Do you know how beautiful you are?"

Nia stares at me with a furrow in her brow, her expression unreadable. She doesn't answer, but I understand. This moment isn't about me asserting dominance over her. It's about her claiming her own power and understanding the queen that she is. It's why I won't do anything until she says please. I am the Dominant, but I have no power at all unless she gives it to me. She wants to be commanded, but I need her to understand that she is the light that guides us through the darkness. Her voice and consent is what gives me power over her. Without her I am nothing.

I take a moment to look at her body, marveling at its beauty and thinking of ways I can both satisfy and mar it. I gently run my hand down her shoulder and arm, then grab her by the hip and squeeze, hypnotized by how her skin flexes beneath my grip. Her eyes watch me, but she does as I told her and never moves. Her obedience drives me while her beauty seduces me, and I feel trapped within her grasp.

"Now tell me what you want," I demand, my fingers still pressing tightly against her waist.

"Can I please kneel for you?" she asks.

"Yes," I reply automatically, desperate to see her drop down and look up at me. "Kneel."

Unashamed of her naked body—exactly the way a woman should be—Nia slowly drops to her knees. Like a trained submissive, she tucks her legs beneath her body and places her hands on her thighs with her palms up. Once she's settled, I walk behind her and pull her locs until they all cascade down her back, then I return to her front, standing above her.

"Is this what you wanted?" I ask.

"Yes," she says, looking up at me with lust and need in her beautiful brown eyes.

"You wanted me standing over you? Controlling you?"

"Yes."

"*Sir*," I snip. "Even if only for tonight, I am your Dom. In fact, I'm your boss. So when you address me, it will be as your Sir."

A hint of a smile flashes across her face before she pulls it away. "Yes, Sir."

"Good, now I have another question for you." I crouch down until we're face to face, my nose only inches from hers. "Do you crave me?"

She swallows hard. "Yes, Sir."

"Do you want to obey me?"

"Yes, Sir."

"You want to do as you're told?"

"Yes, Sir."

"And you don't want to disappoint me?"

"No, Sir. Making you happy will make me happy," she admits, and it sends a chill swirling through my insides. There isn't a person in the world who doesn't want to hear that, Dom or not.

"Is that right? That means you want to be good for me. You want to be my good girl?" I ask, testing the waters of what makes Nia tick.

Being a Dom is about more than just getting what you want. If I don't know what she wants, then I'm lost in a forest of uncertainty. Every sub has a preference of how they want to be spoken to. Some like praise. Some prefer degradation, and my absolute favorites love both. A good Dom will know how to feed his sub what they want, but only when they have earned it. I'm yearning to know what Nia wants, so that I can give it to her better than she ever knew she needed it.

"Yes, Sir," she answers. "I want to be your good girl."

"That's what I love to hear," I tell her as I stand up and remove my shirt. "Do you want to know what will please me right now?"

"Yes, Sir." She nods enthusiastically.

Fuck. Seeing her so needy makes my cock ache with hardness.

"Your mouth," I inform her. Nia's breath hitches at my words, and I smile. "Do you want my cock in your mouth, Nia?"

She swallows hard, her eyes dropping down to my unfastened pants as if trying to see through the fabric with X-ray vision. She wants to know if what I'm hiding is worth opening her mouth for, and I can't wait to show her that it is.

"Yes, Sir," she answers.

"Say the word," I demand in a growl.

"Please, Sir," Nia replies. "*Please* put your cock in my mouth."

At her request and consent, I place a hand on both sides of my pants and push them down, slowly revealing my thick erection to her inch by inch. She watches with eyes that grow wider with every second, until my tip is finally released and my cock bounces free. Nia's jaw practically falls to the floor when she can finally see it in its entirety. She looks at me, then down at it, amazement turning her eyes into stars.

"Open your mouth," I command, and Nia obliges.

With my pants only down far enough to release my cock, I step forward and push myself into Nia's wet mouth, placing a hand on the side of her face to keep her steady. The warmth of her feels incredible, forcing my head back as she begins to suck. Ecstasy wraps me up like a warm blanket as she continues, raising both of her hands and using them as tools to plunge my entire body into bliss. She twists around my shaft with one hand while the other cups my balls, massaging them at the same time. I try to look down and force my mind back into Dom mode, but she's so incredible that I can only look up at the ceiling, my vision turning white from the intensity.

"Fuck," I manage to mutter just as I feel a surge of pleasure shooting forward like a bullet train. I have no choice but to step back and pull myself out of her grasp before I explode far sooner than I intend to.

Once there is a sizable space between us, I look at her in awe of what she just did. I am not a man who orgasms quickly. For whatever reason, I have always been gifted with orgasm control, but Nia managed to pull heaven forward in nearly an instant and I don't even know how to respond. That was unreal. Where has this woman been hiding? I can barely believe we've been living in the same city all this time, both of us into the lifestyle, but my cock never managed to find the nirvana that is her luscious mouth.

"My god," I exclaim, still in shock as the orgasm finally recedes. "That was ... you're fucking unreal."

Nia smiles proudly, eyeing my cock like she's ready to get back to it. But if I let her, the night will end before it has had a chance to truly begin. I refuse to let that happen, so instead of stepping forward and pushing my cock into her mouth a second time, I drop to my knees in front of her.

"Sit on your butt," I demand. "Put your back against the couch and open your legs wide for me. We can't go any further until I return the favor."

Her smile never wavers as Nia follows my instructions to a T. She shifts her body weight and sits down on her butt before scooting back until she is leaning against the couch. Once she's all set, I lay flat on my stomach and slide myself forward, wasting no time engulfing her pretty little pussy with my mouth.

She sucks in a gasp like she just plunged into icy waters, her muscles tightening all around me as her hands shoot forward to grab the back of my head, locking me in place. That's fine. I never want to leave anyway.

It's not a competition, but I eat her pussy like it is. I have to astonish her the way she just did me, and I work myself into a sweat to fulfill the mission. Nia's moans and writhing body spur me forward as my tongue dances across her clit before sucking it into my mouth. I suck and lick it at the same time, building up a rhythm until her breathing becomes labored and her alluring moans are long and drawn out, a beautiful symphony playing above me. The second I push two fingers into her dripping pussy, Nia tightens her grip on my head, her nails clutching me like talons.

"Oh fuck," she exclaims. "Sir, please ... can I please come? I'm about to come."

"Come in my mouth," I tell her between licks. "Let me taste what I've been starving for since the day we met."

"Oh god!" she shouts before her words are replaced by a guttural scream.

Wetness explodes into my mouth as she lets go, and I drink it all down, completely unabashed. I keep going, licking and sucking her pussy and forcing her body into convulsions that fill me with pride. Nia melts for me, and I love it. I want more of it. I need it, and my cock responds accordingly, maxing out in rigidity as I push myself off the floor and move in to kiss Nia's neck.

She pants in front of me, sweat rolling down her face like a cold bottle on a hot day, and her eyes are closed as she tries to recover. I give her a moment, although I'm dying to keep going. Even in this exhausted state, she is still gorgeous from head to toe, and it feels like everything we've done so far has been so harmonic. We fit together. Her submission calls to my Dominance in a way that I haven't felt in far too long. I have no idea what that means or how I should feel about it, but I know that I ache for more.

As her breathing begins to finally slow, I reach up and gently wrap my fingers around her throat. I want to squeeze until she can no longer breathe, but we haven't talked about each other's kinks yet. I could easily assume that she's into breath play, but assumptions in BDSM are billboard-sized red flags. So, I don't choke her. I caress her skin with my fingertips as I pepper her neck and cheek with soft kisses. It's not until her hand comes up and covers mine that I get a glimpse of what Nia truly wants.

"Keep going," she says. "Please, Sir."

Her fingers tighten around mine and I feel her head and neck shift forward. I know what she's hinting at, but I require more if we're going to go down that road.

"You want me to choke you?" I ask, halting the entire scene until she makes her consent clear.

"Yes, Sir," she replies. "Choke me ... while you fuck me."

My body immediately responds to her permission—my cock throbbing, my heart racing, my hands aching to give her the best version of what she just asked for. I place a hand beneath each of Nia's arms and use my strength to lift her until her ass is squarely on the couch with her legs raised in the air on both sides of my waist. The sight of her is enough to send fireworks exploding across my imagination. Her beautiful brown skin is so enticing it makes my mouth water. This is just our first time together, but I'm already thinking about the things I want to do to her as we progress in the future.

Nia places her hands beneath her knees and holds her legs up for me, waiting patiently while I remove a condom from my wallet, discard the rest of my clothes, and position myself in front of her. As Nia watches hungrily, I sheathe my cock with the condom, stretching it to its limits. I place one knee on the floor and one hand around Nia's throat, using the other to direct my cock into her pussy. Her warmth and wetness make me gasp, because I can't believe how good she feels. Everything she has done tonight has been awe-inspiring, and she's doing it without effort. Naturally, she looks this good and feels this incredible. It's like our bodies were made for each other in a lab, and now that we've found each other, our worlds will be colorless if we are ever apart again.

"Show me," Nia suddenly orders. "Please don't hold back. I want it all. Choke me hard. Fuck me hard. Make me come hard. Please, Sir. You have no idea how badly I need this from you. I'm begging. Be relentless."

What the fuck? Who is this woman?

I bite my lip as wicked thoughts in my mind grow wings and take flight. I won't take this sanction lightly. If she wants to be fucked hard, I will show her what it is like to be fucked by a real Dom. I begin with one long stroke that nearly pulls me all the way out of her, teasing my tip and her entrance at the same time. She looks at me with more hunger in her eyes than I've ever seen from anyone before. She pleads with me without speaking, needing me inside of her more than she needs anything else in the world right now, and when I push all the way in, her eyes flutter closed as she moans—an image painted in heaven.

Each and every stroke of my cock is long and hard. I want to give her every thick inch of me. There can be no question about what good sex feels like after tonight. She will never forget. I will make sure of it. I pound Nia's pussy exactly the way she asked for it—relentlessly.

Some guys think sex is all about how fast they can go. Those boys are wrong. When a woman says she wants it harder, it usually doesn't mean faster. I don't make it a race. I take my time, keeping my pace even as I fuck Nia senseless. Our bodies slam together and rock the couch as we both moan, filling the house with the sound of our sex. If she shared a wall with someone next door, they would hear our bliss bleeding through the paint. They would think a god descended from the stars to torture their neighbor. Nia moans without shame, and she doesn't stop when I bring my other hand down on her neck, squeezing it until the muscles in my forearms flex.

"Yes," she croaks behind my tight grasp. "Fuck me, Sir. Oh my god."

"Is this what you wanted?" I ask, completely destroying her.

"Yes, Sir!" she shrieks, her eyes cinched shut as her body rocks back and forth.

"Is this what you needed?"

"Yes. Please keep going."

"Are you ready to come for me?"

"Yes. I'm so close. Can I come for you? Please, Sir. Let me come for you."

I don't answer right away because I feel the surging sensation of my own orgasm galloping forward. It starts in my pelvis and spreads to every limb, and I know I'm about to lose control. It's about to erupt from me with only a few more strokes and I won't be able to keep myself upright before long.

"Do it," I tell Nia as my orgasm begins. "Come all over me while I come inside you. Oh fuck!"

"Yes," Nia yells. "I'm coming again!"

Our screams burst out of us at the same time, doubling the volume to an ear-splitting level. Nia shakes and quivers, causing more and more friction on my cock as I detonate inside of her, filling the condom with all that it can handle. Each time her body moves, it causes me to convulse, the sensitivity of my tip becoming too much for me to maintain control of my muscles. I have to pull out before I collapse on top of her.

With the condom still stretched across my shaft, I sit on the floor and pant like a dog. Nia pulls herself all the way onto the couch and stops moving entirely, the only signs of life coming from the sound of her ragged breathing. That's how we stay until I slide sideways and lay myself on the floor on my back. I stare up at the ceiling as emotions spawn in my mind. Thoughts of everything I've been through come in waves, and I try to blink away memories of Natalia from four years ago, wondering what she'd think about my feelings for Nia.

Is that what this is? Feelings? I barely know her, but I do feel ... something, and I don't know if I like it. I don't know if it's okay that there is a part of me that wants to pursue this and see where it goes, but I'd be lying to myself if I said I didn't. I don't know what the future holds, and I don't know if my heart beats rapidly out of excitement or fear.

The Floodgates

Nineteen

At some point in the middle of the night, I woke up to find clothes to sleep in. I barely remember it, but I ended up back on the couch while Rome stayed asleep on the floor. Amazingly, that's where he stayed until we woke up this morning. I wasn't the only one who had been worn out.

As I watch him quietly slip into the bathroom wearing nothing but his pants, my thoughts don't even care about the present. I'm stuck on last night, memories of kneeling for him vividly re-playing in my mind before rewinding and starting again. I keep seeing the size of his enormous erection dangling in front of me like a tempting fruit, teasing me to the point of ravenousness before he pushed it inside my mouth. I lost my mind once I tasted it, my hands becoming zombified and taking control all on their own. I stroked his shaft and caressed his balls, and the way it drove him insane made me feel like a goddess. Rome controlled my mind and sent me to a place I'm not sure I've ever been. He owned me last night, and I loved it. I wanted to be his and to allow him to have his way with me. I was completely submissive. He did all of that before even attempting to physically satisfy me. It was un-fucking-real, and I wish I had time to fill a page of my diary reciting it all right now.

I wasn't sure how the night would end, because I saw him waver before we entered the house. There was a flash of uncertainty before he snapped out of it and went back to being the confident man I had been sitting across from at the restaurant. It was like he needed to consciously flip a switch and allow a darker part of himself to take the reins, and once the Dom gained control, it was mesmerizing. The way he commanded me, the way he guided me and left no room for misinterpretation, the way he took his time licking my clit, making sure not to rush like boys do. Rome was a man in every sense of the word, and I felt it. My god, I felt it. With a cock at least seven inches long and jaw-droppingly thick, there was no way to avoid it. In the span of less than an hour, Rome made me come twice. I could have cried from how incredible it was. All of my questions about him have now been answered, but there is a new question that has been born as we get up in the morning before having to go to work together.

What now?

No one saw us at Giovanni's. Sierra wasn't waiting outside with a camera to record evidence as we exited, so we shouldn't have to worry about people from Sandcastle looking at us sideways when we enter this morning. But what if someone finds out? Everything at our place of business will change, and we may need to have a conversation about how to navigate those rocky waters if we want to stay afloat at the office.

Next on the list? What does a night of Earth-shattering sex mean for Rome and me? Are we a couple now? Are we going to go on dates and hold hands in public places? Do we have private meetings at Sandcastle behind closed doors so that we can be affectionate? Am I bringing him to meet Jaz and Michael? Will I be meeting his family and friends in the future? Will he introduce me to people as his girlfriend? Do I think of him as my boyfriend? Is there an us?

What now?

The question splinters into a million more and I suddenly feel overwhelmed by the thought. Trying to figure out the future has never been my strong suit, and for all I know, Rome isn't even interested in anything long term. I honestly don't know what he wants after having already been given access to my body. All I can do now is hope that he isn't a player who dumps a girl after making her scream all night. As much as I enjoyed what we did, that would really suck.

When he steps out of the bathroom, his hair and face are wet from washing them in the sink, and his expression is unclear. He's such a difficult person to read that it's slightly intimidating. What is going on behind those beautiful brown eyes? The look on his face makes me want to ask, but his demeanor scares me away. So I just stare at him in the reflection of my dresser mirror. I need a shower, but I don't know if he's planning on leaving right away or not. There isn't much time before we have to be at work, so I don't imagine him staying long, which leaves very little time for us to wade in a pool of floating question marks. I need answers, but how do I break the ice?

I walk into the living room and sit on the couch, waiting for him to put on his shirt and exit the bathroom. When he comes in, his eyes stay low and the same uncertainty I saw in the car before we came in last night resurfaces. What is that?

"So," I force myself to say. "Last night was ... incredible."

Rome comes in, his every step weighed down by an obvious sense of reluctance, and takes a seat on the accent chair across from me. The smile he allowed me to see at the dinner table last night has gone back into hiding, tucked away beneath the expressionless gaze he usually has.

"It was great," he replies as if being forced to admit it against his will.

My eyebrows raise. "You sure? You seem awfully sad right now, and I'm not sure what to think."

Rome forces himself to look at me and maintain eye contact, a smirk wishing it could take over his mouth but being held back. "I'm not sad. Just tired I guess, and I need to high tail it back to my place if I plan to make it into the office on time."

"Yeah," I say. "About that. What's the plan on how we're supposed to act at work?"

"No one will know anything," he replies as if I was already supposed to be aware of the answer. "I won't have my staff accusing you of trying to sleep your way to the top, nor will I have them accusing me of an abuse of power. So, what happened will remain between us. It's just better that way."

I nod, understanding yet frustrated by the response. "Okay. I suppose that's the best way to go about it, because if Sierra says anything else to me, I may just have to slap the shit out of her, and that would be bad for my career progression."

Against his will, Rome smiles. "Well, we wouldn't want that, would we?"

"It depends on what you're talking about. I'd *want* to slap her. I would *not* want to ruin my career."

His smile lingers, turning my insides to jelly. "You're a mess. I love your sense of humor."

"Good, because I love forcing you to smile when it's so clear that you don't want to. What's that about?"

He shrugs, unable to stop the smile now that it has been pointed out. "I don't know. I don't think about it as much as it might seem. I've been through a lot, and I guess the result is that I just don't smile much."

"Well, you should because it's glorious. And I don't mean that in an "we just had sex so I like your face," kind of way. Even before last night I knew I wanted to see your smile, and once you let me I was floored. It's a beautiful thing, Rome. You shouldn't hide it."

The way he looks at me makes me feel like I just leaped from a plane. My stomach plunges into my feet and I can barely think. God, I wish I knew what was going on behind those eyes, and I'm tired of wondering.

"Tell me what you're thinking," I demand.

Rome swallows hard before sitting up straight. "I'm thinking that you're too perfect," he says. "I enjoyed your company too much last night, both at the restaurant and here, and talking to you now feels just as good. You're easy to converse with, and somehow you manage to make me smile. To be completely honest, it scares me. You're too beautiful to have such an infectious personality."

I swallow so hard I feel like I've just downed a golf ball. It's incredible that we've gone from work associates simply maneuvering around each other at Sandcastle to two people who can't stop staring at one another. He was attractive before, but now he's breathtaking. He was always sexy. Now he's mouthwatering. Before, he was just the new CMO of my place of employment, now just looking at him and hearing the sound of his voice fills me with lust. Everything is so different now, all of it changing in such a short amount of time. I'm still spinning from the change up, lost in the rough seas of my emotions and unable to get a sense of direction, because no matter where I look, he is all I see. I don't know what the hell is happening.

I shake my head as we gaze at each other and the temperature in the room ascends.

"You mentioned making it to work on time," I say. "If that's your intention, then you better stop staring at me like that."

Rome exhales before sucking his bottom lip into his mouth. "You think you can tell me what to do?"

I smile. "I don't know. Maybe."

"Tisk, tisk, Nia," he replies, shaking his head with an enticing look in his eyes. "I thought we established that I was in charge."

A shiver runs down my spine thinking about the scene in the office. "Mm. Yes, we did."

"Do I need to remind you again?"

I shrug with a wry smirk. "Maybe."

A devilish smile takes over Rome's luscious mouth. "Fine. Let's see if you remember how to be a good girl for me. Now, take off those pants."

The baritone in his voice makes me quiver as he stares at me. I couldn't turn him down if I tried, and the fact that everything we did last night is so fresh in my memory makes my body react all on its own. It remembers how it feels to have Rome inside me, and it responds without my conscious effort. As I bite my lip and lift my butt off the couch to push my pants down, wetness glistens on the fabric. How am I already this wet for him?

I toss my pants to the side and sit back down while Rome leans back in his seat. He drinks me in, looking at me from head to toe as if inspecting his personal property, but he doesn't let his excitement control him. He's even-keeled as his gaze falls to my wet pussy.

"Touch yourself," he demands. "I want you to see how wet you are."

Oh my fucking god. If I was only a little wet before, that command is sure to open the floodgates. Slowly, I reach down and do as I'm told. I make circles on my clit with my index and middle fingers, the sight of him watching me shooting spikes up my body. Rome sits there without moving, his eyes trained on me. He doesn't reach down and stroke himself. He doesn't lick his lips in an effort to increase his own sexiness. He just watches, as still as a statue, showcasing a masterclass in how a Dom is supposed to be patient and impeccably in control of themselves. He's perfect in his execution, and it makes me that much wetter just knowing that he is what I have been in search of for so long. This is what my friends and I have been toasting to. I have searched high and low, chasing down rainbows, and I have now found my pot of gold.

Rome watches me for two minutes before he moves a single muscle. His only change is when his eyes shift from my face to my pussy, like he finds pleasure in looking at both. By the time I watch him stand up, I'm a soaking wet mess for him, craving his touch in whatever way he decides to give it to me. He has made me need him without lifting a hand.

I keep my fingers precisely where Rome told them to be, teasing my clit further as he begins taking slow, monotonous steps toward me. He pins me to the couch with his gaze, and I find added excitement in the thrill of not knowing what he's going to do when he reaches me. I wait patiently, fingers pressed against my clit, as Rome reaches his destination and takes his time lowering himself to his knees. While I keep rubbing myself, he places a hand on each of my thighs, caressing them gently and sliding them up inch by inch. I suck in a breath when he squeezes, his gaze focused solely on my swirling fingers. Then he dives in, pushing my hand to the side and replacing my fingers with his tongue. The oxygen in my lungs is vacuumed out in a rush, my eyes widening from the sudden unreal sensation.

"Oh my god," I exclaim before slamming my hand over my mouth, embarrassed by the volume of my reaction.

I try to hold it all in as Rome licks and sucks my clit with absolute perfection, but the moans force their way out, seeping between my fingers like I'm trying to hold water in my grasp. All I can do is throw my head back and let the sensation wash over me like the waves on a beach. Rome slides two fingers inside of me, curls them upward at the perfect depth and angle, and fingers me while he tongues my clit over and over again. I am undone as both of my hands wrap around the back of his head and hold on for dear life while he eats me like a starved monster. Time stops, the rest of the world disintegrates, and my body stiffens as the final tidal wave approaches. It rushes forward, a missile speeding toward its target and ready to detonate before I can stop it.

"Sir ... fuck," I stammer, trying to get it out, but Rome cuts me off.

"Don't ask," he says. "Just give it to me, baby girl."

I don't even attempt to say another word. His permission, mixed with the pet name and the overwhelming feeling of his tongue and fingers, sends me careening over the edge of the world's steepest cliff. I fall head-first into a blizzard as my vision turns white from how hard I squeeze my eyes shut. Every inch of my skin prickles before igniting into a thousand suns as I collapse in on myself. I am wrecked beyond repair, the G-spot orgasm ripping me limb from limb and lighting the wick to an infinite set of emotions. I feel happiness, sadness, anger, and bliss all at the same time before everything finally begins to fade away. The fire is slowly put out and I regain control of my emotions as Rome releases me, watching as I crawl my way back to the land of the living and gasp for air.

When it's finally over, my muscles relax and my limbs go limp. I lean back on the couch with my legs dangling off, unable to lift myself up to get comfortable. I just lay there, breathing hard with tears in the corner of my eyes from the devastation Rome just layed on me. I remain in a vegetable-like state, immoble as I watch him stand up and straighten out his shirt. He smiles down on me, clearly proud of himself as he steps forward and crouches so that we're face to face.

"Pull yourself together, baby girl," he says with a devilish grin. "Otherwise you'll be late for work. I have to drive back to my place so I can get cleaned up, so I guess I'll get there after you." With no warning, he reaches between my legs and slides his finger up my pussy, collecting my wetness on his fingertip before sucking it into his mouth. "But a taste like that is totally worth being late for."

Rome leans forward and kisses me on the forehead before standing up straight, turning on his heel, and walking out of the door. I stay on the couch, still panting as feelings of satisfaction, exhaustion, and confusion wrap their arms around me.

He is so incredible, and my body has never experienced the level of pleasure that he has given me over the last few hours. But I still don't have the answer to the question I woke up with this morning. It may be harder to focus on it now that I have been shattered into a million pieces, but it's still there, watching me from within the fog like a stalker.

What now?

Dear Diary,

This is what it feels like to have your mind blown.

Did you hear me? My mind is blown!

A series of unprecedented and unpredictable events has taken place, and I am in a state of total shock. Allow me to sum up.

1. Rome chooses my pitch as the winner of pitch wars, setting up an epic showdown between Nix Malone and I in the near future.

2. After Sierra accuses me of trying to take her job, Rome storms in like one of the Avengers and saves me from her, threatening Sierra's job for her insane lack of professionalism.

3. Rome surprises me by asking me out to a "business" dinner, during which we talk about everything, including the fact that he is ... wait for it ... a Dom!

4. Rome and I return to my place, and he shows me exactly the kind of Dom he is. He's caring, making me use the word please as my form of consent. He never jumps to conclusions about what I want, even hesitating to choke me until I showed him that it was okay.

5. He made me come twice!

6. He made me cum a third time after waking up from sleeping on my floor.

7. He was literally the perfect Dom!

I had the shock of my life, and I couldn't have asked for anything more. The only problem is that I now sit here wondering what will happen next. After giving me the night of my life, there is still a wall of unanswered questions between us. I don't know what all of this means for us, because we still have to work together in front of Sierra, who is already suspicious.

I know what I want. It is easy for me to decide after all of the brutal missteps I've had. But I don't know what HE wants. Rome is an enigma, even hiding his smile as often as he can. What do I make of him? Who is the man behind the Dominant? And the biggest question of all is—will he allow me to find out?

Twenty

J azmine's eyebrows are stuck at the top of her head as she sits across from me, a plate topped with a crispy chicken salad resting in front of her. The muscles in her face don't move and she looks frozen in time with her jet black hair careening over her shoulder, making her resemble a beautiful, dark-skinned sculpture. I don't know what to say to unfreeze her, but I know it was my story about what I've been through with Rome over the past twenty-four hours that turned her to ice.

"I know," I say as I lift up my turkey BLT and take a bite. "I'm not sure what to make of it either."

As a small family is escorted to their table behind us by a hostess with bright red hair, Jaz finally blinks her way out of her frozen state.

"Don't know what to make of it?" she says incredulously. "Bitch, I'm speechless. So all of that talk about the boss from both you and Jeremiah was accurate? He rescued you from Sierra's miserable ass, asked you out on a *business date*, escorted you back to your house, and fucked you senseless right there in the middle of your living room? Then he ate the kitty until you came again this morning? What kind of sexy ass, whirlwind, EL James novel life are you living, Nia? This whole time I've felt sympathy for you, now I'm suddenly jealous. Get it, girl."

I smile as Jaz laughs in the beautifully exaggerated way that she does, smacking the table and throwing her head back. All I can do is shake my head and try not to disrupt everybody in Applebee's.

"Alright, so what now?" Jaz asks. "Because now you've slept with your boss, and I'm sure there's some kind of company policy forbidding that. Plus, when the girls in the office find out, you may be on the receiving end of some hate. Are you ready for that?"

I take a sip from my water to buy myself time to answer, but nothing comes as I pull my mouth from the straw.

"I've been asking myself that question since the morning I woke up with him asleep on my floor," I reply. "What now? I don't know. When I asked him, all he said was that no one in the office would know because he didn't want people talking shit about me or saying he abused his power. After that, all I could think about was how he knew exactly how to find my G-spot."

"Yeah, the G-spot will certainly make everything else a blur," Jaz agrees, nodding as she smiles. "Well, the two of you better make sure you keep it all under wraps then. I'm sure there are some people who wouldn't care, but you already know Sierra would lose it."

"First of all, fuck Sierra," I snip with a raised a finger. "Secondly, I know. She would be the one who would try to file some sort of formal complaint with HR or something, but Rome owns Sandcastle so I doubt it would mean anything. She'd have to make it a lawsuit, but I'm not even sure on what grounds—unless she was fired and Rome promoted me into her position, but that's not going to happen. Legally speaking, I don't think we'd have anything to worry about."

"But your reputation around the office would get dragged through the mud," Jaz says, finishing my thought for me. "As long as you can stay low key and keep it away from Sierra, you should be fine. All worries aside, I'm happy for you, girl. You have had your fair share of rough relationships and hookups. No one deserves a little satisfaction more than you."

I nod as excitement brews in my chest and begins to spread out. She's right. I've been through enough bullshit over the years. I deserve this. I only wish it felt more permanent.

"Thank you," I reply. "I honestly can't believe it all. It happened so fast."

"What has he been like at work? Are you two sneaking away to go fuck in janitor's closets?"

I stifle a laugh. "No, because I haven't seen him since he left my house this morning. He said he'd be late to work, and he must've meant it because we've gone half the day and he hasn't shown up. While that clearly makes it easier to act like nothing has happened between us, it also leaves me wondering about him.

"Even with everything that went down, I swear Rome goes through these brief moments of sadness. It flickers across his face as quick as a camera flash, but I notice it every time. Before all of the good stuff this morning, he looked like he was being weighed down by his thoughts. He didn't really lighten up until we started talking and I made him smile. He's such an enigma, and while that is one of things that draws me to him, it also makes me worry that he has some dark secrets locked away in a closet that no one has the key to. I just wish I knew what was going through his mind. I'm over here ecstatic about it and looking forward to finding out what comes next. But what does all of this mean to him?"

Jaz finishes her salad and pushes the plate to the side of the table to give the server easier access to it. I follow her lead, taking my final bite of my sandwich and stacking my plate on top of hers. The server comes over and whisks everything away before returning with the check. She places it on the table and Jaz quickly snatches it up.

"Thanks," I tell her.

"Don't mention it," she says, placing her debit card on top of the paper. "Anyway, the two of you clearly need to have a conversation that doesn't involve him using his tongue to change the subject or sidestep the issue. I know you're looking to settle down, but what about him?"

"I didn't get the feeling that he was opposed to it," I answer. "And I'm not sure if that was the vibe he had this morning. He just seemed ... sad. It's like his confidence wavers, glitching out like a bad computer monitor before coming back as if nothing happened. It's strange."

"You're going to have to ask him what's up," Jaz informs me. "The last thing you want to do is waste your time on somebody who is only in it for the sex. Not that I think he only wants you for your body, but I think you deserve to know what his intentions are. It's only fair. If he's keeping his emotions out of it, then you deserve to know so that you can do the same. Because while I am happy for you, I will sneak into his office and piss on his desk if he tries to play you." I laugh as Jaz goes on with a straight face. "I'm not playing. The computer, the keyboard, his chair, the floor, everything in there will be pissy. So talk to him and make sure he's not an ass, because piss is DNA and I don't want to end up in jail."

I nod, trying to keep my laughter from bellowing through the place. "I'll talk to him. Well, I will whenever I see him again. I really hope that not showing up to work today isn't his way of avoiding me."

Jaz, sensing my frustration and worry, nods her head. "I'm sure he just had something else going on. Don't worry yourself to death."

"I'll do my best," I reply. "Now let's get out of here before Sierra has an attitude about me taking an extended lunch. Thanks for eating with me and hearing all about my crazy ass life. Oh, and thanks again for paying."

"Anytime, girl. You know I got you. As soon as you talk to Rome, let me know. I'm dying to know what comes next in this saga."

I nod, trying to force away the anxiety blossoming in my gut. "Well, I guess that makes two of us."

Twenty-One

When I didn't speak to Rome the day after we went to dinner and had sex at my place, I chalked it up to coincidence. He never showed up to work after he made me come on my couch, and following lunch with Jaz, I forced myself to believe that he just had something else going on. Maybe he had a friend who really needed his help with something important. Maybe he filled his day with meetings with potential clients from Sandcastle. Perhaps he actually got sick the minute he arrived back at his place after spending the night in mine. Twenty-four-hour bugs exist—maybe he caught one walking out of my house. I didn't have any answers, but I didn't let myself dwell on it too long. He must have had *something* going on.

Now that I've gone another day without a single word from Rome, I don't know what to think. Especially since he came to work and spent the entire day in his office, avoiding eye contact with me and dodging prolonged interactions with anyone who wasn't Sierra, although the two of them have been extremely awkward since the incident in my office. A normal person watching him sulk around the building, his eyes pulled down to the floor by some sort of invisible gravity, would simply assume that he was focused on business. He and Sierra are the top two people at this company, and it makes total sense that he only converse with her about business and deals of high importance. But I guess I'm not a normal person now—not after the night we shared.

After connecting the way we did, I expect the total opposite of what has happened all day today. We should be sharing occasional looks that fill our insides with anxiety-stricken butterflies. There should be quick smiles flashing across the office that nobody sees but us. There should a powerful temptation to sneak into one of the bathrooms or rush out to the parking lot to fuck in one of our cars. I expected excitement and a fluttering heart, but I'm met with a blank expression and disappointment instead. After the conversation at Giovanni's and the sex that followed … what the fuck?

The energy at the office is low, which is typical at the end of the day. We've spent hours hustling around, making phone calls, preparing pitches, sifting through budgets, and planning meetings. No one has any energy left now that we've reached the last few minutes of the day. Anything that is left in the tank is preserved for watching the seconds tick by on the clock, faking like we're checking emails to seem busy. Jeremiah sits at his cubicle with Youtube on his monitor and a hand on his mouse, ready to click to another tab if Rome or Sierra gets too close. I'm sure he's not the only one who has decided they have done enough work for the day. Even I sit at my desk with a black screen and thoughts of what I will do after I leave this office. I've had enough of watching Rome intentionally avoid eye contact with me anyway, so if there isn't going to be any excitement here, I may as well wrap it up, have some dinner, and down some wine. But with only two minutes left before everyone in the building heads for the exits, a shadow fills my door opening.

"Nia, are you busy?"

I look away from the black mirror of my computer monitor to find Rome standing just past my threshold. His expensive jeans and white button-up are as casual as I've ever seen him, but he's still glowing with sex appeal, and I hate the way seeing him makes me want to bite my lip and stare like a teenager with a crush. As beautiful as he is—what the hell does he want? Why come here after dodging me all day, and why the hell would he show up at the very last minute? I want to tell him that I'm busy. I want to remind him that he clearly didn't want to speak with me today, so there is no need for us to talk now. But regardless of the attitude I feel swelling inside me, Rome is my boss. What choice do I have?

I make a show of glancing at the clock right next to his face before looking at him. "Not with less than two minutes left of work I'm not."

He nods, stepping into the office and lowering himself into one of the accent chairs in front of my desk. "I won't take up too much of your time. There's just something we need to discuss before you head out."

I frown—because what the hell is this? What's with all the formality? How is he trying to act all professional after having his cock in my mouth and my legs in the air? He makes himself comfortable just as the day ends and everyone gets up to leave. He couldn't have come to discuss this before the end of the day drew near? What the actual fuck?

As the office begins to look more and more empty, Rome keeps his eyes on me. I can smell his cologne from here, and the gaze he fixes on me gives me far too many memories of what happened on my couch. Hot pinpricks scatter across my face as I wait for him to finally speak up, but my patience runs thin quickly.

"Are you waiting for everyone to leave?" I ask, my brow furrowed as I lean back in my chair.

He shakes his head. "Oh, I didn't even think about it. I apologize. I'll try to make this quick. How is the prep going for the Golden Diamond pitch?"

I let out a long, frustrated sigh. This *can't* be the reason he's in here.

"It's finished and I'm ready. Why?" I inquire, looking up at the clock again.

"Because the pitch is tomorrow," Rome replies. "I've spoken to Nix's people, and they say his only available date for us is tomorrow afternoon. So, are you sure you're ready?"

Even though I'm prepared, the pressure on my body increases and I'm pushed down into my seat, unable to move.

"Tomorrow afternoon?" I say. "They couldn't have made it another two or three days out?"

"You just said you were ready?"

"I am, but ... *tomorrow*?" I let out a breath that does nothing to relax my rigid muscles. "This is Nix Malone we're talking about. Right hand to the madman himself. I just ... I'm nervous."

Rome leans forward in his seat, placing his forearms on his thighs, and I can't help but fixate on his hands. I remember where they've been and what they've done to me. It's an unneeded distraction.

"You're going to be fine," he says. "The way you passionately craft your pitches is exactly why I chose you for this. You're going to do great, and we're going to lock this account. Don't stress yourself."

"Oh, you're mister confidence now?" I ask. "Is that why you've been avoiding talking to me or even looking at me? Was I supposed to take that as I sign that you know I'll do fine all on my own? Because I took it to mean that you didn't want to be anywhere near me after everything happened?"

Nervousness spreads across Rome's face and drips down to his body, forcing him to get up and turn around to see if anyone remains in the bullpen. He spins the other direction and leans back, looking down the hall to make sure Sierra's office is empty. Once he's satisfied that we're alone, he sinks back into the chair.

"I haven't been avoiding you," he says—the world's most obvious lie.

I scoff. "Seriously? What would you call it?"

"Nothing," he snips, his nervousness suddenly mixing with irritation. "It's not you that I'm avoiding. It's ... the situation."

My eyebrows nearly leap off my face. "Oh really? So now I'm just a *situation*? Wow. And here I was thinking that we enjoyed each other's company at dinner and that we had an insane connection afterward. I guess that was all in my head, because clearly all you wanted was to hit it. I'll be sure to remember that and keep it professional now that I know I'm an idiot who was just being used. Great. Are we done here, Mr. Giovanni?"

Annoyance shoots from Rome's pores. "Don't ... I didn't say ... don't call me that," he blares, standing up like the seat just became too hot. "I didn't say that you're just a situation. I said I'm avoiding *the* situation, and it's deeper than you're aware of. Okay? I have my own issues that need to be worked out, and I'm your boss, I'm just not ... right ... at the moment. You don't know what I've been through."

I stand up, matching his energy. "I would if you would just tell me. You act like we had a hard time conversing the other night—like I'm not a good listener who wants to hear all about you. I thought it was clear that I like you and I want to know more. I thought that was the entire point."

"Well, I don't know if I'm ready to give more, or if I'm even capable," he shoots back, emotion suddenly overwhelming his face. "I don't like this. I don't trust this. I don't *need* this. Okay, Nia. I thought that I could give it a try, because you're so incredibly perfect. You stand there looking like everything I might ever need in this life, and I love the way you make me smile, and how passionate you are. I love that you're not afraid to stand up for yourself, and that you embrace who you are with no apologies. You're a real woman, and that has been surprisingly difficult to come by, but now that you're standing in front of me, I just don't feel ready and you fucking scare me. The possibilities of love, laughter, and happiness that waft off of you like rays of sunshine scare the living shit out of me."

The office suddenly descends into silence as we stand on opposite sides of my desk. Rome breathes heavily, as if talking about how he feels has exhausted his body from the inside out. What the hell has this man gone through that has him scared to be happy? We've only been together one time, and he is already acting like I'm a monster coming to ruin his life.

I step around my desk and slowly make my way over to him, careful with each step as if approaching an untrustworthy dog for the first time. I see the discomfort in his eyes and the tension in his muscles. I can sense his apprehension, but instead of being pushed away, it makes me want to move closer. I can tell that he has been through something deep, just as I have, and the common ground makes me want to be there for him. I want to help him heal if that's what he needs.

"Rome," I say, inching my way forward. "If you're not interested in being with me, just say that. It's clear that you've been through something that I know nothing about, but it's unfair for you to judge me based on what I don't know. I'll never get in if you don't let me, but I understand if you don't want to. We barely know each other, and there's no need to make it more dramatic than it needs to be. I like you, and I think you just might be the most beautiful man I've ever seen, but I won't force you to want me. It would suck to have to dive back into the pool of ridiculousness that is the dating world, especially after experiencing you, but I would do it. I'd rather go back than stand here as the reason you crumble. All you have to do is say that you don't want me. Say it, and we'll walk out of this office on our separate ways. We'll act like none of it ever happened. No hard feelings. I promise. Just say it. Tell me you don't want me."

When Rome finally looks up, I think I see tears in his eyes. The sight of it vexes me, but he doesn't let them linger. He swallows hard as he looks me in the eye, his resolve and will returning right in front of me.

"If I said that," he begins, subtly shaking his head. "I'd be lying through my teeth, Nia. I do want you. I want you more than I should, which is why all of this is so hard. I'm not supposed to crave you the way I do, but my body aches for yours. Even more than that, I want to learn everything about who you are as a person. I want us to get to know each other and spend as much time together as possible. And I want to fucking kiss you more than I can put into words right now."

I let out an exhale, surprised to learn that now I'm the one who is breathing hard. The attraction between us is too strong for me to fight, so I don't even try.

"Then do it," I say. "Do all of it."

Rome stares at me for a moment, and I see the battle waging within him. It shows itself in his posture, the way he sways back and forth as if fighting an urge to step forward—or maybe he's fighting the urge to turn around and walk out. He sucks his bottom lip into his mouth, biting down hard before giving in.

"Fuck," he says, before grabbing me by the waist and pulling my body over to his.

Our mouths collide, his tongue immediately finding mine as we kiss even more passionately than the first time, and the rest of the world melts away.

Twenty-Two

"Tell me what you want," Rome demands, fingers wrapped around my throat as my ass arches up into his crotch. I feel his erection through his pants and I lust for it. "Tell me."

He stands with his chest pressed against my back after grabbing my neck and spinning me around. He spent time kissing my shoulders before moving up my neck and licking around my earlobe. His fingers flex against my skin because he knows that I've consented to being choked, but he hesitates now even though his cock is rigid against his zipper. I love that he refuses to go forward without finding out exactly what I want. His need for verbal consent makes my desire for him grow even wider, making it a violent ocean I can no longer escape from. The waves keep pulling back down until I am drowning in my need for him.

What Rome doesn't know is that I have very few limits when I'm with someone who has earned my permission—and he has. I want him in every way. As long as it doesn't involve urine, feces, blood, or anal, I'm okay with it. Even if it is something I haven't tried yet, I would consider it a soft limit that I'm willing to attempt to see if it's for me or not. All we need is to vocalize this so that he doesn't have to keep asking me for approval every time we touch.

"Everything, Rome," I tell him. "Choke me, slap me, tie me up, spank me, flog me, hurt me. You have my consent to do it all. Not only am I a submissive, I'm a masochist, so you don't have to worry about hurting me. I want you to. The only things I'm not into are urine, feces, blood, and anal. Other than that, I am yours to use. I'll let you know if you do something that crosses into hard limit territory. So, please stop asking, Rome. I'm yours."

Rome licks his bottom lip, his eyes twinkling with desire as I look at him over my shoulder.

"That's all I needed to hear," he says, before forcefully pressing his lips against mine again.

We stay that way for a while, kissing deeply with my back pressed against his chest. I can feel his heartbeat, and it pounds as if driven by fear rather than desire, but Rome drives forward, his hand squeezing my throat as he kisses me deeply. He lets out a low growl from the back of his throat, the animal in him taking control as he slides his hands under my shirt to caress my skin. The feeling of his fingers pressing against my waist makes me wish they would go lower. I want him to touch me all over, all at the same time.

"How am I supposed to stay away from you?" he asks in my ear as the tip of his finger lifts the waistband of my pants and slides beneath it. "When you look this good." He kisses my neck as his entire hand finds its way into my pants. "When you smell this good." The tip of his middle finger glides over my clit, forcing a shiver through my entire body. "When your moans sound this good."

Rome presses two fingers down on my clit and begins making small circles that pull a moan from my mouth against my will. He works his hand with perfection, casting a spell on my soul as he alternates between rotating on my clit and slipping his fingers inside of me. It's like he knows my body as well as I do, and it feels so good that all I can do is lay my head back on his chest, close my eyes, and immerse myself in the pleasure. I let him have his way with me, kissing and licking my neck as he plays with my pussy better than any man ever has.

"It feels so good," I whisper, my mouth staying agape long after the words have left.

"No," Rome responds, increasing the pressure on my sensitive nub. "It's not that it feels so good, baby girl. It's that I make it feel so good. I make you moan this way. I make your knees this weak. I make you come. I make you this wet. Now say it."

Goosebumps ripple across my skin and cover my entire body as I say, "It's you, Sir. *You* make it feel so good."

I feel Rome's cheeks lift into a smile as his beard scratches against my neck. "Again."

He speeds up the circles on my clit and I gasp. "You make it feel so good."

"Good girl," he growls in my ear, his voice as rough as splintered wood. "Do you want me to make you come right here in your office?"

I nod my head vigorously as I begin to feel the build up of an approaching orgasm from his fingers massaging my clit.

"Yeah?" he asks. "Then you better hurry up before someone comes back to the office. You never know who may have forgotten something at their desk."

"Yes, Sir," I say, my voice coming out in a whimper. "I'm ready for whatever you want to do to me."

Rome exhales. "God. You make my cock so fucking hard I can barely stand. Why do you do this to me, huh? Are you sorry for how weak you make me?"

I shake my head. "Absolutely not."

"I thought not. Now let me make sure it's worth it."

Rome quickly drops down into a crouch and tugs both sides of my pants down until they are scrunched up at my ankles, then he helps me lift each leg so that I can step out of them entirely. Once I'm naked from the bottom down, he's back on his feet again, his body pressed against my back. I obsess over the warmth of him, losing myself in the moment because he makes the world feel like it isn't even real. He submerges me in his fantasy until I no longer can recognize up from down. Combining every man I've ever talked to on Tinder or FET wouldn't equal one of him, and I am shocked at how easily he has wrapped me around his finger.

I don't hesitate when I feel Rome's hand on my back, pushing me forward until I reach my desk. I place my hands on the top and bend over for him, my legs spreading as he pushes them apart with his knee. Adrenaline pumps through my veins at the speed of light as I realize what we're doing and where we're doing it. We're at Sandcastle, and all it would take is one person walking through the unlocked door to find us right now. My blinds are wide open, as is the door to my office. If someone entered, we wouldn't have a single second to hide, and the thought makes me hotter while filling me to the brim with terror. The two emotions mix together and form a need like I've never felt before. My pussy drips for Rome, and I am lost to the moment.

"Is this what you wanted?" he asks, taking a step back to unbuckle his pants. I see them drop behind me and hear the sound of plastic being torn open. Even with all of this lust wafting into air like smoke from a fire, he doesn't forget to sheath his cock with a condom.

"Yes, Sir," I answer hungrily. This is exactly what I wanted when things between us became physical after dinner. Even before that—I wanted him the moment I saw him stride through the door wearing the most attractive scowl I've ever seen. This is precisely what I've been hoping for.

Out of nowhere, Rome reaches up and sends his hand slamming down into my ass, taking me up on my offer for him to do as he pleases. The sting of the smack reverberates through my body and sends a jolt of pain and pleasure skittering through my limbs.

"Oh my god," I chirp, surprised by how much it turns me on. Given this is the first time he has spanked me or dabbled in impact play, I'd almost expect him to take it easy, worried that he'd hurt me. But he didn't relent. My ass stings perfectly.

"You like it?" he asks.

"Yes, Sir."

"How about this?" He steps forward and pushes the tip of his hard cock against my opening, smearing my wetness all over my clit.

"God, yes," I answer, my desire for him to enter me turning me into a monster that needs to be fed.

"You want it?"

"Yes, Sir."

Rome pushes in one inch, and I inhale softly.

"Say it," he commands.

Another inch.

"Please, Sir." Another inch. "Please give me all of it."

"That's it, baby girl. Beg for what you want," he says, before slowly pushing each and every inch of himself inside of me, stealing my breath and blowing my mind.

My mouth drops open, my lips forced apart as I'm astonished by the thickness of his cock. This isn't the first time I've experienced it, but it feels brand new. It's like I can feel each throb as it stretches me out, making my legs shake as I stand in front of my desk with my arms spread wide, reaching for anything I can use to grip.

Rome doesn't waste any time stroking in and out of me, and he doesn't have to. I'm so fucking wet that there's no need to take it slowly. His pelvis rams against mine like a wrecking ball over and over again, pushing my desk back while I hang on for dear life. He lets out deep, sensual moans between ragged breaths as he fucks me hard, and I yell for him as he slaps my ass in the exact same spot, making it more and more sensitive each time. I find myself craning my neck to look back at the door, wondering if I'll look over and find someone watching us, but there's no one there. So I close my eyes and let the intense feeling overwhelm my senses.

My orgasm doesn't sneak up on me. I feel it coming, climbing its way up my body with each stroke and smack Rome gives me. I don't fight it. I let it build up and take over my breathing until it reaches its peak and is ready to erupt.

"Sir," I say on a shaky breath. "You're about to make me come."

"Say it then," he replies, still fucking me relentlessly.

"Oh god. Can I please come? It's here. I'm going to come, Sir."

"Give it to me, baby girl. Come all over the outside of this condom while I fill it up from the inside."

"Fuck yes ... I'm ..." The rest of the words never escape my lips. They are engulfed by the guttural scream that explodes from my throat as I come. I grip the edges of my desk and squeeze so hard that it hurts my palms as my vision is overtaken by stars that ignite like missile strikes.

As I shake and tremble on top of the wooden desk, Rome lets out a howl as he shatters inside of me. His body trembles as he comes so hard that he has to stop moving altogether. Each quiver is caused by the intensity of his orgasm, jolting his muscles like tiny seizures.

"Fuck," he whispers as he tries to come down from the high. He takes a step back, pulling out and slumping down onto the accent chair.

I gradually return to Earth as Rome carefully removes his condom and stuffs it back into the wrapper, cautious not to let anything spill while I sit down in the chair next to him. Both of us lean back, sweat rolling off our faces as we struggle to catch our breath, and thoughts enter my mind that I refuse to keep locked away.

"That was unreal," I say, to which Rome smiles. "So, what does this mean, exactly? Are we together now?"

The smile vanishes from Rome's lips as he picks his head up to turn and face me.

"What?" he asks, a deep furrow forming a groove in the middle of his forehead.

"After everything we just said and did," I say, unafraid of letting it out because it's clear to me that we both need answers. "Are we together now? Am I your sub? Are you my Dom? I mean, like, for real. I don't want to play games, Rome. I meant what I said earlier. If you want me, I want to hear you say it. If not, then I don't want to waste either of our time."

He stares at me with an expression somewhere between angry and bewildered, and I don't know what he's about to say. I've never met a man that is so hard to read, so when he clears his throat I hold my breath.

"I don't know what we are, Nia," he says, shocking the hell out of me. "All I know is that I like you. Nothing else really matters until I know what to do with that."

Still panting, I say, "I don't know what that means, Rome."

As he gets up clutching his pants, he looks down at me with a solemn expression. "Neither do I." Then he walks out of my office and enters his, slowly closing the door behind him.

Dear Diary,

Am I losing it? Am I allowing the fact that Rome is a Dom push me away from everything I know to be right?

Yes, he's gorgeous, sexy, smart, ambitious, and a Dominant, but there is more to it. There has to be more to it than those things, and I'm starting to wonder if I'm allowing him to get away with things I would never condone simply because I'm so attracted to him.

We had sex again today. In my office.

Geez. Just writing it makes me hot all over again. I won't sit on the edge of this bed and lie—it was incredible. The way he has exhibited such self-control and patience with me has been a thing of beauty to witness. He could've jumped right into impact play, but he waited until I gave him the OK. Then, once he had permission, he let loose. He combined impact play with a little bit of suspenseful voyeurism and I lit up like a sparkler for him. He was amazing once again ... just before deflating my balloon with his antics at the end. All I did was ask him what all of this meant for us, and he couldn't provide an answer. He says that he doesn't know what it means, and doesn't bother to provide any explanation about his confusion. We've had sex multiple times now, and I feel like I've put my desires on full display for him to see, but it doesn't matter. His heart feels so guarded, and that has to trump the Dom traits. Right?

Am I an idiot?

I should do better. He has given me reason to believe that he only sees our situation as a hookup, and I can't allow myself to be played that way. I have to pull myself together—ignore the look in his eyes, the angle of his jaw, and the smell of his cologne. I need to forget the strength in his grip, the depth in his voice, and the way his touch makes my body quiver. I need to be smart. This clearly isn't what I've been searching for.

Except it is.

But if that's true, then why do I feel so shitty?

Damn. I'm so screwed.

Twenty-Three

You're sitting next to him right now? After he left you high and dry yesterday?

Unfortunately, I am. We're on our way to a restaurant called The VP. It's owned by Nix Malone and will be the location for the Golden Diamond pitch. My emotions are all over the place, Jaz.

I bet they are after all that asshole has put you through. I'm surprised you don't have whiplash from all of his back and forth shit. Since you guys are out of the building, let me go ahead and down this gallon of water and head to his office with a full bladder.

As much as that thought makes me happy, I could probably smell your piss from my office, so please don't. Thanks for having my back though.

If you want to thank me, go in there and knock that pitch out the park. Get the new account and show that asshole of a boss that there is nobody better than you in any way. You got this, Nia.

Thanks, girl. We just pulled up, so I guess that means it's go time.

It's all you, boo. Good luck!

Thanks!

I tuck my phone inside the small black purse that matches my outfit and wait for Rome to pull up the parking brake on his car. He shuts off the engine and silence screams in our ears. Awkwardness and tension come to life all around us and we don't even look at each other. After having sex in my office yesterday, I never imagined that this is how we would end up just twenty-four hours later. Even after another mind-warping orgasm, I'm still just as frustrated and confused as ever, and the worst part is that I have to sweep all of my emotions under the rug so that they don't distract me from what's about to happen. Nix Malone is waiting for us inside.

Rome, dressed in a tight white and blue button-up and navy blue slacks, lets out a long exhale as he stares out the window at the restaurant to his left. Tension rests heavily in his shoulders and jaw, making him look even more stressed than he usually does. I wish I knew why he is the way he is, but if he doesn't want to open up to me, I sure as hell am not about to beg. He's not begging for me, so I won't give him the pleasure of me pleading for him. I'm not desperate, although my worst days make me feel like it. No, I'm a businesswoman who any smart man would be lucky to have. So if Rome wants to be dumb, I won't get in his way.

"Are you ready?" he asks, not even bothering to look over at me.

I sigh. "I've been prepping this pitch for weeks now, Mr. Giovanni. I'm anxious because of who the client is, but that doesn't mean I'm not ready. Don't underestimate me."

When Rome turns to face me, his jaw is so tight I don't expect the words to fit through his clenched teeth. Unfortunately, he manages to say, "I'm not underestimating you, Nia. I just want to make sure you're prepared to go in there and face this man. Also, I asked you not to call me that."

"It's not your job to worry about me," I reply with a shrug, feigning nonchalance. "And I prefer to call you by your last name because it's more professional. Clearly that's the way we're keeping it after everything that has happened, which is fine with me. I just need to make sure that the line between us is bold instead of translucent. That way, I can ensure I don't cross it. Now, if you're ready, I'd like to get going. Don't want to keep the potential client waiting."

As Rome begins to speak again, I open the door and step out of the car. I hear him sigh as I slam it shut, but I don't care. Just as he's stepping out, I walk across the busy street, forcing him to jog to catch up. Once he's standing next to me, he mutters something under his breath, but I ignore it and make my way inside.

"Good afternoon," a man wearing a black tuxedo with a gold bow-tie greets us as soon as we're inside.

I start to reply, but Rome cuts me off. "Good afternoon. Rome Giovanni and Nia Washington, here for a meeting with Mr. Nix Malone."

The pale man's smile slowly drops, revealing a much more sinister side as he steps behind a black podium and lifts a black phone to his ear. He stares at us without saying a word before hanging up, his smile returning in a flash.

"Mr. Malone is expecting you," he says, just as jovially as when we first entered. "Right this way, please." The host turns on his heel and begins walking into the dining area, and Rome and I follow.

The VP is much fancier than I expected. I'm not sure what I thought I'd see, but the elegant black and gold decor is quite beautiful. Black leather booths line the perimeter of the establishment, with circular tables scattered throughout the middle. Each table is covered with a white cloth and gold decorations. Even the salt and pepper shakers are golden and look extremely expensive. The customers dining today are all dressed well, lifting decorative crystal wine glasses to their lips and eating steaks that look like they were prepared by Gordon Ramsey. Clearly this place has done very well for itself, but the main dining area doesn't compare to the section Rome and I are led to.

The host takes us to the back of the restaurant, where black and gold doors block off the VIP section of the establishment. We watch as he places a hand on each door and slides them apart, revealing a lavish room draped in gold and white. The walls are adorned with bright pictures of Philly lit up at night and housed in gaudy gold frames. There are lush green plants in each corner of the room, and a long table at the far end, at which a gargantuan figure sits in the furthest seat. When we walk in, he stands up and I feel a sudden urge to turn around and run back to the car.

"Rome Giovanni and Nia Washington," the host says to Nix, extending his arm to guide us to the table.

"Thanks, Jeffrey," Nix says in a voice so deep it makes the room rumble. The host nods, turns around, and walks out, closing the sliding doors behind him.

Nix Malone is larger than life. He has to be at least six-foot-four, and I'd be surprised if he weighs less than two-hundred-fifty pounds, but each pound is made of thick, round muscle that looks built to kill. His shoulders look like two globes next to his head, and his arms and chest stretch the short sleeves of his black button-up. The man is a bear standing on its back legs, waiting for someone to get close so he can pounce and tear flesh apart with his bare hands. His beard is thick and long but very well kept, as is his compact black hair that is highlighted by a wide part on one side. I can see tattoos of what look to be angels and demons clawing up both of his arms, but the stretched sleeves cover everything above the elbow. If there was an image in the dictionary next to the word gangster, it would be exactly what I'm looking at right now.

While I stand back with a racing heart, Rome steps forward with his hand extended.

"It's nice to meet you, Mr. Malone," he says as Nix shakes his hand. "I'm Rome Giovanni, the owner of Sandcastle, and this is Nia Washington. She crafted today's pitch for us."

Nix's eyes shift over to me, pinning me in place until he extends his hand. "Nice to meet you, Nia."

I swallow my fear and step forward. It's game time. "Nice to meet you, too, Mr. Malone. This is a beautiful restaurant. I've never been here, but it looks like I'll have to make my way back for a nice dinner."

Nix's smile breaks through his iron demeanor. "Oh, absolutely you should. Tell your boyfriend or husband that he needs to take you out. A beautiful woman like you deserves to be treated to the absolute best, and The VP is exactly that."

I giggle quietly. "I'll be sure to tell him that once I finally meet him."

"No husband or boyfriend?" Nix says, still holding onto my hand, but no longer shaking it. "I'm shocked to hear that. In that case, maybe I should treat you myself. Everything would be on the house."

"Wow, on the house? I might have to take you up on that," I reply with wide eyes.

I'm surprised by two things: how quickly Nix has unarmed me with his personality, and the brooding anger on Rome's face as he watches us interact.

Nix chuckles before showing me to the seat closest to his, and we all sit down. He orders water from a server who comes from a hidden door somewhere in the back, and it is brought to us immediately. It's clear that this section of The VP is not like the front.

These servers are specific to the VIP section, and there is no waiting when Nix asks for something.

"Can I get either of you anything else while you're here?" Nix asks, eyeing us both.

"No, thank you," Rome answers for us. "As this is a business meeting, I'd like to get right to it if that's okay with you."

I see a twitch in Nix's eye as he looks at Rome, but his amiable demeanor doesn't change. "Ah, right down to business. Okay. I can get down with that. So, you want to be the company that helps Golden Diamond get its feet off the ground with your marketing and advertising. I've listened to three other pitches before today, and Sandcastle will be the last because I don't like dragging my feet. I'm a very busy man, and we need this ad campaign to begin soon so that people know exactly what's coming and what to expect when it gets here. So, if you'd like to *get right to it*, then there's no need to stretch it out. What's your pitch?"

The ice in Nix's voice nearly freezes me in place. As charming as he is, there is no denying that he clearly has a side of him that does not mess around. Now that the greeting is over, all smiles have vanished and we're faced with a demeanor of cold steel. With Nix, business is business, and it's not a game to him.

I have to look over my shoulder to see Rome—which brings back far too many memories of how I did the same thing yesterday while he peppered my shoulder and neck with kisses—and he nods at me, my cue to begin. Each beat of my heart hits like a hammer striking a nail as I am engulfed by nerves. I've been preparing for this for a while, but nothing compares to being in the moment. I'm a woman sitting between two men, awaiting their judgment. Rome and I had sex just yesterday, and Nix looks at me like he would love to take Rome's place today. They see me as a prize to be won, decoration to adorn their arm when they walk into a place as the center of attention. Well, I refuse to allow myself to be reduced to that. I'm a submissive when I choose to be, and even when I submit, I'm still a powerful woman that is not to be taken lightly.

"Our pitch for the Golden Diamond is simple," I start after clearing my throat and sitting up straight. All playfulness is removed from my voice and thoughts of returning to The VP for dinner with Nix are erased. They aren't the only ones who can be all about their business. "The casino and hotel of your dreams is all about the most important person in the place—you. Now, when I say you, Mr. Malone, I don't mean you, the owner. I'm talking about you, the customer. When you walk into any other casino in Philly, the experience is set up to be shared by all in attendance. But at Golden Diamond, you are the king of the casino floor. Each and every amenity in the building is tailor made for your pleasure. Every server treats you like the owner. Every dealer looks at you like you're the only one at the table. Every meal is cooked to your precise liking. Every arrival is fit for red carpet treatment."

As Nix leans back in his seat, I focus on the words I crafted for this pitch with Jeremiah, repeating them from memory with the exact enthusiasm as the first time I spoke it in front of Rome and Sierra.

"The two thousand, top of the line slot machines are jaw-dropping, but they are nothing compared to winning *your* first jackpot. The one hundred TVs to watch games and track the bets you've made are awe-inspiring, but they dwindle in comparison to the feeling of watching *your* bet payout, making *you* the winner and center of attention as if standing in the middle of your own living room. There are thousands of luxurious rooms in the hotel, but the only one that matters is *yours*. In Golden Diamond, *you* are the monarch to which the rest of the world kneels.

"The world's biggest acts will grace the grandiose stage and entertain the masses, but nothing is more exciting than *your* first experience in the grand hall, feeling up close and personal no matter which seat *you* choose. Fifteen fine dining restaurants await *your* arrival, ready to treat you with the utmost respect and care, serving you the most mouth-watering meals you've ever tasted. *You* are their number one customer and you will be treated as such every time you visit as if you were the owner, because *you* are the leader. *You* are the VIP. At Golden Diamond, you are royalty."

I maintain eye contact with Nix as I finish, worried by hesitation as he stares back. He doesn't speak, choosing only to blink and keep me on the edge of my lavish black leather seat. While the wheels spin in his mind, I turn around to look at Rome, who only nods at me to let me know that it's okay. We don't know Nix. We have no idea how he'll respond to this, so all we can do is wait, while the pounding of my heart drowns out all other sounds until the moment Nix speaks.

His eyebrows raise and he blinks quickly as if in disbelief.

"Wow," he exclaims, leaning forward in his chair. "You know what you're doing. I'm impressed."

Relief floods my veins like a water hose as I finally exhale. My shoulders fall and a smile forms on my face like the sun coming from behind the clouds.

"Oh," I say, grinning from ear to ear. "Thank you so much."

"You're very welcome," Nix replies. "That was the best pitch I've heard yet. Very passionate and knowledgeable. It helps that you're easy to look at, but the way you spoke took the focus off of that and put it squarely on your words. You're good. No wonder he chose you to deliver the pitch."

Rome clears his throat before saying. "Umm, yes. She's our best."

When I turn around to look at him, his face shows no emotion.

"Clearly," Nix agrees.

"So, what are your thoughts, Mr. Malone?"

Nix licks his lips, eyeing me before looking at Rome. "Well, my first thought is that you're a very lucky man for having such a gorgeous, talented woman on your staff." I hear Rome shift in his seat, but Nix continues without a care. "Secondly, I loved the way the pitch sounded and I think the idea of Sandcastle doing my ads and marketing sounds like a match made in heaven. But I do have a condition."

I'm so excited by his words that I almost don't hear the part about a condition. Rome and I both sit up, anxious to hear the part that comes before we can celebrate a victory.

"What exactly is the condition?" Rome asks.

"I'll sign on the dotted line right now as long as Miss Washington agrees to dinner with me tonight." I gasp as Nix goes on, ignoring the look of shock on my face. "I'm not asking for anything sexual in exchange for my business, so don't think the worst. I simply would like the opportunity to take you out and show you a good time. No obligations beyond that, of course."

No words are spoken for the next ten seconds while Nix stares at me, and Rome and I glare back. The lavish VIP area suddenly feels like a sauna with the temperature and humidity turned all the way up, sending sweat seeping through my pores.

What the hell did he just say? Please tell me that he's kidding. But even if he is, it's a terrible way to joke, and I'm suddenly disgusted by how brash he is. Nix is clearly unafraid of consequences, and his fearlessness has made him disrespectful. The charm and charisma that I saw earlier are now shrouded in darkness, his true colors floating to the surface like oil in water.

"Are you being serious right now?" Rome asks.

Nix grins. "Do I strike you as an unserious person?"

Fuck. I swallow hard as the two of them glare at each other—two predators ready to fight over their right to a kill. I hate it. It makes me feel like nothing more than meat for them to eat, and I have worked too hard to be thought so lowly of. I want to snap. I want to stand up and yell across the table with a pointed finger that I will not be treated this way, but my fear of everything I know about Nix Malone keeps me silent. So, Rome speaks for me.

"Wow," he begins. "Out of all the things I expected could happen with this meeting, disrespect on this level wasn't one of them."

"Disrespect?" Nix says. "She's a single woman who has never eaten at my restaurant. Don't be so dramatic, Rome."

"Dramatic?" Rome fires back. "You've disrespected my company and my ... employee. It's not something I'll stand for, Mr. Malone. While I am aware of your reputation in this city, truthfully ... I don't give a fuck. I won't allow you or any other man to disrespect Nia. She is worth more than just being *some girl* for you to wine and dine with your money and fast life. Much, much more. So if agreeing to dinner is what is required for us to win your account, then you can fucking keep it."

"You speak for her?" Nix asks with a tilted head.

"Nia is fully capable of speaking for herself, but when a man of your stature and notoriety offends her, I will gladly come to her defense. So, this meeting is over. There is nothing left for us to discuss."

Rome gets up from his seat, and in absolute astonishment, I follow his lead. Nix doesn't say a word as we turn around and head for the sliding door, and I can't believe Rome is willing to give up this account for me. Another boss might have suggested I go through with the dinner in order to secure the money that comes with an agreement this large, but Nix just flushed it all down the drain for me. If he doesn't care for me at all, he has a very funny way of showing it. All I can do is shake my head in confusion as we reach the doors and Rome slides them open.

"Wait," Nix yells from across the room.

When we turn around Nix is walking toward us with a scowl on his face. He glares at Rome, who doesn't budge, digging his feet into the floor and holding his ground against one of the most terrifying men in the city.

"You're a fucking bold one," Nix says. "You said that you're aware of my reputation, which means you know I could close these doors and make you disappear without a trace. No one would ever know where you went. They would say it was like you evaporated into thin air ... and yet ... you're ready to go to war for her. I'm not sure how I didn't see it when you walked in, but I got it now. I understand and I commend your tenacity. I would do the same if I had someone like her."

Rome and I stare at each other, neither of us aware of how to respond. Hell, I don't even know what Nix is talking about. What did he not see when we walked in that is so clear now?

"I apologize for my contempt," Nix says, nodding to both Rome and me. "I hope that you won't allow my coarseness to stand in the way of us doing business together. If you're able to move past it, I'd love to sign on with your company."

My heart hammers with nervous excitement as Rome looks at me, waiting for me to accept Nix's apology. Even now he's willing to forgo it all if I'm too offended to work with Nix.

"Absolutely," I say with a smile and nod. "Water under the bridge."

Nix smiles as he extends his hand to Rome. "Good."

Rome shakes his hand and the deal is secured when I do, too. Joy explodes in my heart as I realize what just happened. We got the Golden Diamond account—the biggest in Sandcastle's history. Rome and I did it together, and he just stood up to a known criminal and gangster for me.

I don't want to feel anything for him. After he left me a sweaty mess in my office yesterday, I told myself that he was too confused to feel anything for me, therefore I shouldn't let myself have any feelings about him. I convinced myself that he only wanted me for sex and nothing more, and told myself that I was a fool for giving it to him. I came here today with no intention whatsoever of submitting to him ever again. I was done. But when a man literally risks his life to protect you when he doesn't have to, it changes things.

Yeah, I'm screwed.

Twenty-Four – Rome

"**R**aise your glass, asshole. I know you don't like to be the center of attention or to have people showering you with praise, but it's only me, and you deserve this moment. So, let's go."

Although I'm reluctant, I do as Nikola commands and lift my shot glass full of tequila into the air. He does the same, and I grin at the proud smile on his face as he clears his throat for a speech.

"Here's a toast to you, Rome," he starts, eyes beaming with pride. "You've been through more than anyone should ever have to go through. You've pulled yourself out of the weeds and risen to unimaginable heights. You're a fucking boss, and you just landed the biggest contract in your company's history after only being there for a few short weeks. You're killing it, bro, and not to get all sappy, but I know both of your parents would be sickeningly proud of you ... and so would Natalia. Here's to you, Rome. Congratulations on the Golden Diamond account. *Saluti.*"

"*Saluti,*" I respond.

When I bring the shot glass to my lips, I hope the burn of the liquor purges me of my feelings. I hope the sting that travels down my throat singes all of my emotions until I have none left to feel. I want to set my insides ablaze and rid myself of the confusion that eats away at me like a cancer. The shot definitely helps, but it doesn't take it all away.

Fuck.

Nikola sits across from me in a white, long-sleeved shirt, and every time he looks at me, I swear he can see through me. My best friend still wields the power to know when something is wrong with me, even if I don't want him to. He eyes me closely, leaning back in his seat and looking across the round table like he's trying to put distance between us to be able to see the whole picture.

"Alright," he says. "So, tell me all about the pitch. How were you able to convince Nix Malone to do business with a small-time marketing agency? From what I understand, this guy plays in the big leagues. Like, the leagues so big that they can erase you from the planet with a nod of the head or the blink of an eye."

"It wasn't me who made the pitch," I admit, already feeling something rumbling within me just thinking about it. "It was Nia."

"Oh, okay ... why'd you say it like that?" Nikola asks.

Shit. Here we go.

"I didn't say it a certain way," I reply, praying he doesn't pull us into a long conversation. Speaking about it will make me feel about it, and that's the last thing I want to do when it comes to Nia.

When I finish staring down at the table, hoping that Nikola will move on quickly, I look up to find that he hasn't. His eyes have that same suspicious glare he always gets when he's wondering about me. I've given him plenty of reasons to worry over the past year, so I'm not surprised. I'm just not interested in talking about it. About *her*. But regardless of how I feel, Nikola's eyes stay pinned to me.

"Come on, man. I didn't say it in any particular way. Stop staring at me," I plead.

Nikola's furrowed brow displays itself in graphic detail.

"Geez," he says. "You should be a lawyer, you're so defensive."

I shake my head as I force a chuckle. "That was a bad joke, Nikola. Do better."

"Uh-uh, don't try to change the subject and deflect it back onto me," he replies. "What's the deal, bro? Who's Nia?"

Fuck. The mention of her name sends memories of her face flashing in my mind like a movie montage. I remember what it felt like to caress her skin—to feel the warmth of her mouth enveloping my cock and sending me reeling—and I instantly yearn to be near her. It wasn't long ago that she was bent over in front of me, her legs spread as she waited for me to slide inside of her. She dripped for me, needing me just as much as I needed her, and I wonder if she still does. What are the chances that she's thinking about me right now?

"Uhh, hello?" Nikola says, snapping me out of my Nia-induced trance and pulling me back to the reality in front of me. "Damn, Rome. You okay? Whoever this girl is, she must be something special if she's got you staring off into the distance, daydreaming right here at the table."

"That's not ... I wasn't daydreaming," I lie, forcing dirty thoughts of Nia back into the closet of my mind. "Look, I don't want to talk about it because I know how you get, and I'm not in the mood to have you judging me or jumping leaps and bounds to get to your conclusions. I'm just not in the mood, okay?"

Nikola's eyes widen as he does an Oscar-worthy job of acting shocked. "I'm not jumping to any conclusions. Goddamn. Why am I the villain all of a sudden, just because you're thinking about some girl?"

"I'm not."

"Then tell me about her. I don't see what the big deal is. We were talking about the pitch to Nix Malone, and then you started having a wet dream at the mention of the name Nia. You're so *not* thinking about her that you can't even tell me about her? Did she do a good job? Did you have to prepare her for the pitch? Is she your best worker at Sandcastle? How did Nix respond to her? Is she nice? Is she mean? How long do I have to keep going with these questions?"

"Oh, my god, Nikola!" I snap. "Her name is Nia Washington, and she did a phenomenal job at earning her chance to do the pitch with Nix, and of executing it with him in person. He loved it and basically hired us on the spot, and he was head over heels for her because ... of course he was. Everything about Nia is amazing. She's stubborn, and smart, and funny, and persistent, and unashamed, and tenacious, and heartbreakingly beautiful. So much so that Nix Malone asked her out to dinner before we left, but I shut that down immediately."

Nikola stares across the table with saucer-sized eyes. "Wow. You shut it down? Why?" he inquires, suddenly fully invested in my story now that I'm opening up.

"Because I'm not going to have my employees dating our clients," I answer.

"Is that against the rules?"

"Not necessarily, but that's not the point. I wasn't going to let Nia fall into his trap. Everyone knows Nix's reputation."

"So, it's not a company rule, and it also doesn't have anything to do with the fact that you're interested in her?"

"I never said I was interested in her."

"But you clearly are."

"Did you hear the way I just described her? Of course I'm interested in her!" I snap as heat sizzles beneath my skin, making me sweat. "God, you're insufferable. Fine, I fucking like her. Alright? Are you happy now?"

"Of course I'm happy, *stronzo*. My question is—why aren't you?"

"Because this isn't what I do," I bark. My voice booms out of my mouth, catching the attention of a few bar-goers. "It's just like I told you at your house, I don't feel anything for people. That place in my heart—the part that has *feelings*—is reserved for Natalia. So, I don't want to talk about Nia or get into the details of our relationship. As much as I know you and Isabella want me to settle down, every time I think about it I feel like I'm betraying Natalia. So, all you need to know is that Nia is an employee of mine who I happen to find very attractive with a great personality. We also just so happen to have had sex a few times and I'm terrified that if I spend any more time with her that I'm going to move past interest and actually start to feel something for her."

"Wait! You've had sex a few times? Are you kidding? You tried to breeze right past that as if I wouldn't latch onto it. You see? I knew I saw something in your eyes the second you mentioned her. Dude, you do realize that it's okay if you have feelings for someone else, right?"

"I disagree."

"Why?"

"Because I was married and my wife died."

"Yeah, four years ago."

"What the fuck is that supposed to mean?" I bellow, suddenly angrier than I knew I would be at this conversation.

"Rome, it's okay for you to move on," Nikola tries to explain, but my brain just doesn't want to hear it. Even after all this time.

"You see? This is why I stayed away after my dad died," I snip, quickly losing control of my emotions.

"Because you didn't ever want to hear the truth? You figured you'd be better off living in your world of bullshit and delusion?" Nikola fires back, using his words as missiles to blow apart the defenses I've built around myself.

"Fuck you," I bark. "You have no idea what I've been through. Both of your parents are still alive, and so is your wife."

Nikola lets out a long, tired sigh. "You're right, Rome. I'm so very fortunate that I haven't experienced loss the way that you have, and I'm so sorry that your father passed away recently and that the pain of that loss is so fresh in your heart. But I've been here for you the entire time. I've seen you overcome the pain, going through it silently only to come out the other end stronger than ever. I've seen you grow and mature, and I've seen you struggle. I've been the one constant in your life, which means that I'm the person in this world that you can trust. And I'm telling you right here and now, that you're a fool if you think Natalia would want you to use her memory as a reason to avoid your own happiness. You and I both know she would want you to move on and find someone who could love you just as much as she did."

I want to reply. I wish I had something mean to say—some sort of quick-witted response that would make him stop talking. But when my eyes sting with tears, I know he's right. Natalia never liked to see me upset, and I know four years is a long time, but my father's passing makes it all feel so brand new.

"I ..." I start, but have to take a second to choke back tears before finishing. "I just don't know if I'm ready for anyone to replace her."

Nikola sighs. "Listen to me, Rome. I knew Natalia, and I loved her, too. She was perfect for you—we all knew that—and no one will ever replace her. Ever. You can't even think of it that way. It isn't about replacing her. It's about finding a way to hold onto her memory while also finding something new for yourself. You deserve happiness, too, bro."

Try as I might, I can't think of anything to say in response. I know he's right, but that doesn't make it easier. I'm broken. The deaths in my life have shattered me into a million pieces, and I don't know how to put myself back together again after this most recent one. I'm sure I've been confusing her with all of my changes in temperature—one second I'm scorching hot for her, the next I'm giving her the cold shoulder. I'm sure it's exhausting and infuriating, and I don't mean for it to be.

"Love hasn't been kind to me, Nikola," I finally manage to say.

"I know," he replies. "But are you willing to go the rest of your life running from it at the cost of your happiness?"

The question is like a ton of bricks falling on my chest, stealing my breath. I feel a thousand pounds weighing me down and it makes me light-headed and unable to focus. I don't want to run forever, but after all this time, I'm not sure I know how to stop.

Earned

Twenty-Five

After thanking me for all of my hard work and doing everything it took to reel in the Golden Diamond account, I didn't hear from Rome for the entire weekend. Two whole days of radio silence from him after defending me from Nix Malone. Nix fucking Malone. I didn't get it then, and I still don't get it now. Even the drive back to the office afterward was quiet and stuffed full of awkwardness. When I asked him what Nix was talking about when he said he didn't notice *it* when we first walked into his restaurant, Rome acted like he didn't know what *it* was. He said it was nothing and kept staring straight ahead, his eyes barely blinking as he focused on the lines in the road. I didn't bother asking anymore questions, because I could tell he wasn't going to give me answers. He'd closed the door again and sealed it shut. So fuck it. I guess we're done for real this time.

I spent both days of the weekend bored out of my mind. It turned out that all of my friends had busy schedules—Jaz and Michael had plans to travel to Kennett Square to spend the weekend in The Bookhouse Hotel just to get away from the city, while Jeremiah had his own sleepover planned for him and Gerald. I was left in Philly all by myself and had to try to dilute my thoughts of Rome by starting Game of Thrones over from the beginning. I ate junk food and sat on my couch, trying to ignore the memories of what Rome and I did on it ... twice. Admittedly, I didn't do a very good job, so I ended up moving into my bedroom, and while I did remember him walking in and out of my bathroom with his shirt off, at least he never laid on my bed. It was a consolation prize at best, but it worked ... a little.

Unfortunately, Monday has returned with a spiteful vengeance like it always does, and I have to see him again at the office. I take my time driving in, leaving the house early so I can travel slower and extend my commute. Philly traffic does its job and makes the trip even longer, but the parking lot still comes into my field of vision eventually. I park my car and take my time getting out, leaning my head against the steering wheel to give myself a pep talk before going in.

"He's an asshole, Nia," I say aloud. "He doesn't know what he wants ... well, besides sex. He knows he wants *that* from you, which makes him like every other wannabe player out there. It doesn't matter what he looks like. It doesn't matter that he defended you against a man that could have easily made you both disappear. He's just a player, and you can do so much better. So since you know better, you have to do better. You got this."

I breathe in a deep inhale and let it out slowly, batting away the devil on my shoulder telling me how incredible he will look when I see him, and I get out with a heart made of stone and my will power filled to the max. I'm ready.

The second I open the door to the Sandcastle offices, the entire room explodes into thunderous applause. As I make my way down the walkway toward the bullpen, I realize that everyone is standing up, and they're all looking at me with excited smiles on their faces as they clap enthusiastically. Jeremiah stands next to his cubicle wearing white on white, beaming like a kindergartener on Christmas as I approach my office. Sierra stands in her doorway clapping like someone has a gun to her head, but she's still involved, and Rome comes out of his office clapping as well, his beautiful smile present in the office for the very first time. The look in his eyes as he stares at me is something new, an affable mixture of pride, joy, and desire, and he doesn't force it away as he walks to the front of the bullpen and quiets the crowd.

"Alright, hold on, hold on," he says to everyone. "Now that she has finally arrived at the office, it's important that we do this right. Nia, please come over here."

My brows knit together, but I'm not mad, just confused, wondering what the hell is going on. The embarrassment of being the center of attention makes me blush, but I make my way over to Rome who has his arm extended for me to stand next to him. As soon as I get close, I smell his cologne and see the lascivious way that he looks at me, but I force my eyes to gaze into the bullpen as every employee stares back at me.

"What's going on?" I ask the crowd.

Rome answers, "I just thought it was appropriate for everyone here to acknowledge what you did on Friday night. Everyone, the one and only Miss Washington has been a part of your team for a long time. You've seen how incredible she is, but I'm new here. I wasn't privy to her skill, resiliency, and fearlessness, but I had the privilege of witnessing it first hand before the weekend came.

"Now, I'd be remiss if I didn't say that Nia had no desire whatsoever to pursue the Golden Diamond account. It was the company's first big fish, and everyone was well aware of the client's reputation. I knew it would take someone with guts of steel to pull it off, and against her will, Nia stepped up to the plate and delivered an incredible pitch that Mr. Malone absolutely loved. He had seen three other pitches before ours, but after Nia was finished, he selected Sandcastle on the spot."

Applause breaks out amongst the crowd once again, the first clap being initiated by an exuberant Jeremiah, who smiles at me from his desk. Once the enthusiasm dies down, Rome begins again, this time turning to face me.

"Nia, I don't mean to put you on the spot," he says, still smiling and making my heart race. "But I just wanted to tell you right here in front of everyone that I was floored by your pitch, and I am immensely proud of you for pulling in the biggest contract in this company's history. You were unabashed and determined, and just like Nix Malone, I was truly impressed. I felt honored to watch you bring this home for us. What you did will never be forgotten. Congratulations on making Sandcastle history."

Holy praise kink.

Rome finishes his speech and starts clapping, leading the chorus of applause for the third time, and all I can do is smile. I wave, making myself feel like an idiot for doing too much, but then Jeremiah says something dumb.

"Speech!" he screams, which causes three or four other people to repeat it.

"Speech!"

"Speech!"

My smile washes away in an instant as I glare at Jeremiah, who laughs at me, totally unfazed by my evil eye. I'll have to deal with his treason later, but for now, I swallow hard and try to think of something.

"Umm, there really isn't much to say," I start as Rome takes a step back to give me center stage. "Mr. Gio ... Rome is right. I didn't want to do this, but I'm a team player who always wants to try her hardest. But, I didn't do it alone. Jeremiah and I crafted this pitch together and it turned out great, thanks to his input. So, shout out to Jeremiah for helping me to make this happen. Also, I hate you for making me give this speech."

The room erupts in laughter and I have to wait for it to fade out before I can continue.

"I also have to thank ... Rome," I say, turning to face him. "You're right. I didn't want to do this. I hated the idea, in fact. But you pushed me, and even more importantly, you believed in me and motivated me to stay on it. This pitch wouldn't have happened without Jeremiah's assistance, but it *really* wouldn't have happened if you didn't encourage me and let me know that you had faith in my ability. So, thank you, Rome. I know you're new here, but you've been a dream come true so far. We all appreciate your drive and ambition, and I truly look forward to continuing to work by your side. Okay that's it. Thanks."

Everyone applauds for the final time, and I don't hesitate scooting my way past Rome to get away from it all. People pat me on the back and congratulate me as I walk through the crowd to get to my office, and once I'm at my desk, life slowly returns to normal. My heart races with pride and adrenaline as I take my seat and turn on my computer. I can't believe Rome orchestrated that entire thing, praising me like that in front of everyone we work with. It was an amazing thing to do, but I know it was more about being a good boss and showing the peanut gallery that he is willing to heap praise for hard work and success. It wasn't about us at all, and as tough as that is to swallow, I manage to get it down.

"Look at you go, superstar!" Jeremiah's unique voice booms into the room as he steps inside. "You handled your business, girl. We're all so proud of you."

"Thank you," I reply with a smile. "But why did you have to make me give a speech, though. You're so annoying."

"Which is exactly why you love me. Don't play."

"I guess."

"Speaking of love," he says. "It looks like Rome has a lot for you."

I roll my eyes. "He has a lot of love for the new client and the money I just brought in. That's it."

"From where I was standing, it looked like he was interested in a lot more than that."

"Then you must've been standing in the wrong place. There's a lot that you don't know about him, but I'm telling you—Rome isn't about that."

"Rome isn't about what?" a different voice asks, startling both me and Jeremiah. We turn our attention to the doorway and find Rome standing over the threshold.

"Oh ... umm, nothing," I stammer, trying to backpedal and making myself look even more guilty of talking shit about my boss.

Rome grins at me before looking at Jeremiah. "Can I speak to Nia alone for a second?"

"Of course," Jeremiah says. He flashes the most ridiculous smile at me before spinning around and walking out, leaving Rome and I alone in my office for the first time since we had sex in it.

"What can I do for you?" I ask, leaning back in my seat and doing my best to put on a stoic face.

Rome looks incredible as always, flawlessly dressed and locking me in place with his unwavering eye contact, but I force myself to remember the pep talk from the car. Rome is just a player who is only sure about how much sex he wants. How convenient for him to be sure about that but nothing else. I can't fall for it again, no matter what he says. If he's unsure about me, I will be sure that he isn't for me.

Rome walks up to my desk and places a hand on it. "Listen, I wanted to apologize."

My eyes widen to twice their size. "Huh? Apologize for what?"

"For being so ridiculous and switching back and forth on you the way I have been."

I gasp, stunned by what he just said and the sincerity with which he said it.

"I've been through a lot," he continues. "And I can admit that I'm not good at trusting people. There's a lot more to me than meets the eye, and I'm sure there's much more depth to you than I'm able to see while working here at the office. I want to explore that depth, Nia. I want to get to know you much better, and I want you to know me. Hopefully, once we get to know each other on a deeper level, you and I can take our relationship to the next level. At least, that's what I'd like to try to do. I guess what I'm asking for is the opportunity to earn you. Can I do that?"

I swallow hard, shocked into complete bewilderment that keeps my words chained up and unable to escape my mouth. First there was the mountain of praise in public, and now this. He wants to earn me? Ugh. How the hell am I supposed to say no to that? I remember the pep talk, but his speech was so much better than mine, and he looks so good in his matching navy blue outfit that fits him to perfection, displaying the roundness of his muscles and flatness of his stomach. Goddamn it, I don't want to keep going back and forth on this, but he's so impossible to resist.

Nodding, I take a deep breath and try to remain focused.

"Okay, Rome," I say. "You've left me confused a lot, and I haven't been sure what to do with that. However, I won't lie to myself and say that I'm not interested in learning about you and what makes you the way that you are. I do, but I won't allow you to keep switching up on me. Okay? If this is you telling me that you want to try to be with me for real, then let this be it. Try now, or forever hold your peace. So, you're sure about this?"

Rome licks his lips, swallowing hard before answering. "I'm one hundred percent sure. Are you?"

"I am if you are."

He smiles, and not just a half smile or a smirk, but a full beam from ear to ear. "Good, then are you free for dinner tonight? I'd like to treat you to a real Italian meal."

I fight back a smile of my own, not wanting to show too much joy even though I feel it.

"Yes, I'm free tonight," I reply. "Where and when did you have in mind?"

Rome turns to the side, preparing to walk out.

"Eight o'clock tonight," he answers. "At my place."

Twenty-Six

W hen I arrive at the address Rome sent to me, I'm taken aback at the house as I pull into its stone driveway. The exterior is black on one side and colored brick on the other. The black, white, and gray bricks mesh perfectly with the all-black overhangs and columns that hold up the balcony overlooking the front of the house, and the underside of the balcony is covered in orange lights that glow like tiny fires. It's clear that the designer had an infatuation with windows, because the face of the home is covered in them, some as tall as twelve feet high. It's gorgeous and completely modern, and I find myself wondering what Rome was really into before he purchased Sandcastle from Mr. Thomas. Like Rome, the house is luxurious, well-kept, and intimidating. Even his house gives off Dom vibes.

The front door is glass with an expansive black frame, and as I approach it I see Rome walking to meet me. He's dressed in black pants and a white V-neck T-shirt, looking absolutely delectable as he places his hand on the door and pulls it open.

"*Buonasera*," he says with a smile. He has been flashing that smile a lot more lately and I'm obsessed.

"Hi," I reply.

Rome steps to the side and opens the door all the way, extending a hand to help me with the small step inside. "I'm glad you're here. Come on in. You look incredible."

A smile bullies its way onto my face as I look down at my outfit, as if I could forget that I chose to wear a white and burgundy dress that showcases a little cleavage and hugs my hips in a death grip. The back is open, but my bare skin is covered by the length of my locs, and I haven't had a reason to wear this dress in far too long. I'm hoping that tonight is the occasion I have been waiting for.

"Thank you," I reply, beaming. "You look great, yourself. Somehow you make a simple combination of a V-neck and slacks look like something from a GQ photo shoot."

Rome pauses to smile—and is that blush I see?

"*Grazie*," he says.

I tilt my head. "Okay, if you're going to start speaking Italian, I don't know how you ever expect us to get to dinner."

The smile on his face doesn't waver a bit and it makes my stomach somersault.

"I'll try to keep it under control," he says. "Follow me. I'm still trying to work some magic in the kitchen and don't want to burn it."

As Rome begins to walk, I follow closely on his heel. "You're cooking? I thought you were going to order in. Actually, I thought you were going to have a chef make dinner. You know how to cook?"

We walk past an open living room that is magnificently designed, making my jaw drop. A gargantuan eggshell sectional takes up the center, with black and eggshell pillows neatly placed on each cushion, while a gray coffee table with a gun metal top rests in the center. Silver end tables with glass tops are strategically placed around the ends of the sectional and matching loveseat, and the entire space is punctuated by the fireplace made of the exact same black, white, and gray brick from the outside of the house. The gorgeous black chandelier hanging from the center adds the finishing touch to a jaw-dropping space that leaves me stuck in my tracks while Rome rushes into the kitchen.

"I'm Italian," he says. "Of course I know how to cook. My mother wouldn't have let me live to see adulthood if I didn't."

I somehow manage to peel my eyes away from the living room and make my way into the kitchen, only to be blown away a second time. Black cabinets next to white marble countertops and mirrored black appliances nearly overwhelm my senses with their beauty, and even though Rome is clearly cooking, the place is as neat as a hospital room. There are no spilled ingredients on the counter or splashes of mystery liquids on the floor. The only signs that he's cooking are the steam rising from pots and a skillet on the stove, and the hunger-inducing aroma spreading throughout the house. I have been in his place all of five seconds and I am in awe of how this man lives. It's almost too good to be true. I've never known a man to be this well put together.

"Rome, your house ... it's surreal," I compliment, still eyeing everything and taking it all in.

"Thank you, I'm glad you like it," he replies. "I just moved in a few months ago so I'm still getting used to it, like a lot of things in my life. But I do love it."

"I bet. Was your last place as nice as this one?" I ask, taking a seat on one of the tall chairs by the island.

"Oh, no way," he says, turning his back to me so he can do something on the stove. "I mean, don't get me wrong, I've never been poor, but my place was average middle class. My circumstances changed when my father passed away."

Damn. I almost forgot that he said he recently lost his father. He told me at the restaurant but clearly didn't want to elaborate. I wonder if I'll be able to get more out of him tonight.

"I remember you told me about your father," I say, trying to tread lightly. "Were you two close?"

Rome doesn't speak or turn around for five long seconds before he answers, "Yes."

"I'm really sorry to hear that, Rome," I say, hoping my sincerity can be heard through my words.

"How about you? Both of your parents still with us?" he asks, looking over his shoulder.

"Fortunately they are," I reply. "And my mom is just like yours. There was no way I was leaving her house without knowing how to get down in the kitchen. We still cook together whenever I go see them. Does your mom still teach you things to cook? I call and ask my mom for directions and ingredients all the time."

Rome stirs a pot before tapping the spoon on the side and setting it down on a napkin next to the stove. When he turns around, his face is blank. "My mom died in a car accident when I was nineteen."

"Oh my god," I blurt out before I can stop myself. No wonder he has such a hard exterior—only thirty-five years old and he has already lost both of his parents. "I'm so sorry. That's horrible. I can't imagine how hard that must be for you."

He licks his lips as he stares at the floor. "Yeah. I certainly have my moments, but ... I manage."

After another few seconds of awkward silence, Rome adds, "Now I have a head full of memories that sometimes make me cry, but more often than not, make me smile and laugh. There is a lot that I wish both of them could've seen, but I know they're still with me in one way or another. I like to think that Mom is here whenever I cook, making sure I don't burn anything. Even now she's looking over my shoulder every time I touch this ravioli."

A soft smile forms on my lips as Rome turns back around to continue cooking. Somehow, I can imagine him and his mother standing over a stove together, laughing as he torches something for the first time, leaving it charred and filling his mother with fits of laughter. It's nice learning something deeply personal to him. It makes him more tangible and human instead of some mysterious, mystic creature that feels like he hopped off the pages of a BDSM romance written by Nasir Booker.

"That's a great way of thinking of it," I say with a smile that he can't see while he cooks. "So, you're making ravioli. Have you mastered the recipe yet or do you have a little book with notes scribbled all over it?"

"I'm making ravioli with Italian sausage ragout," he corrects. "And I absolutely have this down pat. What I love about this recipe from my mom is that it doesn't require a whole lot of effort, but it tastes and looks like it could be a gourmet dish."

"Oh, yeah? Well let me see what you're working with over there."

I get up from my seat and approach Rome from the back, but he holds out a hand to stop me.

"No, no. You stay back there," he jokes. "You can't look at the ingredients while they are separate. It ruins the flavor."

"It ruins the *flavor*?" I ask, giggling. "How does seeing it ruin the flavor?"

"I don't know but that's what my mother always told me, so that's what I'm sticking with. You can see it once it all comes together. Now stay back. I'm just about done anyway."

Laughing, I return to my seat by the island and watch as Rome moves about the kitchen like a trained professional. He grabs plates from the cabinet and sets them down side by side, then pours handmade ravioli in the center of each one. The smells filling my nose make my stomach rumble, but watching him work his magic in the kitchen makes my insides quiver. He grabs another pot and begins pouring from it, but his body blocks my view. I can only smell it, and it's mouthwatering. After everything is put together exactly how he wants it, Rome spins around and presents me with a plate. My eyes bulge.

"Ravioli with Italian sausage ragout," he says like it's an introduction. "It's a sofrito base of crushed tomatoes, mild and spicy Italian sausage, red wine, and a little bit of milk. Trust me, the flavor is like no other."

My eyes remain wide as I look down at the exquisite dish. "Well, it looks absolutely unreal. I can't wait to taste it."

Rome smiles as he brings his plate and places it next to mine, but instead of eating or even escorting me to a table, he begins quickly grabbing the pots he used to cook and starts washing them off in the sink. He scrubs one completely clean, dries it with a paper towel, and puts it in a cabinet under the counter before placing the others in the dishwasher. It doesn't take him long, but he cleans off every single thing he used, leaving nothing behind. It doesn't look like he used the kitchen at all. When he's finished, he grabs both steaming plates and looks at me. "Alright. Follow me to the dining room."

With raised brows, I nod. "Lead the way, Sir."

As I climb off my chair, I follow Rome down a short hall that leads to the dining room, and it is just as breathtaking as the other rooms in the house. A beautiful mahogany table sits in the center surrounded by florid black chairs, with a chandelier hanging over it like a floating centerpiece. Everything in the room looks more expensive than anything in my house. It's stunning.

Rome puts our plates down and says something about going back to the kitchen, but I barely even hear it. My mind is on how unreal all of this is. The house, the man, his clothes, the way he cooks, how he cleaned everything immediately instead of leaving a mess behind that he would have to return to later. He is organized and in control of everything, never seeming to lose his cool or lack composure. In every way, he is methodical and planned out. It's like he read the secret handbook on everything Dom-like and memorized each page. It makes me want to parade him around the world, taking him to every BDSM-centric establishment to show everyone that he is what a Dom is supposed to look like. Everything Rome does is precisely how I believe a Dom should act. Being a Dominant is more than just a title for him. It is his way of life. He dominates everything around him, owning it all without having to announce it or brag. He steps into the room and everyone takes notice—he even owns the people in his presence without needing to beat them into submission. I've never seen anything like it, and it makes me melt every time I'm near him. Although every submissive has their own definition and example of what a Dom is, Rome is everything a Dom should be.

When he returns, he's holding a bottle of red wine and two crystal glasses to go along with our meal. He pops the cork and fills each glass, setting them next to their respective plates before taking his seat. He picks up his fork and stops, looking directly at me.

"What?" I ask.

"You go first."

"Go first?"

"I won't start eating until you do," he says.

Good fucking god.

I battle with myself, trying not to smile as I lift my fork and push it into the ravioli. Rome doesn't move as I slowly bring it to my mouth. My taste buds explode with flavor as I chew, making my eyes widen with shock.

"Good?" he asks.

"Are you freaking kidding me?" I reply. "Rome, this is so good I could die."

"Well don't do *that*," he says, finally lifting his own fork to his mouth with a smile.

"Honestly, what the fuck?" I exclaim, putting my fork down. "How did you get like this?"

Rome chews as he shrugs. "Get like *what*?"

"You know *exactly* what I'm talking about," I snip like I'm frustrated. "This isn't normal. *You* are not normal, Rome, and there's no way you don't know it. You live in this immaculate house that you manage to keep so clean that it looks like a model home. You dress like a model. You cook like a chef. You stood up for me in front of one of the most notorious gangsters in all of Philadelphia. You share fond memories of your mother and show her respect even when she's no longer with us. You clearly have money and know how to spend it like a grown man instead of using it to fill your place with games and toys. Oh, and let's not forget that we've already slept together. You fuck like a porn star mixed with the world's greatest Dom. It's too good to be true. It just has to be. So, tell me what's wrong with you right now before I get up and start opening drawers and cabinets to find it myself. Are you a drug dealer? Is that it? Are you secretly making meth like Walter White? Are you a hitman? Do you have a basement full of jars with people's heads inside? What is it, Rome? Just tell me now and put me out of my misery, because it's starting to look like you should be on the cover of Literally Perfect Magazine."

"Is that a real magazine?" he asks, grinning.

"Stop it!" I say, pointing at him and trying to keep myself from smiling. "I need to know how you got like this. Your mother must've been an amazing woman, because her son is out of this world. Now explain while we eat this ludicrously delicious meal."

Rome sips his wine before leaning back in his chair. "Well, first of all, I appreciate the compliment."

"Oh my god," I say, rolling my eyes. "Yeah, keep voicing your appreciation of my thoughts and words. *That'll* make me less attracted to you."

"I'm just being myself," he goes on with a nonchalant shrug. "It's true that my mother was a phenomenal woman who raised me as well as she could for as long as she could, and my father was no less incredible himself. He taught me all about hard work and putting other people before myself. He instructed me about business and how to keep my head on straight and my eyes on the prize. But the parts of my personality that make me a Dom are parts I can't explain. I don't know where it originates from. Admittedly, I've dated quite a few women, and I've learned something important from every relationship I've ever been in."

"What was your longest relationship?" I probe.

Rome hesitates, swallowing hard. "Five years."

"Oh, wow. Okay. How long ago was that?"

"Four, almost five years ago."

"How did it end? Are you still on good terms with your ex?"

His eyes drop to the table and he clears his throat as apprehension crawls up his neck, stiffening his posture.

"I really don't want to talk about my past relationships," he says. "Just know that the person you see before you is the real me. I'm not putting on an act of any kind. This is who I am. I like to cook and I have a bit of OCD. I need everything to be clean and kept in its designated place or I feel a strong lack of control that bothers me to no end."

"So you're a control freak?"

"Absolutely," he answers quickly. "I think that's one of the qualities that makes me a good Dom."

I nod. "Touchè."

"What about you?" he asks, covering his mouth with his hand while he chews. "You're so focused on how I became the person I am, but you're not exactly a walking mess either. I'm about as picky as it gets, and I knew from the first moment I saw you that you would be my undoing. There's an aura about you that pulled me in, and I was hoping your personality would rub me the wrong way, but it locked me in chains instead. Every time we spoke at the office, it was like you put more locks on the trap that ensnared me, making it so that I couldn't get away from my desire for you. So, how do you explain that? Is your mother an incredible woman, too?"

I let out a long sigh as his words weave their way through me like a magic spell, heightening my senses and lowering my inhibitions. The good food and wine doesn't hurt either, but the way he stares has me in a chokehold, and I don't even want to fight my way free.

"I don't know how you expect me to answer that," I reply. "You can't go dishing out compliments like that and expect me to act like you didn't."

"I have no expectations. I just want to know about you."

After a sigh, I say, "Okay. Well then, yes, my mom is awesome. She is just as strong-minded as I am and always pushed for me to be the same way. She is where I get all of my mental fortitude and strength, and my father is where I get all of my drive. I honestly don't think I get my submissiveness from either of them, if I'm being honest."

"So your parents don't have a D/s dynamic?"

I laugh aloud. "No way. My mom would never say that she has submitted to a man, or anyone else for that matter. This is just a part of who I am, the same way being a Dom is who you are. It's funny because it's natural for me to feel submissive, but I always want it to be earned. It's not something I am ever willing to just give away for free. Once it's earned, I'm at my happiest."

"How important is it to you that you're in a D/s dynamic?" he asks, continuing to eat his food as if we're not talking about deep, explicit parts of our lives.

"It's instrumental," I answer, pushing my fork into my mouth. I cover half my face with my free hand so that I can continue explaining. "Once you've experienced BDSM in real life, I don't think there is any going back. I've seen how good it can be, and my kinks and fetishes have only grown the older I've gotten. I'm not going backward for anyone."

"I agree," he says after swallowing another bite. "While I know that this lifestyle isn't for everyone, I feel like there is no other way for me to exist. Being a Dom isn't like putting my shoes on at the start of the day just to remove them at the end. It's in my blood, still coursing through me even when I'm asleep. I've always made it clear to anyone I was dating that you don't get me without BDSM. Even though I was always open to taking it as slow as my partner may have needed, meeting me here was always a requirement."

"Have you broken up with someone over them not being interested in BDSM?"

"Absolutely," he replies with no hesitation or regret. "I won't have a vanilla life the same way I won't have a life filled with racism or misogyny. Some things are non-negotiable."

"I agree one hundred percent."

"Good," he says with a nod as he lifts his wine glass. "How about other non-negotiable things? What are your hard limits?"

I finish my entire glass of wine and refill it as I start to reply. "It's like I told you before, I'm okay with just about anything that doesn't involve blood, urine, feces, or anal. I'm willing to try anything but those."

"Anything?"

"Just about. I'm very open-minded—fond of paddles, floggers, and riding crops at equal levels. In love with praise just as much as degradation. In fact, I might even love degradation more."

"Oh. Interesting. How about CNC?"

My eyes widen. "I've never done that before, but it sounds like tons of fun under the right circumstances—meaning everything being laid out beforehand so that I'm not caught off guard."

"I see," he says as if making a mental note. "Do you have any soft limits—things that you're curious about trying but aren't sure about yet?"

"I think I've tried everything I'm interested in. I've even done electroshock. At this point I'm only left with hard limits, and I don't budge on those."

"As you shouldn't," he says with a raised eyebrow.

"How about you?" I ask. "Any hard limits?"

Rome's eyes shift up and to the side as he thinks, and I wonder if it's his expression or the wine in my belly that makes it so cute.

"I think we're the same ... mostly," he answers.

"Mostly?" I ask, although it comes out more like an exclamation.

"Alright, don't judge me," he says, grinning. "I'm totally with you on feces and blood, but I have had a sub who liked being peed on ... and I didn't hate it."

My eyes bulge as a slow smile takes over my mouth. "Oh my god! You've peed on someone?"

"I must admit that I have."

"Did she pee on you, too?" I ask, and when Rome doesn't answer, he speaks loud and clear. "*Oh my god*! Rome!"

"I told you not to judge me," he says with a huge, adorable smile on his face. "Wow, I didn't know you were in the business of kink shaming, Miss Washington."

After laughing, I manage to stifle it and act serious. "Ugh. Fine. No kink shaming. I just didn't expect that. Okay, I'm done. Anything else I should know about you?"

Rome hesitates a moment before saying, "No, that's it."

"Do you have a favorite kink?"

"Impact play," he answers, this time with no hesitation. "But specifically with floggers. It's my favorite toy by far. How about you? What's your favorite kink?"

"Bondage," I blab without thinking.

"Oh? Why?" Rome asks as he finishes his food and leans back with his wine glass in his hand.

I take my final bite of food and mirror his posture, leaning back in my seat. "Because it takes absolutely all control away from me. I can't move or shrink away to show my nervousness. I have no choice but to submit—to be completely controlled. To be used by someone of my choosing. To be owned. But I've never been with anyone who has the necessary tools and furniture to truly restrain me. I've worn cuffs and a ball gag before, but there's a lot of stuff out there that I haven't had the luxury of experiencing."

Rome gazes at me for a moment, a smirk pulling one side of his mouth as he raises his glass and takes a long swig of his wine.

"What?" I ask, curious about his expression. "What's that face for?"

Out of nowhere, Rome stands up and sets his glass down on the table next to his finished plate.

"Follow me. I want to show you something," he says.

As exhilaration begins to course through my veins, I finish off my second glass of wine and rise to my feet. Rome smiles again before leading me out of the dining room and through another hall separate from the one that led us from the kitchen. We take a few quick turns and reach a closed black door that he opens with a twist of a gold knob, which leads to stairs that Rome immediately descends. I follow him silently until we reach the bottom and the two of us stand before a large space shrouded in shadows and ominous darkness.

"What is this?" I ask. "I can't see a thing."

"This," he answers, "is my playroom."

Rome turns to his left and flicks a switch on the wall, sending light traveling down the center of the basement like a lightning strike. Once it reaches the far end, it spreads out across the entire room, illuminating the space and jolting my heart like a shock from a defibrillator.

My eyes widen to the size of planets as I gasp and my jaw drops open. "Oh, my god."

Twenty-Seven

My heart is a hammer striking an anvil. It beats so hard that I can hear it in my ears as I stand at the bottom of the stairs staring into what Rome called his playroom. I'm in awe of it, both excited and anxious about the display in front of me. This is like a dream, my most intense fantasy coming to life right before my eyes.

"How?" I ask, although there really is no answer. "You just bought all of this recently? This ... I've never seen anything like this."

Rome steps to the middle of the room, placing himself in the center of the biggest display of BDSM furniture and toys I have ever seen. His basement is practically ... no, not practically ... it *literally* is a sex dungeon dressed in black and gold.

The brick walls are painted black, including the fireplace at the far end next to the massive bed with four pillars reaching for the stratosphere. A gold sex chair rests comfortably next to a black spanking bench. There are two more black pillars in the center of the room, one covered in ropes, the other containing an assortment of floggers of all sizes and materials. A giant Saint Andrew's cross stands in the back corner like a stalker lurking in the dark, while two glass display cases rest atop gold pedestals like decorative statues. Each glass case is stocked with sex toys, from wand vibrators to riding crops, handcuffs to blindfolds, dildos to butt plugs, chains to electroshock wands. It's a collection and display unlike anything I have ever seen, and when Rome looks around, I can see that this is his happy place. He has never looked more in his element, grinning as he takes stock of the room he built for his personal pleasure.

"I owned some of this before I inherited everything my father left me when he passed," he says, his eyes not on me but proudly gazing around the room. "But I needed to buy more when I purchased the house. I just couldn't let this space go to waste, and like I said upstairs, I refuse to live a vanilla life. So, I decided that if I was going to do it, I was going to go all out. I bought everything I could think of, but it was well worth the money."

"Yeah, I bet it was," I reply with a scoff. "I'm sure you've been having a great time with all of this at your disposal."

Rome turns to face me, unarming me with his smile.

"Actually, I've never been down here with anyone," he says.

I frown hard, my forehead wrinkling like a bed sheet. "What? Why?"

"Because I went through a dark, sad, solemn period after my father died," he says, stepping toward me. "I didn't want to do anything but lie in my bed and cry, and that's exactly what I did on most days for a couple of months. But eventually I got up, took account of everything my father left me in his will, and started thinking of what I wanted to do with it all. He left behind a pretty decent amount of money, his house, and two successful businesses. Once I was able to bring myself to sell everything, the sum was astronomical ... but not enough to overshadow my grief. So I started to begin my life again. I bought this house, furnished it, and started going out to try to find out how to live without either of my parents around anymore. I started the process of purchasing Sandcastle, and slowly began to search for happiness again. But I never met anyone that I wanted to bring down here. I've had a few flings, admittedly, but nothing serious, and this ... *this* is for serious."

Rome gestures toward the basement, asking me to take it all in and understand exactly what he's saying. He built this for when he was ready to have someone to use it with. He wanted someone worthy of it, and he has chosen me. He wants me to be the first.

"And you see me as something serious?" I ask, just making sure I'm not misreading the tea leaves.

He clears his throat. "I do, and I hope you see me as someone worthy of your consent."

I've waited so long for this that I can barely believe any of it is real. Rome is a dream escaping my mind and inserting itself into my reality, and this room would scare the living shit out of everyone I know. But I have a growing sense of trust for Rome that gives me comfort while standing in it. That is what this is all about—finding someone you can trust in the darkness. I thought the search for something like this would be endless, but it feels like I just crossed the finish line.

"I do," I reply, copying him. "I see you as *the* person worthy of my consent. You have it ... now what do you intend to do with it?"

Rome's smirk tells me everything I need to know, but I want him to show me. My nerves stand on end in anticipation of his next move, and when he takes a step in my direction, I know my world is about to change forever.

"I intend to make your biggest fantasies come true," he answers. "You said you'd never been with anyone who had the tools required to bind you properly. So tonight, that's exactly what I'm going to do."

Twenty-Eight

I don't feel nervous. More sensitive? For sure. But I'm not afraid of what's about to happen. When Rome takes my hand in his, I don't feel the urge to pull it away and bolt back up the stairs, needing more time for him to earn my trust. I'm placated by it. I feel comfort and safety as he walks me over to the spanking bench and tells me to stand in front of it without moving. My blood rushes through my veins like a raging river, but it's excitement, not timidness that fills my body.

As he takes his time removing my dress, slowly kissing just above the fabric as he slides it off my arm, I quiver, my body's natural response to the amazingness of this moment and the joy I feel in it. He takes his time, no longer using words to prove his point. Everything is done with action, intention, and desire. He drops to his knees to help me step out of my clothes, sprinkling soft kisses down my body, even on my feet as I step out of the dress and stand completely naked before him, totally exposed and left with nothing but trust.

"Have you been on one of these before?" he asks as he stands, using the back of his hand to caress my skin softly.

"No, Sir," I reply with a subtle head shake.

"Good. That means I get to be the memory you have of using it for the first time. Take my hand. Let me guide you."

I place my hand in Rome's and turn toward the spanking bench, inspecting it further now that I'm close enough to see all of the details. There are six cushions with buckles secured to four gold legs, each one made of soft, black leather that looks and smells brand new. Rome wasn't lying when he said none of this had been used before. Four cushions are lower than the other two, clearly indicating where your arms and legs go. The higher cushions are for the user's torso and face to rest comfortably, the largest cushion containing a hole near the back end. Rome helps me as I lift a leg and throw it over to the other side of the bench, centering myself on the torso cushion and letting my arms and legs drop to the lower ones.

"You good?" Rome asks once I'm positioned properly.

"Yes, Sir," I reply.

"Good," he says as he un-secures one of the buckles. "Now, this is the part where your trust for me will be tested. Are you ready?"

I nod, swallowing hard as the thrill of what's about to happen makes my heart gallop like the hooves of a thousand horses.

Rome takes his time securing each buckle and tightening down the straps they are attached to. He binds my left arm first, then my left leg, before moving to the right side and repeating the process. When he's finished, only my head is free to move up and down. The rest of me is totally under his control.

He steps to the front of the bench and crouches down in front of me until our faces are only inches apart.

"Repeat after me," he says, looking me straight in the eye. "*La regina*."

Italian rolling so easily off of his tongue makes me blush, but I remain focused and follow his lead.

"*La regina*," I repeat.

"Good. Again. *La regina*."

"*La regina*."

"Good girl," Rome says with a proud smile. "This is your safe word. It means 'The Queen' in English." As I nod my understanding, Rome continues. "In this dynamic of ours, it will never be forgotten that you are in charge. I am the Dom at your request and approval, a king who rules over his queen by her royal decree. Your consent will always reign supreme, and if you ever feel the need to remove it, all you have to say is *la regina*, and everything will stop immediately. It is my most sacred vow to you. One I will never break. No matter what we're doing or how good it feels to me, you are the priority. *La regina* shuts all doors at once, and I will never hold that against you or make you feel pressured to continue. You are *la regina*. You are the queen, and I belong to you just as much as you belong to me. Got it?"

When I smile, it is filled with so many feelings—lust, happiness, trust, affection, need, desire, joy, excitement, satisfaction. I feel everything all at once, and there's a part of me that wants Rome to undo the straps just so I can throw my arms around him. He doesn't know how long I've waited for him.

"Yes, Sir. I got it," I say. "Thank you."

"Don't thank me yet, my little goddess," he says as he moves his face closer to mine. "I'm about to do very devious things to you."

Then he kisses me hard and passionately, like we're never going to see each other again after this moment. His tongue is as forceful and strong as his lips are soft. It drives me crazy and forces all thoughts out of my head except for one—I need this man.

When he backs away, it leaves me panting and craving more, but he turns on his heel instead. I watch as he heads for the one of the black pillars that is covered in floggers, before going to a golden pedestal and removing a wand vibrator from its glass case. He clutches both in his hands as he makes his way back over to me, setting the flogger atop the gold sex chair before clicking the wand into a nearby device that looks like a microphone stand. With his tools in place, Rome returns to his spot in front of me and removes his shirt, pants, and underwear unabashedly. His aroused cock hangs in front of him in all its glory, a large vein standing out as thick as a pencil.

He watches my eyes as he grabs the flogger and steps forward, and I give my intentions away by struggling to keep them off his thick length.

"You want it, don't you, my little goddess?" he asks.

I melt at the new pet name, hoping it sticks.

"God, yes," I reply to both his question and the name.

"Yeah? Open that mouth for me. Let me see," he demands, inching even closer with the flogger tight in his grip.

I open my mouth, but Rome doesn't slide his cock inside. Instead, he teases me, keeping it just out of reach of my parted lips. While I struggle, he slides the falls of the flogger over my backside, letting me feel the softness of the leather before flicking his wrist and smacking me. My body jolts like it just received an electric shock, but the quick, sharp pain feels so good. When I moan from the feeling, Rome steps closer and pushes his cock inside my mouth. My eyes widen at the sudden new feeling of my mouth being stretched out, but before I can think twice, the flogger crashes against my flesh a second time. The pain starts on my ass and spreads out like lightning splintering across a cloudy sky.

I let out a moan that barely makes it past his cock as my muscles liquefy. I come undone, sinking into subspace faster than I ever have. My mind goes blank when Rome hits me with the flogger again, this time on my back, shocking my senses even further as his cock fills my mouth to its capacity. In an instant, ecstasy wraps itself around me, lifting my mind out of normalcy and into a dreamlike state as the flogger tails crash against me again. Pain and pleasure blend together, creating a heightened sense of euphoria that numbs my nerves. I crave more. I need to be hit harder. I need to come. I am totally unglued as Rome fucks my mouth and whips my body at the same time. Something about having no control and feeling the sensation of him using me however he pleases disintegrates my thoughts until I have no more. I only feel the flogger kissing my skin and my throat being used. Drool falls from my mouth and I don't care. This is heaven.

"Oh my god." Rome's words hit my ears, but they sound like I'm hearing them while underwater. "Look at you. You look so beautiful right now, Nia. You like having that mouth fucked, don't you?"

He pulls his cock out of my mouth just enough for me to answer.

"Yes, Sir," I mumble, feeling drunk from the scene.

"You like being used?"

"Yes, Sir."

"Good. You're mine, aren't you?"

"Yes, Sir."

"Say it, my little goddess. Tell me."

"I'm yours, Rome," I say, and I mean it. It may not be forever, but right now, in this moment, I belong to him. I am a prisoner with Stockholm syndrome. I don't want to be free.

"Jesus," he says, looking down at me. "I love the way you've melted for me, Nia. You're so fucking beautiful. It's incredible how you've given yourself over to me. You make me so proud. I want you to see it. I want you to see how incredible you look while I use you."

Rome steps away, reaching down for his pants and removing his phone from the pocket, along with a condom. He tosses the condom on top of his pants and steps close to me again, fiddling with his phone. "Now open that delicious fucking mouth for me again, my little goddess."

When my mouth opens, Rome pushes his dick inside again and immediately returns to fucking my face. I choke and gag on it, loving every second of the agony as he moves the phone down and records me taking his cock. I don't protest, because there isn't a thing he could do right now that I would object to. I am gladly his whore tonight.

"Do you see it, Nia?" he asks rhetorically. "Do you see how perfect you are with my cock in your mouth? Fuck. I can't get enough."

I don't bother to look at the camera, because I don't care. I am lost in the moment and only want him to continue to use me in any way that he sees fit. I have never felt this submerged before. Men have complained about women not being sexual or kinky enough for their liking, but what they fail to realize is that a woman has to feel a certain level of connection before she can dive into the depths of her sexuality. It has to be earned, and she has to know that her partner can be trusted to protect her when she is at her most vulnerable. I have never gone this far before, and it's because I've never felt this safe with anyone. Now that Rome has arrived, I want to do everything with him, and I have no shame in saying that he owns my body. He absolutely does, because he earned it. He earned me.

When Rome takes a step back, I crave for him to return, and he obliges by bending down and kissing me. Unfazed by the drool stringing from my mouth, he kisses me as if we are already in love. Passion flows between us like kinetic energy, adding more fuel to my need for him, and I groan when he steps away. He walks over to the sex chair and places his phone on top of it, making sure the camera faces us before moving the stand containing the wand vibrator over to me. He twists a knob in the middle of the stand and lowers it, then slides it beneath the spanking bench before raising it again. The wand fits in the hole in the cushion and makes perfect contact with my clit, and I gasp when he turns it on. Shockwaves detonate inside of me, making my eyes roll to the back of my head.

"Oh my fucking god," I blare as the intense vibrations overtake me. If I could clutch something, I would squeeze until my fingers turned blue, but thanks to the restraints on the spanking bench, I can only sit there and take it. I squeeze my eyes shut, trying to gain some sense of calm, but the intensity is so strong I can barely stand it. I sense Rome moving around me, but all I can focus on is how profound the feeling is.

I try to force myself to get used to the feeling, but my sense of control comes crashing down around me when Rome positions himself behind the bench and pushes his sheathed cock inside of me. Every muscle in my body contracts as he begins fucking me hard, pounding me relentlessly from behind while I let out uncontrolled shrieks of pain and pleasure. Between the wand and the size of his cock, I am lost in the wind. I can't move, I can't speak, and I can barely breathe. My mind and body go limp and the world evaporates into thin air—no thoughts, no vision, no stress, no worries, no hearing, no thinking, no existence to speak of. I am nothing until the moment the most Earth-shattering orgasm rips my universe into a million pieces. Stars explode across my vision like a firework grand finale as violent pleasure swallows me whole.

"Oh, fuck," Rome yells, grunting with each powerful stroke as his own orgasm is brought on by the sight of my undoing.

When it's all over, my body is completely limp. My brain doesn't seem to be able to send signals to the rest of my body, so I just lay there, my face against the U-shaped cushion in front of me. Rome gets up, removes the wand beneath me, and hurries away for a moment. When he returns, his condom is gone and he's draped in a black and brown robe, sweat still beading on his forehead as he rushes to remove my restraints. By the time he gets the final one off my arm, sub-drop takes hold in my mind and tears fill my eyes—the result of the overwhelming, sensational high giving way to chemical confusion in my body. An uncontrollable feeling of sadness wraps its arm around me and I begin to bawl as Rome helps me stand, then sweeps me up in his arms. He carries me through the center of the basement like a husband carrying his bride into their new home, but I can't enjoy it. I'm too far gone.

"I got you, Nia," he tells me just as we reach the steps and he begins to climb with me in his arms. "Don't worry about anything. I'm here."

Twenty-Nine

"Ｈow are you feeling?"

Rome's voice is calm and soothing, blending with the serenity of the room. A small fireplace crackles from the opposite wall, shooting beautiful colors of orange and amber onto everything around us as we lay in Rome's massive bed with his arms around me.

I needed this—his comfort and warmth—as I try to regain control over my emotions. As our scene in the playroom ended, I was ravaged by sub-drop, causing my affections to spin out of control like a speeding car on a slick road. If it wasn't for Rome's gentleness, I don't know how I would have pulled myself together without it taking days. Thanks to him and his embrace, I'm starting to feel like myself again.

"Better," I reply with my head lying on his chest and my feet twisted in his black satin sheets. "That was intense, though. I've never experienced sub-drop on that scale—never bawled like that after an orgasm. It was a little scary."

Rome tightens his grip around my naked body, pushing a fortified sense of safety into my veins like an IV. "You definitely had it bad, but it makes sense after such an intense scene. Not to mention that you hadn't ever been restrained like that before. Your body and mind just went through something it didn't understand. As acute as it was, I wasn't surprised."

"Well, that makes *one* of us," I say with a laugh. "I never saw it coming, but I'm glad you were here to help me through it. You made me feel better with your words and arms around me, plus the crackle of the fireplace is just the sound I needed. It's so peaceful in here with the glow of the flames. I love it."

Rome takes a deep breath, raising and lowering my head with a sigh. "Good. I'm glad. You did wonderful tonight."

"I did wonderful? Are you kidding? It was all *you*. All I had to do was lay there and take it."

"No way," he replies. "There's so much more to being a sub than just lying there and taking it. You have to have tremendous mental strength to endure intense BDSM scenes. At any point, your body could have triggered its flight response and started trying to get out of the restraints. You could've invoked your safe word at any point in time, but you persevered and pushed through discomfort. Bondage like that isn't for everyone."

"Oh? You sound like you're speaking from experience. Is it safe to say that you've been with someone who couldn't handle it?"

"I've been single for a long time, so I've certainly experienced a lot," he answers honestly. "I don't know about you, but my experience with the lifestyle hasn't been anywhere near perfect. We all know about the fake Dom epidemic, but the fake sub one is nearly just as bad."

I crane my neck to glance up at him, marveling at his beautiful face being kissed by the glimmer of fire. "Wait, so there are people out there that claim to be subs but aren't?"

Rome smiles with his lips pressed together as if he has seen some truly ridiculous things. "Oh, absolutely. BDSM has sort of gone mainstream. There are a lot of people out there reading about it and seeing it improperly displayed in TV shows and movies, and because the actors make it look like they're enjoying themselves and the people in those shows are doing things that normal husbands and wives don't do, everyone is trying to jump on the bandwagon. The problem is that doing it in real life isn't anything like reading from a page."

"True, but that doesn't keep Nasir Booker from being world famous. Or EL James."

"As far as I know, Nasir Booker is actually in the lifestyle, which is why his books are far more accurate and he's a literary megastar. When people read his stuff, they can get a better sense of what it's actually like. But a lot of people don't care about the details. I've had subs who watched certain movies thinking that because they liked sex that being a submissive was a natural progression. Once they were restrained and hit with a cane, the real feeling of pain and bondage was too much and they learned the value of the safe word."

"Damn. I bet that was a let down in the moment."

"Big time, but I don't get upset when the safe word is used. I already know this isn't for everybody, so it's cool when they point themselves out. It takes a special, devious kind of person to be in the lifestyle in real life."

"Ooh, are you saying I'm devious?"

"*Deliciously* devious, my little goddess," he answers, making me blush. "You made me so proud."

"I'm glad," I reply. "Hopefully in the future I won't cry like a baby afterward."

Rome squeezes me again, bending his neck forward to kiss me on top of my head. "If you do, I'll be here for you."

"Yeah? So you're not scared of a woman mentioning the future? Some men hear that word and run for the hills."

"If you haven't figured it out already, baby girl, I am not like other men."

"Truer words have never been spoken," I reply, giggling.

"As for the future," Rome says, "I haven't really allowed myself to give it much thought. I've just been trying to focus on grieving my father and doing some personal healing. It's a very long process. One that I take extremely seriously. I guess what I'm trying to say is that I'm just taking it one day at a time."

"Your father's passing hit you really hard, huh? I can tell. It wreaks havoc on you every time you mention it."

"It's not just him. I've lost everyone that I've ever loved, with the exception of my childhood best friend. Nikola is like my last hope, and I'm so scared to lose him that it makes me crazy. It's this fear that has kept me from getting too close to you, if we're being honest."

"Oh," I say. It makes sense now. Rome has been through loss, and that kind of thing can affect a person forever. "I was wondering what it was. I thought it was me."

He kisses me on the head again. "No, it really doesn't ... didn't have anything to do with you, per se. There's my parents, but also ... I was married once before."

My eyes bulge. "Really?"

"Yes ... and just like my parents, she died. Four years ago."

The shock of his words hit me like a punch to the stomach. Now it *really* makes sense. But when I lift my head to turn around and offer my condolences, Rome holds me in place, hugging me like he doesn't want to let go.

"No, don't," he says. "I don't talk about it. I can't. Just know that I haven't allowed myself to feel anything for anybody since she passed, and meeting you was the first time I felt like I didn't have a choice but to feel something. It sent terror through me like a speeding bullet, and I'm still scared, but I like you, Nia. I really do, and I want to see where this goes."

"You do?" I ask, suddenly feeling my own sense of fear. "Are you sure? I don't want you to feel pressured or like you have to choose between me and her memory."

"I don't feel pressured," he says almost a little too quickly. "I'm just still healing. Nonetheless, I'm making a conscious choice to be here ... with you. What we're doing right now—lying in bed, entwined in each other's arms next to a crackling fire—I haven't done this with *anyone* since her and I haven't wanted to. In fact, I ran from even the slightest possibility of it. But not tonight. Not now. I don't want to run from you."

Nervous apprehension leaks from my heart and spreads throughout my body, even as I force myself to stay lying on Rome's chest. It's wonderful to know the reason behind why he was so on and off in the beginning, but now I'm afraid of that reason. He chose to marry someone else, and they would still be married if she hadn't passed away. I don't need to know the circumstances of her death to understand why he would be apprehensive about another long-term relationship. It makes me very nervous, but the fact that I'm the first girl he has laid in bed with gives me hope. He's clearly at a point in his healing process that makes it okay for him to choose me. It's worrisome, to say the least, but his words inject me with comfort.

"Good," I reply, throwing an arm over him and pulling us closer together. "I know you've been through a lot—an unspeakable amount—but I don't want you to run either. I think you're pretty incredible, Rome, and if you're willing to give me a chance, I think I can make you happy. I know I could certainly get used to this."

A few seconds pass in silence before Rome clears his throat.

"I know," he says in a whisper. "Me, too."

Thirty

"**G**ood morning, Nia."

I look up from my computer just as Rome walks past my door opening in khaki brown pants and a white button-up with brown buttons. His eyes linger as he goes by, speaking to me without saying a word, and I grin as he continues out of view.

In a flash, I forget that I just got to work, because I'm instantly sent back to last night. Rome and I had the most incredible time together, and I'm not only talking about the sex. While that was unbelievable, what I cherished most was the conversations we had afterward, when sliding out of his arms would have felt like torture. Even now, there is no place I'd rather be than lying in his bed with a fire dancing in front of us while talking about life. It was our first instance of just taking our time and getting to know one another, and after one dose I'm already addicted.

So, Rome and I are together now. There are no more questions about if he wants me or if he doesn't. No more confusion about why he was acting out of sorts. Our intentions for each other have been made known, and this is it. There is an us. While I do have concerns about the fact that he was married four years ago, he assured me that he is healing and ready to be in a relationship. All I can go by is his word, so if he says he is ready to be with me, then I'm definitely ready to be with him.

Now that we're officially together in a D/s dynamic, I wonder what today will be like. We're at work with tons to do. I need to get started on the Golden Diamond advertising as soon as possible, and I'm sure Rome has a million other things on his to-do list, but I can't stop thinking about him, especially if he intends to keep sneaking looks at me while I'm trying to work.

"Good morning, Nia," Jeremiah says as he enters my office carrying a small cardboard cutout. Instead of showing me what's in his hands, he sits down across from me and exhales. "I don't know about you, but I am not in the mood to be here this morning. I'm tired as hell and already in a bad mood. How are you doing?"

I lift my travel mug of coffee and take a swing. "I'm sorry you're in a bad mood. I'm tired, but my mood is okay. It's pretty good, actually."

"Ugh. You and your good moods first thing in the morning," he complains with an exaggerated roll of his eyes. "Why are you happy? Did you finally have a successful FET hookup?"

Jeremiah laughs, convincing himself that making fun of my love life is the most hilarious thing in the world, but when he sees that I'm not laughing along with him, he slowly stops. He goes quiet as his brows draw together like magnets to metal, and he suddenly looks very suspicious of me.

"What are you not telling me?" he inquires, his eyes squinted.

I shrug. "I don't know."

"What the hell do you mean *you don't know*? Here I was getting ready to show you this mock-up for the first Golden Diamond billboard, and you're in here withholding information? Are you dating someone?"

"I don't know," I answer again, just as my cheeks begin to heat up.

"Girl, if you say you don't know again, *I don't know* what I might do to you, and *nobody else will know* where to find your dead body. Stop playing with me. What's going on? Who are you ..."

Jeremiah's voice trails off as I look him right in the eyes, twisting my lips together. Realization slowly dawns on him, and I see the moment the bulb over his head lights up.

"No way," he whispers, gawking at me with tire-sized eyes. Before asking the question he's dying to ask, he gets up and looks over his shoulder to make sure no one is close by. "Rome? You and Rome are hooking up?"

This time, I give him the answer he is looking for.

"Not hooking up," I reply with a smile that I can't control. "We're together."

"Together?" he says a little too loudly. "Like *together*, together? Or just, like, together?"

"What?" I say, frowning. "I don't know how else to say it. We're not just hooking up for fun. We've talked ... among other things ... and it's official. He's my man and I'm his girl. We're together. Officially."

"Oh my fucking god!" Jeremiah bellows, pulling at least one of our co-workers attention to my office. I have to put my finger to my lips and tell him to shush to keep him from screaming it from the rooftop. "Don't tell me to shush. You've been in here holding out on me while you are dating the boss? This is huge. Have you told Jaz yet?"

"Not necessarily," I answer. "She knows that he and I had been talking and that there were some mixed signals being put out there from his end. I haven't told her about the latest developments because it's all so brand new. It literally just became official last night."

Jeremiah gasps. "So I've been given the honor of being the first to know? Usually you tell Jaz everything and I end up feeling left out. Oh, this is a great day—and here I was thinking it was going to be shitty. Ooh, can I be the one to tell Jaz? I have to hear the sound of her voice when she finds out."

I roll my eyes as I laugh. "I guess so. It's not that big of a deal."

"Bitch, what? Not a big deal. He's our boss. Our gorgeous, masculine, sexy, well-groomed boss. This is a huge deal, and Jaz will agree with me when I call her *right now* and say, 'Girl, you're not going to believe who is together.'"

"Who's together?" Sierra's shrill voice suddenly asks from the doorway, cutting right through the good mood like an annoying ass samurai sword.

Jeremiah flinches like he just witnessed a jump scare, and his good mood instantly deflates.

"Nobody," he answers.

Thank goodness. The last thing I need is Sierra finding out about this. All it will take is one perceived special favor and she'll be ready to go to HR and hire a lawyer.

"Oh? But you sounded so excited about it," Sierra prods as she steps into the office.

Jeremiah scoffs. "That's because I was minding my business. It feels good to do that. You should try it."

Sierra glares at Jeremiah like she's ready to slap him, but lets out a long sigh instead before looking at me. "Nia, do you have anything drawn up for the Golden Diamond ad? Rome would like to have something approved before the end of the week."

I start to shake my head, but Jeremiah steps forward. "I have the first billboard mock-up right here. Nia and I were just about to go over it."

"Good. Let's see it," Sierra replies.

Just as Jeremiah raises the cardboard in his hands, my phone goes off with a text alert. Sierra and Jeremiah watch as I pick it up from the desk and see that it's a message from Rome.

> Can they see your screen?

Confused, I quickly type a response.

> No, why?

> Good ... Make sure the volume is down ...

"Nia, you good?" Sierra asks from the other side of the desk. "Can we go over the mock-up, please?"

"Uhh, yeah. Let me—" I'm cut off by another message from Rome. It starts off grainy at first, a pixelated rectangle with no defining features. But when I click on the image, a video immediately takes over the full screen and starts playing. My heart erupts as I let out a loud gasp, and the first thing I see is a closeup shot of Rome's thick cock in my mouth as I'm strapped to the spanking bench in his playroom.

"You okay?" Jeremiah asks, concern all over his face.

"Umm ... yep. Yeah, I'm fine," I lie, doing my best to try and pull myself together, but I can barely keep my eyes off the screen. Rome has his hand cupped under my chin as he strokes his cock in and out of my drooling mouth. It's such a startling image that I don't know how to respond. I can't even think straight. Why would he send this to me *right now*? It doesn't make sense, but before I can even gather enough thoughts to form a coherent sentence, I receive another text.

> Excuse yourself to the restroom. Go inside. Lock the door. And make yourself come to the video of me fucking you senseless.

My jaw drops open as I stare at the screen in total shock. Now? He's Domming me right now, first thing in the morning? When he knows Sierra and Jeremiah are in my office? It's the craziest, hottest thing ever, and now that he and I are officially in a D/s relationship, I know what I have to do.

I clear my throat. "Umm, we'll take a look at it as soon as I get back. I'm sorry, but I desperately need to use the restroom. Too much coffee, I think. I'll be right back."

Sierra lets out a huff as I scoot past her, and Jeremiah looks at me with a suspicious frown, but I don't care. With my phone in hand, I step out of my office and head to the bathroom. As I go, I look into Rome's office, and he spares a quick glance at me with a devilish smirk before going back to whatever he was typing on his computer, his phone next to his hand. I grin as I pick up the pace and enter the bathroom.

Inside, I bend over to look beneath the door of every stall, ensuring that no one is in the bathroom before stepping into the last stall and closing the door. I shake my head, in disbelief of what I'm about to do. But I want to do it. For him.

I play the video, biting my lips together at the sight of Rome fucking my mouth. His moans sound so good, but I have to keep the volume as low as I can. If I was at home, I would play the sound over my stereo just to hear his deep voice telling me how good my mouth feels. Hearing the slap of the flogger against my ass sends my hand sliding down my stomach before pushing itself between my legs like it has a mind of its own. I rub my clit on top of my pants as the video continues.

In only a minute, I can feel how wet I am, and I don't want evidence of it being apparent when I walk back into my office, so I push down my zipper and move my panties to the side.

"Fuck," I whisper to myself as I hold the video close to my face so I can hear it.

The scene on the screen shifts when Rome sets the camera down on top of his gold sex chair, giving me a wide view of the moment he centers the wand beneath me, and positions himself behind me. I watch him stretch a condom over his cock, step forward, and enter me from behind. I have no choice but to rub my clit as I watch him ravage me, remembering how good it felt and how I lost myself in it. As I watch, I can practically feel the vibrator sending me into another dimension of pleasure. Rome fucks me hard and fast, each long strong jolting my entire body forward until the moment my eyes roll into the back of my head when I come in the video. I watch myself melt first, followed by the moment Rome closes his eyes and nearly collapses on top of me from the intensity of his orgasm. Seeing the way his muscles flex and twitch sends me careening over the threshold, and I come right there in the stall, my toes curling in my shoes as I pray no one walks in at this exact moment. If they do, I'll certainly be caught because I'm too wrapped in it to stop. I do my best to hold back my moans, pressing my lips together as hard as I can until I finally come down.

When I turn off the video, I can hear myself panting hard and loud, but the bathroom is still empty. Thank goodness.

"Oh, my god," I whisper to myself, smiling as I lean back on the toilet, still breathing hard.

I can't believe I just did that. I'm at work ... and I loved it. Still beaming, I go to the camera app on my phone and record a quick video of my fingers sliding through my wet pussy, then I send it to Rome. It's the least I can do since he surprised me this morning.

I spend the next few minutes getting cleaned up and making sure my makeup isn't ruined from the sweat beads that decorated my forehead, then I hurry out of the bathroom. When I walk past Rome's office, I turn around to look at him and see the moment he lifts his phone to see my message, and I can't wipe the smirk off my face.

"Sorry about that," I say to Jeremiah and Sierra who are seated in the chairs in front of my desk. "Now where were we?"

"Jeremiah's mock-up," Sierra answers with a little attitude, but it doesn't faze me after what I just did.

The two of them stand up and we begin going over the details of the Golden Diamond billboard, pointing out things we'd like to delete, resize, or move to a different spot. All of us add our input on what the next mock-up should look like, and just before we agree on the changes, my phone chimes again. I take a step back to look at the message from Rome, and smile from ear to ear before shoving the phone back in my pocket. I go on talking to Sierra and Jeremiah about the mock-up, but my mind stays on the message from my Dom.

Good girl

Thirty-One

"I assume you heard the news from Jeremiah."

"Oh, most definitely," Jaz answers after a laugh. "He told me everything in very enthusiastic detail."

"I bet he did," I reply just as I turn my car into Rome's stone driveway and come to a stop.

Jaz lets out a long sigh, and although I can't see her face through the speakers of my car, I imagine she has her eyebrows raised as high as the top of the roof in front of me.

"So, you're doing this, huh?" she asks. "Even after the mind games he was playing with you before? You're sure?"

I smile as I look up at Rome's house, remembering what is down in the basement and how we used it together. Memories work like caffeine making my heart race and I know that there is no turning back now. We've started, and there isn't a hair on my head that wants to stop.

"Yeah, we're doing this," I reply. "Rome and I have talked and he explained a lot. There's a bunch of stuff attached to him that I didn't know before, and now that I know more I feel better. I understand his reasoning."

"He has a bunch of stuff attached to him? You mean baggage?"

"Well, I wouldn't say baggage," I say, trying to correct myself before Jaz can pick up a negative theory about Rome and run with it. "He has been through some really traumatic stuff that has led him to be the man he is. I'm just saying that I know what that stuff is, and it makes sense. He wasn't playing mind games with me, I promise you that. You already know I've been through enough bullshit, and there's no way I would just sit back and let *another* man shit all over me just because the sex is good."

Jaz scoffs. "First of all, good sex will make you do a lot of crazy things. Secondly, I don't want you to think that I'm hating on your new boo. I just want you to be cautious of the way he was acting in the beginning. I want to see you happy, and I'll definitely set something of his on fire if he strips you of that happiness. You've been hunting for a good man for a long time, and I just don't want you to be blinded by the idea of having finally found one."

"Blinded? You think I want to be with Rome because I'm desperate?"

"What? Of course not," Jaz answers quickly. "I know you're not desperate, but you have been searching for a long time while having some pretty tragic results. Going through that could make you eager to attach yourself to something. That's all I'm saying. I just want you to be careful."

Wrinkles as deep as ravines scatter across my forehead as I shut off the ignition to my car. Maybe I'm crazy, but it sounded like Jazmine just called me desperate in the nicest way possible. I *finally* find someone who is exactly what I've been looking for, and now I'm being judged by my best friend for it.

"I'm being careful," I snip. "And I'm not *eager to attach myself to something* either. Rome and I like each other, and we've taken the time to talk and work things out. He explained his issues, and now that I know more about who he is and what he has been through, I'm good. There's a lot that you don't know. But don't get it twisted—I'm not with him because I'm desperate. I'm with him because I want to be."

"I know ... I ... I know," Jaz replies, her tone shrouded in sympathy and regret as she senses my attitude through the phone and tries to keep the conversation upright, but it teeters with my growing sense of feeling judged. "Again, I'm *not* saying you're desperate. I know you're not. Look, get yours, Nia. You're a grown woman and you know what you want. You always have, and I'm so glad that you've found what you've been looking for. Just ... this is the last thing I'll say about it ... now that you have the thing you've always wanted, be careful not to get lost in it. Alright? That's it, I'm done. Go have fun, girl, and don't forget to tell me all of the details. I love you, Nia."

A pregnant pause sits between us while I try to force myself to respond. What am I hearing? On one hand, I know that Jaz is concerned for me. We've been best friends our entire lives, and I know she would gladly sneak into Rome's house and murder him in his sleep if he hurt me. But on the other hand ... could it be that she is so used to watching me flail about, constantly complaining about being single that she's uncomfortable now that I'm not? I've been the butt of their jokes for so long. Maybe they thought I'd always be the one they could look at with sympathetic faces while laughing at the joke that was my love life. I don't know for sure, but I'll definitely be tuned in from now on, making sure that my friends are actually happy for me.

"I love you, too, Jaz," I reply joylessly. "I'll talk to you later, okay?"

"Okay. Bye."

When the call ends, I'm not sure how to feel. I don't want to be one of those people who sinks so far into a new relationship that they can no longer see the rest of the world, their vision clouded by their inability to see past their new sense of happiness. But Rome and I are brand new. I should be allowed to go all-out right now, to announce at the top of my lungs that there is hope for people like me, especially after the shitty relationships I've been through. I'm thirty years old. Haven't I earned the right to cheer for myself when I find success and happiness? I've spent countless nights jotting down my frustrations in my diary, writing it all with so much passion and detail that any random sub could find it and use it as a guide for themselves. I've been in the trenches taking grenades for so long that I don't care what anybody else thinks anymore. I earned this moment, and I'm going to embrace it. Fuck what anybody else thinks.

I have to push my annoyance aside as I step out of the car, but once I'm out, it falls off of me like shedded skin. I refuse to be bogged down by the implications of desperation or worry. I'm standing in front of Rome's house. He's my Dom, and there is a whole new world of excitement waiting for me inside.

When I ring the doorbell, Rome rounds a corner down the hall and approaches the door wearing nothing but a black robe and a villainous smirk. We lock eyes through the glass as he comes forward, and I'm already anxious to be on the other side with him. After our little text exchange at the office, all I've been able to think about is the next time I'll have his hands on me, his fingers pressing into my skin and the warmth of his breath in my neck. I've been craving him, dying to repeat what we did in the video he made me touch myself to. Now that I'm here, I'm not even interested in dinner. I don't need to be wined and dined right now. I simply want to be used by him.

The door unlocks and swings open, and the second that there is enough space, Rome's hand comes flying out. He grabs me by the throat and pulls me inside, slamming the door shut and pushing my back against the glass. I struggle to breathe beneath his grip as he squeezes and forces his mouth against mine, lustful passion flowing through us like electrical currents. I melt in his hands, softening and submitting in an instant. Just like that, my guard is down and the rest of the world no longer exists. There is only him.

Rome slowly pulls his mouth away from me, his jaw tight as he stares at me with his predatory gaze. I don't speak. I simply swallow hard and wait for my Dom to command me.

"I've been waiting for this all day," he says in a voice so low it's more like a growl. "That video you sent of your pussy was so unbelievable—it made me so hard I could barely stand it. I fucking loved it ... however, I didn't ask you to send it. I told you to go into the bathroom and use our video to make yourself come. I never said to send me proof." Rome's fingers tighten like a vice. "When I give you instructions, you follow them to a T. You don't deviate or add to them to satisfy yourself. Do you understand?"

I want to smile, but something tells me it wouldn't be a good idea. I'm not upset that he's pressing me about the video. I know he loved it because he said so, but he's also establishing a rule that I must obey as his submissive. When he wants something from me, he'll ask for it. My job is only to do what he says, and I fucking love that he's setting this boundary. Most people don't know it, but this is what BDSM is all about.

Rome loosens his grip on my throat enough for me to answer, "Yes, Sir."

"Good," he says. "Now tell me—who is in charge?"

I smirk at the memory of the first time he asked me this question in my office. It sent fire through my veins then and heats me up even more now that we're together.

"You are, Sir," I answer.

"Say it again," he orders as his fingers slide up my leg and graze my pussy.

I quiver with anticipation. "You're in charge, Sir."

"Good girl," he says before biting his plump lower lip. "Now get down into the playroom. I have big plans for you, my little goddess."

Thirty-Two – Rome

Have I traveled too far down an unknown road? I'm surrounded by new things—experiences, feelings, emotions, fears—and while the scenery is beautiful, I have no idea where I'm going. All I know is that it's all brand new, my heart is racing, I'm terrified, and I don't want to stop driving down this road.

Watching Nia walk away from me on her way to the playroom, fills me with emotions I haven't felt in a long time. Emotions I'm not sure I *should* be feeling. She's so incredible, and I want nothing more than to keep spending my time with her—but am I disrespecting Natalia? I know she is gone, but she'll always be with me, and that doesn't exclude these moments when I'm with someone else who makes me happy. Nikola tries to tell me that this is what she'd want, but the truth is that she would want to be here. She is not gone by choice, so I have a hard time accepting the notion that she would want anything for me other than being her husband, because that is what she wanted up until the moment she left me. I'm so conflicted, but when it comes to Nia, there is no confusion about it. I crave her.

She rounds the corner, descending down the stairs while I go into the kitchen and knock back a shot of liquor to loosen my nerves from the stranglehold of my memories of Natalia. It takes extra effort to push her away today, but adding this shot to the other three helps significantly. By the time the alcohol hits my belly, I feel better, and I head for the basement with newfound resolve.

When I reach the bottom of the stairs, I am pleased to find Nia waiting at the bottom. Each step I descend shows more and more of her, pulling my mouth into a gape the more I see. She sits on her legs, completely naked with her breasts covered by the length of her strawberry brown locs, her eyes seeing only me as I approach. My god she is stunning. Everything about her calls out to every part of me. In the past, I only wanted one thing from the women I slept with. Nia's spell on me makes me desire so much more. Even now, standing over her naked body, I'm not just thinking about how badly I want to fuck her. I want to tear her apart, then ensure that out of the billions of people on this Earth, I am the one who puts her back together again. In repairing her, I heal myself.

Resting her palms on her delicious thighs, she waits silently—completely still, mouth closed, eyes on her Dom. I feel my heart racing, trying to force my body to act quickly to how unreal she looks beneath me, but I restrain myself. I keep a firm grip on my self-control as I crouch in front of her so that we're nose to nose.

"Open your mouth, my little goddess," I instruct. When she obeys, my cock twitches from the rush of blood flowing to it. "Now stick out your tongue." Again, Nia does as she is told. "Good girl. Now stay just like that."

Growing more aroused by the second, I stand up straight and slowly remove my robe in front of Nia, watching her as a string of drool drops from her tongue. I turn around and place my robe on a hook by the stairs, and when I return there is a small pool of spit on the floor in front of her.

"Jesus," I say. "Look at how beautifully disgusting you are, Nia. You sit there, obeying my every command like a good girl, and you drool all over my floor. You want to be a good girl, but deep down you're just a filthy slut for me, aren't you?"

Nia, keeping her tongue dangling from her mouth, slowly nods while maintaining eye contact.

Holy fuck.

"You want to be my whore?" I ask before biting my lower lip.

When she nods this time, I have to bite down even harder to distract myself from my desire to forgo all of this just to be inside of her. I bite so hard I taste blood, but it does the trick. I have to stay in the moment for her.

"You want to be used?"

She nods as spit hangs from her tongue like a long vine reaching for the floor.

"You want me to use that slutty fucking mouth of yours?" She nods again, and the way she keeps her eyes on me is the exact finishing touch my cock needs to reach a rock solid erection.

In a desperate rush to feel the warmth of her mouth, I step forward and slide my cock over her drooling tongue, pushing myself into her mouth until I reach the back of her throat. The sensation is out of this world, sending my mind into a state of euphoria as she engulfs me entirely. I swear, Nia's mouth is my drug. She is my heroin, my ecstasy, my cocaine, and I am truly at her mercy when she begins to suck. I lose control, dropping the desire to talk and command her, and picking up my need to fuck her mouth. She moans as I grab both sides of her head and use her to pleasure myself.

"Oh my god, that mouth," I grunt above her. "That filthy, disgusting, perfect mouth of yours, Nia. I never want to be apart from it."

Nia doesn't respond with words, only groans of satisfaction and eagerness. I use her mouth for five minutes, stroking in and out while giving her no breaks. By the time I'm finished, she is a drooling, wet mess with a face smeared in saliva. I don't give a fuck. I bend down and kiss her hard as if nothing is there. Who would I be if I acted disgusted by something I caused? Yes, she is my filthy little whore, but I am hers, too.

"You're so fucking beautiful when you're disgusting for me," I tell her when I pull away, although the distance makes me yearn to yank her close again. "All I want is to be inside of you, and I can't take it anymore. There was so much more I had in mind when I opened the door and saw you standing there in that perfect fucking way that you do, but you've ruined it now. I need to feel how wet you are, and I can't wait any longer. Now crawl your disgusting little ass over to that bed and keep your tongue out like the slut you are. Drool the entire way so that I have to clean up after you. Do it now."

Nia pants as I take a step back to let her start her journey to the bed on all fours. She turns around and begins, her bare ass pointed back at me, enticing me, begging me to mount her from behind instead of letting her go. The urge is so strong that I have no choice but to fist my cock as I watch her crawling away. She turns around to look at me, but I don't stop. I want her to see it. I need her to know how insane she makes me. I see the smirk slowly forming on her lips before she turns back around, tongue out as she crawls to the bed and stops when she reaches it.

"Good little whore," I say as I walk over to the bed with her. "Now climb on and stay on all fours. I want that ass so high in the air it reaches the fucking ceiling. I'm about to use your tight little hole."

While Nia puts her face down on the bed and her ass up in the air, I reach into the nightstand and pull out a condom, tearing off the wrapper and sheathing my cock as quickly as I can, because waiting to be inside of her is a new form of torture. As soon as I have it stretched over my length, I step close, slap Nia across the ass, and slide inside.

"Oh, fuck," she moans, and I see her fist the sheets as soon as I start fucking her.

"Yes. This is what I have been in need of all day," I say. "I've needed your pussy, my little goddess. I've craved it. Yearned for it. Ached to be inside of you. The need hurt my stomach like hunger pangs, and now that I'm here, I don't ever want to stop."

"Don't stop, Sir," she pleads as I pound her relentlessly.

"I won't. Not until your tight pussy is completely stretched out."

"Yes! Ruin my fucking hole. Stretch me all the way out, Sir. Use me."

"I'm going to use you," I reply, gripping her hips so tight I know it must hurt. Good. In our world, pain is pleasure. "Whose whore are you?"

"I'm yours," Nia responds loudly. "I'm your whore, Sir."

"Say it again," I demand, smacking her ass.

"I'm your whore."

"Again," I repeat with another slap of her ass, this one causing her skin to immediately redden. Fuck yes.

"I'm your fucking whore, Sir," Nia screams.

"You're fucking right. My perfect, filthy, little whore. Your only use is your holes."

"Yes. My only use is my holes," she agrees, just as lost in the moment as I am. "Please use my holes, Sir. I am yours."

I don't hold back an ounce of strength as I pummel Nia's tight pussy until I feel an orgasm prodding me from inside. As it builds, I go all-out, smacking her ass again before squeezing her hips with enough strength to pop the blood vessels beneath her skin. She lets out a painful yelp followed by a moan of pleasure, then the floodgates open.

"Sir ... can I please come for you?" she begs.

I don't have it in me to deny her and keep going. Just like her, I'm at the edge of my own cliff, and the momentum carries me forward until I am falling with her.

"Come for me, my little goddess," I say. "Come *with* me."

The next sixty seconds are filled with indistinguishable sounds—moans, groans, grunts, and howls fill the air and bounce off one another as Nia and I come together, our bliss in perfect sync. Our bodies vibrate as our respective orgasms force us into seizures that make us both collapse onto the bed in a heap, our arms and legs criss-crossing over each other. We pant up at the ceiling, sweat covering our bodies and sinking into the sheets.

"Oh, my fucking god," Nia exclaims with closed eyes.

"That was perfect," I say. "You ... Nia ... you're perfect."

When I first started the compliment, I meant for it to be part of the scene, switching from degradation to praise now that I'm satisfied. But as the last word comes out of my mouth, I realize that it's something different, and I'm not sure if Nia even catches it.

Perfect. She is perfect, and that's not just dirty talk. I mean it when I say it.

I once told Nikola and Isabella that it would take perfection for me to even begin thinking about settling down with anyone. Isabella laughed and the three of us talked about it as if it would never happen, a longshot at best. But to my utter surprise, it has already happened. She's already here. Somehow, without being in search of it, I've found perfection.

Cubic Zirconia

Dear Diary,

I can't even begin to explain how well things have been going. It's almost too good to be true. Rome and I have been together going on three months now, and I couldn't possibly be happier. It finally happened. After all of my searching and going through horrible date after horrible date, crying rivers of tears that felt endless and thinking I would end up either alone or having to settle, I've finally found a Dom who is worthy of my submission.

Over the past few months, Rome and I have grown together so much. He's unbelievably considerate and always taking care of me. He knows that after he tears me apart, I depend on him to mend me, and he never fails. Sometimes, after specifically brutal scenes, he continues to shower me with love and affection for days, doing his absolute best to ensure my comfort. I honestly can't get enough of him, which is why I go out of my way to spend as much time with him as I possibly can. It almost feels like I'm making up for all of the time I lost while I was floating on my back atop a hopeless sea of immature, unavailable, undeserving men. I'm not drifting away anymore. I've landed. I've found a home.

Not too long ago, I felt like I was searching for BigFoot. I was trudging through the woods with my magnifying glass, examining every bit of evidence left by some guy claiming he was the one. I followed countless leads and got my hopes up far too many times, only to realize I was being led on by a hoax—another man pretending to be something he is not, wearing the suit of something extraordinary only for it to fall apart under scrutiny.

I started to believe that I would never find him—that the type of happiness that I was in search of didn't actually exist. What I wanted was only in books or horrible book-to-movie adaptations with terrible actors. My obsession with finding him kept me going, but the lack of results shook my confidence like a nine on the Richter scale. I felt hopeless and was ready to give up the hunt, assuming my Dom really was just a mythical creature that didn't exist in reality.

But then we stumbled upon each other. Our worlds collided, melded together, and showed me that everything I was ready to give up on was actually real. No one else believed that he existed, but they were all wrong. I knew he was out there waiting for me to find him. And the best part of it all is knowing that this creature that no one believed was real is far more beautiful than anyone could have imagined. All of the legends couldn't hold a candle to reality. He does exist. I did find him. And now he is mine.

Thirty-Three

"Hey, Michael just got off the grill and we're about to sit down and eat while we drink a little bit. Jeremiah is on his way over and I just wanted to reach out to see if you could make it."

I hear the pleading in Jaz's voice. She wants me to come over and hang out with the crew just like we used to do. I have so many memories of sitting on her and Michael's couch with a glass of wine in my hand, the two of them connected at the hip while Jeremiah sat on a chair by himself. We would talk about so much, but there was never a night when the topic of conversation didn't shift to me and my love life at some point. The embarrassing change of pace would ultimately be followed by a toast and a shot, honoring how my life was a train wreck being watched in real time. Then we would go back to laughing and acting like we didn't just spill my business out in the streets for all to gawk at. It has happened so many times that I could predict at what point in the night the toast would take place, and have time to fix my makeup in the bathroom to hide the flushing red of my cheeks. I love my friends dearly, but now that I have Rome, I'm not interested in being talked about or toasted to. Rome and I will toast to us on our own time, and the rest of the world doesn't have to take a shot for us. We're good.

"Umm," I start, and I hear Jaz suck her teeth. My constant rain checks might be starting to annoy her, but she just doesn't understand. How could she? She has had Michael for so long. "I'm sorry, Jaz, but I'm not going to be able to make it. Rome invited me over, and I guess he has something planned. I'm already at his house just waiting for him to get out of the shower."

There's a brief moment of silence over the phone as if someone died, before Jaz sighs.

"Oh. You're already at his house," she says, totally devoid of her usual joy. "Here I was thinking that I could catch you right after work so you could change into something comfy and come right over."

"Nah, I left the office and came straight here," I reply.

Another moment of silence.

"Alright ... okay ... that's cool. Well, we all hope that we get to see you sometime soon," she says. "I feel like it has been a minute since we hung out. Jeremiah and Gerald are getting serious now, too, and he has been talking about all of us meeting him. We were sort of hoping we could all get together and meet his man at the same time that we meet yours. I know you're in this crazy honeymoon phase, but don't forget about us, Nia."

Now it's my turn to suck my teeth, but I make sure my tone isn't as harsh as my emotional reaction is. "I'm not forgetting about y'all. We just have really bad luck with our timing. It seems that every time you and Michael want me to come over, Rome and I have already made plans. I'm not doing it on purpose."

"Are you sure? Because Jeremiah says you still have to hide your relationship from everyone at your office. Maybe it's becoming a habit to keep it all under wraps. But we're your friends, girl. You don't have to hide from us."

"I'm *not* hiding," I snip, unable to keep my annoyance from leaking into my voice this time. "Look, I don't expect you to understand since you've had your happily ever after for so long, but mine is brand new and it consumes my time. I'm not doing anything on purpose or trying to spend less time with you, and I know you're used to me being able to just pick up and run over there whenever you call because I never used to have anything going on. I was the poor single friend whose love life was a circus to be laughed at, but that's over now, and I'm not going to let anything stand in the way of what Rome and I are developing. So, please don't take it personally when I can't just come running whenever you call."

"Nia," Jaz responds, but it almost sounds like a question—like my words and voice don't actually go together. "Okay, I don't know what's going on, but you know that I'm happy for you. You can't be mad at me for wanting to hang out with my best friend. I just miss you, that's all. But I understand what this means to you, so you go enjoy your night with Rome, and give me a call whenever you want. Okay?"

"Whenever I want? What's that supposed to mean?"

Another sigh, this one long and stuffed full of exasperation.

"Nothing, Nia. Have a good night. Talk to you later."

"Yeah ... okay, I'll talk to—" I'm cut off by the sound of the call coming to an abrupt end. She hung up.

What the hell just happened? Am I doing something wrong, or is my best friend expecting me to remain exactly the same way that she has always known me to be, when my life has changed too much for that? I understood all the times I called her over the years, hoping we could hang out, but she and Michael had something going on. I didn't knock her when she got married and I didn't get to see her for weeks afterward. I understood. So why can't she do the same for me? I'm finally happily occupied, and she wants me to still be single and free. Well, I'm not, so they're just going to have to adapt to the new world.

"Everything okay?"

Rome steps out of the bathroom wearing a white tank top and black workout pants, his hair slicked back as the hair on his chest glistens in the light. His lust-inducing fragrance wafts out of the bathroom as he steps out looking like a god, water soaking his shirt and making it stick to his stomach. My eyes immediately fall to his abs, somehow still visible through the fabric of his wet shirt. I was upset before he opened the door and stepped out, but his presence pushes it all back like a bodyguard protecting his most cherished asset.

I swallow hard and let out a long sigh just trying to steady myself. "Umm, yeah. It's fine. I was just talking to Jaz on the phone."

Rome raises an eyebrow as he walks over to the bed and lowers himself onto the front edge. "And is everything okay with her? You haven't mentioned her much lately."

I reach across the bed and rub the top of his hand. "Thank you for caring about my friends," I say with a small smile. "And I don't know if everything is okay or not, but she and I will talk and work it out. She just wants more from me than I'm able to give right now."

"I understand that," Rome says, nodding a long. "But I hope it's not because of our relationship."

"Well," I say, dragging it out as I shrug. "It sort of is. Jaz has been my best friend my entire life, and she wants to be in on everything that happens with me, and usually I'm willing to let her, but it's different now. I've always been the single friend with infinite time on my hands because I didn't have anyone to do anything with, while she was living her best life with her husband. Now that I'm not as free, it seems to have shaken our foundation a bit. But she's still trying. She even mentioned something about wanting to meet you."

Rome clears his throat and sits up straighter. "She wants to meet me?"

"Yeah. Would you want to meet my friends?"

"Umm, sure," he says, sounding anything but. "Yeah ... we would just have to schedule a time to do it. Yeah ... that'd be, uhh ... yeah, that'd be great."

"You sure about that, Stuttering Stanley?" I say with furrowed brows and a forced playful smile.

Rome climbs all the way onto the bed and throws his arms around me, knocking me back against the headboard. "Of course I am. I would love to meet your friends. But right now I'm thinking about you. I have plans for tonight."

"Oh, is that right?" I ask rhetorically. "Do those plans involve us going downstairs?"

Rome nuzzles my neck, then says, "Actually, no. As much as I would love to take you into the playroom and tie you up, I think I just want to reward you for being so incredible. So, when I invited you over tonight, it wasn't to fuck you. It was to pamper you."

"Pamper me? You know I'm not into ABDL."

Rome laughs. "Not *pampers*. I want to pamper you. You know? I want to take care of you. Massage your back. Massage your feet. Rub your shoulders. Bring you wine. I just want you to feel good and taken care of with no strings attached. Sex is off the table."

"It's *off the table*?" I blurt out with wide, crazy eyes. "You can't do that."

Rome's eyebrows jump through the roof. "Oh, I absolutely can. Because ... who's in charge?"

I smile like the devil himself. "You are, Sir."

"And I can do whatever the hell I want to you, can't I?"

"Absolutely," I answer, suddenly feeling like I want to forgo the pampering and swap it out for bondage and orgasms.

Rome grins. "That's right. Now take off everything but your bra and panties, and lay on your stomach."

As a tsunami wave of bliss washes over my heart, I forget all about my tense conversation with Jaz, and I smile. "Yes, Sir."

Thirty-Four

"Tell me how it feels. You like that?"

"Oh, my god. That feels so good. I love it."

"Good girl. Just relax and let me take care of you."

"I'm all yours, Sir."

Rome's fingers press into my skin, pushing all of my stress away. The weight of the world is lifted with each stroke of his fingers, swirling circles on my back that feel like sorcery being weaved against my skin. My hands are tucked beneath my face as I lay on my stomach. Rome straddles my backside with a bottle of massage oil resting next to his leg. True to his word, he hasn't tried to initiate sex, although I'd be more than happy to engage. But he really is all about me tonight. Of all the men I have dated, none of them have ever said that a night should be dedicated to me. It's just another box that Rome has checked off that I didn't even know existed.

"So, now that I've got you all to myself," he says, his deep voice massaging my ears just as much as his fingers on my back. "I wanted to tell you that I think you're doing a fantastic job on the Golden Diamond campaign. The billboards you and your team came up with have been Earth-stopping. Every time I pass one on the highway, it draws my attention."

"Mmm, thank you," I say, my eyes closed as I continue tumbling into the nirvana that is this massage. "I'm practically just adjusting Jeremiah's work. He's the genius behind it all and deserves a raise."

Rome chuckles. "I'll be sure to consider that when the time comes. Admittedly, I'd hate to break up the dynamic duo that you two are together. Even Sierra, who we both know isn't known for handing out compliments, has said that you are doing a great job."

"Wow. Sierra? I never would've thought that. I get a brand new evil glare from her every single day. Hell, everyone does at this point. She hands them out every morning like donuts for the office."

"Oh my god," Rome says behind a laugh. "Has she always been that way?"

"Honestly, I don't even remember," I tell him. "When Mr. Thomas and his sons were there, I think she was better. I remember her smiling from time to time, although she was always driven to succeed and had a personality as cold as a Philly winter. It wasn't until Mr. Thomas left and didn't give the CMO position to her. I think that's when I noticed the change. It was obvious that she was offended about being passed over, and she held onto that feeling even after finding out that he needed to sell Sandcastle instead of just stepping down. Although it was a money move for Mr. Thomas, not being promoted bothered her. Now she's the office evil stepmother, while you're the firm but kind-hearted dad that everyone looks up to and wants to satisfy."

"Oh, is that what I've become? The dad?"

"Well, I'm personally not big on the 'Daddy' thing, but I'm willing to go there if you want."

"Between the pampers and daddy, I think I'm good. Sir works just fine for me, but only you. I don't need anybody from the office catching on to the title."

"Thank goodness."

We laugh together as a thought bubble expands in my mind.

"Speaking of the office," I begin as Rome slides his hands up my back and wraps his fingers around the base of my neck. "We've done a great job of keeping our little secret from everyone at Sandcastle."

"Everyone except Jeremiah," Rome interjects playfully.

"Well, of course. He's one of the besties, and the besties get to know everything. You don't have a best friend that you share everything with?"

"I do," he answers. "Nikola and his wife Isabella are the people I'm closest to now, but we're not as close as we used to be. When my father died I put space between us because seeing them reminded me of everything I'd lost. Now that I'm doing better I try to spend more time with them."

"Good. Everyone needs friends they can talk to, especially when the going gets tough. Have you told your friends about me?"

Rome hesitates a moment. Even his hands stop moving briefly before starting up again.

"I've told Nikola a little about you," he replies.

"Only a little? We've been together almost three months. Why only a little?" I ask. I don't like the tension I feel building up in my neck, especially after Rome just massaged all of it away over the last thirty minutes.

"I'm just private," he answers. "The fact that I've told him about you at all speaks to how much I like you, Nia. Since my dad died, I haven't told anyone a thing about my personal life. I'm taking baby steps, but that doesn't mean that I'm not walking."

As the pace and strength return to Rome's hands, I try to force myself to relax again. Over our time together, he hasn't given me any reason to believe that he isn't all-in for us. He has been insanely considerate while wielding his Dominance at the perfect place and time. He's surprisingly funny and, as far as I can tell, is fully dedicated to the success of our relationship. I know that all of this is true. So why do I have a nagging feeling that I'm missing something?

He doesn't talk much about his parents. He doesn't talk about his friends and hasn't offered to introduce me, and he doesn't talk about his wife who died. These are the most intimate parts of him, but they seem to be under lock and key and guarded by rabid dogs. I want access to all of Rome, even the part of him that hurts the most, but it's crystal clear that he is not ready to show me what he keeps pushed back into the darkness. There is a part of me that understands. Pain and trauma are not easy things to divulge to others. But there is another part of me—a bigger part—that wants to know what that means.

Sensing tightness in his posture, I choose not to keep pushing about his friends. I'm sure he'll tell me everything in time. But when it comes to work, there is still the underlying worry about people finding out.

"What about Sandcastle?" I ask. "I know you're private, but the longer we're together the more likely it is that someone other than Jeremiah will learn about us. Do you have a plan in place in case that happens?"

Rome's hands spread out away from my neck and move to my shoulders. "I haven't given it much thought, to be honest. Everything has been fine and I don't see that changing as long as we stay careful."

"So that's it? Just keep the secret going? You don't think it might be time to let people know now that we've been together for a little while?"

"Not really," he replies immediately. "Look, we're happy, right?"

"I think so," I answer. "I know *I* am."

"Good. I am, too. I really like what we have and I don't want to do anything to ruin it. So, I'm not worried about changing course or giving people information that doesn't even involve them. What difference does it make if they know or not? Even if they knew, nothing would change between us. So why worry about it? Why worry about them?"

When I don't answer, Rome finishes the massage and climbs off of me, lying down beside me with his face flat on the bed.

"Let's not worry about the office," he says with the tip of his nose pressed up against mine. "Work is stress, and that's the last thing I want creeping in here with us tonight. I want a smile on your face and your muscles relaxed. I want joy in your heart and no outside thoughts getting in. You can think about other things tomorrow, but for now I want to know what's your favorite movie."

Looking into Rome's eyes, I'm torn. I hear what he's saying, and while it all sounds good, there's a rock in my stomach that is becoming increasingly more difficult to ignore. "Umm, I love *How to Lose a Guy in Ten Days.*

Rome smiles. "Perfect. Then let's get you cleaned up and tucked into a robe. I'll bring a bottle of wine and massage your feet while we watch *How to Lose a Guy in Ten Days.*"

He kisses me on the cheek before hopping off the bed, and while I'm excited for everything he just said, my brain latches onto something he said and doesn't let go. Until now, I wasn't concerned about people knowing about us. It wasn't something I was fixated on, staring off into space wondering when this monumental thing was finally going to happen. I was fine with our setup, but something clicked tonight. Amidst all the feelings of joy, relaxation, and satisfaction that Rome bestowed upon me, there's something that doesn't make sense.

What difference does it make if they know or not? Even if they knew, nothing would change between us. So why worry about it? Why worry about them?

It keeps repeating in my head, even as I get up to allow Rome to wipe the oil off of my back with a large towel. If he and I will remain the same regardless of who knows about us, then why is he so concerned about other people finding out? He asked the questions himself, and didn't understand that they worked against his argument to keep us a secret. So, as the movie comes on and Rome pours red wine into a crystal glass for me, I sit back against the headboard and repeat the three questions over and over again. The only change is that I'm asking them from the side of the argument that supports us being out in the open instead of hiding, and that makes all the difference in the world.

What difference does it make if they know or not? Even if they knew, nothing would change between us. So why worry about it? Why worry about them?

Thirty-Five

"This is great. Now all we need to do is get with Jackie and have her start working on the social media advertisements, and we'll be ahead of schedule."

Jeremiah stands behind me looking over my shoulder at another cardboard mockup of a billboard we plan to run for the Golden Diamond campaign. Now that construction for the casino is well underway, we need to get going on ad placements on the internet so that people outside of Philly can hear about what we've got coming. As usual, Jeremiah has done a phenomenal job creating another billboard that will catch people's attention as much as his savvy fashion.

"Jackie? You know I can't stand her," Jeremiah huffs, shaking his head as he steps to the front of my desk, his white button up completely devoid of wrinkles like he just stepped out of the dry cleaners.

I scoff as I nod in agreement. "Nobody likes her, but if we get this done now, I don't have to worry about Sierra coming in here and asking me for it. We can beat her to the punch, and I can rest easier at night knowing I made her feel dumb for requesting something we've already finished."

Jeremiah nods, but I see the irritation in his eyes. "Fine, whatever. But it's just after lunch time, and if I throw up everything I ate because Jackie's breath is in there smelling like boiled bologna, I absolutely am going to blame you."

"That's fair," I reply with a laugh. "Just hold your breath as you give her the design."

"Girl, you're trying to make me pass out."

"Is it not worth it to avoid her breath?"

"Ugh. You're the worst," Jeremiah says, his annoyance finally giving way to his smile. "Anyway, how are things going for you? How is sleeping with the boss treating you? Good still?"

I push my locs back over my shoulder as I glance outside my door to make sure no one is near. Simon and Sierra stand over by the bullpen, but I think they're far enough away to have this discussion as long as I speak quietly.

"It's good," I answer in nearly a whisper. "I spent the night at his place again last night."

"Oh, so then you're exhausted," Jeremiah quips.

"Actually, I'm not. We didn't get into anything like that. He gave me a back massage, followed by a shoulder massage, followed by a foot massage as we watched *How to Lose a Guy in Ten Days* and drank wine. Then I fell asleep in his arms and woke up to the smell of bacon and eggs coming from the kitchen. We ate the breakfast he made for us and came to work—in separate vehicles of course. It was an amazing night that didn't need sex."

Jeremiah doesn't respond. His eyes bore into me without even blinking, making him look like a well-dressed mannequin. He stares at me for so long that I get nervous he might actually be stuck.

"Did you just glitch to death?" I joke.

"Shut up," he finally says, snapping out of it. "You spent the night getting *massaged*? Are you kidding me? That man down the hall—that unfairly attractive man sitting in the office over there—ties you up in his playroom and makes you orgasm over and over again regularly, and then pampers you all night? Are you *freaking* kidding me, Nia?"

"Damn," I exclaim with a frown and furrowed brows. "What's wrong with that?"

"Your life is perfect and mine isn't, that's what's wrong with it," Jeremiah says, screaming and whispering at the same time. "You're living the goddamn dream. Do you know that? What you just told me doesn't even sound real. That shit sounds like Nasir Booker wrote it."

My smile is wide and proud as I lean back in my chair and put my hands behind my head like I'm relaxing on a beach. "I can't help it if my life is so dope that it sounds like fiction. That's what happens when you don't settle for the mediocrity that runs rampant in the dating pool. I spent enough time kissing frogs. Now I have a kinky prince. Don't hate."

"No, I do," he fires back. "I hate you. I love you and I'm happy for you, but I hate you. Is that why you couldn't come to Jaz's? You were too busy getting rubbed down?"

I roll my eyes as I sit up straight, the memory of my conversation with Jaz returning to the front of my mind and obliterating my good mood.

"Don't start," I tell Jeremiah. "You sound just like Jaz."

"Girl, she was clearly pissed last night," he explains. "She didn't say much, but we all know that face Jaz gets when she's upset. It was on full display."

"Ugh, whatever. I can't control how Jaz feels, but hating on me for having a man is not what I expected from my best friend since I was seven."

"I don't think she's hating," Jeremiah says. "I just think she's not used to this and she misses having you around."

"I'll still be around, but we're just getting underway and it's still a secret from most people. Once we're out in the open and I introduce him to her and Michael, then we'll come hang out together. But the days of poor old Nia sitting in the corner all alone, scrolling FET while the couples mingle are over, and I don't intend on going back to that. So, she's just going to have to get over it."

"Well, personally, I think you should talk to her. Don't let this fester and grow into a monster that eats your friendship."

I let out an exasperated sigh as I nod, knowing that Jeremiah is right, but also not wanting to even get into the conversation with Jaz about all of this. Although I've made the point before, I didn't require a conversation about our friendship when she married Michael. I was simply there for her and was patient as she dived into her marriage and swam through her honeymoon phase. I never made their relationship about me even when they were dating and I was still heartbreakingly single. All I want is the same courtesy, and not getting it is starting to rub my nerves raw.

"I guess so," I force myself to say, but before I can push anymore words through the filter before they reach my mouth, I see Rome standing by the bullpen looking directly at me. When he sees that he has my attention, he motions for me to follow him.

"I'll figure something out," I say to Jeremiah as I stand, watching as Rome turns and goes into the breakroom. "Anyway, talk to Jackie and let me know when she's rolling on the online placements."

Jeremiah nods before walking out of the office and going straight into Jackie's. Once he's gone, I speed walk through the bullpen, brushing past a sour-faced Sierra on my way to the breakroom. I place my hand on the knob and turn around to make sure no one is coming, then I step inside. The second the door closes behind me, Rome pulls me over to him, wraps me in his arms, and kisses me like he couldn't stand to be apart from me a second longer.

His tongue presses against mine as he kisses me, creating pure lust out of thin air and making me forget that we're in the breakroom at work. It takes a few reckless seconds for us to realize what we're doing before Rome takes a hesitant step back.

"Sorry," he says, but his grin suggests otherwise. "I just really needed that. I've spent all day talking about budgets for each campaign, and I desperately needed something to re-energize me. Turns out, you're just the jolt I needed, my little goddess."

I release a long sigh, doing my best not to focus on his lips or his chiseled jaw. "You shouldn't call me that here. It makes me forget that there are public indecency laws."

"Oh? You know I like having you on edge, so maybe I'll just keep doing it," Rome says.

"Ugh. Always the tease," I say. "Anyway, we shouldn't stay in here long. I need to get back out there and make sure Jackie starts the social media placements and doesn't give Jeremiah any shit for asking. Your place after work tonight?"

Rome takes my hand in his and pulls me close. "Absolutely, and it's not getting here fast enough."

"I agree," I reply, just before we kiss again. I maintain control this time, pulling away before my mind wanders off too far. "Okay, I'll see you later."

Rome squeezes my hand as I try to open the door, making me giggle like a schoolgirl. "Okay. *Ciao*."

I should be embarrassed by how uncontrollably wide my smile is, but I can't help it as I pull the door open and step out. However, my smile vanishes the second I step over the threshold and bump directly into Sierra.

She stands just outside the breakroom, only inches from the door with a disgusted and angry look on her face, and I can see it in her eyes that something major just happened.

"Hey," I say, hoping she'll just greet me like normal and move on, but I have never had that kind of luck.

"I bet you thought none of us would ever find out, huh?" she asks, and icicles immediately form on my heart.

"What?" I reply, but I know it's pointless.

"Don't play stupid with me," she says, making no effort whatsoever to keep her voice down. "I saw the way you rushed into the breakroom after Rome went in there, and I had a gut feeling that if I just happened to glance through the window in the door that I would see something that wasn't meant for my eyes. Turns out my intuition was right. I saw you, Nia. Just now. I saw you kissing Rome in the breakroom."

Thirty-Six

My vision zooms out as the world zooms in, and I'm suddenly off balance. As I stand at the edge of the bullpen with Sierra staring straight at me, I can hear the blood flowing through my veins as my heart pounds like a sledgehammer driving a spike. I don't know what to say. How do I respond to this? For nearly three months we've kept this a secret, and all of it is going up in flames in the blink of an eye. Do I deny it? Act indifferent? Be dismissive? A hundred different flimsy solutions play out in my head, but only one word manages to make it to my lips.

"What?" I say, practically whimpering in the face of Sierra's icy glare.

"Don't play dumb, Nia," she replies, and it's clear that she will not be doing me the favor of whispering to protect my privacy. "I saw you, and I always knew that it would come to this. I saw the way you would stare at him in meetings, drooling all over yourself when he would speak, clutching your fucking pearls when he would say something in Italian. You did a terrible job of hiding how badly you wanted to sleep with him, and now the truth has come to the light."

"Sierra, it's not what you think," I say, trying to force myself to say words that actually make sense, but being caught red handed has me reeling.

"Oh, it's not what I think? You sure about that?" Sierra keeps firing, quickly turning the office into a warzone. "Because what I think is that you've wanted to sleep with Rome since the moment he arrived here. I think you've been lusting after him like a teenager crushing on a rockstar this entire time, and there was some private moment where you took the opportunity to seduce him, and it worked. He is a man after all. Luckily for you, he's single. There's no wife at home wondering why her husband has suddenly lost interest, but that doesn't absolve you. The rest of us are in here trying to get by on our merit, but you figured you could skip the line by shaking your ass and flashing your tits every day."

"Flashing my tits?" I say with a frown as I look down at my white top that reveals no cleavage whatsoever.

"Yeah, that's right. Your tits. Maybe no one else in here noticed, but I did, and I think this is sickening," Sierra goes on. "You should be ashamed of yourself—using your body to get ahead while the rest of us work our asses off to get Rome's attention. If I had the power to, I would fire you right here, right now. In fact, had Mr. Thomas chosen me to replace him, I would have fired you on the spot. Luckily for you, that's not within my responsibility, but now that everyone knows the kind of shameless person you are, maybe you'll just do us all a favor and quit."

With wide eyes, I slowly look around the room and find every person employed at Sandcastle staring at us. We are the trainwreck that no one can pull their gaze away from, and I don't know if it's embarrassment, the shock of being caught, or the fact that Sierra is my superior, but my emotions come to a boil like water in a pot. I want to lash out to defend myself from the insanity of Sierra's accusations about my tits and inability to hide how I felt about Rome. I want to tell her to go fuck herself because I don't let anybody talk to me the way she just did. I want to quit my job, because disrespect is never allowed from a superior—I don't give a fuck how long I've worked here. But I don't do any of those things. Instead, my boiling emotions result in them spilling over in the form of stinging tears sliding down my face.

I hate crying in general, but I loathe doing it in front of other people. I'm not some weak little girl who can't keep herself together. I'm much more powerful than the submissive title gives me credit for, but I'm also human, and the feeling of being overwhelmed is crippling to almost anybody. So I can't speak right now, even as Jeremiah pleads with me through his shocked expression, waiting for me to snap out of it and go off on Sierra for calling me out in front of everyone. I can't. I just lower my eyes to the floor and let the tears fall. They come like raindrops splattering at my feet, and I'm frozen in that position until I hear the sound of the breakroom door opening.

"What the hell do you think you're doing?"

Rome's voice booms into the room like a jet engine, and it is not the same soothing voice I just heard when we were kissing a few minutes ago. This version of Rome's voice is filled with hot coals and spewing fire with each word. At the sound of it, Sierra takes a step back like she might actually flee the scene.

"Umm, I'm not ... I saw you two kissing in there," she says after clearing her throat.

I manage to look up from the floor and witness the moment Sierra pulls her shoulders back and straightens her spine, preparing for a war with Rome.

He takes a step forward, letting the breakroom door close behind him, and stares at Sierra with a look that would certainly make her heart stop if looks could kill.

"So that means you can use your position as VP to belittle a subordinate?" he asks in a quiet roar.

"Well ... no, but this is unacceptable from her ... and you," Sierra says.

Audible gasps spread through the bullpen from the front to the back as Rome's eyebrows raise. I've never seen him angry before. None of us have, and I have a feeling that we never will again after today because the look on his face right now will be avoided at all costs.

"Unacceptable," Rome says, repeating Sierra's word. "I find that awfully ironic coming from you, Sierra. You have the nerve to stand here berating Nia when she wasn't the first person in this office to show interest in me. You were."

Another round of gasps turns our office into the audience of the Jerry Springer show, and my eyes enlarge so wide I think they'll pop out of my head. What did he just say? Clearly he is speaking facts, because Sierra takes another step back, hoping distance will protect her from the truth.

"If there is one thing that annoys me more than a superior abusing their power," Rome goes on, "it's a hypocrite. On only my second day in the office, you asked me out to drinks, and I told you I wasn't interested. That's when you put your hand on top of mine and told me that I'd be interested if I got to know you better. I snatched my hand away, and your mood soured permanently. Everyone in this office knows you haven't been the same since I arrived, even Nia herself questioned what changed in you. But no one knew that you came onto me because I did you the favor of keeping that little situation private out of respect and professionalism. Now, you refuse to provide that courtesy to Nia because I didn't turn *her* down. You've been broadcasting your frustration for the entire company to see, talking down to Nia every chance you get ... out of jealousy."

As my tears dry up, Sierra's eyes dampen like we've traded places. I don't even know what to say as I watch her swallow hard and look around the room, suddenly very concerned with the prying eyes around us. Just like me, she doesn't know what to say.

She clearly thought that time would protect her from what she had done, and the fact that Rome didn't fire her or spread rumors gave her confidence that this would never come out. She should have been thanking Rome for keeping her secret, but instead she was angered by the fact that I was into him, and that anger was doused in gasoline when he began to show interest in me, too.

When the tables turn, they *fucking turn*.

As Sierra stands there silently, her eyes misting over, Rome faces the onlooking bullpen with a stern expression. He looks like a father who is disappointed in his children for their behavior, and no one moves a muscle as he begins to address us all.

"Everybody listen to me right now," he starts, his eyes darting from person to person. "*This* is not what we will become. Sandcastle will not descend into a rumor mill of jealousy, hypocrisy, nosiness, and disrespect. Admittedly, I've tried to keep my relationship with Nia a secret from you all, specifically for this reason. It's not any of your business what she or I do in our private time or in our personal lives. All that matters to you all is that our relationship doesn't hinder the progress and business of this office. None of you can say that you've witnessed Nia getting special treatment from me, and if you're assuming she got the Golden Diamond account out of favoritism, you'd be dead wrong. Nia and I were not dating at the time of the pitch wars. She simply outdid everyone else with a pitch that was so good that she acquired the client. If the pitch wasn't good, we would have never been chosen to represent Nix Malone and his casino. So, you can be mad and make an incorrect assumption if you want to, but you can't deny the results of her pitch to the client.

"I don't care if any of you are dating someone from the office. It's not my business. All I care about is whether or not Sandcastle can grow and prosper with the people standing in this room right now. This isn't high school. So, if you're interested in gossip, rumors, and talking about your coworkers' private lives, please see yourself out right now. I don't care what position you hold or how much you get paid. If you're more concerned about who the boss is sleeping with than you are with your work, the door is behind you. Please walk through it and don't come back. Our goal is to do our jobs and grow this company, ascending it to heights it has never reached before. Nia has taken a huge step in making that happen with her work with Golden Diamond. How many of you can say the same for yourselves?"

When no one answers, Rome finishes.

"So, here is how we'll end this fiasco. Yes, Nia and I are together. We care about each other deeply, and as far as our future is concerned, I don't see an end in sight. So get used to it. We are together. We're a couple ... and it will never affect our work. I advise you," he turns to Sierra, "*all of you*—not to let it affect yours. I don't ever want to have to talk about this again. If I do, you won't have to worry about walking through the exit on your own, because I will gladly push you out. Any questions?"

As expected, no one says a word. The only sounds are breathing and the air conditioner as Rome turns on his heel, steps close to me, and kisses me softly on the cheek in front of everyone. I watch in astonishment as he starts to walk away, brushing shoulders with a stunned Sierra. But before he goes, he turns to her and says one last thing.

"Your decision is easy," he whispers to her. "Either apologize and get your shit together ... or resign. Choosing neither will not be allowed, and you have until the end of the day to make your choice. If you can't decide, I'll take your lack of a response as your formal resignation."

A tear slides down Sierra's cheek as Rome doesn't even give her time to respond before walking away, leaving our entire world in a daze, and my heart dancing.

Thirty-Seven

"What happened today was insane," Jeremiah whispers to me as everyone starts to filter out of the building.

Tension sits heavily in the air like smog, made thicker by awkward silence as the day comes to an end and everyone starts their commute home. Only a couple of hours ago, Sierra saw Rome and I kissing in the breakroom and decided to confront me in front of everyone. She was in her bag with her putdowns, clearly releasing built up anger toward me for showing interest in Rome, only for us to find out that she was into him before anyone else even had a chance to be. Rome stepped out of the breakroom like a knight ready to defend his queen, and Sierra hasn't made eye contact with anyone since. Today was *a day*. Now that it's over, I desperately want to speak with Rome about what happened—about what he said regarding us.

"Insane is an understatement," I reply to Jeremiah. "Did you see how fast she left the building? Usually Sierra is one of the last people out the door, but she was speed walking today."

"Bitch was on her high horse for sure, and rode that thing out of here," Jeremiah jokes, laughing at himself. "I couldn't believe she went at you like that, and you just had to stand there and take it. I felt so bad for you, but then your bodyguard came out the door like Kevin Costner protecting Whitney. Girl, my jaw was on the floor. He snapped."

"He most definitely did," I reply, smiling at the memory of how it all went down. "Then he used it as a moment to talk to everyone about minding their own business."

Jeremiah grins at me so hard that even his eyes are smiling. "I know you loved that shit. That man defended you and checked the entire office for you. I may not be up on the ins and outs of BDSM, but that seemed very dominant to me."

I try to push my grin away but end up pursing my lips instead. "Yes, it was."

I look into Rome's office and see that he's still seated behind his desk, and just looking at him makes my eyes light up. He is unlike anything I have ever experienced, making me feel an array of emotions I never touched with anyone else. Feelings that I thought were dormant due to all of my shitty dating experiences have now been brought to life because of Rome. Being with him has tilted my entire world on its axis.

"Okay," Jeremiah says. He reaches down to grab a few things off his desk before looking back up at me. "I can see that you clearly want to go talk to him from the way you're staring into his office as if I've already left, so I'm going to go. Do your thing , girl. Go talk to your man. I'll see you tomorrow."

I don't even bother searching for an excuse. "Okay. See you tomorrow. Have a good night."

Jeremiah's smile makes me happy. Even though Jaz and I aren't on solid footing these days, Jeremiah has been nothing but supportive since the moment we laid eyes on Rome. He has had my back this entire time, always telling me to go for it and reminding me that no one's opinion on this matters but mine. He has never made me feel bad in any way regarding Rome, and I love him for that. No matter what happens between Jaz and me, I know Jeremiah is a friend for life.

Once he's out the door, I look around to make sure we're alone before locking the door and going to Rome's office. He sits behind his desk draped in frustration, his hand on his head as his fingers work circles over his temples. His eyes are closed and I can see that today's insanity has added weight to his shoulders.

"Headache?" I ask as I enter and sit down on the black couch butted against the wall in front of his desk.

He lets out a sigh. "Something like that."

"Sorry," I say, although I'm not sure what I'm apologizing for. "I can't believe how today went. Everything being pulled out into the open ... and Sierra ... I don't even know what to say. Whatever happened with her? Did she give you an answer?"

"She's staying," he replies flatly, fingers still massaging his temples. "She apologized to me before she left, and she'll apologize to you first thing in the morning."

"Ah," I reply. Well, that fucking sucks. "Why not fire her?"

"Because if she quits after that speech I gave, she has no leg to stand on when it comes to any sort of litigation. Firing her would probably be fine, too, but I just don't want to risk it. Plus, Sierra is a great VP when she's not distracted by her own bullshit. Hopefully she'll see clearer now. If not, I'll do what I have to do."

I nod along, understanding the move from an employer standpoint, but still wishing he would do the drastic thing just for me. But I know Rome is too controlled for that. He won't let his emotions drive him into a ditch.

"So, can I ask you a question?" I ask, hoping I'm not adding to his headache.

Rome finally opens his eyes as he leans back in his chair as far as it will go. "Of course."

"Why'd you admit it?" I inquire.

Rome frowns. "Admit what?"

"That we're together. Even in the face of Sierra's accusations, she didn't have any proof. If you would've come out and said that she was full of shit, we could still have our business hidden. Now everyone knows and will be invested in our success or failure, and you're clearly not the type of person who likes having a world of people watching your every move. I didn't expect you to do that."

Rome licks his lips as he looks at me, making me sink into my seat with his glare as usual. When he looks away, I can tell that he's deep in thought about something.

"Does it bother you?" he asks.

"No," I reply the second he finishes the question. "I'm a little worried about what people may think about me, but I never liked hiding. I only wanted to do it because I knew you wanted to."

His eyes find me again, and they're more filled with emotion this time. "I don't know why I did it. It felt like the right time—like it was the right thing to do. There's just … I couldn't stand there and deny it—deny *you*. I'm not good at explaining it and it makes me strangely uncomfortable to talk about it at all, but I just couldn't stand beside you and tell them that we're not together—that you don't belong to me when you do. You *do* belong to me, Nia, which is why you don't have to worry about what anyone thinks of you. I'll protect you, and I'll fire anyone who disrespects you. All you would have to do is point your finger and that person would be gone. You never have to worry about that."

"You would do that for me?"

"Yes."

"Why?"

"Because ..." Rome's voice trails off, his brain stopping his mouth from saying whatever he was about to. I watch him pull it back, the emotion in his eyes morphing to something more like vexation. His eyes slowly start to move around the room, focusing on nothing at all before he gets up from his chair and comes to the couch to sit next to me. He grabs my hand and looks me in the eye. "Look, I'm not the best at expressing myself these days. I just need you to trust me. Okay? Do you trust me?"

I nearly laugh as I angle my body toward him. "Rome, you're my Dom. I have given myself over to you, and that is not something I would do lightly. You've earned my submission in every way. I trust you with every part of my being."

"Good," he says. "Because when I said that I cared about you out there in front of everyone, I meant it. When I said I don't see an ending for us, I meant that, too. As much as I've tried to fight certain feelings for so long, I fucking care about you, Nia. I care about you so much that it scares me."

"I care about you, too, Rome," I reply as tears suddenly fill my eyes, surprising me.

A surge of emotion courses through my veins and I feel something that I'm too afraid to say. Rome has been through so much, the last thing I want to do is say something that will be a shock to his already-ravaged system, but not saying how I feel doesn't erase it. It's there now, like a leech attached directly to my heart, and now that it's there, it is only going to grow.

As sentiment and passion swell between us, neither of us responds with more words. If I spoke, I would say the thing that scares me most. So instead of talking, I kiss him. A single peck turns into two. Two turns into our mouths pressing together and our tongues colliding, and before I can make sense of my changing world, I'm straddling him. Rome places his hands on each side of my hips, and lifts me off the couch, setting me down on his lap. Our mouths don't separate for a single second as our hands tug and pull at each other's clothes, desperate to find skin as the temperature in the room skyrockets. Sweat beads on both of our foreheads, but it doesn't slow us down a bit. We've lost control of ourselves and have no sense of our surroundings. All we know is how we feel.

"I want you on top of me," Rome commands. "Take off your pants right now."

"Yes, Sir," I reply, immediately standing and pushing my pants down to step out of them. While I wiggle my way out of the fabric, Rome removes his and sits back on the couch, guiding me to him until the moment I sit down and slide his cock inside.

Both of us moan, our heads falling back until we're gazing at the ceiling tile. Rome's hands stay pressed against my hips as I begin to grind on top of him, motivated by the strength in his hands and the movement in his hips beneath me.

"You feel so fucking good," he tells me, lust hot on is breath. "How could I ever deny us when you've turned my world upside down? You're so incredible."

I keep moving, riding his cock with more and more enthusiasm as my pussy responds with a flood of wetness. Rome's hands slowly make their way up my body, squeezing as they go and forcing my shirt over my head. He snatches my bra off like its presence offends him, and lunges forward, sucking my nipple into his mouth while squeezing the other between his fingers. The sensitivity of my nipples makes the entire thing unbelievably erotic, and it spurs me forward.

"God, yes," I exclaim as I pick up speed, cupping Rome's head so that he doesn't let go. "Keep sucking it. Please, Sir. Suck it hard."

"Yeah? You want me to keep going? Say it again, my little goddess. Tell me what you want."

"Please keep playing with my nipples," I say for the first time in my entire life. I never knew I was into nipple play, but my eyes have been opened today even though this is just the tip of the iceberg. There is so much more we could explore in this area, but for now, all I want is his mouth on me.

"Good girl," Rome praises. "I'll give you what you want."

He leans forward again, sucking my nipple into his mouth with an aggressive force that borders on pain. I close my eyes and sink into it, still grinding as my breathing becomes labored.

"Yes. Thank you, Sir. Thank you. Please don't stop."

Rome moans as he keeps his mouth on my bare breast, sucking hard. For reasons I don't even understand, the feeling of his mouth and tongue on my nipple sends me into a frenzy. I ride him faster and faster, focusing on the feeling of his teeth as they gently scrape across the hardened nub of my breast before clamping down harder.

"Oh fuck," I shriek as an orgasm sneaks up on me and clutches me by the throat. "Sir, can I ... I'm coming!"

My ability to ask for permission is sucked right out of me, but Rome is unbothered, sucking and licking my nipple at the same time as I release all of my stress onto him. My orgasm is high voltage, electrifying my entire body and sending me into uncontrollable convulsions in Rome's lap. My hips keep moving as I try to prolong the feeling, and just as I'm coming down from heaven, Rome raises his hips and quickly drops them, pulling his cock out of me as he reaches around to stroke himself.

"Oh fuck!" he screams as he fists his cock. Warm cum shoots onto my ass and back, and I wish the feeling of him cumming on me would never stop. It feels so good that I want it all over my body, and just like that, I've unlocked two new kinks in one night.

When it's all over and Rome and I are getting cleaned up, I realize just how insane this day was. We are no longer hiding our relationship in the shadows, and I have no idea what my relationship with Sierra will be like after all of this. My entire reality shifted the moment she peeked through the window in the breakroom door, but the part of the day that has me sitting on the edge of my seat has nothing to do with that. The biggest shock of the day is something I feel on the inside. Something no one knows but me. I went from hiding my relationship with Rome to concealing something else entirely, and even though Rome and I hold hands as we walk out of Sandcastle together, I'm much more terrified of this new secret getting out.

Thirty-Eight - Rome

"*Saluti!*"

The three of us clink our glasses together before taking a sip of Santa Margherita Pinot Grigio. The mood at the Collazo house is as jovial as it always is, with Isabella working magic in the kitchen to serve Nikola and I the world's most beautiful chicken parmesan with homemade marinara sauce and penne pasta. I've missed dinners here. The occasion used to happen much more frequently—before Natalia died—and while I do feel a stab of guilt for being here without her, I have to admit that it feels good to be back at my friends' table again.

The setting of tonight's delicious dining experience is Nikola and Isabella's gorgeous off-white dining room. The color alone reflects how bold these two are, because I couldn't imagine sitting down to eat in this room without worrying about sauce splattering or wine dripping onto the white seat cushion beneath me. My mind would drive itself insane with worry thinking about the chances that I could trip on the off-white rug leading from the kitchen to the dining room and spill something, creating a permanent stain on any part of the white and tan tablecloth. But somehow the two of them have managed to even keep the white placemats stain-free. I hope I can keep the streak alive as I cut into my chicken and watch the marinara slide across the plate, threatening to spill over the edge.

After my first bite, I look at Isabella and sigh. "*È delizioso, Isabella.*"

She turns to me with a smile, her cheeks tinted pink from the amount of wine she has already had to drink tonight while she was cooking. "*Grazie, Roma.*"

We spend the next few minutes quietly enjoying the meal Isabella prepared, with the only sound at the table coming from forks and knives clanking atop white plates with gold edges, but once Nikola takes a second drink, he finally begins the night's conversation.

"I've got to tell you, Rome," he starts with his wine glass firmly in hand and ready to lift as soon as he's done talking. "I'm proud of you, man. You're starting to look like your old self."

Isabella finishes her glass of wine and sets it down to pour another from the half-empty bottle. "Yes, Rome. Nikola and I were hesitant to say anything, but you really do look good. It's so great to see you smiling again."

"Thank you," I reply, although I'm actually unsure of how to feel. "Things have been going well both professionally and personally, so I don't have much to complain about. Things have been good."

A brief pause elapses, but its pregnancy catches my attention. When I see the look on Nikola's face I feel a hint of suspicion come to life in my gut.

"That's great, man," he says before another apprehensive pause that makes my brows crawl together. "So, uhh ... how are things going with Nia?"

There it is—the question the two of them have been dying to ask me the entire night. Nikola and Isabella have always shown a scary amount of interest in my love life since Natalia passed away, and it has never failed to make me unreasonably uncomfortable. I know that they want the best for me and wish to see me happy, but the topic is always touchy because they knew Natalia. We were all very close friends from the beginning to the tragic end, and I've always been bothered by their desire to see me move on. However, they are right about one thing. I'm in a better place right now. It takes a copious amount of work to be as okay as I am, but things truly are better at the moment.

"Things with Nia are great," I admit aloud for the very first time.

Isabella's face lights up like a child finding their presents under the tree.

"Oh good!" she chirps. "I can't tell you how happy it makes me to hear you say that. You've always been so secretive, Rome."

"But we don't want to pry," Nikola quickly chimes in, and I can tell that they have already talked about how they would approach this conversation. "We just wanted to see how things are going and make sure that you're happy. That's all."

Nikola eyes Isabella as she fills her wine glass to the top and drinks it back down to half.

"I appreciate that," I say with a nod. "Like I said, Nia and I are great. We've been together for three months now, and it's good. I like her."

"That's so wonderful, Rome," Isabella says. "It's great to see you happy again."

"Are you still keeping it a secret at your job?" Nikola asks as he stuffs his mouth full of a thick piece of chicken.

"Actually, no," I answer. "The veil of secrecy came crashing down a couple of days ago when my VP was spying on us in the breakroom. She saw us kissing and called Nia out in front of the entire office, hoping to embarrass her into quitting. But I wouldn't allow that. Since she was in the mood to spill secrets, I intervened and told everyone how Sierra had come onto me just after I took over the company. It was probably immature and unnecessary, but Nia was very upset and I felt the need to step in and protect her from mistreatment. Long story short, it all worked out. Sierra apologized to Nia and I, and everything is back on track with the only difference being that we're not hiding anymore. It's all good."

"Wow," Isabella says, her eyes looking a little squinted. "You stepped in for her? Felt the need to protect her? So can I safely assume that you have real feelings for her?"

"Isabella," Nikola says, cutting his eyes over to his wife like a father threatening their child with a look.

"It's okay, Nikola," I say, trying to ease the tension I see building in his face. "Yes, I do have feelings for her. I like her."

"Awesome," Isabella blurts. "So, when do we get to meet her?"

"Isabella," Nikola snaps, clearly unhappy with the question. However, this time, I don't think it's okay.

As I look down at the table with the question swirling around my head, the first thing I think about is the last time I sat at this exact table with Natalia at my side. She was wearing a black and gray dress that hugged her curves. Her black hair cascaded down her back like a beautiful, endless waterfall of obsidian. Her smile radiated every time she gifted us with its presence, and when we made eye contact my heart fluttered as if we'd just met when we'd known each other for years. That was a month before the brain aneurysm snuck in and snatched her away from me in the blink of an eye. Five years have now passed since that dinner. Five years since I was sitting right here with the woman who was my wife and the love of my life. Five years since the four of us were the best of friends, thinking that we'd have a lifetime of dinners and laughter together. That's it. Just five years. But now Isabella is ready to start up those dinners again—dinners full of drinks, laughter, love, and friendship ... but without Natalia.

"What are you doing?" I ask as flames roar to life in my stomach and quickly travel through my veins to the rest of my body.

"What do you mean?" Isabella responds.

"Rome, it's fine," Nikola says, trying to maintain a grip on the situation, but it's slipping through his fingers like he's trying to squeeze liquid.

"Is it?" I snip. "Is it fine now after nearly five years of Natalia being gone—the anniversary of her death just days away? What, is five years the limit for grief? Once we hit the five-year mark in a few days you'll be ready to replace the woman who was your best friend, Isabella?"

"Replace? What the hell are you talking about?" she fires back, slurring her words a bit as the wine tightens its grip on her.

"Isabella, please stop," Nikola pleads. "This is not what we talked about. Rome will let us in on his relationship if and when he is ready."

"He's never going to be ready," Isabella cuts in, suddenly angry as she drops her fork and sits back, her face scowling. "We've been trying to help him for years, but he refuses to grow up and move on."

"Grow up?" I say with a shocked expression, but Isabella plows over me.

"Yeah, grow the fuck up," she says, pointing her finger at me from across the table. "You're our friend, Rome. We don't want to see you miserable and spiraling, okay? We want you to be happy and with someone who can make you smile, because that's what you deserve. But you know what else? We deserve it, too. Natalia was our friend, too! I miss her, too! So don't you dare say shit about me trying to *replace* her. We will never. But that doesn't mean that we have to die with her."

"Shut the fuck up," I bark, standing up so fast my chair goes flying backward. "Don't you dare talk about her as if you knew her better than me or loved her more. She was *everything* to me!"

"Rome, you have to calm down," Nikola says, standing up to place a hand on my shoulder. "Just have a seat and we can talk about this calmly."

"Oh, I bet you two have been just dying to have this conversation, haven't you?" I ask, my emotions taking over as tears sting my eyes and my heart races like I'm running. "You've been so fucking desperate to push me into something new all this time. Waiting for me to move on from Natalia and replace her with someone new."

"We don't want you to replace her, dumb ass," Isabella barks. "It's okay for you to find happiness and fall in love again. Why are you so against it?"

"Because I'll fucking lose her!" I scream as the floodgates open and tears come like a torrential downpour. "Don't you dare say the word love to me. When I love someone, I lose them. They fucking die. My mom. My wife. My fucking dad died less than a year ago! I will never allow myself to love Nia, because as soon as I do, she's cursed—fucking marked for death. So you two can forget all about your dreams of seeing me in love, making fucking wedding plans, or having children, because I refuse to let it happen. How do you think I was able to get this far with Nia after my dad died? Huh? I vowed to never love anyone else. That's why things are better, because I know I will never afflict another person with the jinxed cancer that is my love."

As I stand by the table with tears streaming down my face, Nikola moves over to Isabella and places both hands on her shoulders as she begins to cry, too.

"Jesus, Rome," he says. "Is that what you think? That you're cursed? Love is not a curse."

"What the fuck do you know about it?" I bellow. "Sitting here with your perfect house and flawless marriage, constantly reminding me of what I'll never have. You don't know how it feels to watch everyone you've ever loved die. You two are the only ones left, and I wake up every day terrified that something has happened to you in the middle of the night. I expect it like I expect the sun to rise in the morning, and it fills me with constant dread."

"You can't live like this, Rome," Nikola says, and I see tears in his eyes for the first time since Natalia's funeral.

"He's right, Rome," Isabella agrees. "It isn't good for your mental health to hang onto these kinds of thoughts. You have to be able to move on."

"I've moved on as far as I can," I reply, turning my feet toward the door. "I've got all the closure I'm ever going to get, and I know what I have to do in order to be happy. Love is off the table, and that's all there is to it. I'm not replacing Natalia with Nia. We're not having double dates or couples nights like the good old days. That's over, and so is this conversation. Thanks for dinner."

"Rome, please don't leave," Nikola pleads.

"Don't do this, Rome," Isabella requests, bawling her eyes out.

I ignore them both. I hate that I'm crying as I go, and I hate walking out on the only two people on this Earth that have been here for me through all of my trials and tribulations. But I'm done. I'm fucking done with everything.

Let go, and Let Love

Thirty-Nine

"I understand that, but I'm not using ten percent of our entire budget on one campaign, Simon. Now get out of my office, and don't come back until you figure out how to reduce the cost. Go."

Every head in the bullpen is turned toward Rome's office as he finishes berating Simon for coming to him with a high-priced ad and marketing strategy he's been working on. As Simon ambles out of the office with his chin tucked against his chest, Jeremiah turns to me with wide eyes. From my desk, I shrug to let him know that I have no idea what's going on with Rome today, and we all get back to work.

Today has been strange. While work has had its usually lackluster moments highlighted by the rare flair caused by a gorgeous mockup from someone on one of the design teams, the air has been thicker. Tension hovers all around us like black smoke from a nearby fire, and it's because Rome clearly woke up on the wrong side of the bed this morning. From the moment he walked into the office, it was apparent that he didn't want to be talked to for one reason or another. He barely spoke as he passed by people giving him their usual morning greeting. When I went to his office to say hello, he barely acknowledged me, throwing me an apathetic, "Hey," before moving his eyes to his computer screen and leaving them there. I'm not the kind of person to beg for attention when it's clear someone doesn't want to give it, so I turned on my heel and walked back into my office where I didn't feel like a bother. I spent the entire day giving him his clearly wanted space, but it doesn't seem to have helped with his attitude, as this is the third time we've heard him have an uncharacteristic attitude with one of his employees. Jeremiah isn't the only person who has turned to me for answers, but all I can do is shrug. Even I have no riposte to his mood.

The day ticks on in uncommon silence. Every chair in the bullpen is filled because no one wants to risk going to the breakroom. They might have to walk past Rome or, even worse, be in there when he enters and suffer the brunt of his wrath. Rome has always been intimidating anyway, so now that he is having his first bad at the office, the usual healthy fear has risen to terror for everyone. Seeing as how we're together now, I wonder what I can do to help, but I'm worried that if I try he'll snap at me. Naturally, I will snap back, and the next thing we know, we're having a freaking lover's quarrel right in the middle of the office, which would send the rumor mill into overdrive as everyone at Sandcastle awaits our demise. I'd rather keep my distance and hope that he'll be better once work is finished.

With an hour left in our day, I notice the familiar look of heads popping up and necks stretching to look over the top of their cubicle walls to see inside Rome's office. I take my fingers away from my keyboard so that the click-clacking doesn't drown out any sound, and I hear what resembles a faint argument brewing. Jeremiah looks at me again, this time with a wrinkled forehead that shows real worry, so I get up from my desk and move to the doorway.

"What the hell is going on with you today?" Rome asks Sierra, who stands at the front of his desk with a piece of paper in her hand hanging loosely at her side.

"I don't know what you mean?" she replies, her voice devoid of its usual fire.

Rome sits back in his chair and scowls in a way that sends a shard of horror through my heart. "You don't know what I mean? I just had to get onto Simon about a campaign strategy that clearly had no thought or direction, and now here you are with numbers that look like you don't give a fuck if this company goes bankrupt by next week. Simon should've never come to me with those marketing numbers anyway, because you are the VP. He should've gone to you, and *you* should've told him that the budget was too high. It's a problem that never should have made it to my desk, Sierra. You need to do your job."

"I *am* doing my job, Rome," Sierra retorts. "I didn't know Simon was going to come in here. He bypassed me."

"And why did he think that bypassing you was something he could do?"

"How the hell should I know? What is with this attitude from you today?"

"My attitude comes from people not knowing how to do their fucking job!" Rome barks so loud I expect the floor to shake.

Sierra takes a step back, shocked by Rome's outburst, and I hear a few gasps from the bullpen as other directors step into their doorways to see what is going on. Angst settles over the entire office and all work comes to a screeching halt as Sierra stands before Rome completely frozen while he glares at her. His face is contorted into a furious expression, but after a moment, it relents. The furrow in his brow smoothes out as he takes a deep breath and puts his head down.

"I'm sorry," he says without looking up. "I shouldn't have yelled at you. That was rude and disrespectful of me, and I apologize."

He looks back up at Sierra and ... do I see tears in his eyes?

"It's okay, Rome," Sierra replies. "Are you okay?"

"I'm fine," he answers. "Do me a favor, please, and send everybody home for the day."

"But we have an hour left."

"I know. Just do it, please. Work isn't going anywhere. We'll get back to it tomorrow. Thanks."

Sierra slowly nods her head as she walks backwards toward the door as if Rome will attack her if she turns her back to him. Once she's out of the office, she turns to the bullpen and announces that everyone is being let off an hour early. I expect cheers, but instead, everyone quietly gets up and hurriedly scampers to the door like a fire drill. They filter out quickly, with Sierra as the last to go. She stops at the doorway and makes eye contact with me before following the rest of them out.

Rome hasn't moved an inch by the time I make it to his office. He sits at his desk with his head leaning back against the headrest of his chair, staring up at the ceiling.

"Bad day?" I ask, hoping he doesn't kick me out.

He sighs, still staring at the ceiling like he's stargazing. "Yeah ... something like that."

"Yeah," I say, looking down at the couch next to me but deciding against moving to it just in case this doesn't go well. "Want to go for a drink? Sure looks like you could use one ... or six."

The corner of his mouth threatens to lift into a smirk, but he forces it away. "I don't know. I should probably just go home. Shouldn't even have come to work today."

"What exactly is wrong?"

Rome shakes his head as if he can't believe the answer himself, but he doesn't let me in on the secret. "Nothing ... nothing that I want to talk about."

I want to pry, and not just to be nosy. I want to know what's going on with him today because I care about him. It matters to me what Rome is going through, but it's clear that he doesn't want to get into it right now. Maybe he will when he feels like the time is right. At least that's what I hope.

"Alright. Well, are you sure? I think a few drinks might loosen the muscles in your face a bit. You look like you're turning to stone."

Finally, Rome's mouth turns up at the corner and he smiles for me. He lowers his head, grinning for the first time today.

"It's dangerous talking shit to me right now, my little goddess," he says.

"What? I just wanted to make you smile. You'd do the same for me. Now come on. We'll hit Heartless Tavern right up the street, have a few drinks to relax, and then you can go home and try to figure out how to not scare the living shit out of everyone in the office tomorrow. Okay?"

Rome grins again, almost involuntarily, before relenting. "Okay."

Heartless Tavern is as empty as I would expect it to be on a weekday just after work. There are a few people scattered across the bar, but when Rome and I walk in, it's easy for us to find two stools next to each other. We take our seats beneath the bright white and red lights reading "Heartless," ignoring the large bearded man next to us who looks like he hasn't left the bar in weeks. The bartender is a woman who is probably in her late thirties, with purple hair cut just above her shoulders and a hoop earring in each nostril. Her black lipstick glistens, reflecting the white lights when she smiles at us, awaiting our drink order.

"Cranberry vodka," I tell her as soon as I'm settled.

"DisAronno on the rocks, please," Rome says.

"You got it," the bartender replies before stepping away to fill the orders.

She drops the drinks off in front of us, and Rome immediately knocks back half of his, sucking in air to cool his scorched throat.

My eyebrows climb upward. "Well, damn. Sierra and Simon had their budgets *that* messed up, huh?"

Rome chuckles, which still manages to fill my stomach with butterflies. "They were, but they weren't. I didn't have to react the way I did. Just a bad day, and … I don't know."

"We don't have to talk about it right now," I say, placing a hand on top of his. "We all go through things that no one else can see. I just wanted to make sure that you were alright. You seem to be doing better already, so my mission has been accomplished."

"I *am* doing better," he says. "Thanks to you. You're incredible, you know that? You have no idea what it means to me to be sitting here with you, enjoying your beauty and conversation. Especially today. It's everything, Nia."

I smile with a playful shrug. "Glad to be of service, Sir. You make me happy all of the time. Returning the favor is the least I can do. Now finish that drink and order another, then you'll be feeling like you're floating on a cloud above all of your problems."

"There you go thinking you can tell me what to do," he says, shaking his head as he smirks. "Who's in charge again?"

I smile from ear to ear. "You are, Sir."

"That's right," Rome says before lifting his glass. "But I *am* going to listen to you and finish this drink. Who doesn't want to float on a cloud?"

Both of us laugh as the door to the bar opens and a small group of guys walks in. Rome and I ignore them, continuing to smile and laugh as we both take long gulps of our drinks and nearly finish them. As I set mine down on the white and red napkin in front of me, I feel the bearded man next to me brush my shoulder as he gets up to leave, followed by another person taking his place. But this person bumps me so hard it nearly knocks me off my stool. When I look over to say something, I pause when I recognize his face. He stares at me, raising his head and looking down at me over his nose. I know those beady little eyes and the douche-bag gaze in them. It's fucking Zane from FET, who I mistakenly almost had sex with months ago.

"Well I'll be damned," he says with all the confidence in the world. "If it isn't Nia, the girl who claimed to be a sub but wouldn't submit. Long time no see. Sorry for bumping your shoulder, but if I'd known it was you I would've done it harder."

My heart speeds up as I let out a sigh, because seeing this asshole is the last thing I need, and not just right now. It's the last thing I need *ever*.

I don't have anything to say to him after the way he treated me at his house—when I had to storm out on his goofy ass because he wouldn't respect my use of the safe word, and tried to guilt trip me into a butt plug. People in this lifestyle do not play about their limits, and it isn't something that should ever be contemned. With that in mind, I roll my eyes and turn around to face Rome, who hasn't noticed Zane's arrival.

"What, you're just going to ignore me?" Zane says, talking louder, his assertiveness unwavering as he still thinks he can intimidate me. "I know we got off on the wrong foot last time, but maybe we could rekindle the flame and try again. What do you say, Nia?"

"I say *go fuck yourself*," I snap, trying to suffocate him with my evil glare.

"Wow. Still so hostile," Zane says. "Nice to see you're still a prude with a shitty attitude."

"Hey," Rome says, looking past me and staring daggers into Zane. "Do we have a problem?"

I place a hand on Rome's chest as he gets up from his seat and stands beside me. "Rome, it's fine. Zane was just leaving."

"Was I?" Zane responds. "No, I wasn't. I was waiting to be introduced to your friend Nia. Who's the guy who *won't* be getting lucky tonight?"

"Zane, walk away," I tell him, because I see the rage growing in Rome's posture, his muscles tightening and jaw clenching as he forgets everyone in the bar, including me, and only looks at Zane.

"Walk away?" Zane continues, totally unfazed. "You don't tell me to walk away. You're just a sub. You have no say in anything because you're just a hole for me and my new friend here to fuck. Now do your job and introduce me to—"

I never see the punch coming. Rome's body moves so quickly that I don't recognize the moment his arm cocks back and shoots forward like a battering ram. His fist slams into Zane's face, and Zane's head snaps back so far it looks like the back of his head touches his shoulder blades. In the speed of a blink, his body crumples to the floor on top of itself.

Everyone around us moves away like a fire just broke out, as Rome reaches down and grabs the unconscious Zane by the face.

"Who the fuck do you think you're talking to?" he blares. "She is mine. Do you hear me? Mine! Don't you ever talk to my woman that way. Don't you *ever* disrespect her. I will break your goddamn neck!"

Even though he's already knocked out, Rome hits him again, sending blood splattering across the floor and staining people's shoes. The bearded man from before grabs Rome by the arm and pulls him back, but Rome turns and pushes him off, not wanting to be touched by anyone. The man puts his hands up to let Rome know he doesn't want any problems, and everyone backs away, leaving Zane on the floor by himself.

Everyone in the bar stares at Rome, wondering what he's about to do next. My heart races as he pulls out his wallet and throws a hundred dollar bill on the bar between our two drinks.

"For the trouble," he says to the bartender, then he grabs me by the hand. "Come on."

Fighting back a smile as I look down at the incapacitated Zane, I grip Rome's hand and begin to follow his lead out of the bar. "Yes, Sir."

Forty

Rome was so upset at the bar that I didn't think he'd follow me home, since we were in separate cars leaving the office. I honestly thought he'd just make a quick turn onto the highway and go find solace in the peacefulness of his own house, so I'm pleasantly surprised when his car pulls into the driveway as I'm walking through my front door.

I don't even know what to make of it all. One second, everything was normal while Rome and I laughed and tried to have a good time after what was clearly a bad day for him. I'd finally gotten him to unclench and start smiling, showing the best, most infectious parts of his personality. The next thing I knew, Zane was there wearing an extra layer of asshole. He decided that disrespect was the only tool he could wield against me after what happened between us, but he didn't know Rome was there ... and neither of us knew that Rome would defend me with violence at the slightest show of opprobrium. Chaos ensued and we had to make a quick exit, leaving everyone in Heartless reeling. Call me crazy, but now that it's over, I'm not reeling. I'm flattered.

Maybe I'm wrong and simply speaking to my bias, but every heterosexual woman wants a man that will protect her and make her feel safe. We all want to know that when other men—the pieces of shit who like to hurt women—are around, that ours will be the one to stand up for us, and kick a little ass if necessary. In a world full of danger for women, safety is paramount, and it is a rarity to find a man both willing and capable of providing it without being a bully himself. Tonight, Rome showed me that—along with all of his other green flag attributes—he is that kind of man.

Unfortunately, when he rushes through the door after me, he doesn't look at all happy about what just went down. His adrenaline is clearly still pumping as he comes in and immediately starts pacing around the room, but the frustration and exasperation that stitched itself in his mannerisms at the office has returned. He looks miserable and on the verge of tears.

"Hey, it's okay," I say as he walks right past me before turning around at the door and doing it again. "Rome, just calm down. It's over. You did what you had to do."

"What if they call the cops? They'll probably call the cops," he says in a panic.

"Okay, then we'll cross that bridge when we get there," I reply, hoping my words will console him, and let him know that if he gets in trouble I'll still be here for him. "But for now, just try to calm down. I honestly think it'll be fine. Everyone saw how he was acting."

"Who was he?" he barks. "I just knocked out a guy I didn't even know."

"He's just some guy I met on a dating app once," I answer. "He was upset that I chose not to sleep with him. I guess the embarrassment still stings even though it was months ago."

Still pacing, Rome says, "Well, he should've known not to talk to you that way. He shouldn't talk to *any* woman that way, but especially you. I couldn't allow that. I never will. You think he's still there? I should go back and make sure he remembers that you belong to me."

With a sudden burst of energy, Rome rushes toward the door like he's actually going to go back to Heartless to do even more damage to Zane, forgetting that he was just concerned about a police presence. As he tries to pass me, I reach out and grab him by the hand to stop him.

"Rome, stop," I say, tugging his arm and pulling him close to me. I wrap my arms around his waist and force him into a hug. "Everything is okay, babe. You're all over the place right now. Just calm down."

Rome finally stops moving and slowly puts his arms around me, wrapping me up and bringing back that feeling of safety that warms my soul. I breathe him in and squeeze, trying to do the same for him.

"Thank you," I say into his chest as I listen to his heartbeat.

"For what?"

"For what you did at the bar. Zane was being ridiculous, and while I didn't expect you to knock him out, I'm glad you did. I always knew you'd protect me, but it was amazing to see it actually happen. I don't necessarily condone violence, but I kinda loved it."

Rome lets out a breath and I feel his tension begin to melt away. "You don't have to thank me for that. You're mine, Nia. I'd throw myself in front of traffic before I ever let a man disrespect you. I mean that with all of my heart."

I smile as I sigh and close my eyes, sinking into him. "I love you, Rome."

Both of us freeze. Time stops as the sound of my heartbeat grows so loud that it is all I can hear. The relaxation that began to take hold of Rome suddenly reverses. Rigidity creeps into his muscles, making him stiffen in my arms until it feels like I'm cuddling a mannequin.

"What did you just say?" he asks as he takes a step back.

It's too late to pull it back now. Although I had the thought days ago, I chose not to say it then. But everything that has taken place tonight just pushed it out of me. Being in his arms after he risked his life and freedom just to ensure that a man he didn't even know didn't disrespect me lowered my guard. The scent of him, and the way his words made me feel worked like a voodoo spell, disintegrating my inhibitions and forcing the words from my heart, and there is no way to put them back.

"I said I love you," I repeat, owning it and basking in how it feels to say it out loud. "I know it's a lot, and I don't expect you to say it back, but it's true. I honestly think I'm in love with you."

"What? Of course I won't say it back," he suddenly snaps, his words slamming into my chest like he just hurled a brick.

It hurts so much that I wince and take my own step back. "What?"

"Why would you say that to me?" he questions as a look of miserable disgust spreads across his face.

"What do you mean? I said it because it's true."

"No, it's *not* true. You don't love me, Nia, and I don't love you either. Alright?"

My face twists into a confused frown that makes my head tilt.

"What ... Rome, what the hell just happened? Where is this coming from? Am I missing something?"

"Besides the fact that we are not in love with each other? I don't know. I can't believe you just said that."

"What the fuck? I don't understand why you're reacting this way."

"Of course you don't understand," he blares, shocking me with the sheer volume of his words and the heat of his anger. "How could you? You don't know me. You don't know what I've been through. You have the nerve to tell me that you love me on the anniversary of my wife's death? Are you out of your mind?"

Understanding and realization hit me like an arrow to the heart, completely deflating every good feeling I had earlier. That's why he has been acting so strangely all day. Somehow, my feelings for Rome have done a fantastic job of making me forget that he is a widower. He loved someone before me and she died, and her death has been the catalyst for his fear of commitment ever since.

I take a deep breath and swallow hard, trying my best not to be offended. "Rome, I'm sorry. I didn't know. I couldn't have possibly known that today is the anniversary of her death. You can't blame me for not knowing that."

"Maybe not," he says as tears fill his eyes. "But maybe you should've picked up on the clues and not dropped this bomb on me. I don't do love. Do you understand? Love has been nothing but poison in my life, killing everyone I've cared about. I refuse to feel it. I refuse to accept it. I don't want it. I don't fucking love you!"

"I'm not asking you to feel it," I say as I begin to cry. "I just wanted you to know how *I* feel."

"Stop it!" he bellows.

"*You* stop it, Rome," I fire back. "I love you, whether you like it or not, but you can't keep forcing me to compete with your dead wife. If you can't give your heart to me, then what are we even doing?"

"We're not doing fucking anything, Nia, because we're done!" he screams as tears cascade down his cheeks. He stands there, crying his eyes out as he stares at me, somehow still defiant even as he weeps.

"Done?" I ask. "We're *done*? You're ending it because I love you? Rome, this doesn't make any sense."

"I don't give a fuck if it makes sense to you. You could never understand."

"Then fucking make me. You don't get to tell me that I won't understand something, and then don't even try to break it down for me so that I can. You don't get to just run away from how perfect we are for each other just because you're scared."

"I'm not *scared*," he shrieks, but his words are barely audible through his sobs.

"Bullshit. I love you, and you know what else? I think you love me, too."

"Stop. No I don't."

"Yes you do. You're just too much of a coward to admit it."

Tears stream down both of our faces as we stand in front of each other like two boxers squaring off. Rome's face is showered in tears, his aura of invincibility completely dismantled as he breaks down and succumbs to vulnerability. I don't know what else to say, so silence screams in my ears until Rome stands up straight and takes a deep breath, trying to regain his composure.

"I don't care what you think," he says, fighting back an onslaught of tears. "But I don't love you ... and I never will."

His words break my resolve, sending me plunging into sadness that cracks my heart. I want to respond—to cuss him out, to fight for us, to call him pitiful and weak, to beg for him not to do this—but he doesn't give me time to. I watch in pure shock and dismay as Rome turns on his heel, opens my front door, and slams it shut behind him. I feel the pain of his absence in an instant, and the cracks he put in my heart give way, shattering me into a million irreparable pieces.

Forty-One

"Hey ... Nia, what's wrong?"

I stare at Jaz with the words on the tip of my tongue, but there's an emotional barricade that keeps them from coming out. When I try to speak, tears seep from my eyes instead. As much as I try to put on a tough exterior to convince both Jaz and myself that I haven't been completely demolished by what just happened at my house, the dam breaks and I crumble beneath the emotions. No words come out, only powerful sobs that wreck my entire body.

Jaz steps over the threshold of her front door and wraps her arms around me, and that's where we stand for the next five minutes, on her front porch with the door wide open, while I cry harder than I ever have before.

"It's okay, sweetie," she whispers in my ear after a while. "Let's go inside and talk about it. Okay? Come on."

The strain of heartbreak has zapped all of the strength from my legs, so Jaz has to help me inside like I'm an injured athlete. Both literally and figuratively, I lean on her for support, even after we've made it inside and taken a seat on her couch.

"Is everything okay?" asks a confused Michael, who's dressed in sweatpants and a robe with a bottle of Corona in his hand.

He gets up from his seat to come inspect, but Jaz shoos him away. They exchange some kind of unspoken, married-people-conversation, and Michael leaves the room without saying another word. It's not until he has made it all the way upstairs and into the bedroom that Jaz finally speaks.

"Okay, sweetie. Tell me what's going on? What happened?"

"Rome," I reply, although it comes out in a whimper that makes me hate the sound of my own voice.

"What happened to Rome?" Jaz inquires. "Is he okay?"

I shake my head, struggling to breathe through the sobs, and I absolutely can't stand the way I'm reacting. I've gone so long telling myself that I'm not weak just because I'm a submissive, and here I am crying my heart out over a man too broken to love me. I want to be stronger. I desire to be the perfect example of what a sub should be—submissive, but stronger than tungsten. Yet, love has weakened my defenses. I could cuss out Zane and storm out of his house. I had no problem telling Marcus that I wasn't interested in his brand of dominance. But I didn't *love* them. Now that the word has fallen from my lips, it has been made real, and true love can hurt more than anything in this world. Maybe Rome was right about it being poison, because I feel like I'm dying a slow death right now, and it is love that is killing me.

"Nia," Jaz says, placing her hands on my shoulders. "Try to calm down, boo. I need you to tell me what happened."

"He dumped me," I force myself to say.

Before I speak again, I repeat the words in my head and let them anger me. I choose anger over sadness because anger is much more useful. Sadness is a bottomless pit that swallows people whole, and you can't move until you learn how to climb out of it with your bare hands. But anger can be the ultimate motivator when it's righteous and mature. I'd much rather seethe than cry, but it takes all of my focus to fight the tears back.

"He *dumped* you?" Jaz exclaims in total shock. "For what?"

"Because I love him," I answer.

The ridiculousness of the statement makes me want to curl up in a ball and break everything in sight at the same time.

Jaz's forehead furrows. "Wait a minute? I don't understand. He dumped you because you love him?"

"Yes. Okay, bear with me while I try to make this long story as short as possible."

"Wait. First of all ... no. Don't try to make the story short. Don't skip any details. I want to know absolutely everything, because bitch I didn't even know you were in love. Secondly, I think we're going to need wine for this," Jaz says.

"Oh, my god. Yes!"

My friend jumps off the couch and speed walks into the kitchen, where she grabs a full bottle of Rosé and two glasses. She jogs back into the living room, sets the glasses on the coffee table, and fills them both to the top.

"Fuck halfway," she says, handing me mine as she brings her glass straight to her lips. "Okay, now go."

I take a giant swig of my wine and sit up straight, then I go over the entire story from start to finish. I explain Rome's behavior at the office—the way he spent the entire day snapping at people for simple work problems that had simple solutions. I tell her about the bar, and how his mood had shifted before Zane walked in and began hurling insults at me like they were bombs. I explain how Rome stood up from his barstool and hit Zane with one lightning quick punch that knocked him out in front of everyone, before screaming at his unconscious body that I belonged to him. It takes time to work my way through the tears that refuse to go away, but I break down everything that happened at my place, emphasizing that I told Rome I was in love with him on the anniversary of his wife's death.

"He said that love had been nothing but poison in his life—that he didn't love me and never would," I finish, and before more tears can fall, I pull the wine to my lips and drink until they retreat.

"That bastard," Jaz says, refilling her glass. "That childish, selfish bastard. I didn't want to say anything, but I was so worried that this would happen."

"I know. I should've listened to you," I say. "You told me not to lose myself in him, and that's exactly what I did. I even let our friendship fade into the background so that I could spend as much time with him as possible."

"Don't do that," Jaz says, placing a hand on my knee. "I should've been more supportive, because I understand what it's like to fall for someone. I did the same thing with Michael when we first started dating, and you took it like a champ—like a true friend. It wasn't my place to tell you not to be all-in for your man."

"But look where it got me. You were right, Jaz."

"No I wasn't. You did exactly what you were supposed to do, Nia. You had finally met someone who checked off every box. When you find somebody like that, you're supposed to go for it. Don't let these Instagram and Twitter girls tell you any different. They don't know shit about being in a relationship or what it takes to make one work. You dived in head-first because that's what you're supposed to do. The only problem was that Rome didn't dive in with you. He couldn't because he was still swimming in a pool of his grief, and until he's able to pull himself out of that, he can never fully be with you, or anybody else for that matter. You didn't do anything wrong, and I'm sorry that I made you feel any different."

"I'm sorry, too," I reply, losing the battle to my tears once again. "Even if I did the right thing, I should have at least listened to you and proceeded with caution. If I would've, maybe I wouldn't have fallen for him so quickly. Maybe I would've done a better job of recognizing the signs. I would've known that there is no winning a competition with someone who has died, especially if they died while still in love. She took his heart to the grave with her. He may not ever get it back now."

"Damn. I'm so sorry this happened, Nia. I truly am," Jaz says.

"Me, too," I reply, as both of us put our glasses down on the coffee table and hug.

"You deserve better," Jaz says, squeezing me tight. "You deserve someone who is willing to love you with the entirety of their heart, not just the bits and pieces left over from a previous relationship. You've been through so much, Nia."

"*Too* fucking much," I reply, and my wall of anger is crumbled by a wrecking ball of misery that sends me right back to where I was when I first arrived on Jaz's doorstep.

My broken heart aches with pain that feels brand new, and I have no choice but to feel it. I hug Jaz as tightly as I can, and I stop fighting. I let myself cry as hard as I need to.

"I'm so sick of this shit," I mumble into her shoulder as memories of Rome storming out of my house replay in my mind.

I don't love you ... and I never will.

"I know, boo" Jaz says as she begins to cry with me. "I know."

Forty-Two – Rome

My bedroom is dark, just like my mood, as I lay in bed with all of the blinds closed and the curtains drawn. The TV plays a show on mute, but even the movement of the character's mouths on screen annoys me to no end. I can't be happy right now. All I know is the pain I feel. All I know is the pain I've caused. All I know is the pain I deserve for being so lost—so turned upside down by my own grief that I would deny happiness to someone who loves me.

Nia loves me. She said it ... and I believe her. I wish it wasn't true because it scares me so much. It's why she called me a coward. She was right. I *am* a coward, but acknowledging it doesn't make it any easier to separate myself from it, because fear has its arms wrapped around me like a fucking bear hug. I feel it squeezing me every day, crushing my spirit as well as my lungs so that I can't breathe or feel anything. I tried to let go of it so that Nia and I could be happy together, but its grip is too strong. Now I've broken the heart of the woman I'm quite possibly meant to be with.

No one knows what it's like to be torn like this. To have Nia on one side—gorgeous, perfect, funny, smart, strong-minded, and loving. She is everything I could ever want in a woman, and it makes no sense whatsoever to choose *anything* over her, but especially fear.

On the other hand, I have the memory of the only woman I've ever allowed myself to love. Natalia was perfect, too. She made me feel things I didn't know I could, and we were happy until the moment she left this life. We were in love the entire time, and that love did not die with her. I will always love her in one way or another, no matter how much time goes by. But holding onto her memory and allowing it to control my life now is ... I don't even know what the fuck it is. Lunacy? Ridiculous? Pathetic? Illogical? All of the above? No matter the adjective used to describe the trap that is our happy memories, I can't let go of her. Five years later, I still feel unable to move on.

And then there is love. I loved both of my parents. They were my entire world, and I don't say that out of obligation. I loved them dearly. We were the kind of family that knew how to laugh together, and chose to do it on a daily basis over stressing out about the troubles of life. We genuinely enjoyed each other's company, so when Mom died it broke my father and I. To say that we mentally struggled after her death would be an understatement, but we still had each other. We leaned on one another even more, still finding ways to laugh when crying felt much more reasonable, and we did everything together. We were inseparable ... until death came for him, too.

My mother was taken from us by a car accident. My wife, stolen from me by a random brain aneurysm. My father, cut down by a heart attack that showed no signs that it was coming before bursting his most vital organ like a balloon in his chest. I loved them all more than could be explained by an encyclopedia of words, and they all died premature deaths and left me on this godforsaken planet to fend for myself. All of them—my world's most important people—snatched away from me. Why would I ever allow myself to feel that pain again, when I'm still broken from all of the times before?

The ringing of my doorbell splits my head open. My soft pillow feels more like a cinder block after the drinks I had last night before bed, and now the tune that plays from the doorbell is a fucking foghorn. I try to wait it out, refusing to even lift my head up, let alone answer, but the foghorn blares again and again.

"Fuck," I whisper as I slowly drag myself out of the bed and walk at a snail's pace to the door. From down the hall, I can see that it is Nikola through the glass, and just seeing him makes me want to break down. He is the last family I have left, and I hate and love him for it, but I would never turn him away, even after an argument.

When I unlock the door, I don't bother conversing in the doorway. I turn the deadbolt and pop the door open, then walk away as he enters and closes it behind him.

"Well, you absolutely look like shit, Rome," he says as he follows me into the living room.

I slowly lower myself onto the couch and lay my head on a pillow, agony filling my entire body like a cup running over.

"Haven't heard from you in a few days," Nikola goes on, sitting across from me on the ottoman. "Isabella and I tried to reach out to you on the anniversary, remembering how hard the day always hits you, and when we didn't get a response or a call back we started worrying. Considering the way you look, I assume things haven't gone well since you stormed out of our house. Are you okay?"

"What does it look like?" I ask, keeping my eyes closed to avoid the light from the sun through the door and windows.

"Oh, it looks like you died and failed at coming back to life. You're like a zombie that couldn't quite make it. You're a *zom*. Get it? Halfway there."

"I get it, *idiota*," I say, but I don't have the energy to make it sound insulting. "Did you come all this way to torture me?"

"I told you, Isabella and I were worried about the anniversary and the lack of communication from you. The wife practically demanded that I come over here and make sure you hadn't done anything stupid. She'll be glad to know that you haven't ended it all, but from the looks of it, you still may have done something stupid.

"You've always struggled on the anniversary of Natalia's death, but you've managed to piece yourself back together again by the end of the next day. Here you are three days later, still wearing pajamas that you clearly haven't changed in days, smelling like farts and cheap wine, with no lights on in the hall you just shuffled down, which leads me to believe that you're lying in your room in the dark like a fucking vampire. Sound about right?"

I frown, but it only makes my head hurt worse. "Oh, my god. Who are you? *La polizia?* I'm suffering enough, officer. I don't need to feel any worse. Then again, maybe I deserve to."

"You see there?" Nikola says, getting up from the ottoman and sitting next to me. "Why would you say that? Even on the day that is your saddest of every year for the last five years, I've never heard you say that you deserved to suffer. So what happened?"

"Do you even know how annoying you are?"

"I don't want to hear that shit from you. You come to my home for dinner and lose your shit at my wife over her wanting to see you—her friend for years—be happy. You stomp out of the house and leave us crying in your wake, then have the nerve to tell me *I'm* annoying. I know there has to be mirrors somewhere in this big, new house for you to look in."

"The sound of your voice is nails on a chalkboard."

"Good. What happened?"

"She told me she loved me," I blurt out. "God, you insufferable prick. On the five-year anniversary of Natalia's death, Nia told me that she loved me. We got into it with some asshole at the bar, and I stepped in to defend her. Knocked the guy out cold before we ran out of there and went back to her place. I guess seeing me protect her put her deep inside of her feelings, and she told me that she was in love with me."

"So you ended it," Nikola says as a statement, not a question.

"Yes. I ended it."

Silence rests over us for a moment before Nikola speaks again, but now there is anger in his voice.

"Rome, as your best friend, I'd like to say something to you," he begins. "And also as your best friend, you can't try to throw me out or storm back into your sad little lair back there. I simply want you to listen and absorb the words I'm about to say—words you desperately need to hear. Okay?"

I sigh, more focused on sitting still so my head will stop throbbing. "Fine."

"Cool," he says calmly, then he snaps. "You're a fucking idiot."

My eyes fly open. "What?"

"Don't talk. I told you to just listen," he says, pointing his finger in my face. "You are a fucking idiot, and a little bit of an asshole. I love you, man, but it's true. You were with that girl for a few months, spending all of your time with her, doing everything couples do. I saw how happy you were. It was written across your face like permanent marker. Isabella saw it, too. You were finally starting to move on and allowing happiness to enter your life. But because the anniversary came up again, you chose to sink. You *chose* to give up and let your fear win, and the fact that you made that choice instead of choosing love makes you a fucking idiot."

"Fuck. What the fuck do you want from me, Nikola?"

"For you to stop being a bitch!" he barks. "And for you to start being the man that Natalia fell in love with."

I sit up and stare at him, anger bristling beneath my skin. "Don't start talking about things you know nothing about."

"Oh, please. Try that silly shit on somebody who hasn't known you their entire life. But *me*? I was there. I know who you were back then. I knew your sense of humor. I saw your humility. I witnessed your strength. I was in awe of your determination and will power, defying your father's wishes for you to become a part of his businesses and staking your own claim. I knew you, which means I knew the Rome that Natalia fell in love with. She married the powerful, motivated, fearless version of you that I remember, and she would run from this terrified, *small* man that you have become."

"You better be careful with the next words you say, Nikola," I warn, but tears sting my eyes as realization dawns on me. I put every ounce of my effort into fighting them back, but I'm too weak. They win easily and begin pouring from my face as Nikola continues to read me like a book I never wanted to open myself.

"When your mother was tragically taken from this world, you were nineteen years old. You wished your mother was alive to see you walk down the aisle with Natalia, but you didn't let it stop you from walking. You were stronger then. You've allowed fear to consume you, man—to weaken you—and you and I both know neither your mother, Natalia, or your father would recognize this timidness in you. None of them would want to see you like this, Rome.

"You used to smile and laugh like it was your favorite thing to do. Now, making you smile is like pulling teeth. At least, it was before you met Nia. She brought your smile back. You knocked out a stranger in a bar for her, so it's safe to say she brought your fire back, too. She made you happy, bro ... and it's okay to let go of Natalia and accept happiness with Nia. Because you don't have to be willing to say it in order for both me and Isabella to know it. You love her, Rome."

The sound of the word sends a spike through my heart that makes the tears fall faster.

"You don't know what you're talking about," I force myself to say, fighting with all of my strength to hold onto the façade.

Nikola doesn't even bother arguing with me. He simply stares at me with his head tilted. "Yes, I do. Lie to yourself all you want, but don't lie to me."

As I stare at the truest friend I've ever had, the walls I've built around my heart begin to crumble. The fear remains, but I allow myself to become more open, and it lets a rush of emotion in.

"But what if something happens?" I ask, unable to even maintain eye contact as I cry like a baby. "What if she dies just like the rest of them?"

"Did the years you spent with Natalia mean nothing to you? Or were they the happiest years of your life and the fondest memories that you have?"

Sniffing, I say, "You know the answer."

"I do. So are you willing to give up having the happiest years of your life over the fear that it *might* not end well? You'd rather be miserable than risk it all for a lifetime of bliss? You're an idiot, Rome, but nobody is *that* big of an idiot."

While I cry, my emotions waging a war against one another inside my heart, Nikola scoots close and puts his hand on my knee. I see tears in his eyes, too, and I realize how much this means to him. I'm in awe of him because he has everything already. He has a wonderful wife that he gets to spend the rest of his life with, with plans to have children in the near future. He has a great job and money to spend. He has it all, yet he is still concerned for me. He still wants to see me happy, even after all of the craziness I have brought to his doorstep. This is what true friendship looks like. This, too, is love. I've tried to run from it, but it has always been here, keeping me afloat when I felt like giving up and letting myself drown.

"Let me ask you a question," he says. "If your mother and father were here right now, and they asked you a simple question, would you lie to them?"

"Of course not," I answer, wiping tears from my wet face. "But what's the question?"

Nikola sighs, staring me directly in the eyes.

"The question is … do you love Nia?"

My face crumples into an unrecognizable mess as I begin to bawl like a baby. I cry my eyes out, terror ripping through my core as I think about the last time Natalia smiled at me. I remember the way she sounded when she told me she loved me, and the way her arms felt around my body as she held me close. I know she would want to see me happy. Just like Mom. Just like Dad. Just like Isabella. Just like Nikola.

I close my eyes, squeezing more tears out as I nod.

"Yes," I finally allow myself to admit. "Yes, I love Nia."

Nikola grabs my hand and gives it a squeeze.

"Good," he says, nodding as a single tear slides down his cheek. "Now what are you going to do about it?"

Dear Diary,

I don't have much to say. It's all too painful. The only word that comes to mind is ... LESSON.

I will let this be a lesson as I try to glue the pieces back together and move forward, and the lesson is that even perfection can be impossible to hold onto. Rome was my treasure. He was what I had searched for with a map and magnifying glass, on a long hunt for perfection, and I was successful in my quest. I tracked him down through failed dating app experiences and bad hookups ... but even perfection can be impossible to hold onto.

Finding him didn't guarantee anything. It didn't mean that he would be mine. All my discovery meant was that my version of the perfect Dom did exist. He had been out there all along, but finding him told me nothing about his heart.

I guess I was too late. Someone else had found him already, and he'd given his heart to her, leaving nothing but crumbs behind for me.

I can't do anything with crumbs.

That's the lesson.

FINDING YOUR PERFECT DOM WILL NOT GUARANTEE THAT IT WORKS OUT. LIFE IS A CRUEL BITCH, AND NO MATTER HOW HARD YOU TRY, A LITTLE LUCK IS ALWAYS REQUIRED.

Okay, lesson learned.

I may not have my perfect Dom, but I do have the perfect friends. I'll lean on them now, and I'm not sure I'll be on the hunt again. It's fine. As long as I have them, I'll think I'll be okay.

Forty-Three

"Alright, I know we don't have shots, but everybody raise your glass of whatever you're drinking."

"No, no, no," Jaz interrupts Jeremiah just as he lifts his cocktail into the air. "We're not doing a toast tonight."

"Why not?" Jeremiah asks with a frown, all the wind being sucked out of his sails as he sees he's the only one with alcohol.

Jaz turns to me and eyes me with a sympathetic look. I hate it, because I'm not looking for sympathy from anyone. I didn't tell Jaz about what happened between Rome and I to garner sympathy votes or hugs, and I didn't schedule an entire week off from work for anybody at Sandcastle to feel sorry for me. I didn't spend three nights in a row at Jaz and Michael's house so that they would look at me with pity in their eyes. I just needed time to recover, and still do. No one knows this better than Jaz, and I smile on the inside as her sympathetic look shifts to a steely glare accompanied by a head nod.

"Because we're just not," she says, refusing to mention Rome's name. At this point, I'd be surprised if we ever discuss visiting the city of Rome, just so that we don't have to say the name. "However, what I will do is thank you for being here with us tonight. Michael and I have an announcement that we'd like to share, if you all don't mind."

Jeremiah checks his phone before placing it on the table face down, while my eyebrows raise in anticipation for what's coming. When I left Jaz and Michael's house after the three nights I spent there, Jaz didn't indicate that she had any news to share. Whatever they're talking about is something new. Perfect. I need as many new and exciting things in my life as I can get to help take my mind off of how dilapidated my love life is.

"If you say that you're getting a divorce, you better sleep with one eye open, Michael," Jeremiah says, only half joking.

Michael frowns. "You think we'd bring you to a happy dinner to announce a divorce?"

"I don't know, man. Just don't ignore the threat," Jeremiah says, exaggerating a squint.

"Oh my god," Jaz exclaims with a roll of her eyes. "The announcement is not that we're getting a divorce ... it's that we're pregnant."

Silence envelopes the table as eyes widen and mouths lift into shocked smiles. My insides turn to glitter as happiness and joyful tears quickly develope.

"Oh my god," I whisper, bringing my hands to my face. "I'm going to be an auntie?"

"Yes, girl," Jaz says, her eyes welling up, too.

"And I get to be the gay uncle?" asks Jeremiah, sending the entire table into a fit of laughter.

We spend the next few minutes hugging each other, and probably annoying the hell out the surrounding tables as we get up and make a scene. We don't care a bit. It's not every day that a lifelong friend announces a pregnancy, so we're going to take our time enjoying this moment. Especially considering the fact that this may not ever happen for me. Now that Rome and I are broken up, I'm taking plenty of time to myself before I even consider getting back into the world's most annoying game—dating. So, more than likely, it will be years before children ever enter my picture, and it may not happen at all. As a result of that sad fact, I will be living vicariously through my best friends, and I intend to be the greatest fake auntie on planet Earth.

As dinner continues, our conversation jumps around like it always does. We converse about every topic under the sun—from sports, to politics, to the seasons changing, to what movies are coming out. We avoid anything that has to do with Rome and the breakup. Even Jeremiah, who is still happily dating Gerald, doesn't harp on the fact that he's with someone and falling head over heels. I see him checking and tapping his phone often, and I know he's texting his man, probably anxious to leave here and spend the night with him. I get it. I used to do the same thing not too long ago.

After a while, the night comes to a close and the four of us get up to head out. Jeremiah and I pay the bill as another form of congratulations to Jaz and Michael on their exciting news, and we start our walk from the table to Michael's SUV, because he drove the entire group in his Escalade.

"That steak was so good," I tell Jeremiah, while Jaz and Michael laugh in front of us as we step outside into the night air.

"Mine was, too," Jeremiah agrees.

"Whatever. You had a sirloin, which is a bag of dog ass compared to my filet mignon."

Jeremiah scoffs. "Eww, you bougie ass. How about you pay me more then, so I can afford the steak that costs more than mine while weighing four ounces less."

As I laugh, we round the sidewalk and make a B-line toward Michael's SUV, and that's when I hear footsteps behind us.

"I love you," a deep voice says loudly.

Our entire group stops and turns around, and I gasp so loud it can be heard a mile away.

"Rome?" I say, my face frozen in a grimace of disbelief.

Jaz, Michael, and Jeremiah all turn to look at me before shifting their eyes back to Rome, who they have heard nothing but bad things about since he broke up with me four days ago. I wasn't planning on going back to work for at least another three days, so seeing him now throws a giant monkey wrench in my plan.

My defenses are weakened by the sight of him. He stands in front of us in all-black sweats, his hair more disheveled than usual, with dark bags beneath his eyes like he hasn't slept since he walked out of my house. Even though he's still extremely attractive, this isn't the Rome I met months ago.

"Rome, what are you doing here?" I ask as my heart begins to rev up.

He takes a step forward and drops a nuke on my emotions.

"I love you, Nia," he says without hesitation. "I know that things didn't go well when you told me you loved me a few days ago. I was absolutely absurd in my reaction, and not because I was so surprised by the admission, but because you were right. I was a coward. I was scared of love and how things could end between us and I let that fear live inside of me, controlling my life and feeding off of me like a parasite for years, and I'm so sorry for telling you that I would never love you. It was the biggest lie I've ever told, because the truth is that I already do, and I knew it then. I was so fucking wrong for how I treated you. I'm so sorry, Nia."

The familiar sensation of tears clouding my vision happens once again, but this time it's not just sadness I feel. I've become close friends with anger, and it accompanies me now to protect me from being hurt again.

"You humiliated me," I say, as my friends watch the scene play out like a movie. "And now you're here putting me on the spot in front of my people. How'd you even know I was here? Following me after dumping me is pretty weird, Rome."

"I haven't been following you," he says, his eyes shifting to Jeremiah. "I contacted Jeremiah and asked him if he knew your whereabouts. I haven't been back to Sandcastle since we broke up, and when I called Sierra to tell her she'd be in charge for a while, she told me you hadn't been to work either. So, I called Jeremiah and explained to him how horribly I screwed up and how much I loved you. To his credit, he went scorched Earth, telling me how big of an idiot I am and how I could never find a woman better than you. He even said that he didn't care if I fired him. He ripped me to shreds, and I told him that everything he said was true. I had to beg him to tell me where you were, and he said he wouldn't do it unless I admitted my stupidity in front of the people who care about you most. We've been texting all night, hoping I could grasp this opportunity. So, here I am."

I turn to face Jeremiah, and he purses his lips together and shrugs. I know he meant well, but I'll definitely slap him upside the head after this is all over. For now, I focus my ire on Rome.

"Fine," I say, still keeping the tears at bay. "Go ahead and tell us how stupid you are. In fact, hold on." As two couples approach the door to the restaurant, I call out to them, waving them over. "Hey! Excuse me. The guy who dumped me a few days ago is about to tell us how stupid he is, if you're interested in listening. He usually likes to hide his feelings and keep relationships away from the public eye, so maybe you could come witness this and tell me if you think he's serious or not. My judgment is clouded since I'm in love with him—like an idiot—so maybe you could be of assistance."

To my surprise, both couples smile as they put their evening on hold to come be the jury for Rome's confession. They stand behind my friends with crossed arms and focus on Rome, who swallows hard as I turn around, daring him to avoid the situation I've caused. Sure, it's over the top, but I don't care. Not right now.

Rome nods his head, silently hyping himself up to do something I know will make him uncomfortable. He swallows again, eyeing the group around me before releasing a breath and focusing only on me.

"Nia, my words can't express how sorry I am," he begins. "The other day, it was the five-year anniversary of my wife's death. The entire day was a fog of sadness and frustration about Natalia's sudden death, mixed with fear of how I felt about you. It was torture knowing that I was in love with you on the day I would usually spend mourning her. I felt conflicted and angry, and I took it out on everyone. I snapped at my employees and didn't get any work done, then I knocked out a guy at the bar for disrespecting you because even though I was hurting inside, my love for you would never allow anyone to disrespect you. Then you told me that you loved me, and I became unglued.

"My heart split in two—one side for the woman I married, the other for you. I panicked, worried that I was disrespecting Natalia on the anniversary of her death, while also fearing that loving you would mean losing you to an early grave the same way I lost both parents and my wife. I fell into a pit of despair and let the darkness swallow me whole, and it took my closest friend to pull me out of it. I clung to him the same way you're clinging to your friends now, and he beat the truth out of me. He asked me how I would respond if my parents asked if I was in love with you, and answering him felt like I was really responding to them. The answer was yes. Yes, I was ... I *am* in love with you, Nia. Right here at this very moment, and saying that I don't care who knows it would be a lie, because I do care. I want *everyone* to know that I'm in love with you. You, your friends, and perfect strangers. I want them all to know."

I quickly wipe away the tears that refuse to stay in my eyes, and let out a long breath.

"And what about your fear? You said you feared losing me the same way you lost them. How do you feel about that now?"

"Fuck fear," he answers quickly. "I'd rather risk it all for us, than live a full life knowing I gave up on the best thing to ever happen to me. Fear will not keep my love for you at bay."

"I don't want to compete with Natalia, Rome."

"And you never will. I promise you, Nia. Because of you, I'm finally ready to move on. I'm sorry I hurt you, and I'm begging you in front of people I don't know to forgive me. I love you, Nia Washington, and I'll never want happiness again if it isn't with you."

Try as I might, my anger gives way to the flood of emotions when I turn around and see everyone standing behind me with tears in their eyes. Jaz covers her mouth with her hand, while Michael puts his head down so that his tears are barely visible in the dark. Jeremiah wipes away a tear before nodding his approval, and even the four strangers fight back tears of their own. Each of them nods to me, not needing to say a word to let me know that even though they don't know Rome, they can see his sincerity.

When I turn around, Rome stands in the exact same place. He hasn't stepped forward, assuming that his groveling would result in instant forgiveness. Instead, he waits for me, his eyes filled with hope and anxiousness at the same time, and the only fear I see in him now is the fear of losing me.

I have new fears of my own. I'm terrified that I will always compete with the woman he lost five years ago. I worry that he'll always have anxiety in the back of his mind when it comes to how long we will last, and I'm horrified by the possibility of being hurt all over again. But all of that pales in comparison to how much I want him. From the moment he strutted into Sandcastle, I have wanted to be with him, and I know that turning him away now would be something I would regret for the rest of my life. I won't allow myself to be that dumb.

"Are you one hundred percent sure?" I ask, my feet already anxious to inch forward.

"I've never been more sure about anything in my life," he answers confidently.

As the final barrier over my heart falls, I run to him, throwing my arms around Rome as our lips connect for the first time in far too long. He spins me around while kissing me, making the entire scene feel like a fairytale getting its happy ending.

"I love you," I say when I manage to pull away.

"I love you, my little goddess," he answers.

Our makeshift audience begins to applaud, and I turn to see smiling faces and tears of joy from everyone. My heart sings with happiness as Rome puts me down and kisses me again. Even though my feet are on the ground, I'm still floating on a cloud.

"So, is it safe to assume that you don't need a ride home?" Michael says, chuckling to himself.

I look at him and grin, my eyes still watering. "I appreciate it, Michael, but I'll be going home with Rome."

Forty-Four

My mind and heart race as the cloud I've been floating on since the restaurant stays beneath my feet, carrying me from Rome's car to the inside of his house, where we kiss the second the door is closed. After four days, our bodies have clearly spent enough time apart to develop withdrawal, now we're desperate to binge on each other.

Rome and I stay connected, our hands pulling us closer, our mouths never parting as we bump our way through the house. We crash into furniture, bounce off the corner of a wall, and knock a few picture frames crooked, but we eventually reach our destination and stand at the top of the stairs that lead to his playroom.

"We don't have to do this," Rome says, even as he kisses me on the neck and I'm distracted by the erection in his pants. "I didn't bring you back here for this."

"No?" I ask, my neck arched to give him easier access to it. "What'd you bring me back for?"

"Because I love you, and I was going to die if I didn't have you near me. We're back together, and that is all I needed. You belong to me again."

"Forever?"

He keeps kissing, making his way up to my ear, where whispers, "For fucking ever."

I know I could go the more romantic route. I could choose to lay with him on the couch and watch movies while we drink wine. I could lay on my stomach in his bed while he massages my back and shoulders. We could simply cuddle, our fingers caressing each other's skin while we bask in a bliss-filled fog of happiness. There are a lot of things we could do after reuniting tonight, and I know Rome is in the headspace of a remorseful Dom who is willing to put aside all of his desires to do whatever makes his sub happy. But the truth is that there is only one thing I want right now, and he and I both know it's the only way for us to reconnect properly.

I put my hand on the doorknob and push it open. "Take me to the playroom, Sir."

Rome's eyes darken as he grins. "With pleasure, my little goddess."

He takes me by the hand and leads me down the stairs step by step, and the second we reach the bottom Rome spins around and pins his mouth to mine. His aggressiveness returns now that I have given him permission, and we kiss our way through the playroom until he brings us to a sudden stop. Without hesitation, I immediately remove my clothes and begin lowering myself to my knees in front of him, in a rush to submit and allow my Dom to use my consent at his leisure. But as I drop down, Rome places a hand beneath my chin and lifts me back up.

"No," he tells me. "Don't kneel. Stand ... and back up."

Placing all of my trust in him, I don't even glance over my shoulder as I take steps backward until I bump into something hard. Rome smiles as he stands in front of me, placing one hand on my hip and the other on my right wrist.

"Take one step to your left," he commands.

When I move, Rome guides me by the waist, then raises my wrist and secures it to a leather cuff dangling from the upper arm of his Saint Andrew's cross. My heart soars as he continues strapping me in, starting first with my other hand before moving down to my ankles. When he's finished I am completely open to him, naked with my arms and legs spread wide. I have no control and I am not free to move.

Perfect.

Rome steps back, assessing my body like a carpenter inspecting his work. His eyes roam my body as he removes his shirt, teasing my eyes and hands. I want to pull him closer. I want his body on top of mine, his fingers in my hair. But he continues backing up until he reaches the black pillar that is covered in floggers. I watch him turn his head and examine each one, scrutinizing them as if they could have flaws that make them unworthy of the scene we are about to commence. When he finally makes a choice and lifts his hand to retrieve it, my mouth drops open and my skin turns to gooseflesh.

"This," he says proudly as the toy dangles to the floor, "is the cat o' nine tails. It used to be a torture device a long time ago. Now it's my favorite version of a flogger." He steps closer to me so that I can see the detail in each long tress. "Before I use it on you, tell me what your safe word is."

I keep my eyes on the flogger. "*La regina.*"

"Good girl. What does it mean?"

"The queen."

"That's right. When the queen is summoned, everything stops. Until then ... don't let fear consume you, my little goddess. I see it in your eyes now, when all I should see is trust. Decide now if you want me to continue."

I don't hesitate. "Of course I do. Please continue, Sir."

Rome smiles again before stepping away. He goes to the spanking bench and retrieves the wand stand he used on me before, and places a wand inside of it before sliding it over to the cross that is holding me captive. He flicks on the wand, making it hum to life before positioning it between my legs. The vibrations hit my clit like a shockwave that ripples up my body.

"Oh god," I say aloud, the sensation almost too much to bear. Just as I relax and settle into it, Rome raises his hand and flicks his wrist.

Thwack.

The tails rip across my stomach, leaving a trail of red on my skin in its wake. My muscles jolt and I let out an involuntary chirp, shocked by how much it hurt ... and how much I liked it.

There is something about this version of pain that people outside the lifestyle don't understand. For most people, the only pain they experience is excruciating. Breaking a bone or tearing a muscle hurts so much that it inflicts people with fear, and the fear heightens the pain. The mind is a very powerful tool, which is why it takes a very special kind of person to let go of fear and enjoy the sensation of pain. Once fear is removed, pain can become pleasure when it is placed in trustworthy hands.

Rome whips the tails again, and this time I don't chirp. The pain streaking across my chest mixes with the pleasure between my legs and I quickly surge toward an orgasm. The two feelings become overwhelming, confusing my body and sending me reeling and wanting more.

"You like it?" Rome asks, steadying himself in front of me as he grips the shaft of the flogger.

The vibrator continues to hum, nearly stealing the words from my throat and replacing them with moans of agonizing pleasure.

"Yes ... Yes, Sir," I manage to say before letting out a groan.

"I like this," Rome says. "I like watching you whimper, the way your body wants to curl into a ball but is forced open for me. I love having control over you."

He swings the flogger again.

Thwack.

"I love watching your skin change colors for me."

Thwack.

"The way your legs quiver from the kiss of the tails."

Thwack.

"The way the conflicting sensations of pain and pleasure turn you inside out right in front of me."

Thwack.

"And I love knowing that you're on the verge of coming, but cannot without your Sir's permission."

Thwack.

I suck in a deep breath as the truth of Rome's words become my reality. An orgasm storms forward, ready to unleash the most pleasurable hell upon me.

"Fuck. Sir, can I please come? Please!" I shriek just as I'm about to lose control.

Rome drops the cat o' nine tails and quickly pulls the wand away from my clit. "No."

I let out a disappointed groan as the orgasm recedes into the darkness, replaced by frustration.

"Aww. Are you heartbroken, my little goddess?" Rome asks, teasing me as he runs the back of his hand down my reddened torso.

"Yes, Sir," I admit, frowning and wincing from the sensitivity of my flesh.

"You wanted to come for me?"

"Yes, Sir."

"You wanted me to let you be my little whore and orgasm all over that wand. Didn't you?"

"Yes, Sir," I say, pleading with my eyes.

Rome's hand continues to slide down my skin until his knuckles graze over my clit and I suck in a whoosh of air.

"Still sensitive for me I see," he says, so proud of himself. "Maybe I should do something about that."

"Yes. Please," I beg, letting go of all senses of shame. I don't care how desperate I look or sound. I just want him to touch me.

"There's my favorite word," he replies, smiling as he looks at my lips. "Say it again. I want to watch that mouth of yours beg me to let you come."

My heart flutters with need and I feel like a child begging for candy. "Please, Sir. *Please* let me come for you."

"The only way you can earn the right to come for me is if it's in my mouth. Do you understand me? I want to taste how much you love me."

"Yes, Sir. I understand."

Rome drops down to his knees and clamps his mouth on my dripping pussy. His lips and tongue are magic on my clit, with a combination of swirls and sucking that make my head spin. I want to reach down and grip the sides of his face so I can ride his tongue like a bull, but the cross has me bound beautifully. All I can do is let him work on me until my need to come returns with a furious vengeance.

"Sir, please, for the love of god, let me come in your mouth," I beg.

Rome finally relents and grants me permission.

"Give it to me, my little goddess. I'm going to swallow every last drop of you."

Rome sucks on my clit and licks it with a flat tongue, and my body erupts as I let go and allow the orgasm to detonate. My head flies backward and slams against the wood of the cross as my arms and legs flex, testing the strength of each cuff as I growl and convulse. Rome doesn't back away. He does as he promised and keeps his mouth glued to me, sucking my clit while I unload down his throat.

"That's my fucking girl," he says as he stands and pushes his pants down, finally letting me see how hard he is. But he doesn't waste time showing off his immense thickness. Rome steps forward and pushes himself into me, stretching me out so fucking good.

"Fuck!" I yell, just as he begins to plow into me without remorse.

Rome fucks me hard and fast, each stroke is a wrecking ball that destroys me. I yell until my throat is fire and squeeze my eyes shut until they ache. He fucks me like he hates my entire existence until he announces that he is ready to come, too.

"I'm about to fucking explode," he roars.

"Yes. I want it on my stomach," I reply, remembering how amazing it felt on my skin before. My new fetish comes forward like a stampede, craving to have Rome's cum splattered all over my body. "Please, Rome. I want you to cum all over me. Give it to me, Sir."

"Fuck!" he screams as he pulls out and strokes his cock in front of me.

I watch as a thick white rope ejects from his cock and lands on my navel, followed by another hitting the middle of my stomach, and another splashing just below my breasts.

The warm cum feels incredible, and it all is like a kinky dream coming true. I fucking love every second of it.

When he's finished, Rome drops down to one knee just to gather his strength again. He takes in huge breaths, looking up at me with love beaming from his eyes. After a moment, he leaves me fastened to the cross and comes back with a warm towel, using it to clean his cum off of me before releasing my restraints. Once I'm free, he swoops me up into his arms and carries me over to the black bed in the corner, where we lay with his arms wrapped around me.

Here, in his arms, I am safe from all harm. The drama of it all is now over, and I am free. I am protected. I am certain. I am in love. In his arms, I am home.

Forty-Five

"**S** o you're not going to tell me where we're going?"

"You'll see when we get there," Rome replies as he exits the crowded highway. I can tell from the look on his face that he's nervous. There is something in his eyes as he stares through the windshield that he hides when he looks at me. Although he hasn't told me where we're going, I can tell it's someplace important to him.

The thrill of last night still hasn't left my body. Disbelief and elation flow through my veins, making reality feel like a fever dream, because Rome showed up to the restaurant and told me he loved me. To people who read romance all the time, this might not be a big deal. But Rome had informed me that he didn't love me and that he never would. He said it with such finality that I had no choice but to believe him, so when the words, "I love you," swam into my ears I didn't know what to do. But when I saw his face and heard his sincerity, I knew I couldn't turn him away. After all, I'd already told him that I loved him, and I meant it.

After what can only be described as make-up sex last night, I woke up to Rome talking on the phone while sitting on the side of the bed. His conversation had been ongoing while I was asleep and he was ending his call, but it was clear he was setting up some sort of meeting. All he told me was that he wanted to take me somewhere special and that I needed to get dressed. So, he freshened up before taking me back to my place so I could, too. Then the drive began, and he has barely spoken since. I've watched him wavering back and forth between excited and nervous the entire car ride, but now that we're getting close, I can see him starting to fidget from the nerves.

We make a turn into Society Hill, one of Philly's most luxurious neighborhoods, and I'm so distracted by the beautiful, gargantuan houses that I don't even notice when Rome turns the car into a gorgeous horseshoe driveway. When it dawns on me that we're at someone's house, I snap my head over to him.

"Are we meeting people?" I ask, knowing how private Rome is and how he doesn't have any family left since his father passed earlier this year.

He turns to me with pure emotion in his face. "Yes."

The idea of meeting anyone who he holds dear makes me feel unbelievably special, but I also don't want him to do anything that makes him uncomfortable.

"Are you sure about this?" I ask. "I know you love me, Rome. I believe you when you say it, and I don't need you to do anything more to prove it."

Rome reaches across the car and takes my hand. "I know, and it's true that I've never done this before. But I *want* to do it, Nia. Not out of obligation, but out of love. Trust me, my little goddess."

I smile as I begin to blush just from looking in his eyes. "Okay, Sir."

Rome flashes a quick grin before pulling me into a kiss, then he steps out of the car and I follow.

Hand in hand, we walk up to the massive, three-story home, and I'm suddenly overcome with my own nerves. Before Rome, I had been on date after date without ever getting to the point of introducing anyone to my friends or family. At the age of thirty, introductions are not run of the mill. I would never take this step without it being extremely serious, and I realize that Rome and I are *that serious*.

Rome presses the doorbell, and the decorative gray door swings open to two beautiful people standing behind it. The man looks at me before reaching out to shake Rome's hand, while the woman keeps her eyes on me only, her face alight with joy. Both of them smile like they just won the lottery.

Rome clears his throat. "Nia, I'd like to introduce you to my best friends in the whole world. These two people are my family. Through thick and thin they have been here for me, fighting to keep me upright when I didn't have the strength to stand on my own. This is Nikola Collazo, and his beautiful wife, Isabella."

"It's nice to meet you both," I say as Nikola reaches out and shakes my hand with a proud smile.

"It's nice to meet you, too," he says.

As I go to shake Isabella's hand, she extends her arms as her eyes fill with tears. She pulls me into a hug that feels as comforting as affection from my mother, before kissing me on both cheeks.

"It's so nice to finally meet you," she says, and I'm moved to tears from the emotion displayed on her face. She turns to Rome and lightly punches him in the shoulder. "You finally brought her over."

Rome smiles, his eyes misting, too. "Yeah, well I told you when I brought someone over that she'd be *the one*. Well ... she's the one."

Isabella pulls us both into a hug a second time before inviting us into their beautiful home. When the door closes behind us, it feels like a circle is being completed, the final pieces of a puzzle coming together to reveal the whole picture—and it's stunning. I'm truly happy, and I have a feeling that Rome and I will be spending plenty of time here with new friends, new love, and brand new joy.

Forty-Six – Rome

The last time I was here, it was right after my father's funeral. I was an emotional wreck, stumbling my way across the grass after everyone had left, with a bottle of Disaronno in my hand and fog in my vision. I tripped over rocks and long weeds on my way, and by the time I reached my destination I was covered in mud, sweat, and tears. It was a living nightmare I couldn't wake up from, especially the fact that I was visiting three people on the same day, at the same place.

I had left my father's freshly dug grave to visit my mother's old one, only to say my goodbyes and visit my wife's.

I hate the fucking graveyard. I don't come here often. Who the hell wants to spend all of their time crying over their dead loved ones, surrounded by headstones covered in tears and moss? Agony floats through the air here, and I made a promise to myself that I would show up on birthdays only, because there is no way I could stay away forever, but I also don't want to spend too much time here mourning the dead instead of living my life. Today isn't my father's or mother's birthday. I'm here for one reason, and as I walk up the hill toward her tombstone, I know this is about to be the hardest thing I've ever done.

Natalia Marissa Giovanni.

Seeing her name etched in stone still fills my stomach with bile that doesn't come up. It's like a cruel joke that I will never believe is true, no matter how many times I stand here staring at it. We were so happy, then it was stripped away in a flash. Here in the morning, gone in the afternoon. How does anyone get over something as sudden as death by aneurysm? I guess if I knew the answer to that question life would have been a bit easier in the days and years after her passing, but I digress. I'm not here to linger on the past. Today is about the future.

"Hello, Natalia," I say, as if she is standing right in front of me. Tears prickle my eyes after just two words, but I won't run away today, telling myself that I'll save the words for next time. Next time may not ever come.

I try not to think too much, knowing that what I'm here to do is vital to my ability to move on with my life after five years of suffering. If I let my thoughts get in the way, they will control me and I won't be able to do this at all, and if I can't do it, then my relationship with Nia will need its own tombstone.

"I know it has been a while since I've been here," I say, looking down at her stone name. "But you know I don't like visiting this place. It's almost like being here fills my head with memories of your final resting place, replacing the happy times that we shared while you were still here. I hate that. I don't want to think of you being buried beneath my feet while I stand atop your dirt-covered casket and cry my eyes out, feeling my heart re-break every time I'm here. This isn't healthy ... and you're gone. You're not coming back. So, this needs to be the end.

"The reason I'm here right now is to tell you how much I loved you. We met when I was twenty-five, dated for three years while we both matured and got our lives together, and then got married when I was twenty-eight years old. The two years that we were married were the happiest of my life. Every hour was full of bliss, laughter, and passion. You taught me things I never knew I needed to learn—things I will never forget—and you made it so that five years after your death, I still couldn't be happy. I'm not ashamed of it. That's how powerful true love is supposed to be. It's meant to be agonizing and long-lasting when it's real. I wear my heartbreak as a badge of honor, because I was never ashamed of loving you—so why would I be ashamed of mourning you? Inadvertently, you made it so that I could never accept anything other than perfection, because that's what you were. You were *perfect*, Natalia, and I never thought I'd find anything resembling it ever again. Until now.

"I want you to know that there is a part of you that will always be with me. I will always have love in my heart for you, but I've finally found someone else. If you're watching, I know that you want me to be happy. You would never wish to watch me wallow in agony every single day for the rest of my life. You'd want me to move on, and you would want me to do it with her.

"Nia is the reason I'm able to smile again. She makes me laugh. She makes me more of a pleasure to be around, and I don't think she knows that her ability to make my heart joyful is more important than her submission. It's true that she's a submissive just like you were, but you and I both know that finding pleasure *outside* of the bedroom was always the goal. I have that now, and I can't fully accept it if my sorrow won't allow my heart to mend. I have to heal in order to have her, so that's what I'm doing now."

As tears drip from my chin, I reach down and place a hand atop Natalia's tombstone.

"I will never forget you. The five years I got to spend knowing you will never be erased, and I hope that you don't take my not coming here as a personal slight. You were the love of my life, Natalia, but I can't die with you, and if I don't let you go, then that is exactly what's going to happen.

"Don't worry about Nikola and Isabella. They are more successful now than ever, and watching me find Nia has helped them to move on, too. They miss you dearly, and I know that they think of you when the four of us are laughing together, but seeing me with Nia is healing for all of us.

"Thank you so much for loving me so fiercely. Our love set the standard. You raised the bar, Natalia, and now I will go on with my life knowing that I have what I have because of the example you set. If something terrible happens and things don't work out between Nia and I, I'll still remember how much you loved me and never accept anything less than the perfection I saw in you. Thank you for everything. I'll never forget you. It's just time for me to move on—to let go ... and let love."

When I turn to walk away, I expect my heart to crumble—to feel the need to run back and hug her tombstone like I have done so many times in the past. But it doesn't happen this time. While I still cry, each step fortifies me. My strength builds as I keep moving, and my sad tears morph into tears of joy and fulfillment. I am made whole now, and while I don't know what the future holds, I know that it is as bright as the sun shining down on me as I climb in my car.

When I start the engine, I don't look back at the grave. I'm letting go. This is the end ... and a brand new beginning.

Dear Diary,

I'm running out of pages. The timing couldn't be better because it seems that I've also run out of reasons to continue writing between these lines. When I first opened you, it was to put my feelings to paper and document all of the insanity I was going through in my love life. I wrote because I needed to get it out, but also as an example that I could go back to if I felt myself wondering about potential red flags. I've been through the gamut of boys wanting to be Doms, falling victim to their many flaws and jotting them all down to laugh and cry at later. It has been quite a wild, stupid, exhilarating, exhausting ride, but I am at the end of the dark tunnel, with nothing but light in front of me now.

There was a moment when I thought my perfect Dom and I wouldn't make it. My desire to find true love in the BDSM lifestyle collided with his broken heart, and while the crash was beautiful to look at, our damage eventually couldn't be ignored. I needed to learn to slow down and evaluate better, instead of diving in head-first and accepting any little thing thrown my way. My bar needed to be set higher. I needed to toughen up and stop looking at the bare minimum as if it were a pot of gold. Rome and Jaz taught me that. Rome, on the other hand, needed to heal. Nikola and I helped him to do that.

In the end, it was more than just our D/s dynamic that pulled us through the fire. It was the fact that each of us were what the other needed to persevere. I realize that is the most important part of it all. We are what the other needs, and that fortifies our dynamic. It makes us stronger, more durable, more passionate, and even more in love.

After showing me exactly what I thought a Dom was supposed to be, I watched the most intimidating man I'd ever met break down over the loss of his parents and first love. I saw vulnerability that I never knew a Dom should have. I saw him struggle. I saw him overcome with emotion, and I didn't think of him as weak for showing it to me. I saw a Dom take the space he needed from the rest of the world and cling to his lifelong friends until he was ready to come up for air.

Then I saw him cry. In front of me and a staring group of strangers, I watched as Rome let go of the notion that masculinity was inherently tied to immovable toughness and emotionlessness. He broke for me, split himself open and bared his soul for the world to gawk at, all while maintaining his sense of self. Through his vulnerability, he showed why he is the perfect Dom. I threw away the ideas I had about dominance in this lifestyle, because Rome broke the mold. How could I possibly say no to such beauty?

There is nothing in our way now. After taking another week away from work just to solidify our reunion, Rome and I walked back into Sandcastle hand in hand. The entire office gawked at us as we strided in and made our way to the HR department to make it official. Rome thought it was unnecessary seeing as how he is the owner, but I convinced him that it was best to avoid potential issues, just in case Sierra or anybody else decided to cause a stir. Although the obligatory administrative stuff is now out of the way, we continue to maintain our professionalism and try to keep the public displays of affection to a minimum in front of our coworkers. Even Sierra has come to see our relationship as normalcy.

Each of us has added more friends into our lives. I've been over to Nikola and Isabella's luxurious home a few times now, and I absolutely love creating memories with them. It's easy to see that they love Rome. It's apparent in how they poke fun at each other while also being unbelievably caring. It's incredible how the four of us meshed so well together since Rome introduced us two months ago.

As for Rome, he is now a part of the Jaz, Michael, Jeremiah, and Nia crew. While Jaz and Michael usually host, we've convinced them to come over to Rome's house and spend time with us there. It is a blast every single time we get together, no matter whose house we're at. Rome and I just make sure the basement door is locked whenever they come over.

There are very few pages left here, and I'm fine with that. I think it's the perfect ending, actually. I've used my writing as a way to cope, but now I confide my feelings in Rome. There is no need to keep a diary now. So, I guess this is the end. It's time to move onto bigger and better things, to see what beauty life has in store for Rome and me. Seeing as how I used to come back to what I'd written in these pages to try to avoid repeating mistakes, I don't really see a need to keep it at all.

I'm not the same person I was when I first started writing. However, I refuse to throw this away. Just because it's not for me anymore doesn't mean it couldn't help someone else. Instead of trashing all of this, I think I'll put it somewhere. Maybe it would be best on the shelf of a library, hiding between other books like a treasure map for someone else to find and use to their advantage. Perhaps it will help another submissive avoid some of the pitfalls I fell into, while also giving them hope that what they're looking for can be found. It may take time, but refusing to give up has never been a bad idea.

As I sign off, I'm starting to believe that this is what was always meant to be for the words I've written. As much as they were for me, they were for someone else who is truly struggling and in need of evidence that what they're going through isn't specific to them. I struggled, too, and now I've written my way out of the book. So, I'll head to the library and find a shelf to stick this notebook on. All it needs now is a good title.

I think I'll call it ... A Good Girl's Guide to Dominance.

THE END

Acknowledgements

Well, we've come to the end of yet another book, and I can barely believe it. *A Good Girl's Guide to Dominance* was a long time in the making, and I couldn't be prouder of the way this book turned out. This is the first book that I created from the outline phase to "The End" with no attachment whatsoever to the military. This was 100% me in author mode full-time, and it feels amazing to bring it to completion and have it being anticipated the way it is. I'm so unbelievably fortunate to be able to do this for a living at just forty years old, and it's only possible because of the fans who have been flocking to me lately. I am truly honored, and I hope this book gives you everything you have been looking for in a romance novel.

My goal with *A Good Girl's Guide to Dominance* was to use Nia as a way to explain to women what a Dom is supposed to look like, while also giving examples of how a man can wear the suit of a Dom without actually being one. Everything I write is for the female gaze, but deep down, I do this for the men. I desperately want men to get their shit together both inside and outside of the BDSM lifestyle, and I know how badly women want the same thing. Women are yearning, more than ever, for men to not suck, but I'm not seeing improvement. I'm trying to help, so I hope that men will read this and pick up on what Nia is saying both in her diary and in her inner dialogue about the men she dated. She points out all of the flaws, red flags, and clues that she sees, so men can self-identify their own fuckery and learn to do better. For my female readers, I hope this helps you to play "spot the difference" when it comes to men who are legit versus the ones who are full of shit. Keep your eyes open, ladies. They're out there, but it will not be easy to find because the sea is full of catfish. Be careful.

As usual, I have to thank my one and only true love in this life, my wife Isabel Lucero. Thank you for always helping me with this and allowing me to bounce ideas off of you. Getting to work next to you each and every day is a dream come true that was eleven years in the making, when we first started our book journey together back in 2013. It's so incredible that we get to live this life together after starting off in that trailer in 2003. We've come so far, and now we're living the dream and raising our kids inside of it. It truly doesn't get much better than this, and the crazy part is that I retired from the military only six months ago, so it's really just getting started. We have so much more to accomplish, and we get to do it side by side. I can't wait to let them see what we do next.

I have to send a huge shout out to my assistant, Jasmine. Thanks so much for all of your help with everything. You take on the parts of my job that I absolutely want no part of, and I see how stressful it gets every single time we have a rollout. I appreciate your patience and support very much. See you in Kentucky!

Thank you to The Author Agency, who I have worked with for my last three releases now. Becca and Shauna, you two always do such a great job and I absolutely freakin' need you. Thank you for all of your support in helping me spread the word about this release. I appreciate you both.

Thank you to each of my beta readers for *A Good Girl's Guide to Dominance*. Chandra Quimby, Lindsey Acree, Scarlet Pennywell, Sharon Davis, and Sierra Ramirez Beasley—thank you all for your kind words and motivation during the beta phase. I can't overstate how important that phase of the process is for my confidence leading up to release day. I'm hyper-sensitive while my betas are reading, ready to latch onto any perceived negativity and drown myself in sorrows over it. But all of you were super positive and made me feel like the release would be a good one. Thank you all so much!

Shout out to my agent, Stephanie, for all of your support. This is our first go 'round, so I'm anxious to see how these wheels spin since the change up. I have all the faith in the world in you, and you and I both know we have something massive on the horizon that I'm about to start and can't wait to get to. For now, let's do this romance together and snatch up all the bags! We'll see you soon, NA fantasy!

Shout out to all of the organizers and coordinators for every book signing that I have coming up—Authors in the Bluegrass, Indies Invade Philly, ApollyCon, RomantiConn, Electric City Love Con, Book Harvest, and BRAE. There will be so many more coming, and I'm beyond grateful for all of your support. You make my dream life a reality. Thank you!

Lastly, I want to thank each and every WS Greer fan out there. Thank you all for believing in me and rushing to buy every book I release. If it wasn't for you, absolutely none of this would be happening. I get to write books for a living because of you, and I will never be the person to take that for granted or forget it. There was a time when I would publish books and next to nothing would happen, and if something did happen it didn't last long. Now, I'm ecstatic every time I publish because of you and your support. People call me their favorite author, and it's the biggest compliment I could ever get. Thank you all so much! If there is one thing I can promise you going forward, it's that there is so much more to come. I will only be doing more and more, and working to get better. Trust me when I say ... I'm just getting warmed up.

Until next time. Embrace your kinks!

Author's Note 2

Nix Malone and Solomon King are mentioned heavily in the first half of *A Good Girl's Guide to Dominance*. I work hard to keep all of my characters in the same universe so that I can guide my readers to gems they might have missed. This is the case for Nix and Solomon. The two of them have a story of their own that is much darker than *A Good Girl's Guide to Dominance*, and Solomon is still one of my favorite characters to this day. He and Nix are more ruthless than this book could ever show you, but they have a story of their own that I hope you feel inspired to read after hearing about them in this book.

Their tale is called *Madman*, and it shows you everything that the people of Philadelphia come to know about their infamous antiheroes. Nix is all business in *A Good Girl's Guide to Dominance*, but you get to see his true nature in *Madman*, and you'll see why Nia was so hesitant to work with a man of his reputation. If you're interested, turn the page and read chapter one, and I hope it makes you want to keep reading and find out more.

Chapter 1 of Madman

The world is gray.

No surprise there. How else would I expect it to look on my seventeenth birthday?

I step out of my rundown house and breathe in the chilled air, nearly freezing my lungs in the process. On the other side of the door that's closing behind me, is my thirty-four-year-old mother, who's passed out on the filthy living room floor with a needle in her arm. Again. Whitney—the woman I have no choice but to call my mother—decided to use my birthday as an excuse to push more heroin into her veins. It was a time to celebrate, she said, as she pressed the plunger and fell into a lifeless stupor on the couch, just before losing control of her bodily functions and sliding down to the floor where I left her. Happy Birthday, Solomon King.

I can see my breath as I step off the squeaky, dilapidated porch and zip up my new coat. It's thick, with a Philadelphia Eagles logo on the back. Really nice. It's mine, but it wasn't always. Because who are we kidding? Isn't it obvious? Whitney is a junkie, so we all know she would never save enough money to buy me this coat. But it's freezing in South Philly in December, so I needed something to keep me warm. I also needed these Timberland boots and sweatpants, just like I needed this Eagles beanie, and when you live in Strawberry Mansion with a junkie for a mother, you do what you've got to do. You take what you need, and make no mistake about it, I take what I want, when I want, from who I want. So let's just say I needed the clothes I'm wearing more than the little rich prick I took them from. I'm sure his mother and father love him to the moon and back, so he probably has five new Eagles coats to replace the one I stole from him. Don't feel bad for him. I don't.

I walk out of my yard, closing the rusty fence behind me, and start down the street toward Aaron's Arcade. It's only a block away from the shit-pile I call home, and as I walk on the gray sidewalks that are glistening with pellets of ice, bypassing rundown house after rundown house, I pass a group of bums on the corner huddling around a metal trash can with a fire blazing inside of it. The flames release tiny embers that float around the entire group as they warm their hands and skinny bodies. There's four of them, and as I walk past, one of them notices me. He's the smallest of the four at maybe five-six or seven, and probably the youngest with the most to prove, but his glaring eyes catch the attention of the others, and before long, all of them are looking me up and down. They see my fancy coat and Timberland boots. I bet they're thinking about how warm I look, because all of them have little thin jackets that look like they're not offering nearly enough warmth. I see them watching me out of the corner of my eye, but I press on without care.

"Nice coat, kid," the little one says. He steps away from the crowd as if he might walk towards me. That's when I stop walking and face them, smiling.

"Aww, that's so sweet of you to say. I bet it'd fit you nice and snug," I say with amusement dripping from my words. I smile at the little black kid, and he glares back, but it slowly fades and morphs into confusion. He looks like he doesn't know what to think of my smile, then turns around to look at his crew.

The biggest guy in the group is lanky with a thick beard that could use the love and affection of a comb, and he leans forward, squinting his eyes to see me better. His face freezes when he recognizes me.

"Come back over here, Darnell," the big one says to the little one. "That's Solomon."

"What? I don't care who he is," Darnell spits back, trying his best to stay tough, but the tall one won't let it go.

"Yes you do," he replies. "Just come back. Let it go."

"Oh, don't let him discourage you, Darnell," I interject, taking a step towards him. "I'd love to play."

Little Darnell frowns again, before finally listening to his inner-self and stepping back over to the burning trash can. He re-enters into the empty space he just vacated and flashes me his best tough-guy-frown. I tilt my head, poke my lip out and pout in disappointment, just as I turn and continue on my path. As I walk away, I hear the tall one say, "Don't mess with that kid, man. I've heard about him."

The rest of my walk to the arcade is quiet. Nothing but the sound of my own footsteps and rows of broken down houses. The cars that pass aren't fancy or flashy, and the passengers inside are just as beaten down as the automobiles. The trees have no leaves in December, and they seem to represent Strawberry Mansion perfectly—dead and ugly, but still standing, barely.

Most people are inside because it's too cold to be out here, so I don't see another person until I reach Aaron's. As I approach the arcade, my first thought is that I'm probably going to have to punk some kid for his money, because I only have two bucks in my pocket, and I'm going to burn through that pretty quick. But as I walk past the narrow alley just before the entrance, I see something out of the corner of my eye.

In the middle of the alley, I see commotion that surprises me. It's two boys and a girl, standing perfectly between the entrance and exit of the grimy alley. They're arguing about something I can't make out, but my eyes are drawn to the girl. She doesn't look like she's from around here. She has blonde hair, full lips, a thin nose, and blue eyes I can see all the way from over here. She's wearing a white sweater and has a look on her face that says she isn't even remotely afraid of the boys who are laughing at her for some reason. She's holding her own, and I like the show the three of them are putting on in front of me, so I decide not to go into Aaron's just yet. While I watch in amusement and wonder, I reach into the pocket of my sweats with my right hand, carefully bypassing the gun I keep there, and pull out my lighter, while simultaneously pulling my cigarettes out of the other pocket with my left hand, making sure to avoid the box cutter I keep in that particular pocket. I light one up and lean against the side of the brick building, just as the blonde girl reaches back and slaps one of the boys right in the face.

Not a second later, the heavy-set boy she hit pushes her, sending her falling backwards onto the cold, slick cement.

"Bitch!" the boy yells. He's filled with a lot of pride for a guy his size picking on a girl her size. He even puffs out his chest a little. When I look at him, two things stand out to me. One: he has a hard time growing facial hair, but he's really trying because he thinks it'll make him look tougher. Two: he's done this before and has signature moves for being intimidating, and sticking out his flabby chest is one of them.

The other boy is tall and slender, and he has the look of a kid who spends his free time dressing up in a Nazi uniform and doing that stupid salute to himself in the mirror, with his thick blonde hair and dreamy blue eyes. He screams something about money at the girl, so from the looks of it, I've walked up on an attempted robbery. My, my. This is just the kind of thing that puts a smile on my face, but usually it's me who's doing the robbing.

When the Nazi boy reaches down to try to dig into the girl's pocket, she kicks him in the chest and he stumbles back, hitting the dumpster behind him. I smile as I watch this girl get up and throw a punch at the chunkier boy, hitting him in the jaw. The only problem is that this girl is just too small, and the chubby boy is pissed off now. He draws back and slaps her across the face, but to my delighted surprise, she doesn't scream out in pain, and she doesn't run away. She stands up tall, and tries to punch him again, but the Nazi grabs her arm and throws her back down to the ground. The two of them jump on her and start trying to dig into her pockets and take off her watch. Whoever bought her those nice clothes is going to be pissed when they see how dirty they are now. The boys are too strong for her, and she's being overpowered by both of them, and that just doesn't sit well with me. I put out my cigarette on the brick wall beside me and start down the alley, clapping my hands in delight.

"Well done!" I shout, grabbing their attention. "What a show! I was quite entertained for a moment there."

"Hey, just get the hell out of here, man," the slender one says to me as he leans over the girl, still taking off her watch. "This has nothing to do with you."

"Maybe it does, maybe it doesn't," I reply, swaying my head back and forth. "But I'm here now, and the sight of two boys pushing around a little blonde girl—well that doesn't put a smile on my face."

"Hey bro," the chunky one says as he stands up straight and turns to me, showing me his linebacker physique. Now that I'm closer, I can tell he's a thick kid, not just chubby. I can see he's broad-shouldered even under his black leather jacket. "You sure you want this to be your problem?"

I let out a laugh that seems to rattle both of the boys, and it puts a frown on the girls face.

"Oh I'm sure," I answer, still smiling like a kid on his birthday. How perfect. This is my present! "Nothing would bring me more joy."

I've never been the type to rely on a lot of talking. Instead, I let actions speak for me, which has built me a reputation that obviously hasn't reached these two. So I decide to show them.

Without another word, I charge at the thicker kid and tackle him. The two of us bounce off of a dumpster before crashing to the ground, and the second we land, I start swinging. My fists connect with his chubby face over and over again, and he's defenseless with me sitting on top of him. Blood explodes from his face and flies all over the ground of the alley. Every time I hit him, more blood splatters on my fists and face, and for some reason I can't explain, it makes me laugh. The sight of his bloody face is hysterical to me, especially after he was trying so hard to be tough on this little blonde girl. So I punch him and laugh like a birthday-boy should!

You see, other people are about trying to force you to believe something without showing you it's real. They have no evidence of what they're trying to convince you of. They want you to fear them so that they don't ever have to show you just how weak they actually are. They hope to scare you away before the fight ever begins because deep down inside, they're even more afraid than you are. Me? I want to show you. I want you to see it firsthand so that it's engraved in your mind forever! I want you to fear my actions first and foremost. Once I stop talking, that's when you should be running.

It seems like a full thirty seconds goes by before I realize I'm still punching this kid in his face. From the looks of it, he at least has a broken nose, and maybe even a broken jaw, though I'm not certain. It's hard to tell with all the blood. My breathing is heavy, and just as I go to get up, the slender kid takes a step towards me, finally ready to try to get me off of his bloody friend. As soon as I see his foot move in my direction, I pull my nine millimeter out of my pants pocket and whip him across the face with it. Blood flies through the air and splatters on the girl's sweater, making her jump back. The slender kid cries out in pain as I stand all the way up and aim the pistol at the back of his head, while he holds the gash on his cheek as it drips with blood.

"Oh, I'm sorry," I say to him as he hunches over, crying. "Did I get you there? Oops. Look at me, Slender." When he doesn't turn to face me, I get annoyed. "I said look at me!"

The boy has tears streaming down his face as he turns around. I can see the gash on his cheek, and I'm sure he'll need some stitches. Perfect!

"Momma's going to want to know what happened there," I say with a chuckle. "I'd like to shoot you right between the eyes, but that'd take all the fun out of knowing you're gonna have a big scar on your face for a long time. When people ask you what happened, you tell them that you met someone special. Someone who changed your life forever with just one encounter. Tell them his name was Solomon King. Now go." The kid looks down at his friend for support, but that's useless. "Looks like your friend needs to sleep our encounter off for a while. You'll have to go without him."

The slender kid nods his head, turns on his heel, and runs the other direction.

I take a deep breath and let out a loud exhale as I tuck the stolen gun back into my pants. The blonde girl is still on the ground looking up at me. I can't make out what her eyes are saying, but she's staring at me like she's never seen anything like me before. Little does she know that she hasn't.

I don't ask her if she's okay. I saw what happened and I know she is. Doesn't really matter to me anyway. I didn't do this for her. Before I leave, I reach into the half-dead chubby kid's pocket and take a twenty-dollar bill he has, then I look at the blonde again because she's still staring without saying anything.

We exchange a long look into each other's eyes, but I eventually get bored and start to walk back the way I came from, just as she starts to get up and dust herself off.

"Hey," she calls out before I turn the corner. Her voice is smooth and pleasant. Not something I'm used to. "You come here all the time? To this arcade, I mean."

I look over my shoulder and answer, "Guess so."

"I have to go now, but if you come here often, I guess I'll see you around."

"Guess so," I reply as I turn the corner and walk into the entrance of the arcade with blood on my face and hands, and an extra twenty dollars to spend. Happy Birthday, Solomon King.

About the Author

WS (Will) Greer is the author of bestselling novels such as The Therapist Series, Kingdom, Interview with a Sadist, and The Darkest Kink. He's also a USAF veteran since enlisting in 2004, and retiring after 20 years of service in 2024.

WS prides himself on being a man who writes spicy romance with the absolute best of them, while also understanding and appreciating that he is a guest in the house of romance that women built.

WS grew up in Clovis, NM, and now resides in Delaware, where he lives with his wife—bestselling author Isabel Lucero—and 3 kids.

More from WS Greer

Thank you for purchasing *A Good Girl's Guide to Dominance*! Please leave an honest rating and review wherever you purchased your copy. It would be very much appreciated!

Check out these other titles from WS Greer

Madman

The Therapist (The Therapist #1)

Shameless (The Therapist #2)

The Fallout (The Therapist #3)

Toxic (The Therapist #4)

Kingdom

Interview with a Sadist

I Love to Hate You

The Darkest Kink (The Darkest Kink #1)

How May I Please You (The Darkest Kink #2)

Want more from WS? Visit WS-GREER.COM for much more!

Made in the USA
Columbia, SC
04 October 2024

6aa99236-aa7e-442f-8dff-7c5df2d60d5fR02